Also by Stephen Swartz

THE WARRIORS BAUMANN

A Flu Season Saga Novel

[BOOK 7]

Stephen Swartz

MYRDDIN PUBLISHING GROUP

UNITED STATES ◆ UNITED KINGDOM ◆ AUSTRALIA

ISBN-13: 978-1-68063-043-5

www.myrddinpublishing.com

Cover Design by Stephen Swartz

The FLU SEASON Saga

I.
The Book of Mom

II.
The Way of the Son

III.
Dawn of the Daughters

IV.
The Book of Dad

V.
The Granddaughter

VI.
The Grandsons

VII.
The Warriors Baumann

TABLE OF CONTENTS

This is the way the world ends, not with a bang but a whimper.

— T.S. Eliot, "The Hollow Men"

THE WARRIORS BAUMANN

PROLOGUE

JUST KICK'EM. Put your boot down there and give'em a kick. Stir the embers, make'em spark to life. Let'em glow up in the dark. That way the creatures of the night will know you're aware of them and won't be so quick to pounce. And you have your sword ready.

Stank Baumann lifts his boot, leather rough-worn and scarred, taps the edge of the campfire, making the embers glow. He chuckles, pulls his wolf-fur wrap tighter about him, settling his greatsword across his knees, ready for what will come.

Across the camp fire sits his older brother Rory, also wrapped in what furs he could fashion into garments without the aid of a good woman who knew the stitching art. He gives a grunt to the glowing embers, knowingly, and likewise takes up his blade.

"Let them come," Rory mutters to his brother.

The dark folds around them. pressing in, yet the quiet betrays the enemy. A snap of twig, crackling of dry leaves. Coarse rumble of guts full of fear. A raspy breath. Their mount stirs nearby.

Then comes the forest-splitting war cry.

From out the fetid bowels of Hell spring six half-naked savages meting wooden clubs and stone knives, breaching the circle of ember lightfall with their foul fury.

The brothers rise as one, swords swinging with purpose: severed limbs flying, blood splattering, moans multiplying – until the stilted silence reigns again save for the heaving breaths of the victors.

"More this time," says Rory, almost sadly.

"Ay, they wished for death," Stank mutters.

He studies the fallen bodies: savage creatures not quite men. All they've seen for weeks. Ozark is no paradise.

"Getting worse. What is this place?" asks Stank as he wipes off blood from his greatsword on the rags of the dead.

"We're not in Kanza no more," says Rory.

"Ain't it a truth now," Stank responds, adding a grunt of disgust at the mess around them. "Come twenty days on and only this place full of savages. Glad we ain't like them. Never be like them."

"We got us the Glory," Rory agrees.

"And the best swords ever forged," says Stank, examining his greatsword. "Longclaw wins the night once more."

"All Hail the Lord Fritz!" Rory cheers.

"Hail Lord Fritz, patriarch of our clan."

Rory laughs. "Clan!" He starts to gather their meager belongings into their packs. "What clan? We're only two."

"An army of two," Stank says with a growl.

He gathers one of the packs, pulls it onto his back by the straps.

Rory throws the other pack over his shoulder.

Stank regards his brother. "Wherever the Baumann brothers go, the clan goes!"

"Have patience, Stank," says Rory. "For we shall find us wives in due time. We shall make us a clan. I promise you that. We will build us a kingdom. We will be kings! Now let us go and bend the world to our whims."

"The world is ours!" roars the mighty younger brother.

After hot tea and cold biscuits, starting to put up the camp, Rory drops to the ground with a groan.

"What's your woe?" calls Stank, about to mount his warhorse.

Rory looks up at his brother, a tortured look on his face. "Seems the savages got me. One did." He reaches back, feels his ribs, hits the wound. "Not bad, but it's something."

Stank goes to see. A cut in his brother's tunic reveals the spear that got through. It bleeds, seeps down his back to the waistband of his trousers. It will need sewing. "You got thread?"

"Wash it first," Rory insists.

"Have no worry. I know what Mama taught us: fix your wounds first with medicine then with thread."

"Ay, she did." Rory grimaces at the pain. "She stitched many."

Stank spits into the wound, wipes it dry. Blood bubbles up again. He goes to his saddle bag, retrieves needle and thread. Can't make a fine shirt but he can close a wound, has done so many times after a battle. He sets to work on Rory, rolling him over on his belly on the leafy ground, folding the tunic away and wiping his skin once more.

"Bite hard," says Stank and hands him a fallen stick.

"Don't need it," Rory growls but he clenches his teeth when the needle enters.

"Odd how a blade makes no noise yet a needle makes a grown man scream," says Rory, trying to laugh.

Stank stitches the wound, blood trying to escape.

"We'll get you to a town, find a physician to do it right. This will stand for now."

Stank helps his brother to his feet, gives him a boost up into the saddle. Stank leads Winnie on, tugging the reins, and they set off down the road like nothing untoward has happened.

1

THE REMNANTS

Setting out from Wichita in the year 2353 – from a hovel on the west side; the eastern two-third put into ruins from the air-burst that hit the city a couple hundred years before, when the people tried to rise up against their masters and were put down (they still sing of the episode to this day) – Stanley Kirk Baumann, having a few marks of woe to bear and provisions in a pack, swearing off breadcrumbs and widows' lusty gazes, set his mighty steed eastward without regrets. Ned and Beck waved farewell. So did the boys down below, a hand raised out of their bunker. Marva Quincy dared show her face, the nasty scar from forehead to chin not deterring him one bit from a night's romp in service to the remnants of a once great nation. Her father begged him to lay with her, hoping for a child to carry on. On to what? he'd sneered, amused. He'd heard the tales, believed half of them. They wanted him to stay, be their protector, being a big man with a quick sword. Folks out west survived the best, he knew from his mother's stories, yet his destiny lay to the east. To the other side of the savage lands.

His mount was a fine stallion, feisty yet half-mad with fear, dun coat with a black mane and tail – regal-looking, Stank decided. They eat horses, no matter how grand a beast, so he kept watch as he had during his evening with Marva, got a pouch of coins for his service and a bag of foodstuff: dried potato wedges, some wilted greens, and the last cow cut into strips grilled over a brazier. He rode high in the saddle passed down from his grandfather, rider to rider.

The path he trod unfolded easily, golden grain stretching to far horizons, like a dream he'd once had. He could scan the wide fields for approaching opponents, could gallop ahead or stop and await the fight. He won every encounter, vagabonds being what they were: a weak excuse sick with hunger and unskilled. Yet he never would eat the flesh of any man or woman who'd fallen. The line had to be held somewhere in a desperate world.

He rode through the day, whistling happy tunes, past bison herd and antelope squadron, over mounds and through washes, pausing at creeks to drink, under scattered groves of cottonwood for shade, the sunny days welcoming him, a rare traveler in dark times. He skirted any collection of buildings that might constitute a town in older days. There were many of them, now in ruins, people fleeing to safer locations. An army in white robes swept through the area in years past, killing anyone who foolishly wished to stay. He recalled that time when he'd met his cousins Jango and Fatt in a couple of skirmishes, fighting side by side.

They'd talked of their families, hidden away to keep them safe. Had to fight to protect them. That was all Stank remembered. Those cousins died in a later encounter with waves of white-robed fighters. Religious fanatics, all could see, determined to spread their curious beliefs northward into the vast lands of the Americus. His mother told him about earlier fights his people had with the fanatics they called Slammers. Being young, it was only a fanciful tale. Yet every year after, he saw the wounded return, the boxes of the killed set on wagons, home from battle, and he had to wonder whether the stories were true. "Your mother wouldn't lie to you," he recalled her saying each time he would give her a cross look or a hesitant smile.

So he rose like his brothers: Clem, Stu, Kyle, Mel, and Don. They rode into battle in Colonel Deeds' battalion, put the Slammers down at Belle Plaine, south of Wichita, and rode home victorious. They'd made a stand, fought hard, drove them back. This was the line they should never cross. Plans were made for a new offensive, expecting to push the Slammers further south and draw a stronger line. His brothers felt safe and not excited to go back into the fight. Then he'd gotten a notice from Rory, the eldest brother, requesting assistance.

He rode across the prairie, the only man on horseback he saw for days. As though the entire world had been sucked up in a whirlwind never to return. Like a cleansing flood. Or a great plague. The world was much lighter now, he mused. Few were he and his clan among the prairie, just remnants of what once was.

He rode past a battlefield strewn with old bones, tattered cloths, and rusty swords. He couldn't recall the place, or when the battle was fought. There had been so many during the past hundred years, back and forth, making these plains red with blood, pushing people from their homes, leaving them with half a family. Olden times. All events become stories, he considered, then quickly catalogued and soon forgotten. And men like him simply move on.

Camping for the night, he lay against his saddle, watching the fire, cooking his dinner, and thumbing at an old pouch of bullets he pick up off the battlefield. He held one of the brass things up to his eye, studied it. Such little things could cut through a body – even through armor, he heard. But you needed a catapult, the launcher, for the metal thing to fly through the air to its target.

A sword was better, he thought, but you had to be close. He liked being close enough to see his opponent's face as he struck him down. If only he'd had one of those launcher things, he could send this metal flying through the air into his enemy. It was like the machine bows he'd seen in the larger towns, a device that flung darts into a target at high speed. He looked over at his horse, sad at the wound it once bore, hit by such a dart as he fled a bad episode in an ugly village after giving service to a worthy wench without her husband's consent. The man had raised the dart launcher after him.

He cursed at the memory. They'd an agreement. He took no fee, after all. Only supper.

He stirred the pot, strips of dried cow and a sprinkle of greens.

"Bygones," he grumbled, fetching his dinner from the fire.

He munched on a strip of meat, chewing loudly as darkness drew down around him and crickets rehearsed their chorus.

"Winnie," Stank called to his steady steed, untethered, taking up the fine flora of the grove. "I'll apologize again for getting you in that bit of trouble. No lasting harm done." The horse turned to him, gave a sad snort as though understanding. "Weren't like he'd any right to you. He was supposed to pay me, not the other way around, eh? Ah, different villages, different rules."

He chewed on the fat a while.

"Handshaking used to do it fine. Maybe best we write it up from now on. But where you gonna find a scribe these days?" He feigned looking around for a man of letters. "Rory'll know where we can find one. Rory knows everything."

His brother – half-brother, truth be told – was the odd one of the brood. Reddish hair and blue eyes, like one of the Iowa clans. Not a black-haired, brown-eyed man like Stank. If legends were true, Rory came down through a line of reds going back a couple hundred years to the old capital in the east, long destroyed now. Fate brought that ancestor out to the western territory, and when that man had grown enough he took up with a local woman of the Comanche clan – like Stank's line seemed to be. But they knew they were brothers – half-brothers, and just as good.

Stank pondered his mother, in his mind wearing a humble dress, passed down, hair tied up, a weak, regretful smile on her tan face. Like the day he left, riding with his brothers to battle. He could play those images over and over, back and forth, sped up or slowed down, change the colors of their clothing, make them smile or frown. It was a foolish ability, he knew. Like those colorful bands of pretenders coming by to give a show and gather some coin.

What? See things inside your head? Things from the past? Things that never happened? Things you wish happen? It's magic – a kind of evil magic, his mother cautioned. Best never tell anyone you can see things. His mother told him how she saw things like that. A rare gift from the Great Spirit, she called it.

In the morning, as the chill faded under a bright sunrise, Stank saddled up and rode off. Another three days to meet up with Rory.

That time when he'd gotten up from the mat, started pulling on his clothing, leaving the woman to watch him, clucking like she'd been well-satisfied.

"What's your name, sir?" she'd begged, giving a lusty toss to her thick blond hair, sending the mane back over her shoulder.

"Stanley K. Baumann," he'd responded, hitching up his trousers.

"Stanley? What's it mean?"

"Name my mother gave me."

"Ain't no meaning to it?"

"It means warrior," he said, uncertain. "You can call me Stan."

"Just Stan?"

"Awright, Stan K."

"Stan *Kay*?"

"Stan K. Like the letter K."

"Stankey.... I like it."

"No, not Stankey. Stan-*KAY!* It's Stan K. Letter K. K for Kirk."

"So *Stank*? That it?"

"It's Stan. Call me Stan K."

"Stank? That your name?" She gave a throaty laugh. "Thought you washed up before we lay together."

He'd felt insulted. "I did."

"Well, you still smell like horse."

"And you ride like a girl," he came back.

He smiled at the memory, setting eyes on the horizon.

As he'd ridden off across the plain with another pouch of coins in his saddle bag, the husband happy to have a child on the way, he'd decided he liked the name: Stank.

Rory was different. He was named Aurora when he was born, on account of his flame-orange hair. Yet playing with other boys he got teased a lot, got into fights, because of his name. Better it was given to a girl, they said. But as he grew tough and could best those boys, they agreed to call him Rory.

All the other brothers had plain names, whatever their mother could think of while a village scribe waited patiently for a name to be spoken. He had eight half-brothers with the same mother; others in the village were called cousins but he treated them like brothers. A pair of sisters, as well, but he paid them no mind.

Lost in thought, Stank let two riders approach too close before taking notice. Two like him: strongmen, warriors. They halted with a respectful interval between them, shouting news back and forth, news of battles to the south and east, how they'd fared. One lifted his arm, showing a hand was missing and wrapped in stained cloth.

"None west," said Stank. "You can go in peace."

The warriors thanked him, bid him a joyous journey.

Another day, toward dusk, Stank passed a creek and down the slope came a pair of vagabonds that thought they could steal his horse or worse. One sniveling man rushed to grab the reins. Another man, older but no larger, had a lance, tried to spear him or his horse but Stank maneuvered Winnie sharply to his left so the lance struck air over the rear of the saddle but cut his fine tunic. Angered, Stank swung his sword down, severing the lance. On the backswing he separated the vagabond's arm below the elbow, the hand grasping the lance dropping to the ground. The man who'd reached for the reins, failing, rushed to his partner and Stank rode on.

"Always trying the easy way," he said with a sigh. When would these simple folk understand? If you're a sniveling snot two steps up from a worm you got no business testing your measly mettle against a strongman brandishing a greatsword forged in Tulsa!

2

BIG BROTHER

TWO DAYS ON, he approached the village of Independence, what had been a tribal gathering place in olden times, but now a town of tribal and non-tribal survivors alike. He stayed a night to have a look at his latest offspring. A girl was born to Helena Vander, wife of Nate Vander, a weasely man who'd begged Stank to get on her so they could have a child. Nate moaned how he inherited the wasting curse from his family's history of getting bad medicine, all the way back to plague times and whatever poor potions people were given hoping to not die from the virus. Nate put her on the mat, on elbows and knees, and turned up the bottom of her skirt to show him her rump. The man waved him over, then sat to watch the episode, to cheer them on, applauding when the act came to its conclusion.

"That should do it," said Stank. "Felt good. Likely be a son."

Nate thanked him, gave him the agreed fee and supper.

"Got any others in town need a pregging?" Stank asked, wiping supper grease from his lips. But no others were in season.

Returning to Independence, Stank went to the hovel, called out the woman's name.

"Enter," came a man's thin voice.

He pushed the curtain aside, the brightness of the hearth briefly blinding him. The mother sat, back against the wall, a babe at her breast sucking away. The husband stood gazing down upon them, a big smile on his narrow face.

"Looks a success," said Stank. "Sorry it weren't a son."

"We are happy to have any child," said the husband. "We will be happy to raise her, wed her to a fine fellow in another village, if we can. You have blessed us, sir."

"If you want another, I'll be back this way in a couple months."

He tipped his leather helmet and left.

Continuing eastward, Stank rode over to Altamont then turned up to Parsons to see another babe he'd fathered: a boy of three years and running wild. Had the same look, taking after him more than the mother. Someday, he told the mother, he might return to collect the boy and train him to fight. He already had enough sons for a full squad of warriors.

The road to the southeast was harrowing, vagabonds challenging him left and right. A toll gate had been set up which he rode around despite the heehawing of the toll collectors. Stank raised Longclaw, waved the blade at them. A warrior was allowed to pass.

Down to the village of Webb, the farthest he'd been eastward. He grew excited as he urged his steed up the main street, seeing people give him a fearful look, most hiding. He hadn't come to hurt them, but they didn't know. Best to keep safe.

Somewhere in this dire gathering of wooden shacks would be his brother Rory. Likely in a tavern, drinking his favorite dark ale – if they still made it. It was famed across the territory. A high price in Wichita if you could find a bottle. He took stock of the tavern, saw two more establishments down the street. He caught eyes watching him. None came out to greet a weary traveler.

"Meet in Webb," Stank muttered, getting frustrated.

He stomped into the nicer looking tavern, scattering the guests at the sight of his brusque figure and his greatsword, a fearsome weapon most couldn't wield with two hands. Stank had the strength to lift the blade in one hand and use it devastatingly.

He felt the eyes on him.

"Rory?" he called out. Silence came back to him.

Stank stared at the man behind the bar, white as a ghost.

"You know Rory Baumann?" asked Stank.

The barman gave a nod, remained stiff. Then tilted his head to the right.

"Next tavern?" asked Stank.

The barman nodded.

"Figures. Never find him in a place this nice. Clean and neat."

He turned to go, heard the shuffling of guests returning to their activities: cards, dice games; whores flirting, men drinking.

Out the doorway he went, down to the next tavern, an ugly hole-in-the-wall joint that better fit his brother's style.

"Rory!" he cried out from the street.

A woman poked her head out the doorway. "He says come in."

So Stank entered.

The dark interior kept him from seeing the man at first, but his arms knew what to do, were always ready, and Longclaw swept the room in six broad slices, laying four assassins on the floor, a woman getting in the way and suffering a gash across her belly. She held in her guts.

"You best get to a physician," he told her.

She pulled herself to the doorway, fell outside, got up, staggering away, shrieking in agony.

Stank stood tall, no hard breath. What was that? They must've known he was coming and laid a plot. What happened to Rory?

He rushed out, got to his steed, mounted. He held Longclaw high to let everyone know who was the warrior.

"Rory!" he called out, loud enough to be heard across the village. "Where's Rory Baumann?"

People came out, stood at a safe distance from the warrior.

One man grew bold, strode into the street, smoothing his green scribe's apron. "He's not here. Left a few days ago. Headed east."

"How you know?" demanded Stank.

"Because the sheriff gave him a decree of absence."

"Decree of absence?"

"The order to depart. A writ of no return."

"What's that?"

"Ordered to leave this town and never return. On pain of death. For crimes done here."

"Ordered to leave?" Stank let out a great guffaw. "That's so Rory, that red devil. What did he do?"

"Fighting. He laid a few low." The man pointed down the street: eastward out of town. "He left that way. Few days past."

"I was to meet him here," said Stank, glaring at the man.

"If you're a Baumann, you better be gone, too. No Baumanns are allowed in Webb. It has been so ordered."

"On what charge?" Stank demanded.

"Mayhem."

"Mayhem, eh?" He grinned. "Wish I'd've been here for that."

"It was not a pleasant episode," the man declared.

"Not for some like those in the...what's it called? the *Mouse and Muskrat*? Whatever that hole-in-the-wall's called. Not my choosing. They came at me first. After all's said and done, you best get your gravesman here."

"Gravesman? What happened?"

"I was attacked. But no worries. They did not succeed."

"Someone attacked you?"

"I said it. You deaf? Anyways, you best clean up there before the rats come for supper. They'll surely make a mess of what's left of the fallen pieces."

"Pieces?" The man's eyes widened. "You left them in pieces?"

"They chose," replied Stank.

The scribe watched the warrior ride down the street, then saw a pair of men jump from an alley with lance and halberd to take him down. Yet two swings from that mighty sword laid them in the dirt, a dust cloud rising over the bodies.

Stank turned in his saddle, shouted back: "Two more for your gravesman. And I ain't paying for them."

The road turned through forest and field, hill and dale, as the sky clouded over, darkening, and a gritty rain soon fell. Stank made his camp under a thick stand of oaks, hefted the saddle off his horse.

"Sir Winthrop the Bold, offspring of Bad Apple, sired by Raging Harmony," he said with a wry chuckle. "You lost your name like me. Just good ol' Stank these days. Ain't it right, Winnie? Ah, how many more years you got in you? Battles take their toll, eh?"

The large warhorse gave a satisfied snort. They'd been together several years, both in battle and across plains. Sometimes it seemed to Stank as though his horse could read his thoughts and it spooked him sometimes.

Winnie strode over to the saddle bag upon the ground, sniffed at it until Stank fetched an apple from the bag, handed it up.

"You're too clever by half, Winnie."

Stank sat with his broad back against a tree trunk, sword across his knees. He wiped the blade clean, admired it.

He thought back to the village scuffle, wondered what part was true, what part was just Rory making up one of his plans. He was a sneaky fellow, full of schemes. Always inventing a new tale.

In the early days, Rory fought with him, taught him how to fight although Stank, even at a younger age, was bigger than Rory, eldest of the brothers. Their mother always told them they'd better learn to fight. War was coming – yet wasn't war always coming? Quebeckers from the north attacking Chicageaux. The Missourites forging west. Slammers from the south. Likely some odd folks from the forbidden zone to the west would march eastward to take what his family had fought to hold. Only a small square of land, enough to grow some crops, raise a few hogs and chickens, enough to keep the boys fed as they grew. That's all he wanted.

"A mama's task is to raise boys into men," June-May would tell them. The boys made a habit of thanking their mother every day, giving hugs and kisses like oaths of fealty. They grew big and tall, strong and well-formed, ready to be warriors. She felt proud.

They were ready when a Slammer party snuck north to consider taking their village, but the brothers stood up and none of the squad of white-robed fanatics managed to return to their holy horde. They remained in Kanza land serving as food for the hogs.

It was good their mother took on any man who came by, adding more warriors to the village's guard. It was her calling, June-May accepted, to bring forth life into this horrible world, and hope one of her brood might be clever enough to fix everything, make the world right-side-up again. Instead, she only managed to bear strong men more fit to fight than solve the world's troubles.

Their mother swore after each birth that she would keep bearing all she could until her body gave out. The world needed more people: people to grow food and protect food growers. And whatever June-May said was law and none of her boys dared go against her.

Rory was the only son that ever stood up to her, made her cry in his anger. He called her a *whore*.

"Not any different than a man taking up a woman wherever he finds her," she countered. It was a profession, everyone knew. One of many professions needed in the new world. She was doing her part. All the men who stopped for a night meant nothing to her unless the meeting started a babe growing in her. While full of child, she was given food allotments and didn't have to work. Others of the village accepted June-May as the most fertile of the women.

One day Rory announced he was leaving, had to go. He'd decided he was going away to find his fortune. In fact it was on June-May's birth-memorial: the first day of Sixthmonth – the laboring had run mostly on the last day of Fifthmonth but she crowned after midnight so the birth occurred on the first of Sixthmonth – hence her parents, Ana-Luann and Dergon, put the name June (old name of the month) ahead of May.

Fortune? the brothers asked Rory. What would that be?

"It's what Lord Fritz wants for us all," Rory responded, angrily. His brothers always doubted him. "Fame! Glory! Wealth! And don't forget power! Free electro for all! Most of all, it's being lords of our own lands. A clan of brothers and cousins. A high stone wall around a high house. With two towers for looking at the stars. And another tower even taller, tall enough to wave 'good morn' at the God of All."

"That seems like an awful lot to hope for," said Clem, unable to think clearly about such a big idea. He looked to Stank for support.

"How you figure?" asked Stu, stroking his long mustache.

"There's lots for the taking out east," Rory replied, smiling wide-eyed like he'd already laid his eyes on a pile of gold.

"You fixing to just take it from somebody?" Kyle challenged as he flexed his arm muscles, lifting the anvil, setting it down.

"If I have to," Rory answered, getting frustrated with them.

Mel, the chubby one, pointed to Rory's belly. "Food, too?"

"Of course, food," Don with the big nose full of snot told Mel with a slap to Mel's knee, then emptied his nostrils on the ground.

"All of that," said Rory. "Enough for you and me, and all of our women and kinder, our horses, and any dogs we find. Maybe find real guns to use instead of those screw-bows you like using."

"Screw-bows are faster, more accurate," Stank spoke, holding the device across his lap. A screw was turned to tighten the bowstring, pulling it back then releasing the string with a finger lever, sending the dart straight into an enemy with the punch of a mailed fist and the cut of a blade. Those devices had become the preferred weapons of the Slammers now that guns and bullets were scarce.

"Don't you mind them," said Rory, the only full red-head among the brothers; Clem and Don had slight red to their hair and beards.

Rory came forth from June-May two days after her only husband wedded. An ordinary man named Baumann, given the name Frank, came from the western reaches, being what they called a 'cowboy': a wrangler of bovine foodstock and producer of leather goods. He came from a village called Skinner Canyon. It no longer stood after windstorms destroyed most of it and wildfires took what had remained. It was said this Frank who bore the same name as others did in the family line, bore also the red hair of his father and others of his line further back, all the way back to that first redhead son some called the Red Devil, a notorious criminal. Thus Rory had a fair portion of conniving in him, the will to scheme, always too clever for his own good, and he blamed this ancestor for all of it.

The Baumann clan was thus known as criminals. The whole clan outcast, yet they did what they could to contribute to the community – for without everyone sharing and working together, they would be lost and left to a cruel fate. This was no time to go it alone. Only by standing together would they survive, June-May declared.

And this Baumann woman produced strong men able to fight, so they welcomed her participation in the community, praised her with each son's birth. Mourned with her when a son was lost in battle.

Stank noted how his mother's status rose with each son's birth. He wondered if he might do the same but from the opposite side of the bed. Offer his services to widows and barren women, help them gain a child. His mother thought it a silly occupation for a virile man like him but couldn't stop him. The young man had a knack for the sack, skill in defeating will, a way with women that none could explain. Fit as a god wouldn't describe all of him; he had a look, part devil and a quarter demi-god, like the giants of ancient times, and irresistible to most women. He was polite, too, so husbands were put at ease. He would keep secrets, visit later to check on the offspring, and in that way gained a good reputation as a sire.

"And we'll surely need this fellow," said Rory, waving at Stank. "He will make many sons. Many sons will form us an army."

Awaking to the dull orange light of dawn cracking through the dark woods, Stank realized he'd fallen asleep.

"And we will be kings!" echoed Rory's voice from the dream.

Stank got up, stretched his sore back, began packing the camp.

"Rory, you bastard," he grumbled, then let out a yawn.

He set his steed on the road once more.

3

Ozark Rage

STANK TRAVELLED the eastward road at a leisurely pace, always watchful of vagabonds hiding in the brush ready to pounce. They'd hear his approach and know he wasn't a man they dared trifle with, nor could they expect to defeat him.

"Ay, Rory," Stank grumbled as Winnie strode forth, "what've you gotten hid up and down your sleeves?" He believed Rory told truth, telling him to meet in Webb, only to be driven from the town. Then they lay in wait for Stank. Or were they expecting Rory to return?

Rory must be in some trouble if he sent a message all the way to Wichita. He'd boasted of going east to find his fortune, then needed help? Not likely. Perhaps the message was only a ruse to get Stank to travel to Webb where pumperknockers could attack him. Maybe it wasn't Rory at all who'd sent the message. He could be riding east for nothing. Rory could be sitting on cushions in his house far from here, thought Stank, and not even know his brother was riding east to find him.

"This is a road?" Stank grumbled as leafy brush intruded upon the dirt path.

He pressed on through the woods, keeping his eyes alert to signs of ambush. A floral path like this was game for a trick. Easy to hide vagabonds. Must've not been trod for a while. How could this paltry trail be a highway to the capital city of Louis?

Must've made a errant turn somewhere, yet it was the same dirt he followed. Rory was setting him up again. Another prank. Always getting him in trouble.

Stank came upon a junction with another trail, the dirt crossing trampled by hooves and boots. A painted sign of wood stood marking the directions.

This way to Carthage, that way to Granby. Mere hamlets, likely abandoned. Or ahead to Springer's Field. He knew the town only by reputation: gambling houses for rich folks on holiday. Rory would go there, he suspected, yet it was the farthest of the choices.

He looked closer at the signpost. The white paint was old, flaky, yet appeared as though pieces had been scraped off – scraped off by claws or fingernails. Wild animal? Or a desperate man? And there on top, caught by a shard of splintered wood: strands of red hair. A man's hair, he saw, looking closer.

"Ah hah!" cried Stank. He tugged at the hairs, ripped them free, studied them, rolling them between his fingers. "Rory, you bastard."

As he sat high in the saddle, shadows flickered over the crossing.

"Cut me down," came a voice from above.

Stank looked up, saw a man tied to the branch by ropes, looking like a hog ready for slaughter. He laughed at the sight.

"Rory!"

"I've had better names," said the man hanging from the branch by his hands and feet.

Stank dismounted. He slid Longclaw out of its leather scabbard and swung the greatsword upward to cut the ropes. Rory shook free and slammed down, his back against the tree trunk, one rope still holding him aloft. He cried out for safety but Stank swung his blade again and the red-haired brother crashed to the ground.

"Scoundrel!" cursed Rory, laying there. He remained unwilling to move until he had assessed damage to his body.

"I saved you," Stank shouted, and went to help his brother up.

Rory held out his hands for his brother to cut the rope binding his wrists.

"You said meet in Webb." Stank cut the wrist ropes.

"I was there," said Rory, shaking his hands loose and rubbing his wrists. "Then I was bid move on. In a rather unfriendly way."

"I met those movers. They had no fear of me."

"Nor me." Rory frowned. "Yet I've not the brawn of you, brother."
Stank returned to his horse, then regarded Rory. "Your horse?"

"Stolen."

"You rode Betty? Who'd want that old nag?"

"Elizabeth's a fine mount. Trustworthy. Fearless."

"But old."

"As we all shall be one day at a time."

"Where to?" asked Stank, giving a glance behind himself for any
approaching attack. "Back to Webb to set them straight?"

"No, we must keep on east. I have an appointment with destiny.
We both do, actually." Rory had his cheating grin on. "There are big
things we must do. The biggest ever tried in our whole lives. And it
shall set us up for the remainder of our lives."

"You're always bolstering talk." Stank mugged at Rory. "Another
scheme? A plot with no holes? I feel you're about to cheat me out of
something."

"No – no games. Not this time."

"Then tell me. We've plenty a ways to walk – least until we find
you a horse."

"Should be a farm coming out from these woods. Or a vagabond
camp. Then I'll take a mount for the remainder of our journey."

They walked on in the direction of Springer's Field, deciding how
to get a mount for Rory. No farms along the way. In fact, the land on
which they traveled had no farming on it, only savagery. They kept
wary. And mostly silent. Talking would draw vagabonds to attack.

Stank handed Rory his spare sword, a shorter, lighter and faster
blade than Longclaw.

"Feels good to have a weapon in my hand again," said Rory.

Sweeping aside the undergrowth as they went, Stank asked him
what his plan was.

"It's a long story," said Rory, acting annoyed, like his brother
should just trust him and follow whatever plan he had, needing no
explanation. "I got a wind of changes in the capital. The King there
has a daughter—"

Stank gave a snort. "You begged me out this far for a chance at a
wife? Fine enough fare in Kanza. Your eyes judge too harshly." He

tugged Winnie to follow.

"No, this one comes with land. I'll be a duke or something."

"So this plan of yours takes us to Louis?"

"Naturally. That's the capital these days — as close as we have."

"Should've packed more, long journey such as this."

"And I need a horse."

"That problem is entirely your own creation."

"I didn't create nothing. They ambushed me, took what I had. I was hauled out into the woods — as you saw — left to die. I knew you would find me. I believed in you, brother. In your dogged quest for the answers to questions. You're a curious fellow."

"I like to know things."

"What you like is to lay with wenches, widows, and wives."

"That's a truth. Yet I always ask them to tell me things. I learn a lot that way."

"Sure you do." Rory laughed.

They came upon a clearing, gazed out at empty fields beyond the woods. Others had stopped there, left remains of a campfire. Stank waved his brother to sit on one of the logs and rest. He tied up his horse and sat on the opposite log with a loud breath.

"So what do you need me for if it's you wedding the lady?"

Rory stretched his arms back, smiling.

"She's the daughter of the King. Majory's her name. A might fair maiden. Hair like spun gold. Chest like the Ozark hills. And a good head on her. Keeps the King's library. Sings songs she thinks up, too, and plays the lute."

"Sounds like your type: well out of your pool."

"Don't laugh." He tried to look Stank in the eye. "I need you to be my champion. You're a fine fighting fellow. I'm asking for Majory's hand in marriage. Actually, all of her. It is important. Important for all of us. That marriage will make me a member of the Court."

Stank tightened his lips. "Have you even met her?"

"I saw her once." Rory smiled like a fancy lad full of tales. "Up on the balcony. Not long, I'll admit. Yet she gazed down at me."

Stank shook his head. "Looking at an odd rube, no doubt."

"Perhaps. I smiled up at her and she smiled back."

Stank almost blinked. "First sight, eh?"

"There's another member of the Court – he's a duke already – he also wishes for her hand. Thus, I need you to fight him – and win – so I can proceed."

Stank sat up tall on the log. "That's a queer deal. What if I die?"

Rory shrugged. "Then that duke gets her and I don't."

"And what do I get?" asked Stank, leaning forward.

"You? You get a fine funeral with the best of everything."

Stank stared hard at him. "A funeral? I'm here, meeting you like this, to go have my own funeral?"

"Well, when you put it that way...." Rory grinned. "Ay, I'm sure it won't happen that way. You'll defeat him."

"You said champion. Does that duke have a champion?"

"He fancies himself a fighter, so I'm betting he'll go against you himself. But me – look at me? I'm a wiry fellow, not a brawny figure such as yourself. I need a true champion. You're just the right man. When I made my decision, I thought to myself: Who is the finest fighter I know? Well, it's my brother Stan. He's the man."

Stank glared at his brother a while, until Rory looked away.

"You don't want to help me? Help us? The whole clan?" He met Stank's eyes again. "We will be kings! All of us. I know we will. Help me win Majory's hand. That is the first step in my plan."

"You seem more bold than foolish now. I worry on you."

Rory waved him off. "Bold and foolish, you might say. Yes, it is a difficult target yet it is the only target worth firing on."

Stank shook his head, acting tired. "I have no fear of any Court duke. I shall likely win. I always win. I wonder only what reward I shall get for my effort."

"Why, you Sir Stanley shall also be a duke. With land you call your own. And a wife with a castle, and a high tower to look down on your holdings, all your subjects. And offspring you can keep for yourself. Keep because they'll be yours. You will teach them how to fight fair – moreover, how to rule. You see? It will be a grand life. You'll see. Life will be grand."

"I fight this duke fellow, beat him to a pile of pulp—"

"No, you'll have to kill him."

"—and you're certain this princess will want to marry you. Then you become a duke and you appoint me to be a duke, as well. Is that your plan?"

"Indeed, Stan. You see the plan. You're the man."

"If I can...." Stank rubbed his cheek, trying not to smile. "What training does this duke have? I mean in the combat arts."

"He's a bookworm. But he has a countenance Court ladies prefer. No battle scars, let's say. He can fence, sure, but only with a rapier. He couldn't lift a broadsword."

"Is he a wiry fellow? Quick and sneaky?"

"I wouldn't think so. He goes by rules. Won't be laying a scheme. Won't be cheating. Believes in righteous acts."

"Then it sounds easy." Stank grinned. "And I'll be a duke, too."

"And, being a duke, you will have many lady suitors."

"Then I should like to meet this duke. Meet him and slay him. It feels right. Why should we go about our days like this? I would wish to lay about, pampered like royals, get the top grapes from the vine, with pretty girly feet to smash them into wine! And drink away all of my days!"

"There you go, Stan! You've got it. You must think like a duke to defeat a duke."

Seeing fields beyond the cover of the forest, they decided to press on. Two footmen leading a horse made a comic scene. After crossing the fields, they took turns on Winnie, the other walking beside. They found a new road cutting across the acres and took it with the sun showing them the way, blazing behind them.

"I've only a single bedroll," Stank reminded his brother.

"I don't mind," Rory came back. "We slept together for years in that straw bed in Wichita."

"We was babes then," Stank snarled.

"Well, now, I'm the elder brother, so I should get the bedroll."

"I'm the bigger brother, so I'll fight you for the bedroll."

"Half a bedroll, then?"

"I'll take the larger half."

"You do know half means equal portions, don't you?"

"I'll take what portion I want. It's my bedroll, says I."

"Then find us a good patch of grass and I shall lay myself down like a dog. You can have your bedroll, brother. Keep it."

They did not find a patch of sweet grass to lay on and followed the road into the next forest. Alongside the dirt path old houses and barns leaned in their final days, weathered and crumbling, ready to fall into piles of broken boards. Rusty hulks of old motor carriages sat idle in the yards, sad reminders of past days when the world was still new, before the plague and all was forgotten. Rory had to take a close look, *tsk*ing at what horrors he saw inside the machines: a few old bones, tattered clothing.

"Could've ridden one of these carriages," Rory muttered. "If we'd been born sooner. You pour in the fuel and let it burn. The burning turns the wheels and away you go."

"So how far you figure to Louis?" asked Stank to pull his brother away from the ruins of the past. "I rather not walk the whole way."

Rory looked back at him. "Gotta be a week of walking. If we had carriages like these, only hours. But even if we found one that could operate, we couldn't find any fuel for it."

"Why did they leave them to rust?" asked Stank. He'd seen a few of the machines left around Wichita.

"No more fuel. Like I said. Fuel was dead."

"That's what I heard. That's what they said."

"So we raised horses. What remained that weren't eaten during the lean years. They fuel themselves in a grassy field or a hay bin. It is likely a better way."

"Until you're down to a single mount," Rory teased.

They made a camp in the next wood, found an old fire pit, set out a dinner of what foodstuffs still filled the saddle pack. Not much. In the morning they would continue on to Springer's Field where they could get more. Maybe get a horse for Rory to ride, something cheap. He was becoming annoying, Stank decided, lifting off the saddle and setting it on the ground.

Rory sat back against a log, letting out his bad air. "What a life!

Won't be long before we're riding in fine carriages with teams of fine horses pulling us along, eh?"

"If you say so," Stank responded. He set up the camp while his brother relaxed. "You comfy now?"

"Just fine, thanks, brother."

"No sweet grass to lay on."

"I may need that bedroll, after all."

"I'll let you use the blanket, but the bedroll's mine. All mine."

"Yet I'm going to make you a duke!"

"I must fight for my dukedom, eh?"

"Well, if you put it that way...."

"You keep putting it that way, Rory. Your victory rests only on my shoulders."

"And what broad shoulders they are!"

Having little to eat for supper, they grumbled about every woe from the past that put them in this precarious position. A long list, as it turned out. Stank was full of regret, Rory prodding him to feel bad about most of his decisions in life. Stank reminded Rory of his own past failures. As eldest brother he should set a high example to follow, yet he was a clever one, a schemer, always looking for the useful angle. Granted, he didn't have the size to be a warrior, so he had to rely on his wits, his way with words, his perfect powers of persuasion. But Stank could see through him: like spying a fish in a quick-rushing stream.

"And what of Clem? The others?" asked Rory, begging for news.

Stank let out a big breath, shaking his head. "Clem? He's in the factory, a steward of sorts. Ill sorts, says I. He's game for the trade, seems. Likes working with his hands."

"How about the others?" Rory pressed.

"Ay, lemme think." He stared up through the branches a while. "Stu took up with that homely wench Ginger. With the face full of frecks. You'd like her. Red like you. Says they're gonna breed many, make a clan. But he's got no skills, not even fighting. Thinks he can be a teacher of some sort."

"He'll come round. Learn himself a trade. Get a set of skills. He'll make something of himself. Or she can lay out for some coin. They'll make it work. Stu's a good lad."

"Kyle's as hot as ever, gets into roundabouts and hog-tossing like a proper rogue. Doesn't clean up too well. Mama's happy for him. Militia came by to look at him, thought he would do to take some training, join him up, but he blew it all up with some foolish devilry. You know how he can be. They'll consider him the next year. Mama begged them to come back."

"And Mel? Don? What're they up to?"

"Mama sent them to the school hut, won't let them back home 'til the end, no matter they want to go play their games. What games? I heard they like to spy on the girls washing in the stream. Then get caught so often they get beaten by the school master."

"School master? Is that Father Thyme?"

"Naw, he kicked off. Right in the middle of a numbers lesson, I heard. But the kids didn't tell no one for a couple days so they could play instead of have lessons. But he got to stinking and they gave up the body. Put him in the ground soon after. It's Mister Knob now."

Rory laughed a while, then stopped. He listened to the woods as darkness settled around them.

"Cousins ain't no better," said Stank in a lower voice, watching the woods beyond Rory. "Militia actions. Down south twice this year getting after Slammers. Push them back, way back. Trying to move them south of the Red River, call it even."

"That's good," Rory responded in an even quieter voice.

"Fatt got a wound. Arm. Stitched him up, back into the fray."

"He's a tough lad."

The fire was burning low, embers glowing but fading.

Stank lifted his boot, gave them a tap, made them glow up.

Rory had a sense about him, his eyes informing Stank. They took up their swords just in time for the attack.

4

FORT BRANSON

"GO EASY," Rory complained, jostling the saddle on Stank's mighty warhorse.

"It's a flesh wound," said Stank, leading Winnie along.

"It pains every jolt and sway."

"It'll hurt a bit, then go quiet."

"I may not endure so long."

"Then what should we do? I stitched you a fair length of thread. It'll hold a might longer."

"I can't wait for it to heal. We must make way."

"To your fight. Rather, to my fight. And your wedding."

"Yes, yes, we must." He endured another few minutes. "Oh, how can I do this, our great plan, with a wound in my back?"

"It's part of the plan. Ask Lord Fritz."

"Lord Fritz doesn't know," Rory grumbled loudly. "He only sets a thing in motion. Never changes them later. We do as we like, go as we should, fix things ourselves and hope for the best."

"Then Lord Fritz intends you to go through this hardship."

"Not this pain!"

"Ay, a pain to make you smile. Endure it, brother."

"Perhaps we should find a physician, after all. A true stitcher." Rory seemed serious. "Check on your threads."

"It's good stitching."

"Perhaps it needs something more. A poultice, perhaps."

"I'm game for it. I'll confess I know little about medicines."

Rory moaned. "Any farm wench can make a good poultice."

"That's an old wives' tale."

"Old wives have the best tails, says I." Rory tried to laugh but the pain made him stop.

"I'll stitch it again. Make it tighter."

"No! No more needles!"

"Then what? You want me to kiss it? Like Mother used to?"

Rory took a long breath, let it out slow. "Must find a farm around with a wife knowledgeable in poultice patting."

"There's none I've seen along this road. Only those farms that've fallen. No wives there but ghosts."

"Must be a farm somewhere on this road."

"It ain't farm country, not with these thick forests. Would a wood witch be of service, you think?"

"I don't trust them. Could slip me a bad poultice. Then I'd surely be worse. No, must be a farmer's wife."

"Lot easier to stitch you more."

"You've no light touch, brother."

"I can wield a needle as good as Longclaw."

Rory winced in pain. "We must stop for a spell."

"Then where?"

"This road goes east. To Springer's Field, where they had the big battle sixteen years ago. Seven princes slaughtered! And many more commonfolk. And 'twas Flanigan, King of Louis, came out victorious. King of all the Missourites after that. All Hail!" He craned his neck around. "There's bound to be a crossroad pointing us south. Then we'll reach Fort Branson. I know the physician there."

"Fort Branson? I thought it burned down."

"No, still stands. They repaired it. Need it to guard the southern reaches from the Arkans."

"So many of us, pushed into these bands that fight against each other." Stank let out a weary sigh for the first time in years. "I only want to go hither and thither providing my services in the name of family growth. Not have any need to fight. I'm tired of the militia's demands."

"Ay, you're one to talk! You'd be a captain if you stayed."

"Don't want that. I fight to protect."

"And help me wed a princess." Rory winced again. "If I dare can make it to Louis."

"The lady will surely be impressed by your sustained vigor," said Stank and laughed loudly.

"I'll be quite well by then. You'll see."

"First, then, to Fort Branson to find you a bigger needle."

"And a sweet-smelling poultice."

"Maybe a sweet-smelling maiden to rub it on you, eh?"

Stank led his brother atop Winnie through the wooden gates of Fort Branson, what seemed more a village than a military encampment. As they approached, he'd regarded the long lake, twisting through the dense forest like a lizard's tail, wondered if it joined a river that flowed to Louis. He could put his brother on a boat and off they'd go. He knew there was once a wide river passing Louis, although it had slipped to a mere shallow stream over the years, only a tract of mud in some seasons.

"Haven't been here for a couple years," Rory sang, pleased to find a bit of civilization in the wilds of Ozark. "Looks almost new again."

"Where is the physician?" Stank asked his brother.

Rory shook his head. "Must be here somewhere."

"Here is somewhere."

"I mean he is here in some place."

"We's here and he's somewhere. In a place."

Rory grew angry. "I said that: *here somewhere*. He's someplace."

"So where's this physician?"

"I'm not fibbing," said Rory. "There must be a physician here."

"Here where?"

Stank stopped Winnie, called out from the middle of the street, making people halt their daily going about to stare hard at the pair of unsavory travelers.

"Anyone?" He looked at their faces staring back at him: likewise weary, fearful of a big man, unwilling to help. "Ain't gonna hurt you.

Need a physician, is all."

"Billy's his name, I think," said Rory, and Stank called out the name but got no response.

"It's like they're all deaf as dung," Stank grumbled.

"It's a work day. They have things to do."

"Physicians got things to do," said Stank. He tugged the reins, leading Winnie down the main street, reading off the shop names as they went.

"*Doctor William F. Payne*," Stank read on one storefront. "Not a physician I would recommend. Not if you want a smooth outcome."

"It's just a name. Not a treatment," Rory barked.

Chuckling, Stank helped his brother down off Winnie, leaned him against the storefront like a bundle of sticks. Rory cried out in pain, cursing.

"You're acting worse than a militia recruit smelling cannon grain the first time," Stank snarled at him.

He helped Rory awkwardly inside the medicine-scented shop, dark but for what light came through the dirty front windows, and dropped him on a three-legged stool by a high table.

"Anyone about?" called Stank, hands on hips.

A buxom woman in a white gown came out from the back room, stopped at another table where she gathered up several items and returned into the back room with them.

"You saw us, did you not?" Stank called after her.

She came out from the back room again, regarded the pair with a frown. Yet at the sight of Stank, her eyes widened. She acted prim, brushed her gown and stood straight, as rigid as a commander. It must be clear to her that Stank brought an injured friend.

"What need you?" she asked in a dry voice, clearly putting away her first impression of the warrior.

"My brother's got a wound," Stank announced. "Vagabonds gave attack in the forest. Fair number of miles behind. I stitched him as best I could. He wants a poultice for the pain." He grinned at her. "I think it's just a ruse to get me to delay our journey. We're off to the capital."

"Capital, eh? Which one?" she asked in a plain voice.

"Louis," Rory called out. "There is no other."

"Oh, there are many, each making claim," she said with a smile, giving a grateful glance at Stank.

"Louis is the only one that matters," Rory insisted.

"He claims he's got business there," said Stank and Rory pinched his lips. "Then this happens."

He lifted Rory's tunic, showing the wound on his lower back.

"Flesh wound," she muttered, and Stank laughed.

"In a raw spot," Rory explained. "It's a prodigious pain."

Stank gave a snort. "You're a great pain, brother!"

The woman winced, snuck a wily wink at Stank. She obviously had seen worse wounds. Stank startled.

"Not much to brag on," said the woman.

Stank couldn't resist regarding her buxom profile as she leaned over to examine Rory sitting on the stool.

"You can fix him?" asked Stank.

"And a poultice," Rory added, voice desperate.

"Poultice isn't required," she said sternly.

"Are you the physician?" asked Rory, concerned he wouldn't get a poultice. Stank glared at him; he liked having the woman present, liked her medicinal fragrance. He sniffed close to her.

"I'm the doctor's daughter," she responded without cheer, giving Stank another wink. "I'm learning the arts. I know most treatments. He leaves the minor work to me. Father is out presently."

"You can repair him?" Stank checked. "Ready to ride again?"

She started to smile, caught herself, maintained her stern façade but snuck a look at the big man. "Ride? I wouldn't know whether he could ride again. Couldn't he ride before?"

A full smile burst upon her face – standing so only Stank could see. Puzzled, he watched this curvy woman, her face brightening. After a moment he understood what she said, smirked at her.

"We came on one horse because *my brother* lost his in an earlier fight. Before this wound found him in yet another fight."

The woman gave a nod. Too many wounds to repair, she seemed to be thinking. Stank watched closely: the dip in her cheek, the glint of her eyes, the fullness of her lips, the way her strong throat slid down to those luscious mounds—

"So much fighting," she was saying as she examined the wound. "Men such as yourselves always fighting."

"We don't seek it," Stank replied. "We end it." He gave a pat to the hilt of Longclaw. "Like any good swordsman."

"Ah, so you've a good sword, have you?" She grinned at Stank.

"Will there be a poultice?" Rory spoke to break up the flirting. "I will need a poultice to soothe this pain."

The woman gazed up at Stank, her eyes making him twitch. She turned her attention to the wounded brother.

"It's stitched fine," she said. "If you're to have a poultice, you'll be bed-ridden for a day or two. It'll make you weak. Too weak to travel. That's so the medicine can heal you. Have you time to stay a while?" She gave Stank a strange look. "Time for a rest?"

"It's not our plan," Stank replied, not quite sure of her meaning. Perhaps there were two meanings in her words. "But if we must, we must." And he saw her smile.

"No – we must be going on our way as soon as possible," insisted Rory. "Just slap a poultice on me and strap me up and I'm good for going – and on we go."

"You'll grow faint," said the woman with amusement. She batted her eyes, shifting her gaze to Stank. "You could fall off your horse. That would make the wound worse. Then you'll need to stay longer in the *front resting position*." Her eyes rested on Stank.

"Wouldn't be the first time," Stank said with a chuckle.

The woman looked at Rory's wound closer, bending over. "Maybe a poultice is not necessary. Looks to be a good stitching. No swelling. No pus that I can see. I can drop some germ killer on it."

"Germ killer?" Stank hadn't heard that term before.

"Yes, pain is caused by *germs*." She noticed he didn't understand. "They're very small things that bite you deep down inside you. Often dozens of them. Hundreds in a bad case. Much too small to be seen without a special eye-glass. It takes special medicine to kill them."

"Like tiny demons, eh?" Stank screwed his face up in wonder.

"Yes, demons. Tiny little demons. We call them germs."

Stank couldn't help but lean back, sneaking a view of her grand posterior as she explained about germs. He got caught as she stood up straight again. She gave him a wink as though she didn't mind his looking, seemed to enjoy his attention.

"No poultice is needed," she declared, brushing her hands.

"But I need a poultice! One of the good ones. To make dead the pain. I can't go on without it. And we must go on."

Stank turned to her. "Can you make up something for him?"

Her smile slapped him awake. "Something?"

"To shut him up," he spoke. "I don't care if it works or not."

She smiled again, gave him a wink as clear as a horse kick, then turned and stepped into the back room.

"There. You satisfied?" said Stank to Rory.

"Thanks, brother."

"Don't thank me. Your pain was causing me pain."

"I appreciate your concern."

He gazed around the office, staring at the shelves of bottles and jars, wondering what they all were. He never believed much in those pills and ointments. He'd been lucky in fighting. Some cuts, sure. A bad puncture once. All healed up nicely without any poultice.

With his brother receiving the poultice and resting on his belly to let it start healing, Stank was free to wander about Fort Branson. It actually stood as a fort, built for defense, no longer just a village. There were high wooden walls and guards walked the landings with bows. Outside the walls, the forest had been cut back to allow open area the guards could keep watch over, leaving a chorus of stumps. Beyond the cut-down area, the forest gloom could hide an attacking force, Stank decided.

He continued strolling down the main street, carefully stepping past filth and garbage tossed out or dropped behind dumb animals. A certain smell wafted through the streets, reminded him of home. The people he passed looked glum. Yet they moved with urgency, as though they'd better finish their tasks quickly or else be punished. None gave a smile or a greeting, looked at him in a way letting him know he didn't belong, wishing him gone.

He found not a single tavern although a food shop had a corner with shelves of bottles for sale. He saw signs on several streets that warned of drinking in a public area. Now, if only he had a room for the night, a place where he could drink some good brew and roll on a soft bed with a sweet-smelling serving girl. He grinned to himself. The only one fitting his present wishes was that woman doctor.

What was her name? She never said. More of the coldness of this fort-town. People kept to themselves. Ah! If one's name were known, one might be called out, sent for unpleasant duties. Better to be like a ghost, nameless and secretive.

Fort Branson had the feel of a place under siege, as though they expected an attack. Wichita, the west side, had little fear of attack. Nothing anyone would want there. People lived happy lives, or so he thought. Care-free, he called it. His life was a happy one, and to him that was all that mattered. People in this fort-town, however, didn't appear happy. Better to leave as soon as he and his brother could.

He strolled back to the physician's office. Inside his brother still lay flat on his belly on the high table, snoring away, loud like a well-fed hound.

"Haven't slept much, being on the trail for days," Stank told the woman doctor at her quizzical look. She appeared annoyed by Rory's behavior.

"Not many do," she said, giving Stank a longer look. Something about her: the pink of her cheeks, the brightness of her eyes. That figure pressing against her gown, pushing the cloth to its limit.

Stank turned his eyes to Rory. "How long before he can go?"

"Let him sleep it away. The poultice will make him sleepy."

"So hours?" Stank grinned at her.

"At least a few." She gave another wink.

"What's your name, miss?" He tried to offer a polite smile.

"Mona," she answered hesitantly.

"You don't like your name?" He stepped closer, then realized his road scent was strong and took a step back.

"My name is fair. I don't mind it." Her smile was strange, unlike when they'd first entered the office. "What's yours?"

"Stan." He forced a smile when she didn't seem to like the name. "That's short for Stanley."

"I like Stanley. Suits you better than Stan." Then she grinned in a new, bolder way. "You're a large fellow. You need a large name."

"Yes, I think so." He liked her, wanted to know more. "My poor brother – and folks that know me – they call me Stank. Because of the K of my middle name. It's Kirk."

"You have a middle name?" Her smile spread wider. "You must be some kind of royal."

"We once was." He hoped he didn't look like he was lying. "Well, it was long ago. After the plague but before the new capital. One of my kin was the vice-president in the old capital. It's written so you know it's true. And my mother recounts it. A long story."

He noticed how she'd sidled up to him, gazing up at his face and he wished he'd trimmed back his scraggily beard.

"Mine is a long story, too," she said, her voice hazy. Hearing her voice soften pleased him. "Do you like long stories? I do. The longer the better. How long's yours?"

"Will you tell it to me?" Stank asked too innocently, feeling her warm breath before his face.

"You wish to hear it?" she asked, leaning in.

Stank gave a curt nod. "I do."

"Father is away," she said, her tone different. "He is past due. I can tell you a story while we wait. The long one, if that interests you." She blinked. "First, you should clean yourself. There's a basin in the back room. You have time for a bath."

"A bath?" That surprised him. He expected something else.

She smiled at him, daring to show her teeth, still white and even as a saw blade. That pleased him.

"Yes," she said.

"Yes...?" He remained puzzled.

"You do want a hot bath, don't you? To wash off the trail?"

"I'm used to it," he said quickly, then stopped to think.

"I'm not used to it," she said, feigning revulsion. "I shall help you bathe. I'm good at it. It's what we call 'water therapy'."

"Oh?" Then, catching on to her wiles, he stammered: "Why, yes. Yes, I do. A bit of therapy would be good."

"I knew you were a royal," she said cheerily.

He chuckled, feeling flattered. "I'm game for a dunking." He had to stare into her eyes. "One thing: Will there be soap?"

"Soap is the magic potion." Her eyes brightened, held his gaze. "It makes everything slide together easy. You want everything to slide easy, do you not?"

"Easy is a good thing, I think."

"It is."

"Unless you crave something hard."

"That is my wish, Stanley."

"Is it?"

"First...."

She took his rough hand into her soft hand, led him to the back room. More shelves stood there, filled with odd jars and bottles, boxes of medicines, rolled up scrolls – magic spells, he imagined. Looked like an apothecary. Yet in the center of the room sat a large metal basin, sized for three-quarters of a grown man. To the side, against the plaster wall, stood a heating unit with a metal chimney going to the roof. Orange flames boiled from wooden sticks piled in the tray beneath the grill. A big pot sat over it, steaming.

She let go of his hand to fetch the pot of hot water.

"Once you're clean, I will tell you my story."

"Seems a fair deal. I like stories where everything's easy. They're the best ones."

They heard stirring in the outer room, kept silent to see if it would pass but heard a body fall, crash to the floor, and a man cry out.

"Damn poultice! Sent me into dream land. Into that horror with no mission. What a dark place!" Rory grumbled. "What'd she put in this poultice?"

Mona got herself up from the soapy water, stood dripping down over Stank as he lay back in the wash basin, arms behind his head, contentedly numb. She grabbed a towel, juggling her breasts to keep them covered as she hurried to dry herself.

"I've seen them already," Stank chuckled. "You've nothing to feel shame for. They're the finest I've ever seen." He pointed his chin at her lower portion, the lawn overgrown. "Yet you leave the southern paradise uncovered. It's a mystery."

"I have only two arms to cover myself, sir," she said, acting coy, then stepped from the basin, wiping her legs and feet.

"You're a fine looking woman, Mona," he said, smiling happily as he lay back in the sudsy water. "I liked your story. A fine romance. I liked how it ended. A happy ending. I shall return another day for the next chapter."

But she was out the door, hurrying to the patient.

"Mona?" he called, then again after a while.

He slipped into a slumber. When he awoke later and got himself up and dried, he stretched his arms and legs, did his training moves. He stopped to listen for sounds from the outer room. Hearing none, he pulled on his clothing.

"Where are you, my dear?" he called, stepping out to the shop.

"You don't need to call me that," his brother muttered.

Rory lay upon the high table again, covered with a sheet.

Stank watched him, turned back the sheet to inspect the wound. The poultice remained in place. Looked no better than before.

"It's fine now," Stank told his brother, replacing the sheet.

"Ay, a poultice is a good thing." Rory tried to look up. "Told you it would be. I feel much better this morning."

"It's the same day. Still after noontide," said Stank, chuckling. He spied the time device on the wall, clicking at every minute. "Two hours only have passed."

"That's all?" Again Rory tried to look up from the table.

"Yes, but enough."

"Yes, a poultice serves us well."

"Indeed." Stank grinned to himself. "You were right. A good stop for us. And I got me some therapy, too."

"I do smell a flowery scent. Pricks my nostrils. Is it you? What've you done to yourself?"

"Only a bath." He laughed dismissively. "Right fine therapy, I'll confess. I'm fresh as daisies, ready for the remainder of our road."

"Then we best be off before I fall into dream land again. Aargh, it's a frightful place. I was surrounded by demons though they had

47

the appearance of comely maidens. Danced for me, got me excited, made me spill my seed, then tormented me by turning into red-faced devils with pitchforks, all coming at me, crying they'd have me for dinner before I could awaken."

Stank shook his head. "That is a frightful dream."

He looked around the shop, expecting to see Mona.

"Where did she go?" he asked Rory.

"A poultice sleep will do that. Ay, I'm back again, no worse."

"Glad to hear it." Stank looked around the room. "Now where did our fine doctor go off to?"

"All I heard was some man coming to tell her news," said Rory. "She rushed out. Seemed important. Didn't say nothing to me."

Stank stood boldly in the shop's entryway, gazing up and down the street, not seeing her.

5

THE WOODS HAVE KNIVES

"IF YOU'RE READY, we can go," said Stank, seeing his brother off the table and sitting on the stool. Another glance at the doorway. "I wonder why our lady doctor hasn't returned. Where could she be?" He mused a while. "I thought I treated her fine. No complaints."

Rory reached back to check on his poultice. "What's this? You and her?" He grumbled. "It's no wonder she gave me a fine poultice that sent me far away. She wanted time to dally with you."

"As I recall, it was you that wanted a poultice," Stank said. "And she wanted me. Said as much. And giving me the wink-eye. As long as I had a bath first."

"A bath?" Rory made a face. "That's her wile, is it?"

"It wasn't a wileful thing. Many partake."

"And did you?"

"Have the bath? Ay, did."

"That's the awful smell that stings my poor nose. Like the death of flowers. A graveyard of them."

"It wasn't unpleasant." Stank grinned. "She had the healing arts under her belt, to be sure. I'm much refreshed."

"And you were rightly healed? What was your injury?"

"She found a wound long left untreated. That's what she said. So I allowed her to ease it."

"Oh, 'twas her wound, not yours, eh? A ruse."

"That's what she said."

"Ay, a woman'll say all manner of things to get a warrior into a bath. Then comes the drowning. Or a portion of poison. You better be on guard for all manner of wiles."

"I was, brother."

"You're a tempting target for wiles."

Then Rory had to launch into the tale once more of his dalliance with Daniella the Fair, as he continued to call her. The senior maid in the household of the Robinson family, she of the silvery hair and snowy cheeks, pink in all the right places, as he described her each time, with eyes like shimmering jewels. She had but one flaw: she wasn't impressed with Rory. He tried for two years to woo her and got rebuffed each time. Even so, he built up in his mind that she was secretly in love with him and would soon let down her guard and tell the world of their love, then marry him in a lavish ceremony the whole community would attend.

"That was only a dream," Stank spoke when the telling had gone on too long. "A dream without a poultice."

Rory told everyone he eventually grew tired of her, when it had always been her rejecting him. He explained to anyone wishing to know that he was no longer interested in her. She wasn't as fair as he'd believed. She was free to do as she wished. She could marry that doorman of the household and Rory was fine with it. Not one ounce of envy in him, he insisted. Of course she would forget him.

"I pray this princess in Louis doesn't have the same trouble with you as that maid in Wichita."

"Not at all," said Rory. "We met. Our eyes met. I'm certain there was a connection. I can feel it even now."

"Like an arrow shot into your heart, eh?"

"Ay, like that. Not a real arrow, mind you."

"Naturally. An arrow of the mind."

Stank looked out the windows of the shop for Mona's return, saw none on the street appearing as her. Only grim villagers going about their tasks. He thought back through her actions: she heard Rory stir, got up from the bath, dried herself and pulled on her gown, out to check on Rory, picked him off the floor and onto the table again, then...left? It didn't make sense.

"Where could she be?" he asked the dirty street.

"Ay, she's done with you," Rory sang out, feeling they were even on the jabs now.

"Done perhaps." Stank continued to survey the street. "Yet it's a mystery I would solve before we leave."

Rory grumbled. "And pay for her services?"

"I might've paid already," Stank said with a dry chuckle.

"Perhaps it's best we go on." Rory attempted a laugh. "Before she returns. We can avoid payment."

"I shall pay the woman in coin," Stank said firmly.

"Perhaps you already paid her with your time as a healer."

"I said that. 'Twasn't that kind of healing," he muttered, staring out the window. "She wouldn't leave the shop unattended. It's odd."

Stank turned to his brother.

"I'll go out, search for her. You wait here. Tend to yourself. Sit still and let the poultice heal you. I'll return shortly."

"As you wish." Rory had a big smile. "Mark my words, brother: I fear she has a pull on you. Hooks cut deep. Take your greatsword."

"I always take Longclaw," Stank barked.

Atop Winnie, Stank rode slowly up and down the major passages of Fort Branson, looking for Mona and getting only hateful stares back at him. He kept a smile on his face and his sword unbrandished as he went, clopping through the muddy streets. He never called out a name nor asked anyone about the woman, only looked.

Not until he came to the main square where a throng of people gathered, carts and tables set up for market day. A steady exchange of produced goods and credit notes, some coins, some fair barter. It seemed orderly, unlike the markets in Wichita. Maybe there were laws in place here to keep people civil. He watched a while, shoppers noticing him atop his war steed. Who is this guardian?

Seeing enough, he turned Winnie to return to the shop.

"Ho! Guardsman," Stank called to a man in a gray uniform with a heavy musket leaning on his shoulder. "Have you seen a woman in physician's garb traipsing about the streets in the past hours?"

"I'm not a guardsman," the man snapped, presenting the musket as his frilly crimson epaulets danced on his shoulders.

"Pardons, I took you for a guard of this fort," Stank replied and gave a mock salute.

"I'm sergeant of the battery," the man boasted.

"A fort should have a battery. A good idea. I say: have you seen such a woman about?"

"A few women pass by, as usual, though I hardly give eyes to them. A waste of time. My duty is to mind the garrison."

"Yes, indeed. But have you seen her?" Stank held out his hand. "She's stands yea tall, has a fine bosom." He grabbed air breasts to mark the size. "With brown, brown*ish* hair, cut rather short for a maiden, and wearing a physician's white gown. Rosy cheeks...." He paused to think of more description.

"There was a woman in white going to the main gate a while ago, I recall. Don't know about the rest of her."

"To the main gate?" Stank looked up, tried to see down the street to the gate but the street bent.

"Yes, out the gate. Seemed in a great hurry."

Stank stared down the street. "My thanks."

"Best of luck finding your wife," the sergeant chuckled, setting the heavy musket upon his shoulder once more.

Stank grinned awkwardly. "Oh, she's not...."

The sergeant had started marching away, calling to his charges to get in ranks, so Stank turned Winnie, going toward the gate.

If Mona had left the fort, what could be the reason? If he were to follow her, what would become of Rory back in the shop? Perhaps he should go and tell his brother he was riding out to search for her. Perhaps his brother would fear he was abandoning him. Perhaps the argument that would ensue would delay him too much to make good in his search. Perhaps he should simply go out and find her, then return to get his brother. Rory would have a welter of words for him either way.

"A pesky pox upon thy purple pustule," he cursed, and urged his steed on to the gate.

Guards waved to him as he passed under the arch, out of the fort and turning up the road. The forest beckoned, deep darkness hiding his next adventure.

"Where are you, Mona?" he called, keeping his voice low. He was unwilling to rouse the spirits of the wood. They might be displeased by the interruption. "Step forth for me, Mona," he begged, glancing side to side as he passed.

He set down a path where trees reigned overhead and the leafy brush rising from the fecund ground formed a lush tunnel. He kept his hand on the hilt of Longclaw, ready for ambush. The greenery overwhelmed his eyes, a dizzy mosaic of hues. Narrowing his gaze, he believed he saw vagabonds behind every leaf. He dared not call out for Mona now.

He set his steed to a trot, enough to pass through the green way into a more open part of the forest. He could see between the thick trunks here, better assess the branches, detect danger awaiting him among the foliage. He startled a pair of deer which darted away.

"Are you here, Mona?" he sang in a light voice, hand on the hilt of his greatsword.

He tramped along the trail. The vegetation closed on him, twigs brushing his arms and knees as he rode on. Perhaps this was the wrong trail. Wasn't the one he and Rory had traveled going to the fort. He sensed he might be lost. Better to return the way he'd come, start again from the gate.

He whirled Winnie around, rattling the brush. With a last look back, he noticed the rustling of bushes.

"Whoa," he called to Winnie.

He set his steed facing the movement. Merely wind or a person of interest? His gloved hand curled around the hilt of his sword, slid the blade free and held it ready.

"Come forward, if you dare," he called ahead.

The bushes ceased their shivering, lay still a moment.

Stank was ready for the attack: a quartet of foul fur-clad beasts beset him from three sides. Winnie took out the attacker coming up behind them with a well-directed kick. Stank sliced downward with Longclaw, separating mind from matter. One savage fell apart upon the ground. The mighty upswing took out the lance thrusted toward him, and the downswing left the lanceman armless. Two arms with one cut. The savage would thrust no more.

"Now be at peace," Stank shouted. "You should know not to test a warrior from Wichita! Foolish fools acting foolish."

Leaving the bloody pieces splayed in the foliage and fallen upon the ground, Stank set his steed to return to the fort.

A cry arose from somewhere in the wood. A woman's voice!

Stank listened, locating its source, then fixed the direction and stomped through the brush, greatsword ready.

He broke into a clearing where a camp had been set up. Leaning branches with ragged skins lain over, a poor man's hovel, not a brief overnight shelter. The fire pit smoked. From atop his steed he didn't see any inhabitants. Perhaps they were the savages who'd attacked him moments before.

Dismounting, the only person he found was in one of the leaning shelters: a mid-aged man looking beaten and faint. He was tied up, hands behind. Stank checked for weapons, found none, and cut the rope loose. He helped the man up. Before he could thank Stank, the woman's cry arose again.

"It's my daughter," the man spurted.

Stank went to the next leaning shelter and found Mona thrown down on a bed of grass, her white gown torn, her hands tied in front. He cut her free. She beamed at the sight of her father behind Stank. Reaching for her hand, Stank helped her up.

"Father!" she cried out, standing wobbly before them, then went to hug the man.

Although touched by the reunion, Stank whirled about to guard the entrance, found none approaching.

They stepped from the shelter, stood in the clearing.

"Thank you, thank you," Mona called to Stank.

She wept against her father, his arms wrapped tight around her. They muttered words to each other, chiding the misfortune of trying to do good works in the wilds and the danger they'd found.

"Sometimes it's best not to do good work," Stank offered. He had to recall the times he'd helped here and there, for nothing more than a smile, a bed, a supper, or all three. And today's adventure.

They ignored him, consumed by their mutual joy at being freed, but Mona's brief smile was all the thanks he needed.

"How'd you get caught up here?" Stank asked, then saw how her happy expression changed, as though fear once more enveloped her.

He spun around in time to cleave the rushing savage into two halves, shoulder to hip as Longclaw bit.

"Any more?" Stank shouted across the camp and into the woods.

Only silence answered.

"That's all, I'd guess. Savages!" He turned to Mona. "You were an hour away from the shop. I worried."

"They held my father until I appeared," she said breathlessly. "I got a message. I had to hurry to my father. They captured me, too."

"Captured you both, eh?" He looked her over, searching for any wounds she might have as she held her torn gown together. "An evil scheme! Yet you are safe now."

"Thank you!" She reached for him.

He held up his free hand. "Stand back. There may be more."

As she stepped back, two more savages rushed at them from the dense flora, brandishing spears. Stank swept his blade at the nearby shelter, cutting the skin covering off the frame and tossing it over the rushing savages as they arrived. They fell under the skin and rolled into a bundle. Stank stove the bundle twice and retrieved a bloody blade. He listened for cries of pain, stabbed the blade again.

"Let us leave this horrible place," he told Mona once he was sure the savages were done. He reached back for her hand.

Her father stood behind them, looking weary, rubbing his wrists.

"Come, Father," she said, going to him.

"Ay, happy reunion," Stank sang, nodding in satisfaction. "How'd you get into this trouble?"

The father started to speak: "I feel called to administer medical treatments—"

Mona broke from her father's hug, continued for him: "My father often goes forth to the woods to help these poor folk."

"Poor folk? Hah!" Stank made a nasty face. "They nearly took my soul – would've if they'd had any training."

"They are sickly," said the father. "They have—"

"My father treats their ills. Many ills which you can get living this way, hiding in the woods."

"Their minds are addled," said the father. "The sad effects of the terrible virus passed down for generations. This is the best they can do. So I...I try to help them."

Mona's face changed. "This time they sought to keep him. They wouldn't let him go after giving them treatments. I got word just as I tended to your brother, so I ran out. Forgive me for leaving you. I thought to return shortly."

Stank frowned. "It's a fair reason. Go as you must."

"I came to free him."

"You should've brought me with you," he said.

"I expected to speak to the folk. They would free him."

"Not what happened, was it?"

"Then I was captured, too. I feared for him. They would hurt him. Then you came. I thank the spirits of the forest that you came after me, helping us – saving us!"

Stank's face brightened. "Seems I was born to save the weak and weary, to cut down evil forces. Whenever the force is with us. And, not only that, but to sire the next generation of warriors."

"The land needs more saviors." She swept against him, her arms around his mighty chest, but he kept his arms free, sword held out. "Thank you, Stanley!"

"I thank you, as well," said the father, reaching for his free hand to shake. "Praise to the gods for you!"

"All is well," said Stank humbly. "Let me be free. Free to fend off the next attack."

He pushed her away, shook the father's hand loose, stood ready, surveying each direction.

"The woods have knives," he muttered, searching for danger. It always seemed to follow him. He hated greenery.

They put the father up into the saddle and Stank led his horse on through the forest with Mona walking behind them. He kept his sword ready, the trail being narrow. His eyes checked each dark patch among the greenery, expecting to see eyes watching him. He listened for any unnatural movement.

He waved Mona to silence whenever she tried to speak.

"Now you may speak," said Stank as they broke from the forest and saw the gate of Fort Branson ahead.

Stank gave a nod to the gate guards, knowing him by sight.

"He saved us from Zarkers," Mona called to them.

The guards seemed impressed, saluted them.

Arriving at the physician's shop, they were confronted by Rory, sitting up on the high table, angry that the poultice had no further effect. He glared at Stank.

"Good you returned from your holiday," Rory complained. "I'll be needing a new poultice. If your mistress can fix up one."

6

PLANS IN PERPETUAL MOTION

THE SUPPER MONA prepared for them was a hunk of meat, likely from a hog, with cut potatoes and greens. They pulled out a bottle of wine to celebrate their freedom. Dr. Payne gave a toast to Stank for his bravery. Stank said it wasn't bravery; the Zarkers were so poorly trained they had no chance against him.

"Still, we thank you for coming after us," said Dr. Payne. Then he shook his head slowly. "I dare not think how it would have ended if my younger daughter, Lotta, was captured. Lotta would not have lasted long. Good that she snuck away with that jester fellow, a bard named Cooper, now free to do her tricks. A couple years gone now. They go town to town gaining coin for their amusements. No telling what transpires after the shows. It is an awkward thing to endure."

But Stank's eyes were set on Mona. He liked watching her move about the kitchen, between kitchen and dining table, and returning: the way her simple dress swayed, the way her mousy hair had been let down, ranging over her shoulders, how her bosom barely brushed the pots and pans as she leaned to tend them.

"She can cook, too," Rory sang, enjoying the first bites of a good meal in many days. "And doesn't taste like a poultice."

"Enough with your poultice, brother!" Stank snapped.

"She's a fine poultice patter." Rory smiled at Mona. "A fair maid with a fair touch. Fit for such as my brother."

"I'm not a fair maid, sir," Mona responded in a polite voice. "I've trained in the medical arts for years. Most of my life, you might say, at the side of my father."

Dr. Payne beamed at her. "It is truth." He sat visibly happy but remained weary from his adventure. "After her mother fell ill, she was desirous of learning how to aid the sick and treat wounds. I had no son to follow me, so it was Mona who took up the medicine bag."

"Someone must keep the villagers healthy," said Mona.

"Lotta was useless. Only a bag of tricks for her," said Dr. Payne.

"It's a grand thing to follow your father into a profession," Stank said with a long look at Mona. "My father was a warrior, and so am I. It's what I've trained for."

"And he's the best!" Rory cheered, then went on describing some of Stank's more exciting exploits and boastful highlights, even as Stank tried to wave him to end it.

"All well and good to be able to fight," Dr. Payne spoke up when Rory stopped. "An important set of skills, much like a surgeon. That affords you the opportunity for success."

"Ay, success in battle is paramount," Rory cheered.

"The same for medicine," said the physician.

"A community needs all manner of professions, I would think," Mona spoke, gazing at her father.

"To defend and protect family and community is paramount, as well," her father offered. "There is a need. Especially in these dark times. Why, just look at the Zarkers. See how poor they've become. Regressed to such a barbaric state, living like animals. Dressed in furs and not much else. In a camp of animal skin shelters. We have a fortified village with high walls and a strong gate, with enough services to allow us to carry on."

He looked at Stank, then Rory. They nodded in response.

"We will carry on," said Dr. Payne. "We will grow. We are not yet ready to give up on a society based on equality and mutual love. We used to have that everywhere, if my reading of the history books is true. But it's been ages—"

"You've a history book?" asked Rory incredulously.

"Ay, that mutual love is a good thing," said Stank, giving a wink to Mona, who blushed. Dr. Payne noticed.

"I have several," the physician replied. "They are very old and I dare not open them often." He smiled at Rory, turned to Stank.

"I intend to find a good husband for Mona," said the good doctor. "She deserves both a calling in medicine and the pleasures of a wife. In whichever order she thinks best."

"Oh, Father," Mona exclaimed, blushing.

Stank grinned. "You wish her to have a husband who lets her continue treating people's ills, eh?"

"Exactly that. He must allow her to follow after me, regardless of what arrangements the two of them would make in the home. I will support any plan that lets her carry on after me."

"A village needs a physician," Mona quipped. "I should be happy to carry on after you, Father. Yet you've a long span yet to go. You needn't worry." Her eyes shifted to Stank. "I shall find a husband, one who wouldn't get a sour mind for me treating people of whatever assails them. I've pledged to do that."

"Seems she'd be good on the journey, eh?" Rory nudged Stank.

"That is all I'm asking of you, daughter," Dr. Payne replied.

Stank cleared his throat, ignoring his brother, grinning at Mona. "She's a fine...a fine woman. A physician, too. A worthy catch for any lucky man. A man with tolerance."

"I shall be the catcher, Stanley," said Mona too boldly. "Of a man who comes to my bed clean and sober. A man who wakes me to go to the clinic then welcomes me home at dusk. Who beds me well."

Dr. Payne nearly choked. "My dear...."

She gazed at Stank. "Will you help me clear the table? A good warrior must also be humble."

"Ay, humble." Stank nodded, stood and began gathering plates.

Past the bathing basin which he regarded with affection, Stank stood beside Mona at a smaller wash basin. Sweeping the plates free of remaining sauce and splashing them with hot water poured from the steaming kettle sitting on the brazier kept them busy. Rory and the physician continued the conversation in the outer room.

Stank pondered what Mona had said, smiling to himself.

"You're pleased," she said, noticing.

"Pardons for my brother's outrageous behavior," said Stank with his hands in the sudsy water. "Your father seems an honorable man.

If I were someone else, I might ask him for your hand in marriage."

"Your brother is turned askew by his condition. Nothing to worry about. As for my hands, warrior, I shall use them to heal."

"I believe you. And I welcome your healing touch. And perhaps more." He gave her a knowing look.

She smiled flirtatiously. "You've no wound, have you?"

"Only to my heart," he said, then feigned a sad sigh.

"Hearts are easily mended if that is all that ails you." She smiled deeply at him, pausing the washing. "If you've need of a treatment, there is a method."

"Oh, a method, eh?" He took her seriously.

"Yes," and she lifted her hands from the wash water and placed them around his grim face, wetting his beard. Leaning into him, she pressed her lips to his. Lingering, then parting. "How is your heart now, sir?"

"It beats faithfully," Stank replied. "Perhaps a bit quicker now, in truth. Is that a sign of trouble?"

"You can tell me. Is it? Have you want of trouble?"

"I've had enough of trouble for a day."

"Indeed you have, sir." She set her eyes hard on him. "Saving my father and me from those woodland savages is more than one day's work for most anyone. I cannot thank you too much. A supper and a kiss, I give you. That's the best I can do now. I might be persuaded to consider more...if Father were not so close."

"He needs to rest, I'm sure." Recalling the bath they'd shared, he glanced back through the doorway. "Talking with my brother shall make your father sleepy. Rory has a way with that. Then we can see what plans can be made for the two of us."

"The two of us? Have plans?" Her laugh was like holiday bells. "I think we already have plans." She gave him a wink.

He winked back at her, felt odd doing so. "Before, you mean? It was a bath, wasn't it?" He lifted the last plate up from the water, handed it to her. "Or only a bath? I thought more."

"A bath is part of the treatment," she said, wiping the plate with a towel. "You knew that, I'm sure."

Stank watched her hands slide smoothly over the plate – like they had over him in the bath. "There was no more sliding about than necessary. As you said. Forgive me for thinking of more." He studied her as she set the dried plate on the stack of dishes. "There must be a plan. The way you disrobed to join me in the bathing. The soap you so lovingly lathered over me. Those bubbles...."

"You had an unpleasant smell," she said sternly, then she turned playful, sniffing him. "I did sense a need in you. I'm good with that talent, and with touch. A touch to soothe your battle wounds. They will accumulate. The wound is inside."

"Inside, eh?" He thought a moment. "Never think of it that way. You may be right. Yet I welcomed refreshment."

"Refreshment? Is that all, warrior?"

"Ay, that and anything more."

"It was an easy chore and better done in the manner in which I did. As my father said: I am a professional. It was not to be seen as an invitation."

"Invitation? To what?" Feeling insulted, Stank glared at Mona, then brusquely wiped his hands on a fresh towel.

Mona held her smile firm.

"I am a practical woman, as you may have determined. I do not make idle prattle with random strangers. You, sir, were a stranger at that time. Seems days ago, granted. I still thank you for rescuing us. However, I had no further plan with you. Not then."

"No plan, eh? A play thing that happened by, eh?" He calmed, stood puzzled: her harsh words and yet the cheery smile, the rosy cheeks and fierce eyes. Was she a demon such as Rory warned him about? Longclaw was in the outer room.

"Oh, I suppose I gave wing to a fleeting fantasy," she spoke to his dour face, "yet it fluttered away as soon as I stepped into the bath. A large figure such as yourself left little space for me. Finish bathing and be done, I said to myself. Then your brother called forth about his poultice." She chuckled, blushing. "He loves a good poultice."

"Ay, he does." Stank shook his head. "And now? Have we a plan? You and me? Will we continue? Should I return here after seeing my brother to his destination? Will you wait for me?"

"Ho! You've got plans already set. Rein your steed, sir."

Stank grinned at the mention of his horse. Winnie was tied up in front of the clinic, a pail of water set before him, a bundle of hay for dinner bought from the livery on the next lane.

"Winnie is content," said Stank. "Now for you and me."

"I, too, am content," Mona spoke with another wink.

"Then let us make a plan – a new one – that I shall return to you in a short time. Away no longer than I must. And then? Perhaps we shall see each other anew and make still a newer plan. Perhaps that plan shall light up the world. Do you think it's possible, Mona?"

A boisterous smile swept across her face; her hand rose to hide it. "You, sir, are full of plans. I shall be here, doing my work, by my father's side. As always: tomorrow and the days that follow. And if you should happen by once more, I shall take another look at you. If I find you fair, I shall invite you in for a good supper."

"Supper only?"

"A good supper is always a start."

"An invitation then?"

"Perhaps."

"Then that shall be our plan. Agreed?"

She dared a winsome grin. "Let me give you a bit of spittle to remind you of me."

Fighting the hot flush of her face, she stepped up to him, slid her arms under his arms, almost clasping across his back, and stretched up for a kiss. He wrapped his mighty arms around her and their lips pressed hard.

They hadn't gotten far up the road to Louis before Rory, perched on the reddish mule Stank had to buy so they could continue on their journey comfortably, dared opine once more.

"She's fine making a poultice, yet what wife or daughter isn't? As for her wiles, she seemed well-trained. Hmm, perhaps taught it by a mother now gone? That's a clear mark of trouble, I say. You best keep away from her. That's my advice."

"You've no standing in this matter, brother," Stank responded.

"I'm your brother, as you just now called me. I look out for you. I give advice as befits my love for you. That's a duty of the first-born."

"Granted, and thanks."

"You only just met the woman, and she getting to her middling years, at that. You've not much of her youth left to enjoy."

"Ay, many a woman's taken within an hour of meeting. There's no claim of quality either way. Even after years of knowing each other and some stab you in the back, eh? Sometimes it's better to go to bed before she can get to know you too well."

Rory caught his brother's insinuation: a past romance.

"I still love her," Rory moaned. "Only a misunderstanding. That hairy Harriet, the hirsute whore, is a peculiar case. Bad timing. It won't happen with Majory, I feel very confident."

"Ho! You don't even know her."

"Not shared a hot bath, true. Yet that will come in due time."

Stank laughed. "After I defeat that duke in duel, eh?"

"Ay, that's the plan. And a fine plan it is."

"We shall see what plan you have when we arrive."

"I feel obliged to give you my opinion of your woman. Brotherly duty. She has skills – medical skills. Useful. Bodes well for a steady employ, as well as battlefield assistance. She can remain close by for mending you. Mend others, as well. Then again, perhaps you don't want her mending others, getting close to other burly men such as yourself. That hot bath you shared? Likely's her trap. Give him a taste, a good look, then let the poor man stew a while, giving up all his dignity before she drives her dagger into him. I can see it—"

"You have a way with words," Stank roared, "which go counter to any worthy purpose."

"Do I now?"

"You have much to say that need not be said."

Rory complained but Stank ignored him, urging Winnie into a quicker pace. The roadway opened from the forest, the fallow fields spreading outward, showing abandoned farmsteads and a few still open with hands working them. Stank gave a wave to a pair of boys cutting hay. They knew a warrior rode past, and would likely report to their parents what they'd seen.

"Now as I was saying," Rory started up. He proceeded to describe Mona, listing all of her good and bad traits.

Stank had enough of it and shouted at him to end it.

"I'm only concerned for your safety."

"Perhaps you got too much poultice," Stank called back. "Makes your tongue fall in fever, waves in the breeze like milkweed. Going nowhere and everywhere all at once."

"Now you've got the fine tongue, brother!"

"I'll not have you speaking of Mona in that way. She's my lucky problem, not yours."

Rory laughed. "So you confess she's a problem?"

"A fine problem to have. What to do about Mona?"

He sang out a happy tune, waving his free hand along.

"I should be so fortunate to have her as a problem. Long have I wished for a good wife. For a woman who could bear my faults, and overlook my flaws yet still find love for me. Not a twig of a woman a middling breeze could topple. Not a woman too hefty for me to carry to the bed. Nor a woman painted with pox. Nor one without a sturdy womb. She must have a fine head upon her strong shoulders, full of knowledge and the will to speak it, use it. A strong will to survive. Also to assert herself in appropriate situations. And I wouldn't mind if she should out-shine me, for we would know in our hearts how we fit together in our own time and place. Like two halves of a split peach. Naturally, I would wish her to have a fine body that matched mine: taut yet flexive. I've no need of a too-pretty lady, not like you seem to require, brother. Rather, if she has a basic, fair body and a rather fine smile, good teeth in the front, I would be grateful and appreciate her for all the days of my life – of our life together. Let her be a person of herself yet love me the same, as I shall love her no matter my calling in battle or bedroom. I wish for nothing more."

"It is a worthy wish, brother. Outlandish yet worthy."

"I dare wish for nothing less."

"You might aim low, and I applaud you for seeking simple traits which can satisfy you. But I require more, as you say. A beauty that stops men in their tracks, holds their eyes firm. A figure that tempts men to err, that keeps them awake at night in lust. Yet she is solely mine. Ay, I would want such a woman who can bring out my best, whatever it may be, then lay back to receive my best."

"You want a comely whore," Stank snapped, looking back. "Like our mother. I never would've guessed that." He laughed and Rory reddened close to the hue of his mule. "We all want our mothers, yet in a different body, so there's no shame in what we do."

"Come now, Fergie," Rory spoke to the mule. "Don't listen to my brother. He's full of the love virus, can't think clearly, can't be polite to man nor beast."

The reddish mule was neither young nor as fit as Stank would've wished, but the price matched their coin. Now they were low in the pouch. He'd waved off reward from the good doctor; his actions were merely the proper thing to do and he wouldn't want money for doing what's proper. He checked the mule's hooves and mouth, saw worn teeth. The animal had ribs showing but a good meal came with the price so he believed the mule could serve them for the journey. Get Rory to Louis and the mule need do no more.

"Ay, Mister Ferguson," Rory sang. "Son of Fergus, a Count of the Sedalia clan, breeder of tough mules. Pardons for forcing you on this labor. It isn't a wagon of heavy timber, at least. Only a poor man in search of his princess. You can bear me for that, can't you?"

"He won't have any opinion on the matter," Stank called back.

"Opinions are common as bad air," said Rory.

Stank roared with laughter. "And you've a supper of beans!"

Feeling insulted, Rory rose off the saddle and let go his gas, the noise startling the mule. "Ay, Fergie! There's a bit of fresh air."

Stank reached for his sword, eyes surveying the road ahead and the fields on either side.

"Let us stay silent now lest we draw the vain and curious to wish us harm." He kept his voice low. "There are many who dare to fancy themselves fighters. They'll wish to test their mettle against such as us. Stay ready, brother."

Rory got the message. "Ay, ready as ever, brother."

7

VAGABONDS ALIKE

AS THE ROAD turned up to hills trying to become mountains, the forest returned, thickening and pressing against them on both sides, slowing their travel as they had to keep watch with weapons ready for a skirmish.

Drums echoed through the trees and they paused to listen.

"Zarker," Stank muttered as Rory drew beside him on the mule. "They don't sound drums when they're preparing for attack. Must be a ritual feast."

"A wedding, perhaps?" Rory suggested, grinning.

"They don't marry, I heard. Just everyone takes everyone at wild whim. In a great circle, in a field, at midnight. They call a start and let them make play in the hay, then call a stop. A mating dance, it's called. Ring of poppy, I think. All fall down at the end."

"Seems a serious lack of organization," said Rory with a chuckle. "I could make a chart for them to follow, assign them partners. I can see it now: me, the ring-master. They'd thank me."

"You don't want to get involved with such as them. I saw one of their camps, remember, when I rescued Mona and her father. Worse than overnight stops we've set up. Savage living. One step above the beasts of the forest."

"Ay, yet living it is. A place set midway between man and beast."

"They'd eat you and me if they got a chance. Not even wait for the roasting, or making a savory sauce."

Rory shook his head. "Not a dinner I'd accept an invite to."

"You wouldn't have a choice," Stank grumbled. "Chewing on you before you were completely dead."

"Ay, a poor dinner. I would see that they tossed me up."

Stank laughed, then got quiet again.

They rode onward a fair distance more as the sun slid toward a cold horizon. The land had risen, leaving gaps between hills for the sunshine to hold steady a little longer. Yet a cool wind blew against them from the north.

Stank waved them to halt, needing to check the territory ahead, searching for a suitable campsite. He decided they should head to a spot across the field by the edge of the wood at the bend of a creek.

Rory stared at his brother, not following.

"What?" Stank called back.

Rory frowned, then urged his mule forward.

"Do you have it?" he asked Stank, coming alongside.

"Have what?" Stank seemed annoyed, wanting to hurry on.

"What you always carry with you. I recall you do, even in battle. You said before it reminds you of who you are and who you follow. A strange habit, yet you persist. I refer to the image."

"The image?" Stank made a face. "It's called a *picture*. An image set on paper. Mother said it shows the faces of our kin long ago."

"Yes, standing before a shop in their town," said Rory.

"How long ago, I do not recall—"

"A time is written upon the paper, is it not?"

"Ay, yet it's faded over the years. Cannot be read now. More than a hundred years ago, certainly. Perhaps longer."

"Maybe two hundred years. You think?"

"Could be." He patted his tunic, unable to feel the folded paper in his shirt's breast pocket. He became concerned, wished to reach in to be certain it remained there.

"Fetch it, then." Rory waved him to pull it out. "Let us give our eyes over to the memory page."

With a survey of the road ahead, Stank bit his glove, pulled it off and slid his hand inside the tunic, slipping into the pocket. A sigh of relief that it remained there despite all they'd been through the past week. He retrieved the folded paper from his pocket, held in a clear envelope of a strange material meant to protect it.

He held it up for Rory to see. "This?"

"There it is," Rory cried happily like he'd won a wager. "Open it. Let us gaze upon the faces of Lord Fritz's brood."

"Lord Fritz is much older than these kin on paper," said Stank, carefully unfolding the cardstock. "Mother called this kind of paper a *photo-graphic*. Back in those days they had a device could capture a scene with light, and then another device put it on paper like this. We can see this image from the past. Ah, can we do anything half of this now? Even in a city like Louis, full of all manner of modern machinery? Have they such devices there?"

"When I'm made a duke," Rory said proudly, "I shall require the invention of such a device. Then we shall arrange ourselves just like those folks and make a *photo-graphic*. I promise you, Stank. You'll be in the image same as the rest of us: me and Majory in our royal finery, and our brood. You're tall, so we'll put you in the back."

Stank studied the image. It had faded over the years yet he held it dearly, gazed upon each face. He lingered on the man standing at the center of the family portrait. Below the image, names had been written in blue ink by a steady hand. He counted the names, came to *Jacob Baumann, DDS*, the man in the center, looking as much like Stank himself as any of them although he wasn't nearly as big or strong. The tan-faced woman beside him must be his wife. *Trina* was the name written for her. The youth, four boys, their sons, stood tall, looking different from each other, having hair of black, brown, red, and yellow.

He showed the paper to Rory.

"Ay, them's the ones. Our kin. Lords of old. What happened to them? What a life they must've had back then."

Stank took a deep breath. "They lived. They had their lives. And they grew old and one day they died. We have no more accounting of them. Only this image on old paper that Mother kept, handed down to her from Great-Grandmother Augusta. In a way, brother, it's the most valuable thing left to Mother after the air-burst rained down."

"Lucky they lived on the west side, across the river," Rory spoke in reverence. "Pity others weren't on the west side. Then you and me might never've been born. Nor our mother born. Nor hers."

"It's a long, sad line of folk sharing our name," Stank spoke. "A clan named Baumann. Going all the way back to Lord Fritz and his great horn, calling warriors to battle from an Old Country. Ay, wish I could've seen that, heard its song roar in the olden days. I would've fought fiercely!"

"You would've," Rory agreed, patting his brother's shoulder.

Stank folded the cardstock, slid it back into the clear envelope, and returned it to his inner pocket, giving it a secure pat. He took up his glove once more. "To camp."

"Ah, they were simple folks," Rory continued thoughtfully as the mule followed Stank. "Not warriors like us. Simpler times. An easy life they had. Plenty of wine and roses, I suppose. Yet how far we've fallen from those days. How far, Stank...."

"Should've gone north, up to Springer's Field," Stank said, tending the campfire. "Then continue to the northeast on the Royal Road, as bad as it is. Our path through the hills is slow. And full of danger."

"We may be delayed too much," Rory assessed.

"Then you'll miss your chance, eh?" Stank chuckled. He would do anything for his elder brother but he still recognized the foolishness for which Rory was well-known. He would get big ideas in his head that couldn't be satisfied short of a long, hard effort. Like this queer journey. When his idea was proven false, he would dismiss it like a bad apple, never taking any blame for all that had transpired.

Stank regarded his brother a while as the man sat back against the blanket roll, puffing a stuffed weed.

"This leaf is a bit dull," Rory mumbled, holding up the roll.

"You best snuff it." Stank shook his head. "Zarkers can smell it."

"It's a small fog, nothing beyond this campsite, I assure you."

Stank glanced at Longclaw, always within reach. "I take little of your assurance to heart."

"You will be rewarded, brother. Have no worry. All hardship will prove your worth."

"That's not what ails me."

"Then what does?"

"This path – what we've ridden through the hills to Ava, a poor hamlet of fallen shacks and a few unburied bodies. Then onward to Mansfield, a village of burnt houses and burnt fields. That old man calling to us, begging for food."

"You gave him a bit, so no reason to feel glum."

"Not the food. We've plenty for now. It's the sight of those places, how they were dealt such horrific blows. The land scoured of people, beasts driven away, taken elsewhere." He regarded his brother. "I'm beginning to wonder if it was by order of the King. But for what?"

"For disobedience." Rory let out an uneasy chuckle. "Well, that's what it usually is. Common folk not obeying some obscure edict from afar. And those folks don't read."

"Ay, preyed on like vermin. Yet forced to labor in the fields for a slim portion of the produce. Not enough to carry on."

"When I am a duke, I shall end all of that. I promise."

"When you are a duke, eh?"

Rory moaned. "You have little faith in me...."

"Faith, yes," Stank laughed. "Not much confidence."

"Everything I've told you is truth. How could you doubt me? Ay, I know some of my efforts in the past haven't ended so well, yet I believed them true and worthy projects. This time, I am much more certain of success than ever before."

"Let us get to Cabool and Willow Springs, Mountain View, and to Van Buren, if we can. Then we'll find the way north."

"Van Buren?" Rory paled in the firelight. "I've heard bad things about that place. It's in the deepest, darkest part of the great forest. Zarkers are many. They're organized. Better than the savage bands you had to fight. These have chieftains and cadres of warriors. They bested Duke Billy's battalion just south of there."

"True?" Stank sighed, thinking. "Then we avoid Van Buren. Try to go north. Hope to meet the Royal Road."

"That would be...well, perhaps back through Winona, then north. It would be hard going, but we'd arrive in Rolla sooner or later. Take three or four days."

"Better we go north from here than go east first. We'll pass Fort Leonard that way. We can restock supplies. We won't make Louis with what we have."

"Good plan, brother," said Rory. "I knew it would be good to send for you. Nobody I'd rather be with on a hard journey."

"Yes, good idea." Stank grew weary. "A hard journey requires a good sleep. I'll take first and last watch."

In the darkest portion of the night, Stank awoke. Stretched on the ground with a blanket under him, Longclaw at his side, he listened to the beasties in the branches fiddling away. A skitter had crossed the camp, squatted to nibble at his boot. Stank kicked it away with his other boot. He sat up, rubbed his eyes, and noticed that Rory had fallen asleep when it was supposed to be his watch.

The man was snoring, or what passed for nose noise, a low roll of phlegm forever cursed to remain imprisoned within his throat.

He watched him. His brother mumbled something, words Stank couldn't make out. Not until:

"No, Majory," Rory spoke out, "I don't want to go to the garden. There are snakes in the garden."

At that, Stank stopped being kind and kicked Rory's leg. Kicked it again when Rory failed to rouse.

"What?" Rory cried out, then put his hand to his leg.

"You fell asleep on watch," Stank cursed.

Rory rolled up to a sitting position. "I'm awake now."

Then it was Stank being kicked awake.

"We've guests, brother," said Rory, holding up his short sword at the Zarkers coming into the camp.

Stank grabbed Longclaw, started to pull it from its scabbard – as a dart shot by a Zarker hidden in darkness hit his hand. Cursing, he broke the dart and snatched out each end, clenched the handle of his greatsword. The wide blade at the hilt blocked a fresh dart.

"What's this?" he roared, getting to his feet. The space was tight, not open enough for him to swing the blade. But he could thrust it, and thrust he did: into a throat, between ribs. And pulling the sword back towards himself, he let the great pommel poke the eye of the Zark coming upon him from the rear.

"Watch out," Stank shouted, moving his arm and the blade away from the eyeless barbarian.

Turning back, Stank thrust Longclaw forward, straight into the nose of the next attacker, running the blade deep into the skull then shaking the man off the blade.

Stank twisted around, catching a dart in his chest. Although the tunic was pierced, the heavy leather braces he wore over his shirt and beneath the tunic halted it.

Behind him a knifer leapt, blade poised, struck the leather brace and saw the blade turned away.

"Enough!" Stank spun and punched the Zark in the face, leaving a bleeding nose bent severely to the side.

Rory defended, held his own against the attackers, short sword slashing this way and that, cutting into bellies, leaving guts to flow, a misplaced hand dropping to the fallen leaves.

"Ay, brother!" Rory sang. "Our morning exercise."

"I'd rather sleep," Stank growled. "I'll not be attacked daily."

Stank stepped back, surveying the camp. He saw another Zarker rushing him and raised Longclaw to offer a new way to the attacker. Instead, a surprise dart raced past him, striking the savage in the throat, knocking the man back, gasping for breath.

Snapping his head around, Stank spied a strange man holding a machine bow. He raised Longclaw for a fatal swipe.

"Whoa!" called the man with the machine bow, lowering it. "I am your friend, not your foe."

8

A DANDRUFF PROBLEM

THE MAN with the machine bow dipped his head, then met Stank's angry eyes. The man's black hair lay coiled a dozen times, hanging down his back, his brown forehead bare. Bewhiskered like a man on a journey without razor, he grinned like a bobcat seeing its prey. He wore a pair of scuttled trousers, kid boots to his calves, and a twin-tailed coat like a fine gentleman but dirty from days on the road and torn in places, the original blue hardly showing. A vagabond of high esteem, Stank assessed.

The man raised his free hand in greeting, keeping the machine bow at his side.

"Lucky I found you," he called across the camp.

"Who's this one?" Rory demanded.

"Lyle Danderoff," said the man, "at your service."

"Service? What service's it?" Rory refused to lower his blade. "We took care of this business by our lonesomes."

"You haven't heard of me? Lucky Lyle? Out Joplin way? What a few folks know as the Theater Guy?"

"Theater guy?" Stank questioned. "What's that?"

"I am, good sirs, an actor!" The man affected a flinch toward a pompful entry.

"Actor?" Rory screwed his face. "Seems more a bowman." Then he broke into laughter. "Baumann! Get it? He's a Baumann."

"I carry this weapon for such moments as tonight," said the man whose name was not Baumann. "Lucky I happened by."

"How you happened by?" asked Rory as Stank studied the man. "Following us? What for?"

"Why, I travel like you. My camp is just over there." He whipped a hand behind himself. "I was awakened by those awful creatures as they traipsed through the woods. I followed them, knowing them to be trouble. And I found them set to attack the two of you."

Stank narrowed his eyes. "So you thought to help us, eh?"

"A bit slow to start," Rory added. "Waiting to see which side to join, eh?"

"No," replied the man. "I hesitated. But once I saw you two could defeat them yourselves, I stood watch, ready to protect you. As I did when this large fellow failed to find the fiend falling fast upon you. So I acted – as it were."

"And glad you did," said Stank, giving a curt nod. "Thanks."

"What'd you say your name was?" asked Rory, regarding him.

"I'm Lyle Danderoff. The Actor. Although, truth be told, I've lost my troupe. All dispatched day after day by the ragged fiends like these you've laid low. I'm the only one remaining."

"You say you have a troop? *Had* one?" asked Stank.

"Oh, I mean *troupe*, not a troop. A theater troupe. A collection of actors, clowns, jugglers, magicians, storytellers, singers and the like. Not a troop as in a band of soldiers. Not like that, at all – although I did my youthful duty in a militia. The Golden Battalion, they call it. Fine gold uniforms, we had. Precision marching. With a drum line and golden trumpets. Quite a sight! 'Twas in my youth. Then came the days we had to fight. Necessary then. Had to protect the *colonia*. I'm lucky to escape it. Not my calling. Getting too many close calls. The next might've ended me. Yet I survived to join the theater. I'd much rather pretend to fight than actually fight, you see."

"Ay, we see," Rory said, giving a disappointed chuckle. "A pretty boy, eh? Loves to pretend."

"You've militia experience then?" asked Stank.

"Brief. And of a certain kind." He held up the machine bow. "It's all I know how to use. No swords for me."

"Ay, can imagine," said Rory.

"A stage prop sword I can manage," said the actor.

Stank laughed and the actor turned sour.

"I've often been told I'm not big enough in the shoulders to swing such a weapon. I heartily agreed, so they gave me this clever device. They said I could still be useful. I've skill with this weapon. Draws back the bow for me. I shutter to think how many dastardly foes I've vanquished from afar. With this device I can kill from fifty paces. Fifty! While you, sir, even with your greatsword's reach with your outstretched arm can barely extend six paces."

"You were useful," Stank remarked, frowning. "In a timid way."

"Likely they chased him over to us," said Rory.

Stank held up his hand, checking the wound the dart made. He'd not worn his gloves while asleep so the small arrow had penetrated between the bones. He flexed his hand.

"You're hit?" Rory asked, alarmed. "Hard to put a poultice on a hand. You'll be out of the fray a while. What about the duel?"

"No poultice." Stank continued flexing his hand. "No damage. A bit of ointment to kill the beasties, all I need."

Rory gave him a sly look. "Are you saying we should return to Fort Branson for treatment by a fine lady physician?"

Stank shook his head. "Not saying that. The next town will do."

Danderoff spoke up: "I know a winsome wood witch who would absolutely delight in taking care of your wound."

Rory nearly laughed. "No wood witches, if you please."

"What was your name again?" Stank demanded.

"Danderoff. Lyle Danderoff. Actor."

"Dandelion?" asked Rory, adding chuckles.

"It's Danderoff, *if you please.*"

"Man's got a right to his name," Stank declared. "Dandruff it is."

"Close enough, sir. I shall answer to it."

"Answer what? I only wished to thank you for your last dart. Far worse the outcome if not for its flight."

"Worse?" asked Rory. "We would've been done with these vermin another minute or two. They were falling faster than flies fat with dung." He waved at the bodies and pieces of bodies that littered the camp. "Look at this mess. Who's going to clean it? Not us. Savages best gather the leftovers and take them home for digging."

"These types don't bury the dead, they eat them," said Stank.

"They eat the dead?" asked Dandruff. "How barbaric!"

"And you, as well, if they managed to strike you down." Rory had a grin for the new fellow. "Not much meat on this one. Dark meat, to boot. How tasty!"

"They'll dine on any flesh, no matter the color," said Stank.

"Ay, meat's all the same under the skin," Rory offered.

"That is the way of the Zarkers," said Stank, thoughtfully. "How low a tribe can fall in, what? two hundred years? Living off the land, becoming animals. Day to day surviving. A pity."

Rory nodded grimly, then brightened. "Not like us who travel far and wide in our Sunday garb to impress delicious princesses in high castles, eh? We've fallen low, too. Not as lowly as them that lay in cleaved parts here, but do fall a little from our high horses."

"You, sir, have a wit about you," Dandruff cheered.

Rory spun around, searching for a fresh enemy. "Where? Show me this wit! Where hides?"

Stank broke into laughter at his brother's antics. The new man looked offended at first, then joined in the joke.

"Ay, look at this," Rory spoke, ending his amusement. Holding his sword arm, he showed the long cut there. In the morning light the wound continued to bleed. "They got me, the foul fiends!"

"Oh dear," cried Dandruff and stumbled back, faint with alarm.

Stank set his brother down and looked at the wound. "Serious as a slice of sheep. Need a number of stitches for this one." An errant blade had drawn a red line down Rory's forearm from elbow to wrist. Not deep but a cut nevertheless. Partly hidden by his loose sleeve, pain soon introduced the wound.

"I'll submit to your needle," said Rory, looking worried. "Then I must have a poultice for the pain."

"You are the pain, brother," Stank snapped.

He dug out his sewing kit from the saddle bag, got tools ready as Dandruff stood straight, trying not to watch.

"We haven't finished introductions. What would be your names, good sirs?" asked Dandruff, trying to recover from alarm at seeing the blood on Rory's arm.

"Don't know what they *would* be," Stank spoke, eyes fixed on the needle and thread, getting them to mate. "Could be whatever they want. But Mother told me I'm Stanley K. Baumann. Stank for short. And this one crying out from this minor cut is Rory Baumann. My smaller yet elder brother. He's soon to be a duke so you'd best give him respect."

Dandruff bowed, theatrical in his whimsy. "Your Majesty."

Rory grinned unhappily. "Now he's toying with us."

"There'll be no toying in this camp," Stank growled. He put the needle to the skin and Rory howled. "No wolven beasts neither."

He stitched one loop after another. Rory bit his tongue, holding back his screams.

"Don't be a prissy like that Dandruff, brother. Be strong. Only a needle, not a blade. You're a Baumann!"

"Not so prissy," said the bowman. "I've killed a few men."

"Only a few?" Stank continued working, not looking up. "I kill a few to break my fast."

"Indeed, sir. I can count them this morning."

By the time Stank finished the stitching, morning had filled the camp. The bodies began to stink.

With stitching complete, they packed the camp, loaded the horse and mule, led the beasts away. They followed Dandruff through the brush back to his camp, wary that he may be leading them into an ambush. Yet the path proved uneventful.

They packed the actor's camp: a frilly tent, carpet, bench, and a dozen pillows. They packed everything into a tiny painted cart he'd parked beside a path, a place for his worldly possessions, pulled by a pitiful piebald pony better put to children's amusement.

Dandruff climbed onto the seat, took the reins, and called to the pony to pull, waving at Stank and Rory to go ahead.

"Fair away with us, for a ways," Stank declared.

Satisfied with the arrangement, the group headed west to meet the road north to avoid more of the savage Ozark land. Eventually they came to a crossroads.

"This way, gentlemen." Dandruff waved at the signpost. "Here's the road to Springer's Field. We can meet the Royal Road there."

"We?" Rory muttered.

"I'll pass Springer's Field," Stank announced. "Let us go askew, and not enter that place."

"You can get medical help," said Dandruff. "It's a great town. It's grown so much over the past decade. An excellent arts district and a grand theater. I've played in several productions there, including, I dare say, what most will swear is the best performance of the ages ...by me! I played the lead role in *The Way of the Son*."

"Way of what son?" asked Rory, unimpressed.

"It's a play. On a stage. Actors play the characters."

"Oh, a fake story," Rory responded, glancing at Stank.

"Not fake," said Dandruff. "It's art. We give you the semblance of verisimilitude: an act so akin to actual events that you would never know the difference were it not up on a stage right before you as you sit comfortably in cushioned seats in a large hall."

"Sounds like a waste of good time," Stank decided.

"He won't go into Springer's Field," said Rory, flicking his thumb at Stank. "Bad feelings and all. A lady—"

"Enough!" Stank bellowed. He calmed himself. "We've wasted too much time with this backing track. If you intend on reaching Louis, we must not dally in Springer's Field."

"Dally," said Rory to Dandruff, chuckling. "We've done little but dally since we met up. Fort Branson: ay, a meager adventure. This fellow: smitten. Yes, by a lady doctor who gave me the most pleasant poultice I've ever had the pleasure of a pat upon my posterior."

"Enough with your poultice!" Stark cursed.

"I've need of a new poultice, brother. For my wound. And you, as well. Don't let your hand stiffen with pus."

Stank raised his sword hand, flexed it within the glove. "Feels fine. No pain. Not stiff."

"He's a brave one," said Dandruff. He called to Stank: "A stop in Springer's Field would be good for all. You can mend. And I shall greet my theater brethren. Perhaps we can put on the play for you. Would you like that?"

"A play?" Stank roared with laughter. "Why look at a thing you already know is false?"

"It is a review of a thing, not an attempt to trick you," Dandruff explained. "A remembrance of things past. It's an entertainment."

"The cocks of poppies," Rory snapped, then to Dandruff: "He will turn. Get him fixed in comfort. A room in a fine inn. We've coin for that. And he'll be ripe for a fake story about real folks, eh?"

Dandruff took no offense. "That is my suggestion, as well. A rest. Medical attention. A fine play. Good food. I hear the braised mutton is famous there."

"Mutton?" Now Stank showed interest. "Braised?" He turned in the saddle to face Rory. "Could enjoy a shank of mutton, I suppose. If it came with a pair of taters."

"I have no doubt they can find a few potatoes," said Dandruff.

"And a personal attendant later," Rory added. "For exercise."

"Not at all," Stank shouted back. "I've no interest in laying with another dalliance. I've my own lady awaiting me now, as you know." He nodded at Rory for Dandruff's benefit. "After I take this one on to Louis, I am free to return to her."

"Mona Payne," Rory announced. "Good name for a physician, eh? Moan in pain, eh?" He laughed even as Stank growled at him.

"Then we shall abide a while in Springer's Field," said Dandruff from the cushioned seat of the cozy cart. "Get you both medical care. Have a fine meal of mutton. And see a play."

"Are there worse ways to spend your life, brother?" Rory called to Stank. "We've just been through some of those worse ways. Lived to tell about it, eh? They can make us into a play!"

Rory had traveled the Royal Road previously and had tales to tell of past adventures, none too pleasing to Stank who was content to laze on the hard bed they settled for, the cost of three being princely. The cost of livery for a horse and mule, plus a pretty pony and cart, did nothing to ease their arrival.

Yet Stank endured the stories, trying not to swing a fist at the theater fellow with each feigned laugh, clearly offering homage to his brother's ridiculous talk.

Stank watched the two jabber on and soon spied a mark on the actor's bare leg, hosiery rolled down to his ankles.

"What's that from?" asked Stank from his cot.

Dandruff turned, surprised, then understood. He pointed to the scar just below his knee.

"This is when a sword came through my trousers during the first Battle of Winfield. I was just a youth."

"A battle, eh?" Stank cheered.

"Yes," Dandruff replied. "Tripped and fell upon a blade left in the grass."

"You tripped and fell?" asked Stank with a wry grin.

"I said it was in my youth. I was not a soldier."

"Ay, but he was there," said Rory.

"And what's that one?" Stank pointed to another mark upon the actor's calf, round like a musket shot.

"That one? I was gored by a bull. At my uncle's farm. Big, black beast bounding at me! I still have night terrors from it."

"A farm wound," Stank announced.

Dandruff seemed offended. "You wish to see war wounds? Is that it?" He pulled his shirt off, exposing a plethora of marks upon his chest and belly. "Plenty to ponder."

"That's more like it," Stank declared.

Dandruff pointed to a three-inch line. "This one is from my sister and I practicing with small swords." He pointed to an X. "This was a few boys in our *colonia* giving me a mark to say I was a weakling." A jagged line ran down his belly into his trousers. "This was the time I climbed over a barbed fence and slipped down." He pointed to other marks, told their causes, all from boyhood errors.

"Let me show you war wounds," Stank roared. He pulled off his shirt, pointed to one mark after another. "This is the Battle of Arkan and this is the Battle of Enid. Both when I was sixteen. This is from the skirmish at the Emporia. These, here and here, are when I rode with Chief Lex over in Green Country, fought Slammers at Miama. I got a few arrows tried to get into me there." He turned to show his back. "See these? Now I wear a leather vest to stop them. Always wear it under my tunic."

"That's a good choice," said Dandruff, impressed by the warrior's marks. "You do have marks, sir."

"I got this one," said Rory, pulling up his pantleg and pointing to his shin. "Got broke when I was a kid, but healed right up."

"No sword wounds," Stank bragged, waving his hand casually down his body, turning to show front and back. "None get so close to me. It's those pesky darts from afar that get through." He rolled up his pantleg, showed the mark of an errant dart in his calf. "And here—" He pulled off his boot, lifted his foot to show the sole. "—got a nail in my foot. That's a farm wound. My only one."

He put on his boot, sat down on the cot with his shirt still off, and lay back for a nap.

"He's a right tough one," said Rory to Dandruff's gaze.

Rory saw what had Dandruff entranced: the swath of dark hair across Stank's mighty chest. Rory had red hair on his, but not much even as a grown man.

"You lads be off for a while," said Stank, putting his arm up over his eyes to shield them from the light coming in the window. "I've a destiny with Old Father Sleep."

Rory nudged Dandruff. "He'll be out for hours."

"Let us go see what is new in Springer's Field. I'll show you the theater. Perhaps a few friends will be there. Then we can return and fetch your big brother for the play."

"Ay, he's big, awright," said Roy with a twist of his lips. "Yet I'm the senior brother. He gets his height and strength from a different father than I. It's the way of our clan. Each of us a different father. Same mother, though, dear one she is. You could say we Baumanns are a legion."

9

"THE WAY OF THE SON"

SPRINGER'S FIELD was the largest city Rory had ever seen other than Louis. So large it had outgrown the original stone walls put up around the great field to protect the last piece of arable land from savages bent on destroying everything they could. In those darker days many believed the world was ending and wished to go ahead into the light before the final flames. The sooner they could destroy everything, the quicker they could depart.

They grew crops on that last acreage, fed themselves, and others from across the land came to join them, seeking a place of survival. A village rose around the great field, grew into a town with all the necessary services and the accompanying flaws of any town. Streets ran in a neat grid, cobblestones maintained on the main avenues. Buildings of wood and stone kept up. Even a few towers rising to ten floors. The green flags with the white blossom flapping everywhere, especially around the central square where the governor lived.

Called His Lordship for the leadership he displayed in building the town, Desmond Conklin, now quite aged, had been a handsome fellow by anyone's standards: dark eyes that could see through you, dark hair like he'd been born of the southern wastes, a tall man of standard proportions but with a wry smile of assurance for any who came seeking advice or redress. He held Court weekly for the public to come forth. The rest of his time was spent in the Council, arguing with seven councilors how best to solve this problem or another one, or else give ample praise to their successes, or often be amused by the occasional dancer or theater troupe.

"I've played here six times," said Lyle Danderoff, explaining the long history of the place for Rory's benefit. Rory seemed intrigued by all he saw as they strolled about at a gentle pace, as though both were fresh dandies prancing down the broad avenue – Broad's Way, the signs announced. Many fine carriages rolled past yet there were no splashes of mud coming at them as he'd expect in other towns.

"Ay, a shiny city on the hill," Rory spoke, head craning around to see everything as they strolled.

"It's actually built around a central park – the original field that was protected for decades so people could grow food," said his guide. "It still exists, but now it's more of a grand sports yard for the youth to play their games. The town's needs increased so the farming had to expand outside the old walls. We saw the fields as we arrived."

"Yes, yes, that makes sense," Rory muttered, surveying all.

Dandruff went on explaining more than Rory wished to know, making his head fill up with unwanted facts he'd never use.

"It's a bit off Broad's Way," said the actor, waving Rory on.

The next street, Barker's Street, where they turned, led right up to the theater.

"Theo Barker was a famous actor in his day," said Dandruff with a dip of his head to the sign. "He was the first to play Sandy here. I was a fresh-faced lad back then."

"Is it so?" asked Rory, not too impressed but being polite.

"My last performance, I told you and your brother, was the role of Sandy in *The Way of the Son*. It's a play in five acts based on the opera of the same name. A very old work of music. You see, long ago it was the custom in higher venues to sing all the lines, the text. In this version, we speak the lines, although there is one song, a set piece, in Act Five. It's a variation on the music from the opera."

"I fancy a good tune," Rory said with a whimsical nod. "Mother had some talent with a flute, many have said."

"There was a band of five or six that played an overture as well as exit music for the performance last time. They also played during the song I mentioned. I believe they included a flute."

Dandruff led Rory to the front of the grand building. Wide steps led up to triple doors. Above the doors spread a long signboard with the words *Grand Theater*.

"Must be the Grand Theater you've been talking of all this time," Rory said with a happy grunt. "Has a grand appearance, it does."

"The same," Dandruff sang. "It's like my home, this place."

"Then welcome home, lad."

"Now this play," Dandruff started in, eyes stuck on the marquee, "is about the adventures of a young man and his family during the great plague centuries past. History books tell us it all began in a magician's den." He regarded Rory, who appeared fascinated by the telling. "A tiny demon escaped, spread throughout the land, vilely touching each person. Half the populace died. Others fled the cities, went to the countryside to survive. Our protagonist fled to an island along the coast and tried to live safely there, so the story goes."

"Seems like what I'd do in the same situation," Rory responded.

"However, this island was ruled by a mad prince. One day that prince – for reasons that remain unclear to this day, yet most people suspect it must have been pure jealousy – he banishes our hero. The old prince insists our hero's wife stay on the island and become his bride. Her name is Hannah. She already has a baby. Sandy is the father. Can you believe? In a time of plague?"

"Well, people gonna do what they gonna do," said Rory.

"His wife, Hannah, goes with him, she and their baby. Banished from the island, sent into the savage outerlands. End of Act One."

"I know a bit about them savages in the outerlands, I do."

"Worse in those olden days." Dandruff took a breath, filled with performance fire. "They suffer much on the journey, always seeking a safe place. They return to one family member's house, their aunt, but she is sick with plague and dies. So they travel on. Yet they are attacked by savages. The wife is made to lay with one of them but our hero frees her and they escape from the camp. They—"

"Now that's a fine tale!"

"They use an old chariot left behind and travel over the hills to a town where warriors of two armies clash in the streets. There they meet Hannah's sister, who they had thought died years before. I like this scene. That's Act Four. In it, the baby gets to speak. Yes, the baby addresses the audience from her mother's arms. That special child is named Isla Augustine."

"That's a queer thing," said Rory adding chuckles.

"Not in a play, sir."

"A babe may speak, yet none can understand."

"You see, that baby was so named because she was born on that island at the beginning of the play, and it was in August in the old month of the old calendar. Not like we have now."

"Seems a clever child. To know of your own birth like that."

"Oh, yes. In the play, she leads her parents to safety. She is able to see the future. They travel to a great forest and make their home there. They dig into the side of a hill, make a burrow and live in it for many years as Isla grows up. The play ends with Isla wedding a boy from another forest family. It's a great feast. But it's interrupted by the arrival of vagabonds bent on thievery. The wedding folk put them down and the feast goes on. And that song I mentioned? It's in the wedding scene. The whole community sings of their joy and how they made a happy life there."

Rory gave a nod. "That's a good end for it."

"Have I told you that I played the Sandy role?" Dandruff grinned proudly. "Each time it was performed here."

"Is it so?" asked Rory. He gave his companion a curious look.

Dandruff blinked, like a tic from drawing a bad memory.

"There was one time this crusty old actor showed up, wanting to take the Sandy role. And I, still being young, had to give it to him. But he was much too old to play that role. You see, the character of Sandy is only supposed to be nineteen. Not thirty-six like that Finn Bolger. He was half-insane by then, did you know?"

Rory shook his head compliantly. "I did not know."

"Well, he was." Dandruff broke into laughter. "Did you know he died on stage, right at the end of a long soliloquy? Not in *The Way of the Son* but in another play. It was in *The Music Lady*, I do believe. A play about the woman who wrote *The Way of the Son* as an opera, as I told you. Lots of music back in those days. He played the villain, Mad Bill, who goes after her, expecting her to love him just because he gave her a special horn. Called it a *tuba*. Like Tuba-Cain, that ancient giant. At the end of the play Mad Bill destroys her prized horn. He puts on a red coat and drives a team of eight horses over it, smashing it. She loses her powers then, can't make music after that. Anyway, that Mad Bill gives a long speech about his undying love for her – and that Finn Bolger drops dead right there on stage. The audience thought it was part of the play! Then other actors stopped the play, realizing he'd died."

Rory perked up. "I want to see that play."

"Another time, perhaps. Tonight's play is *The Way of the Son*."

Dandruff pointed to the marquee above the doors.

"There you go. *The Way of the Son* is playing. See? We should go see it. I wonder who is playing Sandy this time?"

"Not you?" Rory quizzed. "Why not you?"

"Oh, I had my turn. Thanks. Time to move on, find other troupes to play with. I'm not worried. Plenty of actors across the land."

"Ay, many have roles to play, eh?"

"Each in our own times and places, what say you?"

"I'm game for an entertainment. Let's see this play."

"It doesn't go on until evening. We can enjoy a supper, then go to the theater like gentlemen. You could be my crusty old uncle, and I the happy prince."

"Ay, it's a duke I aim to be and very soon. As soon as I wed the princess. That'd be Princess Majory of Louis."

"Princess Majory?" Dandruff laughed like he'd heard the jokes everyone had heard but Rory. "The King's youngest daughter? The one who has the stink eye? And thick ankles?"

"You've seen her ankles? How dare you!"

"No, no, good sir. It is only a rumor."

"You take it back!" Rory grew red. "She's my darling. She'll be my wife. Just as soon as my brother slays the wretched duke in fair duel. Then she'll be mine. And I will give her all she wants and love her to the end of our days."

"That's a bold boast, is it not?"

"There's no better boast than a bold boast, young man!"

They returned to the inn, roused Stank, told him they would attend a play in the evening. Stank was not amused.

"I'll not sit in a chair for hours to watch people pretending," said Stank, rubbing the sleep from his head.

"You misunderstand, sir." Dandruff grew bold. "It's a fine review of history. A great moment from our past. You can learn much from watching. I see Jason Langley on the marquee. Perhaps he plays the Sandy role. He's one of only a few great actors left in our nation who can play the role."

"There's no nation," Stank grumbled. "Not no more. Only a few cities with strongholds, reigning over the surrounding land. The rest of the country is nothing but a horde of savages. Wild lands. Hasn't been a nation for near two hundred years. There's been far too much pretending. A grand ruse that leaves us all vexed and dour. And I won't go."

"It'll raise your spirits, brother," Rory urged. "Come on."

"A few hours caught in a spell will do you great benefit, sir," said Dandruff, affecting a role.

"Caught in a spell?" Stank laughed. "I just woke from that."

"No, this would be like a waking dream. You suspend your sense of disbelief and accept what you see, what you hear, as truth. Only for a brief time. You will feel so much. It will move you. You leave the theater refreshed, your head energized. Nothing more required of you than to sit and watch the stage. React as you may. Let the troupe entertain you. Like a prince."

"Like a prince, eh?" Stank grinned and Rory urged him on. "I'd sit like a prince and let these strangers entertain me, eh?"

"Yes, precisely," said Dandruff. "Sit yourself back and watch the entertainment."

"Perhaps I should grab a bit of this entertainment you so wildly praise. What could go wrong? Will there be fighting on the stage? A bit of mischief and mayhem? Love-making?"

"All of that in this play, I assure you," Dandruff explained. "I've performed this play several times, so I know it well. I've been Sandy, but I've also played Sergeant and the doctor from the island. Yet it is decidedly the role of Sandy that has any meaning for me."

"You do not present yourself on the stage tonight?" asked Stank.

"No, sir. I'm afraid I've no role in tonight's performance."

"Then I might as well go see it, see what the fuss is about."

"There you go, sir." Dandruff beamed. "We can get a good supper at the Lion and Shark before the show."

"Lion and Shark? What's that?" asked Stank, getting himself up.

"A dinner place. A restaurant known for meat and fish."

"From the surf to the turf," Rory explained.

"Then I shall sup to my belly's bounds!" Stank roared.

Parading down the street they went like three stooges, grinning at folks they passed as the evening spread over them. First to the Lion and Shark, where two bawdy wenches served them. Stank tossed a handful of coins to them. A slice of red-berry pie came as dessert. A plop on Stank's lap by one of the wenches, a sloppy kiss to his cheek, hoping for more coins. He slid her off and she dropped to the floor with a loud *oomph*. Not a happy moment, and the three had to rush out with the tavern master shouting after them.

They laughed in the street, then quickly fell arm in arm as they continued merrily down the avenue to the theater.

Many had gathered before the theater when the three arrived, yet Dandruff knew what to do, got tickets and led them inside.

"I see Rockwell Hudsucker has the role of Sandy," Dandruff said with some disdain, studying the play card. "But Doris Dale should be spectacular in the role of Hannah. She's played it before, looks right for the part. Kitty Luo plays baby Isla. Must be a child actor. Never heard of her."

"What's this say?" Rory asked Dandruff, sitting beside him and holding up the card with all the words printed on it.

"It's the program," said Dandruff. "Tells you the story. And about the actors. And who pays for the production. Can't you read it?"

"Ay, my eyes can't focus in this poor light," said Rory.

"I already told you the story. You can follow it, I'm sure. The rest is who the actors are. Only the principal players matter. I see Jason Langley gets the Island Prince role."

"Too many rules," Stank grumbled, sitting on the opposite side of Dandruff from Rory. "Get on with it."

"Oh, dear," said Dandruff. He flashed a worried look. "It's not the full play. It's only a review. They're playing only selected scenes. But at least they are the best parts of the play."

"Not a full play, eh?" Stank spoke loudly, to the consternation of audience members around them. "I'll demand our coin be returned. Let's go out."

Stank started to get up but Dandruff caught his arm.

"It will be fine. You'll see. It's like they are only performing the arias from the opera, not the less interesting recitatives."

"Aria, eh?" Stank took his seat again. "Sounds like a fine maid."

"It's a song," said Dandruff. "A set-piece. I'll bet they include the final wedding scene."

At that moment music sounded from the front of the stage. The small group of musicians had assembled, a man waving his arms to get them to play the opening song. A lively flourish of flutes and violins, then a horn....

"This is what's called the overture," said Dandruff, keeping his voice low. Guests around them *shush*ed him. He waved apology.

The song played on and Stank and Rory sat patiently listening. Then Rory leaned over and asked Dandruff when the actors would come on stage. He was about to answer when the first actor split the curtain and stepped to the front of the stage.

It was Doris Dale, playing Hannah, seventeen years old, in the illusion of being stuck on a coastal island during a plague. Her dark hair lay uncombed, her dress in tatters. She stood barefoot and her belly was big. She addressed the audience in her character's voice, complaining of life on the island. She told how she and her family came to the island – not an easy travel. Her teenage cousin Sandy and his mother, Polly, came to save them in a town ravaged by the virus. Yet her mother had died so Polly took her with them to the island where they sought refuge.

At that point, the actor playing Sandy came on stage to comfort her. She cried against his shoulder as he told the audience his love for her. He referenced the unborn baby, rhapsodizing how this child would save the world from all its horrors.

"Oh, will she?" cried Hannah. "Will she push back this scourge?"

"Let us pray she will have miraculous powers," said Sandy.

Then a group of villagers came on stage to mock them, threaten to beat them into submission. Back to work! They must work hard if they wished to stay on the island, a sanctuary for a few. Otherwise, off they go into the savage outerlands.

"Oh, no," cried Hannah, holding her belly.

Parting the group of villagers came the prince of the island, an older, fat man in a fancy robe.

"There is my darling." cried the prince. He went to her as Sandy fell back. The prince wrapped his arms around her, tried to kiss her but she held back. "You shall come to me in due time, my dear."

"I won't ever be your bride," cried Hannah.

Sandy stepped forward, holding a sword.

"She will never be yours!"

He swung the sword, obviously not sharp, and the prince fell.

The group of villagers cried for justice, pointing off-stage. "Go! You must go off our island. You are banished forever."

Defiant, Sandy took Hannah by the hand and they exited stage-left, behind the curtain.

"That's not how it really happened," Dandruff whispered to Rory. "Not if you've seen the opera. The daughter is born before they leave the island." More *shush*es from neighbors.

A new scene: Sandy and Hannah on a boat, crossing the strait to the outerlands, bemoaning their fate. They arrived on the opposite shore and surveyed the ruined village there, made their new home in a fallen inn. An old man arose from the ruins to teach them how to survive. He showed how to catch fish, how to grow vegetables in pots, how to collect rainwater in a barrel. He gave Hannah a guitar and taught her to play. Then, when the old man was dying, he told them they must go on. Marauders would descend on the inn.

"They've cut out a lot," Dandruff told Rory as a new scene began.

The scene was about finding others hiding in the forest, coming together as a community. A lovely song of mutual kinship was sung. Dandruff wiped tears from his face. Rory grinned. The magical child arrived on stage, appearing already seven years of age. The actors danced together as music played. Then marauders appeared, waving their spears.

"They used guns back then," Dandruff explained.

The actors playing marauders took Sandy and other men away, saying they were needed to fight against the evil Duke of the North. The women wept. The child called after her father.

It was a touching scene. Even Stank was heard to sniffle. Rory wiped tears. Dandruff felt pleased his companions were caught up in the play.

In another scene, set several years later, Sandy returned, weary from war and time in a prisoner camp. The child had grown, didn't recognize him at first, then did. It was a fabulous reunion. Yet when he met Hannah again, she had five new children to show him.

"I couldn't wait for you, not for a ghost who may only haunt my nights," she told him, dabbing her eyes. "I could only presume you died in a battle long ago."

He forgave her, just happy to be home in the forest once more.

In the next scene presented, it was the daughter's wedding day. Isla Augustine, as everyone knew, married a forest boy by the name of Little Joe. It was a great celebration, with feasting and dancing. The child actor was switched for a teenage girl.

"This must be Kitty Luo," said Dandruff. He sat transfixed by her beauty, standing in a simple white dress. "The marauders come during the wedding. That's what happens in the opera."

Shushing from neighbors, rougher in tone.

"I'm explaining what's different in this version of the story," he responded louder than a whisper.

The audience applauded. Some stood as they continued to clap. Dandruff jumped to his feet, clapping. Rory got up, too. Stank looked around, decided to stand just to fit in. He towered over everyone.

Afterwards, Dandruff led his companions to the back of the stage hoping to greet the cast. He knew a few of them, by reputation or because he'd worked with them previously. Rory didn't mind, never having gotten a close look at real actors.

"If you would take a good look, sir, I am a real actor," Dandruff responded, unamused.

Rory tugged at the bandage on his forearm. "Ay, but you wasn't on the stage there."

At Rory's arm scratching, Stank lifted his wounded hand, flexing it to test how much he could endure of the pain.

"I liked this pretending. I almost believed it," said Stank. "I liked the fight scene most of all, when that young man takes on the band of marauders all by his lonesome to save his daughter. A noble deed, though he failed in the end."

"That is the tragedy of the story," said Dandruff. "In this version of the story, the daughter has magical powers. You saw how she just waved her arms and the marauders all fell down. A bit of hyperbole for the sake of the audience's cheers."

"Never knew she had magical powers," said Rory.

"This is what makes a play such an enlightening experience. You can feel so many things all at once," said Dandruff.

Eventually the actors streamed by, going to their private stalls to remove their facepaint and wigs. Dandruff called to them, giving a silly gesture to Stank and Rory.

"Rocky," Dandruff called, to the actor's chagrin. The man turned, spied Dandruff in the crowd of fanatics, and stepped over.

"Do I know you?" asked Rockwell. "You look familiar."

"Yes, yes," cried Dandruff. "I performed this very same play with you only two years ago. You were Frank in that production. I played Sandy then."

"Yes, that's correct," said Rockwell. "You don't look the same."

"Rough times, rough times."

"Indeed." Rockwell frowned. "We all are having them these days. Venues shutting down. No place for us to perform. It's a dull world we've come to."

Dandruff praised the older actor's performance as young Sandy, not mentioning the age difference except by allusion. It is what an actor does, they both understood: you become what you are not.

"Nor you, Lyle, with your swarthy skin and that raggedy hair."

Rockwell put forth with a wide grin. "It is all in the game, is it not?"

"Quite so. Truth in glory," said Dandruff.

Then Doris Dale, the actress who played Hannah, came forward, joining Rockwell, taking his arm in hers.

"Superb performance," she cooed to him. "Again."

"Thank you, my dear, as always." He patted her arm as he began introducing his old colleague. Polite responses all around.

"And these two," said Dandruff brightly, gesturing at Stank and Rory, "although appearing as typical rogues, are actually of a high pedigree. They are actual descendants of the opera's composer. Yes, the very same as this play. Allow me to present Mister Stanley K. Baumann and his brother: Mister Rory Baumann. You hear their name? Baumann?"

"Oh my!" Doris exclaimed. She had eyes for Stank, quite clear for all to see. Rockwell was taken aback by the huge muscled man.

Dandruff saw the look on Rockwell's face, stepped forward with an overwrought smile intended to prevent bloodshed. Stank grinned politely at Doris, who was about to swoon.

"Such a grand fellow," Doris sang. "We must have him in a play. Simply must!"

"I'm not an actor," said Stank, affecting a delightful scowl on his stern face. "Yet I'd happily bed you for a fair price."

Rory pulled Stank back. "She's not like that."

"Come, my dear," Rockwell demanded, taking her roughly by the arm and leading her away.

"Apologies," cried Doris, quickly departing.

Rockwell had hold of her arm, tugging her away while sending a frown back at the three guests.

"See you next time," Dandruff called after them. "Somewhere."

10

ANOTHER WAY TO GET AWAY

STANK SEEMED DISTANT as the trio returned to the simple room in the inn.

"Ay, he's smitten again," Rory grumbled. "A fair lass doing that pretending always gets him." He laughed like it was only a joke, but Dandruff thought he was sincere.

"I'm pleased you enjoyed the play." He turned to Stank. "You did enjoy it, didn't you?"

Stank had pulled off his boots, let the room fill with his feet. He let down his trousers, pulled off his shirt, stood naked before them.

"I liked parts. Other parts not much. Too much singing."

He went to the basin of water set on the stand, washed himself using a small towel and a cake of soap, splashing water on the floor.

"You liked Doris, didn't you?" Dandruff asked. "She made a fine Hannah, don't you think?"

"If that's Hannah, then I'd say it's so." Stank regarded Dandruff, whose eyes had fallen down along Stank's muscular body. "You said Hannah was eighteen. That actor lady, she looked thirty."

"Well, as Rocky said, that's what acting is. You become what you are not." The actor threw his hand into the air as if on stage. "Look at me: my color and my hair. Not like the real Sandy at all. He had light brown hair, it is written; a 'sandy' color. And yet, I've been praised for my performance in the role each time." He ran his hand through the dozen coils of black hair that fell down his back. "This hair has gotten me many roles, I'll have you know."

Rory laughed. "Never seen hair like that much in these parts."

"You will in Louis," said Dandruff. "Plenty of us around that city. Women, too. Come up the river from the swamp lands. Your brother will likely make friends there, those who crave a child. Louis lands were hit hard by the air-bursts."

"I'm not in that business any longer," said Stank. Staying naked, he flopped down on the cot by the window, filling it completely. "I've a woman now. Mona. Mona Payne. Physician. She's waiting for me, and I for her. After this poor adventure – mind you this, brother – I intend to return to her and we shall make many sons together."

Rory smiled from across the room at Dandruff. "He only met her once. 'Twas at Fort Branson."

"And you've a better account of your infatuation?" Stank roared from his cot.

Dandruff was confused. "What infatuation?"

Stank laughed. "My brother believes he will wed the princess in Louis and thus become a duke. I'm to fight another duke, put him down, as it were, so my brother's free to wed with her. Remove the obstacle, the rival, as it were."

"I see!" Dandruff seemed surprised but held back any ill-thought words he might be tempted to speak. "It is a good plan."

Stank snorted, folded his arm up under his head. "We're away in the morning, good plan or not."

Rory agreed, but Dandruff hesitated.

"Might I continue with you?" asked the actor. "There are several possibilities for me in Louis. Many theaters. Different roles to play."

"You? Go with us?" Rory snickered as he threw himself down on the other cot.

"Why, yes. You saw what happened to me when I go alone."

"You'll have to keep your machine bow ready," Stank said.

"Yes, of course."

"He can come along," said Rory. He blew out the candle by him. "He sports fair amusement."

"Say you, brother?" Stank grumbled.

"I'm the leader of this expedition," said Rory. "And I approve."

"Then he's your burden to bear."

"Thank you," Dandruff responded, feeling his way in the dark to the cot where Rory lay. "Seems I must share it with you."

Rory gave the thin mattress a pat. "There's margin for you if you wish it. If not, there's also a floor."

The Royal Road beckoned them, fresh from a fine slumber, a hearty meal of fried wheatcakes and bacon setting them well for a journey. The small cart pulled by the privileged pony, Dandruff on the bench, followed after Rory on the red mule and Stank on his mighty steed.

"Come on now, Fergie," Rory urged his mount. "You can keep up with that warhorse, can't you?"

"I'll not be racing with you," Stank shouted back.

After a while Rory turned, calling to Dandruff and asking what was so important he needed to bring it in a cart. The actor explained the cart held his costumes and props, the working tools of his noble profession.

"I used to sleep in it when we stopped for the night," he added.

"Who's 'we'?" Rory begged.

"There were four of us originally, when we set our way from Old Joplin. And you know what happened to them. Only I remain to tell the tale."

"Ay, the tale," Rory grumbled.

"Killed by savages?" Stank asked, turning in his saddle.

"In a most gruesome way." Dandruff choked up. "Once captured, they were slain. Splayed and roasted."

"Ay, that'd be savages, awright," said Rory.

"I hid in the woods, watched through the branches."

"They didn't take the pony?" asked Stank, disbelieving.

"I suppose they didn't see it," Dandruff called up to Stank. "We'd stopped for the eve. My colleagues went forth to seek game for our supper. The savages captured them while they ventured deeper into the forest. I remained with the cart and the pony. Only later did I smell the roasting and went to investigate."

"Must've been a sight for hungry eyes," Stank laughed.

"It's not a joke, sir."

"Not meant as a joke," Stank called back.

"Leave the poor man be," Rory told Stank.

"I shall regain my humor once we reach Louis and I gain a role in one of the companies there. It's good to step outside myself for a while, be someone else, take on their problems and forget my own."

"You're destined to play many roles, I'm sure," Rory called.

"From your mouth to the theater gods' ears!"

The Royal Road rose roughly with each mile. As they continued on, more travelers passed by them south-bound and they gained fellow travelers north-bound, each stream keeping to its designated path. A long line of lingering stone marked the ancient way, each side of the twin roads broken, long-crumbled, unusable for wagon wheels or horses' hooves. Yet the ancient way showed the direction: up hill, down dale, up hill again: a steady exercise pressing onward twenty or twenty-five miles each day. One or another day barely ten miles or less, as they were forced to work around the fallen bridges of old, maneuvering over rugged terrain not mended in generations. Fellow travelers banded together to help each other over obstacles, giving cheers at their successes.

Stank complained. "Hardly a royal road."

"Ay, it's long overdue for refitting," Rory said.

"We can at least see how it used to be when it was new, smooth and shining," the actor added in theatrical voice.

"Those old metal carriages rolled along it," Rory reminded them, pointing to ancient rusting hulks left here and there off the road.

"Shame they haven't any today," said Dandruff. "We could be at Louis in hours instead of weeks."

They set up camp each evening, other travelers nearby, in parks set aside for overnight stops. Some nights they were left alone. On other nights, fellow travelers would come over to have a look at the fancy cart or admire the mighty warrior. A few dared speak to them, asking where they were heading. Rory was quick to dismiss their inquiries like their destination was a secret.

Everyone on the Royal Road going east-bound was set for Louis, as sure as morning followed night. They could see this warrior must be headed to Louis to join the tournament and win the prize. There was much talk in the overnight camps, and annoying questions as they traveled during the days. Many wished the warrior well.

"Be gone with you," Stank would snarl when chatter grew too loud. Yet children in those families delighted in rousing him, then running away before his fury. He had to draw out Longclaw a few times to silence them, causing many a mother to admonish him for his cruelty in threatening children.

He sheathed Longclaw and pronounced wisdom: "Kinder should be threatened from time to time. Makes them smart."

"Come on now, Stank," called Rory. "Be civil. Save your rage for the royal ring."

Sometimes it was Dandruff and his lavish cart of oddities that got the attention of fellow travelers, and the actor was never shy in presenting himself or performing a scene at their request – or as he presumed they'd requested. He had to keep up his acting skills.

"It's all in the head: the whole ball game, as it is said. We must always practice our roles, run the lines, be ever-ready to go upon the stage, no matter where we may find it."

"Ay, the mark of a professional," Rory said with chuckles of glee.

Further on, they welcomed old Fort Leonard, where long ago the King's battalions trained for war. They sought only a good night in a fair inn, the cots arranged as before with Dandruff on a mat on the floor. It is his venue, Stank noted: warrior on the best bed, schemer on the next best, the 'great pretender' below. Dandruff didn't mind; he was pleased to be in their company and gain their protection on the road. As payment, Dandruff was determined to entertain them.

Upon rising in the morn, Stank discovered a serious breach of protocol: An empty pouch.

Barely half-dressed, Rory stood in shock at the announcement.

"What is the problem?" asked Dandruff.

"No more coin," Stank grumbled. He dug his fingers in the pouch trying to dislodge an errant coin from a corner. Nothing.

Rory counted up their expenses. A few tolls – Stank passed free, being a warrior, but Dandruff's cart was due the fee. And the inn for a night. A fair supper in a middling tavern. A round of drinks. A tip to one of the lustier wenches, smaller tip to another. Fresh bandages for Rory and Stank's lingering wounds.

"You've no coin of your own?" Stank demanded of Dandruff.

"No, sir." The actor seemed to be playing it straight this time. "I confess to none. I hoped to gain a role and thus be paid my fee. Yet I haven't gained such yet. I would repay you in Louis upon a new role. My promise to you."

"Smoother to pay as one," Rory said, "and you repay us later."

Dandruff balked. "I—I could perform for you, sir. Make it up to you in that way. I could perform the final speech by Prince Hal in *The Fourth Night*. Or, better yet, the weeping soliloquy of Jezebelica the Moon Queen when her sons are captured by the Moon reavers." A quick survey: not interested. "Did you know that *Moon Reavers* is completely made-up? There aren't actually any people living on the moon. It was commissioned by—"

"I knew that." Rory made a nasty face.

Stank shook his head. "We're out. The pouch is empty."

"What do we do now?" asked Rory, seemingly afraid of having to sneak out of the inn. He knew Stank could never sneak out of any place, as large as the man was.

Stank shook his head again, thinking as the others kept silent, not daring to disturb him.

"I shall need to work," he said after a while.

Dandruff looked at Rory for answers. "Work?"

Rory nodded. "Ay, work."

"What kind of work? He's a warrior. Is there a battle to join?"

"Battles everywhere," said Rory, staying focused on his brother, "but that's not what he means. He means to offer his services to any woman wanting a child. He's good at that."

Dandruff went smug, gave Stank a longer look. "Yes, I get it."

"You don't get it. It's for the women," Rory explained. "For any's wanting a babe." He addressed Stank: "You're up for it? How about your pledge?"

Stank remained stern, stoking himself. "It must be done. Doesn't break my pledge. This is business, not for love."

"Agreed," his brother responded, nodding.

Stank spun around to Rory. "Mark us another night here then put forth the call. I'll go at once to any address deemed worthy. Or the less worthy, if needs be. Yet they must be in want of a babe, not for mere play. And be in season."

"That's a hard requirement to meet," Rory mused.

Dandruff looked between the two brothers. "He will sire a child? That's his work?"

"It's a side line," Rory muttered, worried for his brother.

"Yes, I see that now," said Dandruff, amazed. "I can see how one winsome woman would want the wanton wood of a warrior. Good on you, sir."

"It's not my desire to sow seed this way," said Stank in a rough voice. "Not now. Not from these days forward. I did make a pledge."

"A pledge?" asked Dandruff, daring to raise Stank's ire. "Pledge to what?"

"Ay, you missed the story," said Rory, checking with Stank who waved him off. "Our friend is smitten, as I said before, but with the lady doctor named Mona. Her."

"Ah, yes!" Dandruff smiled. "You said. Yet I seldom hear of any warrior owning up to his pledges."

Stank grumbled loudly.

"But we've no coin," Rory moaned. He saw Stank was serious.

Pushing Dandruff aside, Rory made the wash basin ready, bid Stank clean himself.

"I shall go make arrangements."

Dandruff quickly followed Rory from the inn, both offering a silly grin to the desk manager as they stepped out.

"You can't be serious," Dandruff pressed.

"He used to do it all the time," said Rory. "Put away a lot of coin for when it rains. You know: to buy a rain bonnet."

"He will lay upon a woman? At her willing?" Dandruff seemed to hold the image in his head. "Just like that? And she allows it?"

"Moreover, her husband allows it. It's how the kid gets born."

"The husband?"

"Yes, for many, the couples who cannot bear a child, Stank is a welcome guest. Paid well for the service. Besides, it's how we grow the populace."

Dandruff remained fixated. "I couldn't ever do such a thing."

Rory gave him a mocking look. "Of course not. You're not built well. Nobody wants a child like you." He laughed to make it a joke so Dandruff wouldn't feel too bad. "Me, neither."

They went to several places in the town, delivering the word.

"Anyone wanting to welcome a child in nine months? Anyone at all? M'Lord Stanley, the Wichita Warrior, is this very day in town, fully available for breeding services to any woman, married or not, if she wishes to have a babe henceforth. Come quick to his chamber or he to yours before he departs for Louis, where he is bid to join the Grand Tournament!"

Although some women were wont to signal their desire in plain view of their colleagues, families, or husbands, several caught up to Rory and Dandruff outside to make their arrangements. Rory would assess their viability, as he had many times before for Stank. This one too old. This one, sorry, much too young; wait a couple years. This one had bad bones. Another with a pox upon her face. This one too plump, that one spear-thin. Not in season. Not a good candidate. Yet he knew they couldn't be too selective if they were to get enough coin. He decided to accept one woman having a lot of coin who only wished for sport.

"I've three good marks arranged for you," Rory announced upon returning to the room. "Two with husbands agreeing to it. The third unmarried but approaching the hill. All good bodies, clean teeth, the rose in the cheeks like your Mona."

"Enough!" Stank bellowed. "Never speak of this again. And you never put her name in the same statement as my service."

"That's fair," Rory replied humbly.

He explained the arrangements. The two women with husbands would welcome him in their homes, one insisting on watching, the other ashamed of the idea and unwilling to watch. The unmarried woman, not wishing her neighbors to notice, would visit him in this inn's room. All offered good coin.

"So we must leave?" Dandruff asked, got a stern nod from Rory.

Stank dug out his best garment from his travel bag, shook it out, and proceeded to dress in it. He looked handsome as he stood before them in his service appearance. A quick trim of beard, comb through hair, and he was pronounced ready to go forth and fornicate.

"We go with him," Rory told Dandruff. "In case there's trouble. A man atop a wife leaves himself vulnerable to changes of heart, you can understand."

"That I do." Dandruff was about to launch into his own story of an errant tryst, but Rory cut him off.

They arrived at the first house and found the husband standing at watch, checking the street for neighbors looking out their noses at he and his wife's private business.

"Ah! Warrior indeed," cried the husband albeit in a lowered voice and standing aside so they could enter before anyone noticed. "This is our humble home, yet without the laughter of children. We follow a regular schedule of unions yet nothing after seven years. Wife says I'm to blame. You see, my family was one too deep into the plague times long ago. I may have carried it forward. The wife thinks so."

Stank stood tall before the husband, unimpressed.

"Let's see your gear," said Rory like a professional inspector.

The husband, seeing Stank's stern face, obeyed.

"There's your problem," Stank spoke in his deep voice, making it as deep as he could, part of the play. "Even if your seed was viable, you wouldn't reach far enough to make it worth the effort."

"That's part of the curse," said the husband. "Those medicines of long ago set this in motion. They were trying to wipe us out. Keep us from having children."

"It's a ruse," Rory responded.

"Don't worry. Stanley's here. We shall fix her right up. Is she in the interval?"

"Yes." The husband turned to Rory. "It's a good time for her."

"I asked her," said Rory. "She's ready."

"Then let us meet," said Stank, puffing out his chest and giving his loins a pat.

The husband waited nervously with Rory and Dandruff sitting outside the bedding room, listening to the noises Stank and the wife made. They kept exchanging glances.

"She never sounds that way whenever we are together," said the husband. "I pray he doesn't hurt her."

"Nobody sounds like that when my brother ain't involved," said Rory with a laugh. "Yet he is gentle as it matters."

Finally, the noise ceased. After a further half-the-hour, the door opened and Stank came out, fully dressed and combed. No grin upon his face. He gave curt nods to Rory and the husband, continued on through the house to the front entry.

"That's all," said Rory. "Now the fee, sir."

The husband stood, unsteady on his legs. He gave a glance into the bedding room, saw his wife laying back calmly. Closing the door, he stepped over to a nearby cabinet and retrieved a pouch of coins. He handed it hesitantly to Rory.

"It's all we have for now," said the husband.

"What's it?" Rory was angry. He juggled the pouch in his hand, assessing its weight. "The agreed amount?"

"Yes, it's all there," the husband assured. "But it's all we have to give now. We will earn more later. But having a child born to us is worth every coin we have. Thank you, good sirs."

"Not him," Rory thumbed at Dandruff. "He's not a sir."

The husband gave a nod and Rory and Dandruff exited.

Outside, they found Stank standing away from the house, as was his way, not wanting to draw attention to the house he'd visited. He was always conscientious of how his service would look to the strict members of a community. His clients appreciated his ability to keep secrets.

"So how was she?" asked Rory brightly.

"Fair to middling," came the response. "Got the fee?"

"Seems close."

"Count it."

Dandruff stood to block the view of their coin counting from the street, spreading his cloak out. Rory poured the pouch into his hand, counted the coins.

"All here." Rory returned the coins to the pouch. "Said this is all they've got but worth it for a chance at a child."

"Then it was a fair bedding," said Stank, distant and cool.

They went to the next appointment. The wife took him straight back to the bedding room, swiftly past the wispy husband who could barely watch her flee and the door close loudly behind her. Noises from within unnerved him and he had to escape, saying the fee was on the side table. Rory got up to count it.

When Stank finished, the husband hadn't returned, but they left anyway, seeing the wife blowing kisses to Stank.

"You best lay still a while," he spoke to her.

"Oh, I'm barren as a salted field, sir," she chuckled.

"What's that?" Stank stopped to regard her.

"I can't have children," she said. "But I still enjoy a good shove. You were the best, sir."

"Damn you." Stank stalked off and Rory and Dandruff hurried after him.

"Cheer up, brother. Perhaps she'll have a child now. You being a better seed than that nervy wisp of a husband. She'll be surprised. I bet she has twins."

The third woman, unmarried and worried about neighbors, came to the inn at midnight to meet Stank who still had strength left for a proper session. She was the prettiest of the three, he'd say later. Her form reminded him of Mona and he had to close his eyes. She was at the edge of the motherhood window, so he took his time, remained patient, and delivered to her multiple opportunities.

Rory and Dandruff waited in the corridor, passing the hours by exchanging bawdy tales until they leaned back against the wall and fell asleep.

11

FEMININE MYSTIQUE

STANK TURNED WINNIE around to await Rory on his red mule.

"Let us be vigilant about our coin. I'll not wish to go through another night like that one."

"Ay, you're getting old, are you?" Rory teased.

"Old enough to know some things."

"Ay, the things men know...."

"Things we never think to think, so we've never thought those thoughts."

"Now there's a thought!" Rory shook his head. "I think you need a good draft."

"I think you've had a good thought, brother."

As they continued on, riding the Royal Road, Rory reined Fergie until the colorful creaking cart pulled by the patient pony passed alongside. Dandruff sat aslump on the bench, reins lazy in his hand, other hand catching a yawn.

"Wakey wakey!" called Rory.

"I dare declare I'm awake," Dandruff responded.

Their travel north from old Fort Leonard was slow going with the land rising steadily. Fewer fellow travelers occupied their eyes, ever watchful of threat and amusement. They'd gathered a crowd of travelers eager to keep with the warrior and his friends. He would protect them.

"Likely we will stay overnight in Rolla," Rory told Dandruff.

"Another fine inn?" asked the actor, holding back a yawn.

"Likely less. His Lordship wishes to save his hard-earned coin."

Dandruff chuckled at the sobriquet. "He must still be exhausted. A man to admire, surely. If only I were in possession of such a list of appointments."

"Ay, as well," Rory responded cheerfully. "Yet I, too, am pledged to another and shouldn't engage in service." Rory studied the man. "And you? Have you no love for the lorn?"

"Here and there."

"We've time aplenty. So tell us."

It never took much prodding to pry a tale from Dandruff, true or less than. He mentioned a few encounters in Old Joplin, youthful acts not to be judged, then more in Springer's Field as an apprentice actor, all the others in this troupe or that one. Never could be sure if the feelings were true or merely an act.

"Ay, never trust an actor," Rory mugged.

"Most of them."

"They're full of themselves."

"Full of many *roles*. They draw upon them as needed." Dandruff grew sullen at the memories poking him. "It seems as though they have no sense of themselves. Cannot be their true selves. Always on stage, whether upon a wooden floor or in life itself."

"Ay, we're all on a stage, acting for others," Rory groaned. "I once or twice heard of an actor saying as much. Might've been you."

"Could be," said Dandruff, grinning. "I've been known to talk."

They fell silent as they proceeded up a steep grade, almost losing sight of Stank. But they had nothing to fear in the past few days so they worried not but let their beasts keep pulling. Over the crest of the hill, Rory could just spy the top of Stank's head.

"Halt, you vagabonds!" a shrill cry arose from over the rise.

Rory drew his blade. Dandruff reined the precious pony.

Mounting the crest, they both saw standing in their way a young warrior of diminutive size yet full of unexpected ferocity. A pint-size pumperknocker waving a wooden sword and talking bold. In fact, a woman warrior, her hair chopped short and what remained of it tied back in two golden wheatshocks.

"Stand fast," the girl cried, waving her sword over her head.

She couldn't have been more than twelve years, likely less, Rory assessed, yet she had the verve of a full-grown man.

"What's this?" Stank pressed forward. "We're no vagabonds. Let us pass."

"All are vagabonds if you haven't paid the tax," she cried.

"You're but a child," Stank retorted.

"No child stands with sword in hand!" shouted the girl, standing in a dirty shirt and ragged trousers, looking like a boy.

"But what you have is.... It's a wooden sword," Rory called out.

"A sword to slay you!" she declared.

Stank laughed and drew out Longclaw, making a show of it, inch by inch, the full length freed from its sheath, held in a single hand. He lifted it up into the bright afternoon sky.

"Here's a sword to slay *you!*"

The girl did not budge, nor fall timid, but grew bolder. "If you be a warrior, you know the code. Speak it! Or go back to your slop pots and sleep on dirt."

"You've a nasty mouth," Rory shouted from his mule.

"That's no warhorse," she announced, pointing her wooden sword at Rory. "Barely a toy."

"Fergie's a fair mount. Gets me up the Royal Road, doesn't he?"

"You shan't go more up the Royal Road 'less you pay the tax."

"Oh, it's about a tax, is it?" Stank spoke. "What's the damage?"

"Three coins. One for each of you," said the little toll collector.

"That's a bit high for mere passage over this hill," said Stank. "It isn't such a grand hill, at that."

Dandruff got off the cart, stood by his patient pony.

"You," she addressed the actor. "Back on your toy wagon."

"I step down for a rest, given all this commotion. Was just in a napping mood," said Dandruff.

"Ay, a good time to rest," Stank called to his companions.

"There's no stopping here," explained the girl, a moment showing confusion. "You should travel on. But first you pay the tax. Then you may pass."

"What if we don't pay it?" Stank challenged from atop his great steed, urging Winnie a step closer to the girl.

"You shall not pass!" she cried, again waving her wooden sword.

Stank leaned down from his saddle and the bratty girl stumbled back as the warhorse towered over her.

"Have you a mother? She about?"

The girl seemed distracted, then glanced around.

"Ah, it's a ruse," Stank called to his companions. He sat up in the saddle, still holding Longclaw. "She stops travelers, then her family or whatever they've got rush at us and rob us. Stand alert."

"It's from an old school," muttered Rory, holding his blade out.

Dandruff got the message, returning to his cart and fetching the machine bow and a handful of darts.

"Where's your kin? Have they a plan for taking us?" Stank asked the girl, who appeared less confident now.

Yet she grew fearsome in a flash, slashing her wooden sword, striking air. Winnie snorted, tripped back.

"I'm the only warrior here!" she declared, standing defiantly.

Stank tumbled off his horse, stood as a giant before her. She rose only to his hip, yet dared swing her sword against him. He stepped back, Longclaw in his hand, a twisting dance as she swung at him and he stepped left and right to avoid a strike.

She grew angry, swung harder, missing.

"What's your name, child?" asked Stank with one hand raising Longclaw, the other pressed to his hip.

"I'm not a child," the girl cried. "I'm a warrior!"

"Oh? Look at me, little girl," Stank ordered. "I am a warrior. I've got plenty of battle marks to prove it." He stared down at the girl. "What've you got, little girl?"

"Not a little girl!"

"Then what are you? You're not a warrior. Not by any measure."

Stank turned to his companions, laughing. Being momentarily distracted, his shin caught the hard edge of the wooden sword.

"Ah hah!" the girl shrieked happily.

That was enough. Stank grabbed the wooden sword with his free hand, wrenched it from her hand and tossed it aside. He grabbed her by her shirt, lifted her as high as his shoulder, leaving her dangling from his hand.

"I'll not be attacked daily," Stank grunted. He looked her in the eye. "Now you will tell me first your name. Then your family's name. Then your year of schooling. Speak it now."

She swung from Stank's hand, well above the ground, and gave a look down to guess at the pain a fall would cause.

"Lower me and I shall talk," she said like a mature negotiator.

"Are you sure? I think you're a liar."

"Girl like her, no doubt a fibber," Rory joined in.

"She appears to be a fine actor," Dandruff added.

"She'll say anything to get away," said Rory.

"I'll talk truth," said the swinging girl, "if you lower me."

"I shall lower you, little warrior, after you say your name," Stank declared. "Go on. Speak it."

"I'll tell my name once you lower me."

Rory laughed. "She's not a warrior. She's an arbiter."

"Ay, that she is," said Stank, again amused. "Name?"

"Not 'til you lower me."

"Ah, you grow heavy," said Stank, and immediately lowered his arm, keeping hold of her by the shirt. But as he brought her lower, she slipped straight out of her shirt and plopped on her bottom upon the ground, hitting the hardpack road.

"Whoops," laughed Rory. "Slippery one, that."

The girl got to her feet, defiant despite wearing no shirt. She rubbed her bottom, wincing.

Stank tossed the shirt at her and she pulled it on, showed him her meanest face.

"Nothing to see," said Stank. "Maybe she'll grow out someday. Could be a boy, though. Still not a warrior. Now, tell us your name."

Her face burned in anger. "I'm Mabel Maddox. Warrior. None may pass without paying the tax."

Dandruff chuckled at the display of amateur acting. He called to Stank: "You could've stood at a spot on the road like her, demand a tax, instead of earning your coin as you did back in that town."

Stank gave Dandruff a nasty look, then softened speaking to the girl: "Perhaps that's more fair. Yet this girl has the tax jig locked."

"It's my hill," she insisted. "And you shall pay the tax."

"We've little coin," said Stank mournfully. He glanced about as if looking for an attacker or two, saw none. Only one child acting too bold. Perhaps it had gotten good result in some instances.

"Mabel Maddox?" Stank quizzed, feigning surprise.

She held her head high. "The same."

"*The* Mabel Maddox? Famous woman warrior?" Stank displayed amazement. "Why, your very name strikes fear far and wide. I had no idea 'twas you. Pardons." He ceremoniously took a knee. "I'm so sorry for having challenged you. Forgive me."

"It's fair you recognize me by now," she responded as though she believed his ruse. "I shall allow you to rise."

Stank stood tall, towering over her. She gazed up at him until he grinned.

"You're a wee one. Why the warrior wag? Lazy day with nothing to do? Hiding from the schoolmaster? Or have you a mind to become a warrior?"

The girl grinned. "All you've said."

"So you are a warrior?" asked Rory, acting coy.

"Mabel Maddox," Stank spoke, "have you a mother? She about?"

"I've none. None since I came upon this world."

Dandruff snickered. "Came upon this world? Are you an angel?"

"I'm a warrior," she said with a snarl.

"You've no mother then?" Stank continued gently. "Who cares for you? A father? You've any brothers? sisters?"

"None you've said." She stood confidently. "I care for myself and need no others."

"Surely you have someone," Rory offered. "How do you eat?"

"I eat like any warrior eats. With my sword close by."

Stank roared with laughter. "She's a warrior, awright."

Mabel stood firmly before him, wooden sword back in her hand. Stank still held Longclaw in his, and as he sought to replace it in its long sheath, his elbow out, the sharp edge caught the girl's arm.

"Ow!" cried the girl.

"Stand back," said Stank. Then he spied the spot of red upon her arm, a nick only yet he felt bad for the wound. He went on sheathing his greatsword, then focused on her. "Now you're a warrior. You see that? A wound from a warrior makes you a warrior."

She didn't cry, shed a tear, nor grab at the nick. "So let it be said among warriors that Mabel Maddox was here today made a warrior at the hand of.... What's *your* name, warrior?"

"I'm Stanley of Wichita," he said, expecting her to be impressed.

"*Sir* Stanley," Rory called to them.

"Never heard that name."

Stank gave a shrug. "Well, we are far from there."

"We are the warriors Baumann, I'll have you know," Rory spoke.

"You? ...Perhaps." Mabel looked at Dandruff. "And him?"

"I am, to be sure, not a warrior, but an actor. I'm traveling under their protection."

"He's with us, but not because we protect him," said Rory. "He's a weird fellow, and amuses us."

"Come, let's repair you," said Stank and got out his sewing kit.

He took it seriously, as though he might need to perform a dire surgery, yet it wasn't a nick so grave as to require any thread. He cleaned it and stuck a bit of bandage over the mark.

"Come now, Mabel," said Stank. "All better now."

Mabel glared at Stank, seemed surprised.

"Well?" he demanded.

"I'm a warrior!" she erupted.

Stank frowned, expecting her to be grateful.

"And you're all alone, are you?" Rory jumped in.

With a flip of his hand at her, Stank mounted his steed.

"Let us be away," he said, and noticed the line of other travelers waiting patiently, trailing down the hill behind them. "We've tarried enough on this hill. With an ungrateful child, too."

Rory regarded him. "But this child...."

"I'm not a child, I'm a warrior," Mabel shouted.

"She cares not for herself, only gathering tax," said Stank. "She'll do well in coming years, perhaps meet a fine lad and together they shall have little warriors. For now, we are late to a tournament. So says the red-head."

Rory gave a dismissive glance at Stank. "Ay, brother."

"You're leaving her?" cried Dandruff from the bench of the cart.

"She wishes nothing more," Stank bellowed.

"Not at all, Sir Stanley," Mabel spoke loudly. "I'm a warrior. You are a warrior. We should go warrioring together." She regarded the mighty warrior on his warhorse. "I shall need a mount such as yours to finish my warrior posting."

"We're fresh out of steeds today," Stank said with a grunt.

"Ay, perhaps you ride a bit with the actor," said Rory. "We may yet come upon a suitable mount for such as you. Not too high, not a beast stronger than you can handle."

"That would be fine," said Mabel, a whimsical grin painting her face. "If the horse should be white or gray, I would like it all the more. With a black mane and tail, too."

"You've no further requirements?" asked Stank, annoyed.

"Leave her be," said Rory. "Must be gentle with little warriors."

"She'll get what she gets."

"She can ride with me," called Dandruff. "I won't be bothered. We can talk of many things. The poor pony never listens."

Mabel studied the man on the cart, remarked on his brown face and black coiled hair. "You vouch for this man?"

"As much as we can," laughed Rory.

"I am an actor," said Dandruff. "I've no ill intents. Not a warrior, though I did my part in battles past. I'll teach you the machine bow, if you wish. It's a fine weapon and can be used by anyone, not only a warrior."

"Then I shall ride with that one." Mabel smiled, and slipped her wooden sword under her belt.

"You're taking her with us?" Rory asked Stank. "She's just a kid. Shouldn't we ask about?"

"Ask about where? There's no village in sight."

"I've no village," she announced, sounding proud.

"Hear? No village." Stank turned Winnie toward the road. "None would have her." He roared with laughter.

Mabel climbed onto the cart, took a seat next to Dandruff, giving him a longer look. "Does your hair hurt?"

Dandruff explained how he formed his hair into the style it was as Rory and Stank discussed their plan.

Back and forth they argued. We can't simply lift a child from the road and be off with her. Three rogues like us? Not a fair turn. Eyes will judge. Even if she claims to be free, no parents about, it won't look good should we come upon a constable or the King's militia. All we have is her word for her true condition. She could tell false tales, make us criminals. None would believe a child's tales. We say we're merely taking her onward to a family member in another village?

Rory was adamant. "What then? I still don't like it."

"Sirs," called Dandruff.

Stank and Rory stopped their discussion and turned back to the cart. There on the bench the girl had leaned against Dandruff, her eyes closed, apparently asleep.

"Full day," Stank grumbled.

"Poor kid," said Rory.

"Let the kid nap as long as she will," said Stank, weary from the episode, "and we can make many miles before she wakes."

12

A WHIMSICAL WARRIOR

IT WASN'T THAT THE ROAD became easier to traverse. Rather, those who might consider attacking them took one look at Stank on his mighty steed and had turn-about come into their heads. Yet one morning's calm was shattered on a patch of open ground by the war cry of a ragged pair of reavers, racing roughshod from the wicked woods, long lances laying in line for the attack, and Stank—

"Why, he sat up tall in his saddle," Rory told it as the campfire crackled. "Showed who he was, and without any stopping or slowing they raced in a wide circle as if showing their middling mounts and returned hastily into the woods whence they came. Like it was all a circus trick."

The group laughed, Stank most of all.

"And those old women, pretending to be with injury to get us to stop," said Rory. "Offered them help only to get knives put on us."

"Thankful my leather vest stopped the blade," said Stank.

"But you punched them in the face," Dandruff said with a gasp much like what he'd given upon witnessing the punches.

"They needed a lesson," said Stank. "It was free to them."

"They weren't truly old, just dressed so," said Rory.

"You did them true," Mabel spoke up, standing so as to be seen within the group. "They should've known better."

"Ay, should've," said Rory.

"Desperate times call them to desperate acts," said Stank.

"Everywhere along this Royal Road are vain vagabonds bent on boosting our booty," said Dandruff. "I wouldn't survive were not for your protection, good sirs. I thank you for allowing me to travel with you." He dipped his head in thanks.

"Ay, like them over there," said Rory, thumbing at the next camp a few yards away. "And them." Pointing to another camp.

They had collected other travelers like dust on their boots, folks seeing a warrior-on-steed and wishing to accompanying him to gain safety. Stank wasn't bothered by it – as long as none bothered him. He made a formidable guide: frightening to the weak and devious, a gentle giant to the righteous and simple.

"You should charge them a fee," Dandruff suggested.

"And charge you?" asked Stank gruffly.

"I offer entertainment as my fee, sir."

"Well, I haven't had to fight any of them," said Stank. "Only the two incidents did a weapon come at me."

"You're a brave one," said Mabel brightly, gazing at Stank. He'd treated her fair, had christened her a warrior, and now she admired him like a god, understanding she was not actually a warrior. "Like a true warrior. He protects the weak, fights for justice, and takes his fee only where it's fair."

Stank felt humble, nodding as he kicked at the embers of the fire as was his habit. He reached for the hilt of Longclaw, pressed into his hip, and removed the sheath strapped around his body, set down the greatsword beside him on the log.

"There is much to learn," said Stank to everyone but intending his words for Mabel. "Yet what is not taught are the moral things. The things from the heart. 'Tis commonplace those are taught by the mother and father, not a militia captain."

"Then you were taught well, sir," said Mabel. "Those people over there appreciate you."

"Ay, there's different kinds of appreciation," said Stank.

"They should've paid a fee for protection," Rory spoke up, raising his voice so the other camps might hear him. "A man can't keep on absorbing attacks without fair compensation. Like that rogue in the bushes, crouched with his machine bow, like a dirty fox—"

"I should have taken that one out," said Dandruff.

"'Tweren't no bother," said Stank. "Longclaw had reach. Snipped him a new one. He'll not sing much. Sent him to his nurse."

"You struck the rogue's throat," said Dandruff, reliving the shock of the incident.

"That one flung his bow, thus he discovered consequences," Rory responded with chuckles. "It is the way of the world."

"The world's ways wash over clean and unclean alike," mused Dandruff.

The camp grew quiet. Mabel, who wasn't the least sleepy, asked about their destination. Rising into talk once more, the men gave a lot of answers until she held up her hand like a school mistress to halt them.

"Yes, my dear?" asked Rory.

"You go to Louis? For the tournament?" she asked in summary.

"That is our story," Rory replied.

"Is it not true?" asked Stank of Rory, giving his brother a look. "You didn't tell of a tournament."

"I said you had to fight the duke." Rory looked around the circle. "To remove the duke.... To open the way for me.... For me to wed the princess. That's the truth."

"You didn't tell of a tournament," said Stank, playing with him.

"Yes, I did. You must defeat the duke.... That happens to be in a tournament. It's not a falsehood, brother."

Stank laughed. "You led me on. Made me think of a duel."

"It is a duel. Not a joust or within a mêlée. Only you and him. I imagine it coming in the courtyard. You call him out. And you'll be surrounded by the Court watching from balconies and landings, and around the main floor. It will be a fine battle."

"A fine battle," Stank mused.

"I have no doubt in your victory, brother."

"Neither do I."

"Then there's nothing for you to worry about."

"Ay, nothing. If I won't be fatigued by this journey. Fighting my way to Louis. All manner of rogues and vagabonds and wood witches harassing us. I'll not be set upon daily."

"You can get your warm-up exercises," said Rory.

"I'm warm enough for many days," Stank grumbled.

"Then I shall protect you," said Rory. He laughed, thinking it a fine joke. He waved his hand at Stank. "Behold: My prize bull. My champion. My best man."

"I'll be your best man, but I won't steal that woman for you," said Stank. "Only the duke. I'll fight him, and—"

"And kill him," Rory cut in.

"And you go wed your Majory, and good luck to you both. Have a brood of sons. I'll find my way home."

"Ay, home to your Mona," said Rory, a twinkle in his eye.

When they took up the road again, yet more vain vagabonds and random rogues dared assailed the travelers. Now the growing band of journeyfolk dissuaded most attackers. The group bound for Louis counted fifty men, women, and children, and the warriors Baumann, an actor's courtly cart, and a girl who fancied herself a warrior.

Dandruff ceased his recitation of Sandy's soliloquy in *The Way of the Son* as they came up to the stone gates of Rolla, a walled town built on mining enterprises.

"Now we find us a fair inn," Rory announced to the group.

Those who accompanied the warriors Baumann either continued onward or likewise stayed in the town for the night. Some camped outside the gate. They agreed to meet at the gate in the morning to press on together.

It was a rustic inn, even for such a fair town: matched their coin well. They lugged their bags up to the room, its window overlooking the town's square. Stank let out a huge sigh, grabbing his tunic and pulling it up and over his head. He was ready to sleep on the level again, choosing the cot by the window.

Then he regarded the girl.

"We can't have a girl sharing the room with us," he said.

Rory looked at him, then at Mabel. She seemed worried.

"It'll be awright," Rory told her. Then to the men: "We just won't take off our clothing tonight."

"I wish for a bath," said Stank. "Even a wash at a basin will do."

"There's an old woman across the hallway," said Dandruff. "She may host the girl for the night."

"An old woman?" Stank considered a moment. "What if she's one of those witches?"

"No witches in a town like this," said Rory.

"She's in an inn, brother. She's not from here." Stank frowned. "Could be just her thing to have a girl to abuse."

"The innkeeper thought she was our daughter," said Rory. "One of us. Never asked questions – a good thing, I suppose."

"Then we play it true," Dandruff offered. "We are her fathers."

"Father and two uncles," said Rory. "One red, one brown, eh?"

Stank laughed. "I'll take her underwing. 'Twas I who made this girl a warrior."

"I thank you, sir," Mabel spoke, relaxing now that they'd decided to keep her. "I've seen men before. Not a good sight, but I have."

"You've seen men before?" asked Rory. "Was it your father?"

"I steal among the camps at night," she spoke.

"You steal from the camps?" asked Dandruff.

"If there's good coin to be found," she answered unabashedly.

"A true sneak." Rory chuckled.

Stank let out a great exhale. "Well, I for one shall not be put at dis-ease by her presence. I shall go about my usual tasks. She can look or look away." He finished pulling off his leather vest and shirt, stood bare-chested before her.

"You look fine, sir," said Mabel.

"See? She's got no ill-will toward her father." Stank laughed, and turned his back to her to drop his trousers.

"That may be the case," said Rory, but holding a concerned face. He turned to Mabel: "How's we go for a walk for a while? Look for a treat for you while my brother does his washing?"

"That'll be fine," she said, sneaking a look back over her shoulder as Rory escorted her out of the room.

"Might I join you?" Dandruff called, coming out after them.

"Let the minstrel join us," said Mabel, nose in the air.

"I'm not actually a minstrel, my dear," Dandruff tried to counter as they went down the stairs to the front entry. "I'm an actor, as you surely know by now."

They strolled about the town, looking into shop windows, getting dismissive looks and a few cross shopkeepers waving them away. In one shop Rory bought a yellow candy for Mabel and she gave him a wonderful smile. Yet when Dandruff put his hand on her shoulder to steer her out of the street as a cart came by, she spun around ready to cut him. He admonished her for continuing to bear the wooden sword tucked in her belt.

"A warrior must always be ready," she responded.

Rory grinned. "She's a lively one."

"When you touched me, I didn't know it was you in that instant," she told Dandruff. "I didn't hurt you, did I?"

He brushed his sleeves, straightened his jacket. "Not at all."

When they returned to the inn, Stank had finished his washing and lay upon the best cot unclothed. He startled at the door opening, then swept the blanket over his midsection.

"You've had your tour then?" he challenged the three.

"Uncle Rory got me a candy," said Mabel. "I can't show it to you because I ate it already."

"Well, a candy is only good if you eat it," said Stank. He swung his feet to the floor, keeping the blanket over his lap.

"Someone's coming," Dandruff announced.

The burly innkeeper arrived at their open door. He crossed his thick arms as he scowled into the room.

"Missus says you've a girl in here," he spoke, filling the doorway with his girth. "Need to see papers for her."

"Papers?" asked Rory. "She's our daughter. Rather, I'm her uncle and he's her father."

"Father, eh?" He looked between Stank and Mabel. "That one's got dark brown hair and tan skin. The other's pale with yellow hair. I'll guess they ain't related."

"Her mother had the yellow hair," Rory said.

"You've no papers on her?"

"Papers? We didn't think we need any kind of paper. What kind of paper's that?"

"Official papers. With a stamp. From the town registry."

"Oh, he means a birthing document," said Dandruff.

"Long lost," Rory answered for Stank.

"Then she'll have to stay with a woman tonight," the innkeeper said with a thumb thrown behind him. "There's a few here. I'll ask around."

"We won't be leaving her with a stranger," Stank bellowed.

At that Mabel grew bold, slipped her wooden sword out from her belt and held it up.

"Mind you, child," the innkeeper warned, "I'll not be having none of that play fighting in my inn."

"See? She's her father's daughter," Rory laughed weakly.

"She'll not come to abuse," said Stank firmly.

"She will not come to abuse staying with a woman guest, either," said the innkeeper. "It's that or you all can leave. That's the rule for inns, decree sent out from Louis."

"Oh, is it?" Dandruff pondered.

The innkeeper turned to Dandruff. "I didn't see you come in. Are you the servant?"

"No, I'm not a servant of anyone," Dandruff declared, standing in a theatrical pose. "I'm an actor. I do my own plays. I'm not owned by any theater."

"I meant a servant to these two gentlemen."

"We ain't no gentlemen," said Rory. "We're warriors."

"Warriors I can bed," said the innkeeper. "Servants can stay, too. If you vouch he's yours. Otherwise, he needs to go down to the servants' room below. Plenty of rugs for them to sleep on."

"I am a highly praised actor!" Dandruff said with a raised voice. "Not a...a servant!"

"He's a friend." Rory glanced at Stank as if seeking approval. "I'll vouch for him."

"Thank you," said Dandruff with a theatrical flourish.

"But for her, she needs to stay with a woman," the innkeeper persisted. "It's the rule. I'll ask around."

He turned to leave, stopped at the room opposite, knocked on the door. An old woman opened the door, spoke with the innkeeper. She looked over his shoulder into their room, saw Mabel standing with the wooden sword in her hand. The woman shook her head.

"I've no patience for a feral child," said the old woman.

The innkeeper gave a nod, thanked her, and left for other rooms.

"Well, that's a foul turn," said Stank.

"We are a fair bunch – despite us being men," said Rory, looking around the room. "None of us would abuse a poor girl."

"I'm not a poor girl," Mabel shouted. "I'm a warrior."

"Come now," said Stank from the cot. "Even warriors must obey rules from time to time. It may be you'll need to stay with a woman. And leave your sword here. We don't want any fights or harmless entertainment to answer for."

Mabel switched to a brooding face, sword in hand at her side.

"Don't cry," said Rory.

"Warriors don't cry," she snapped.

The innkeeper returned. "I've found a woman who'll see to her."

"I must meet this woman and inspect her," said Rory, then gave a wink to Mabel.

Off they went to the other room. The innkeeper knocked on the door. A woman of middling age wearing a proper mistress gown and waxed apron answered, gazed down upon Mabel and smiled.

"This one?" She had a grin like she was pleased. "I'll be glad to host her for the night." She bent down to speak to Mabel. "I've got two daughters myself. One's about your age. They're back with my husband in Clair County. We've a farm there. I'm only in town for shopping. Fabric goods and such. Do you like to sew?"

Mabel wasn't taken by the woman. "I do not sew."

"Well, then...what's your name?"

"I'm Mabel Maddox, and I'm a warrior!"

"Yes, I see." She shot a frown at the innkeeper. "Even a warrior must know how to stitch. What if there was a battle wound needing thread? Would you know what to do?"

Mabel thought a moment. "I suppose it's a good skill to know."

Rory leaned down. "Sir Stanley stitched my wounds, he did."

"Then I'll learn it," said Mabel.

The woman straightened up, gave nods around. Deal made.

"I'll come for you at dawn," said Rory. "First light. Then a meal to break our fast and on we go. We're getting closer to Louis."

Pounding on the door awoke the three men. Stank scrambled up to answer, his blanket on the cot, standing bold in his altogether before the innkeeper who wore a nightshirt, holding a candle.

"Your child has begot trouble," the man growled.

Stank pulled on his trousers and followed, leaving Rory snoring and Dandruff watching curiously from the floor.

Arriving at the other room, Stank found the woman up against the wall, frightened like she'd seen a wraith. But it was only a girl who stood before her. Mabel held up the wooden sword.

"This has been going for the past hour," said the innkeeper.

"I hadn't heard, not past my brother's snores," said Stank.

"This one's a wild girl," said the innkeeper. "Completely wild, I'd say. Not a normal child. And that wooden toy she swings to and fro. Did you put her up to that?"

"I've not done anything. She chooses to play at being a warrior." He yawned. "Like her father."

"Perhaps. Yet it's trouble. I've had to call the constable. He will be here momentarily."

"The constable? Was that necessary? She's only a child."

"A feral child. Dangerous, too."

By then they heard heavy boots stomping up the stairs.

Around the corner came the constable in a red and gold uniform and his deputy in tan and brown, short swords drawn.

"Ho!" called the constable, a man with long black mustache, bare chin, and beady eyes. "What is the trouble this hour?"

His deputy yawned, brushed his long white hair back, adjusted his official jerkin.

"This child," said the innkeeper.

The constable stared into the room, saw the woman against the wall and the child keeping a sword on her.

"Followed the rules. Put this child with this woman. All agreed."

He gestured to Stank. "Her father."

"What's the trouble?" asked the constable again.

"She's been shrieking the whole past hour. From this child's wild acts. The poor woman's afraid for her life."

"From a child? Holding a play sword?"

"I'll not have my guests being upset during the night," said the innkeeper.

"What's the trouble, girl?" called the constable, speaking over the innkeeper's broad shoulder. "Can't you get into sleep?"

Mabel spun around, a wild look on her face. "She grabbed me."

The woman appeared disheveled, welts on her face. "I only tried to pull the blanket over her. Then she attacked me."

The constable seemed to hold back rude laughter. "Girl, why did you attack this woman?"

"She touched me," Mabel shouted back. "So I sought to teach her a lesson."

"With a wooden sword?"

"Yes, with my sword. She'll never touch a girl again that way."

"What way is that?"

"In a devious way."

"Let's put the sword down, shall we? Tell how she touched you. Was it like a harmful act or was it like a gentle touch?"

"Like a harmful act." Mabel broke from her warrior persona. "I don't like that."

Stank stepped forward and the innkeeper moved out of the way.

"Mabel, my dear. What about her touching disturbed you?"

"It...it awoke bad dreams...."

"Ay, bad memories. Of what? Earlier times?"

"Yes." Tears started to fall down her cheeks.

Stank turned to the constable, hands out. "She's not feral. Not a wild child. She's headstrong, as you can see. And I'm not her father. Truth be: we met on the Royal Road. She's an orphan child, so we chose to take her with us for her safety. I know nothing about her parents other than she said they were dead."

"Dead parents?" The constable thought a moment, fingering his mustache. "Perhaps that's the trouble. Either she's needing a spank, or she's had too much spanking." He stepped into the room, staring at Mabel. "I see a child who got poked by a certain fear. Is it true? You burst into rage at a memory. Is that it?"

Mabel sniffled back tears, sword still in hand but arm down at her side. "I don't know anymore."

Stank called to her: "We shall keep care of you, if you wish. You are still my warrior apprentice." He faced the constable. "Maybe she has a memory of bad things and this woman brought them out, even at random, with no ill-will towards the girl. The child only acted out of that fear."

"You, sir, have wit about you," said the constable. "Like a witch. Conjuring all manner of spells to cause troubles. Poke a memory...."

"I have heard such from witches," said the deputy.

"Isn't it commonplace here?" asked Stank. "Children have bad dreams, awake in the night screaming, acting as though in a fight."

"We've none of that here," said the constable. "Children sleep in peace here. We've no witches casting spells here. Where might you be from, sir?"

"I and my companions are from Wichita."

"Ah hah! The witch village. I've heard much of it."

"Surely a witches' gathering place if they dare name it so," said the deputy.

"No, it's not a witches' town. The name comes from those tribals living there long ago. No witches there."

"Yet you have this idea that dreams cause actions. That's a poor amusement. And in the middle of the night, at that." The constable gazed at the girl then spoke to the innkeeper: "We shall take the child, put her in a room for the remainder of the night. In the morning we shall call a priest to examine her for any devil's marks. Ask a few more questions to determine if she is a threat."

"Threat? To what? A night of good sleep?" Stank demanded.

"A threat to anyone. Look at this scared woman. She's soiled her nightgown. I'll not have that in my town. A feral child must be held to account."

"If she's feral, how can you hold her to an account?" asked Stank with a scowl.

"The feral child shall speak from the devil's throat," explained the constable, as though in a church spell.

"As it is written," said the deputy with a grin on his face.

The constable went into the room, grabbed Mabel by the arm. She swung her wooden sword at him but he swatted it away, out of her hand. Then he gave a backhand to the child's cheek.

Stank roared at the constable for that slap, ready to punch the man, but the deputy raised his sword to him.

"You wish to join the child?" growled the constable.

13

A RASH OF INJURY

AS THE SUN ROSE over the town's walls, the squad of four night-stalkers escorted the wild child to the cold constabulary, the girl full of complaint, candles lighting windows at her noisy passage.

"She won't be any trouble," Stank insisted, matching stride with the lanky constable. "We can leave here forthwith and not return. There will go your trouble."

"Yet the trouble has already occurred," said the constable with a smooth smirk. "Punishment must follow."

"For waking the populace? Frightening a hostess?" Stank shook his head, noting he didn't bring Longclaw with him when he left the room to go with the innkeeper to where Mabel raged. He felt naked, walking barefoot and shirtless outdoors. If the need came, he could wrestle an attacker. Or offer a well-placed punch upon a face.

"Child or not, the law remains the law," the constable spoke back as they arrived.

The constabulary had the terse trappings of an old church, with colored-glass windows rising above a grandiose entrance. Inside sat several rows of benches. At the far end of the room stood a wide dais with a prominent podium perched in proper position for a preacher's pomp and sermon stance. Behind the podium rose a tall window of colored glass, a myriad of perfect pieces put together to create the fantastic image of a god with raised hand blessing a mortal man on his knees. Stank paused at the sight: not too realistic.

"Come," called the constable, "the law awaits."

"The law waits for no man," said the deputy, dragging Mabel by the arm past Stank. She had ceased crying, perhaps too afraid now what her punishment would be, yet staring in awe of the place.

"What is this vain law that wounds a child the same as a grown person?" Stank tried to hold his anger and be polite.

"As it is written," replied the constable, then told his deputy to retrieve a copy on paper of the laws for this rube who knew nothing about how a polite society operates: a society which must be ruled by law – then offered a snooty guffaw.

"What will you do with her?" Stank inquired cautiously.

"When the magistrate rises and finishes his morning meal, he'll be over to us and render a verdict. You may give your reasons, if you wish, for dismissal of the charges. The child may speak, as well, if she wishes. And both of you must answer all questions put to you."

"What charges?" asked Stank, fighting back his anger.

"The magistrate shall determine."

"Is this how you steal children?"

"Steal children?" The constable laughed like he'd laughed at the same question before. He regarded Stank.

"You had better robe yourself before the magistrate arrives, lest you find yourself with charges."

Stank grumbled. He wished his companions might find the way to the constabulary and give him aid. He wasn't prepared to speak in a court. Not his battleground. Those judges and the vain men who pronounced lies he'd encountered in the past only looked at him as a warrior and thereby took all violence he'd done as evil which must be rendered powerless. Judge Matthews in Wichita said as much.

That judge believed – wanted to believe – that all violence must be removed from the earth. He soon learned that violence removed was only half a plan, for violence would still arrive in other forms. It could never be removed completely. Days later it was Stank who'd stood between the judge's family and those murderous marauders. Violence was perpetrated without judgment upon those murder-men and seven bodies quickly lay in quarters with Longclaw red-stained. Saving the judge and his family caused the charges of mayhem to be dismissed. Yet the judge, although thankful, remained afeared of a heavy blade in strong hands and ordered Stank to leave town, never to return. Eventually Stank was granted the right of return to visit his mother once a year.

"There's always someone coming to take what you've got: your wealth, your family, your life," Stank muttered, drawing a look from the constable. "You must prepare to defend against that."

"What are you saying?" asked the deputy with a curious look.

"Thinking my thoughts," said Stank, "and responding to them."

"That's a witchy trait," said the deputy.

"To think aloud? To answer yourself? To make truth stand apart from the hail of nonsense by public examination?" He wasn't happy. "It's how I think out ideas. And now you say I must prepare for the judgment. I gather words. So I prepare, nothing more."

Mabel sat on a nearby bench, a sullen look on her face. She sat calmly, perhaps gathering strength, ready to rage again. The deputy stood before her, two guards behind him ready to catch the girl if she should attempt to escape.

Stank watched her as he decided what to do, what he would say to the magistrate.

A commotion erupted at the entrance to the constabulary.

Rory and Dandruff bulled their way through the doorway, loudly complaining about having to come there in the middle of the night.

"There you are!" cried Rory, ignoring the guards and gesturing wildly at his weary brother, whose grin burst fully upon his face.

"Ay, brother," Stank called, "here we be."

"That innkeeper, he told us you came this way. Better you find your way to a bedding house, eh? Yet here you be. And at dawn, too, that fat coin-catcher! Trying to charge us for the full night when we had barely half of it."

"There she is," Dandruff exclaimed as though he was her father. "Miss Mabel! Are you well? Unhurt by these bad men?"

The constable took exception to the accusation. "Who are these?"

"You do not recognize me? I'm Lyle Danderoff, famous actor! And this is our star player: Miss Mabel Maddox—"

"Who's it?"

"—the most famous child actor in all the land, a central member of my theater troupe, the Danderoff Players. We have just completed a run of spectacular performances in Springer's Field and we are on the way to Louis to perform for the King himself. You had better not delay us, or His Majesty shall hear of it and bring punishments on you. It is fair warning."

"He's an actor, awright," said the deputy, mugging.

"Never heard any of that," said the constable.

"Attend plays much?" Dandruff challenged, putting his hands on his hips and tilting his head. It was a serious accusation.

"What play?" quizzed the constable.

"*The Way of the Son* in Springer's Field. Miss Mabel here plays the magical child Isla who knows all and thus guides her parents to safety only to be captured later by vile vagabonds and made to serve their perversions yet survives in heroic fashion."

"Ay, that's a story," Rory interjected, playing along.

"I'll be needing my clothes," Stank spoke to his brother. "And, of course, Longclaw. You best bring everything on Winnie, so we may depart the instant this matter is settled."

"Under the finest care in the town," Rory responded. "Same for Fergie. They'll be sad to depart this place."

"So this child is one of your pretenders?" asked the constable of Dandruff. "No, I don't attend such witchy things. They're bent upon screwing our heads around. Make us believe things that aren't true. I abhor such displays of mirth."

"There are no displays of mirth allowed in this town," the deputy added, foisting a deathly frown upon the group. "It's in the law."

"More laws to forget," Stank grumbled.

"You must release this child at once," Dandruff spoke, affecting the role of the island prince in *The Way of the Son*. "Such trauma as this episode shall unduly harm her ability to perform."

"Nothing happens before the magistrate arrives." The constable gazed up on the wall at the time counter, measured the bars. "Only one hour, thereabout."

Stank noticed a child sitting high on the wall, posed on the small perch there, like a decoration. Yet the child appeared to flex fingers in a rhythmic pattern, as though counting. The child moved the bar up a peg, returned to counting fingers.

"That is how you use children?" Stank demanded, pointing to the child up on the wall.

"It is a job best suited for the smaller ones," the constable replied dismissively.

"And you've other jobs for children?" asked Stank.

"There are—"

"We must leave here immediately," Dandruff declared, his words cutting through the discussion. "Already this frightful night has left our star performer weak and unable to perform. She will need time to recover her delicate skills. His Majesty shall be disappointed. Do you wish that?"

He pulled a rolled up parchment from inside his great cloak and presented it to the constable.

"Look. Here is our Royal commission. See it? Now read it: 'The Danderoff Players, a Royal troupe; With all Rights and Privileges due a Performing Act.' See the seal? The Royal stamp of approval? It's all there. I and Miss Mabel are members of the troupe."

The constable stared at the words drawn in elegant style, full of curling lines, hard to read that way.

Dandruff grew impatient. "If you delay us further, there shall be repercussions to pay. Do you wish to pay repercussions?"

"Ay, he's a clever one," Rory muttered to Stank.

"Repercussions?" the constable asked Dandruff.

"To pay. And I hear the cost is higher for those who impede His Majesty's entertainers."

"Entertainers?" The constable studied the scroll. "It does seem a true thing. The ink is long dried."

"It is a true thing," Dandruff insisted, pinching the corner of the open scroll to retrieve it.

The constable held fast to it. "We must await the magistrate. It is the law." He glanced up at the time counter, saw the child raise the bar another peg and resume counting fingers.

"Do you ever feed them?" asked Rory, looking up at the child.

"They get a meal at the end of the shift," said the deputy as the constable continued looking over the scroll. "Every twelve hours."

"That's not a fair way," said Rory.

"Fair for children," the constable said, looking up from the scroll. He rolled it up, handed it back to Dandruff. "Seems fair enough. It's easy work. And they don't need much food."

Dandruff accepted the scroll, slipped it inside his cloak. Turning to Rory and Stank: "Now let us collect our star performer."

"You must wait for the magistrate," the constable reminded.

"How much longer?" asked Rory, leaving Stank frustrated.

"We must be on the road," Dandruff spoke, "or else we shall not arrive in time for our Royal performance. His Majesty shall be much aggrieved, and we shall be obliged to disclose the reason for delay. We shall name the names of those who delayed us." He looked at the constable's jerkin, reading the name tag pinned there. "Mister Cane, is it? Constable Cane."

"And this one's Mister Lane," Rory added with a chuckle at the deputy. "These are the names we shall name."

"You need not name names," the deputy grumbled.

"No naming names," the constable added.

"Some names need to be named," said Dandruff.

"And we shall name the names," Rory barked.

"No need for names," the constable insisted.

Dandruff stood firm, acting the island prince. "You are prepared to accept the consequences of causing delay to His Majesty's Royal troupe from its scheduled performance?"

The constable didn't smile as he stared at Dandruff.

The deputy balked, spoke to the constable: "Perhaps it's true."

"It most certainly is true," Dandruff pressed. "Word will find you and the word will be with you. Quite a pair these: Cane and Lane, His Majesty's grievous pair of dolts."

"We don't want to be dolts," said the deputy to the constable.

"No, never dolts," the constable conceded.

A sudden breeze blew into the hall, hot like hell, as doors opened and closed, black cloak storming as the magistrate entered, followed by a four-clerk retinue in black robes and bearing ledgers.

"You've risen me early!" the beefy bearded magistrate bellowed, approaching the constable and deputy. "All your noise!"

The constable grew bold. "Sir, it was the child making the noise in the night, not—"

"All I see is a girl sitting calmly while you dolts harass my sleep in a decidedly tawdry manner."

"Beg pardons, sir," said the constable, dipping his head.

"Not enough pardons for disrupting my sleep. You cut short my dream before it reached a fine climax. Unforgivable."

The magistrate stood catching his breath. Great lungs heaved as he brushed his gray beard then struck loose whiskers from the black robe, patting his large belly.

He let out a long sigh. "I'll not get that dream again."

"We *are* dolts," the deputy mumbled to the constable.

"Again, pardons, sir," said the constable.

"What's the charge?" demanded the magistrate. He gestured for the clerks to take their stations at the back of the hall.

The constable started to speak, but the magistrate waved him to silence. "Let me get in place."

They watched the weighty magistrate waddle up the wide aisle, gaining the dais after a while, stepping onto the platform with an awkward buoyancy. He grabbed at the podium to steady himself, to avoid the fall, then swung himself down upon a well-cushioned seat. Little more than the top of his peaked cap shown above the top of the podium.

"Now," the magistrate said at long last.

The group had followed the magistrate up the aisle, and stood in their designated positions by the time he finally faced them.

"What's our business this morning?" the magistrate spoke, then yawned for a while.

"The child before you caused mayhem upon the night," spoke the constable in an official voice. "The first charge. The child before you caused severe fright to her hostess in the inn where both stayed over the night. Second charge. It should be noted the child arrived in the company of three men, these men here present, thus they were told the law requiring them to send the child, a girl, to overnight with a willing woman, which the innkeeper found. Furthermore—"

"Wait. Stop." The magistrate wiped his wrinkly brow, trying to focus. "Where's the woman the child frightened?"

The constable looked at the deputy who shrugged, then regarded the magistrate. "She remained in the room. We did not bring her."

"So she's not so frightened to remain in her room, perhaps return to sleep – unlike some of us who'd rather get a fair night's rest."

"Yes, sir." The constable cleared his throat.

"Proceed."

"The hostess was frightened by the violent acts of this child. Acts which include outlandish screams, thrashing about as if taken in a witchy manner, and, lastly, wielding a play sword with malice, thus causing a welt or two upon the woman."

"Stop," the magistrate barked. He rose to see over the podium, to gaze at Stank. "Why is this man half-naked?"

The constable started to speak. "He was—"

"I've not yet returned to my room in the inn, sir," said Stank. "I came with the child to protect her."

"Many were interrupted on this night," the magistrate decreed. "And yet here you stand, coming after this child. To protect her."

"Yes, sir." Stank stood straight, his mighty muscular chest filling the magistrate's eyes. "She's an orphan child, thus I've adopted her, and will train her as a warrior, which is her wish."

"Ah, dear sir," Dandruff spoke, holding up a hand. "The child is a player in my troupe, as was appointed by Royal decree."

Stank shot Dandruff a nasty look. "She is both, sir."

"Ah, true," Dandruff cleverly conceded. "First a player on stage, then an orphan. Her parents were both players in my troupe, you see. Then untimely slain by savages assailing our camp while upon the Royal Road. This fine warrior came by and saved us or else we, too, would be slain. He offered his protection so we might make our way to Louis to perform for His Majesty, King Karl."

"Stop," the magistrate ordered, waving his hand for everyone to be quiet. He turned to the nearest clerk behind him. "Bring me the elixir."

The clerk popped up, rushed away, returning momentarily with a tall beaker of something that steamed in curling clouds.

"There," said the magistrate in a gravelly voice. "Let me drink a bit of this first. Then we may continue. You see? Your rapacious rills ruined my morning ritual."

He blew into the beaker twice, then sipped. Pausing, he regarded the girl, sitting on the front bench, dozing. He took a longer quaff. He admired the girl and her child-sized puffs of snore.

"Seems this one is the calmest of you all. I envy her sleep." He drank more from the beaker. A rich aroma drifted out to Stank and the others. Rory's belly gurgled.

Stank stood tall, Rory beside him, then Dandruff, as though they were the ones to be given punishments. The constable grinned, his night's effort about to pay off. The deputy smiled beside him.

"I see a child of good humor, fair at rest," the magistrate spoke, "while the bunch of you – this crooked constable and his dolt of a deputy, a half-naked warrior, a costumed fool with two many coils of hair to count, and that red-head ruffian."

"I'm no ruffian, sir," Rory tried to argue.

The magistrate looked them over, frowning.

"I do not see the woman who was wronged."

He turned to glance at the child high on the wall, moving the bar another peg higher.

"I see the hour is early and a full day of cases to hear. I will not waste more time on this one."

He struggled to stand but made it, breathing hard, hands on the podium which swayed against his weight.

"I now order all of you – you three men and that sleeping girl – to leave this town within the hour and never return, not for a single night, under penalty of a fair flogging."

The constable's face went white. "But sir!"

"I have made my ruling. Obey it."

The constable bowed his head. "Yes, sir."

"Go on now. All of you. Out of my sight. Be gone!" He waved his arms, the black robe's sleeves flying like an angel exiting the gates of heaven.

14

THE RIVERLANDS

WITH A GRUNT, Stank reined Winnie to let the creaking cart and plodding pony catch up. When they met side by side, the warrior gazed down at Dandruff and Mabel perched on the bench.

"You've a Royal commission?" Stank questioned him.

"I do," came Dandruff's reply, sounding smug. He kept his eyes on the road. "It's a true commission."

"That was luck for us," Stank called down.

"It was true. A real Royal commission. A little past the date, I'm afraid. Yet they didn't notice. Or they couldn't read it."

"Past due?" Stank pondered. "It's false?"

"Not at all, sir." Dandruff regarded Stank atop his warhorse. "It was real. I did start my own theatrical troupe a few years past. We did perform for His Majesty, King Karl. He enjoyed our performance and gave us the commission."

"So what happened?" asked Stank with a sly grin.

"We had many plays in the capital. I told you of my fellow actors being ambushed by savages. However, I could not save them. That was the end of the Danderoff Players, you see. It is only I now."

Mabel gave Dandruff a stern look. "And me."

"Sad thing, to lose one's comrades," said Stank.

"The commission is correct, sir, yet valid for only three years. I saw that period come to an end three years ago. We could not return to Louis to play for the King again and so renew our commission."

Stank glanced ahead. "Another sad thing."

"He can play again when we get to Louis," Mabel spoke up.

Stank nearly broke into laughter at her enthusiasm.

"What're you rattling on about?" Rory called from his red mule. He leaned down, speaking to the mule: "They're hatching schemes again, I've no doubt. Stand ready." He chuckled at the luck that fell upon them, the case against the girl being dismissed by the sleepy judge. "Ay, that one brings us luck!"

"His commission," Stank called to Rory. "Seems a true thing."

"Ay, another true thing," Rory muttered. "Too many true things. Saving us or cursing us. I wish the world was only a play."

"You'll play for the King once more?" Stank asked Dandruff.

"If we are allowed." He glanced at Mabel, the girl now bearing a childish grin. "However, we've not a full company – thanks to those savages. Only me and this famous child actor." He added theatrical posturing to amuse her. "She has a rare talent."

"I'll be that magic child," she declared.

"Do you know the play?" Dandruff asked her.

"Never heard it. Never saw it. Never knew it lay about the land. Never knew actors. Never found paper things splattered with words. Never got taught what's wrought or what's naught—"

"The magic of a play, my dear, is not yet in your experience," the actor spoke with theatrical glee. He then let out a disappointed sigh, acting overwhelmed.

Mabel laughed at his performance.

"Coming into the riverlands soon," said Stank. He gave a nod to them and urged Winnie forward to retake the lead.

Though they left immediately from Rolla in that grim hour, the sunrise not yet a suggestion, some of the campers in their traveling band managed to rise and follow. Others couldn't ready themselves and lost the chance to travel with a warrior. Stank looked back at the line of those that followed Dandruff's creaky cart: six families, a dozen others in a loose line stretching back many yards, all seeking protection as the group continued to the capital.

Stank heard Dandruff telling the story of Isla the magic child to Mabel, switching to recited lines from the play they'd attended then reverting to telling the story. He spoke lines of various characters –

as though he himself played each of them. He sounded proficient to Stank's ears, though he only knew the story from childhood. All the children in the village were told the story, part of their education: a warning and an inspiration.

As he reached Rory, Stank rode in tandem.

"That one's corrupting the youth," Stank chuckled.

Rory glanced behind at the cart, saw Dandruff and Mabel fixed in their talking. "Ay, she could play the warrior princess, I'll bet."

"Seems a true child now, not a warrior princess."

"She's both. A girl becomes a woman, ay, and bears both within her: the elven child and the warrior princess. It's for the man to see which she plays and give her what she wants."

"You're preparing for marriage," Stank said with amusement.

"Ay, it's a lesson to remember."

Stank turned serious. "When we reach Louis, we must part ways with those two." He gave a glance back. "Enough of the distractions. I must prepare for a duel, as you've so graciously arranged for me."

"It's a tournament, as those travelers have told," said Rory using his humble voice. "You needn't worry. You can enter with a mark of your name on the ledger. You can write a name, can't you?"

"I have my mark. So does Longclaw."

"Then comes the duke."

Stank let out a big breath. "The duke!" He glared at Rory. "Tell me of this fellow. What's his weakness? How shall I defeat him?"

Rory smiled. "With a strong blow to the head, I should imagine."

It was good to have his brother back again, free of interruptions that always come with a long journey. Now that they were as far as the riverlands, they could focus on the task at hand.

"Duke Lindo is the first son of Duke Dave and Duchess Denise, a landkeeper of lower drainage. They maintain a residence below the city. Closest village is Mehlville, south of the King's residence. One of many standing hills among the marshes."

"The riverlands stretch wide there," said Stank, thinking of what he knew from his school days. Children in the village learned where places were. The city of Louis stood on a bluff overlooking a muddy plain that once held a wide river within its banks – still did during the spring, yet only a swath of mud and sand the remainder of the year. A wide bridge bore travelers from the city gates over the span to the eastern shore, into the wild country of the Illini tribes.

"They stretch more so in the north," Rory added. "Ay, two mighty rivers as strong as you but as rivers, crashing into each other there, spilling their waters over the lower lands, forming a vast marsh. It cannot be crossed. As well, that river which once flowed south to the far marshlands is but a muddy ditch these days. Indeed, the King lives between swamp and marsh looking down from his bluff. I see the Court set beneath a great silver arch built in ancient times. Those pleasure gardens so famous across the land are there."

"Pleasure gardens?" asked Stank, showing interest.

"Ay, pleasure for members of the Court. They play sports there. I have watched the sporting lads play. They kick the balls there. It's a spectacle for the amusement of the King."

"Certainly. Everything is for the amusement of the King."

"Duke Lindo, on another hand, takes a different bluff south from there. Has a view of the ditch, the muddy stream winding its way south. Never you mind that. They're members of the Royal Court for generations."

"What's he like, this Duke Lindo?"

"I haven't met him, as you can guess. Only seen him from afar. Had to endure watching him kiss the hand of my Majory. A sight for my sore eyes. Protocol, you understand. Many protocols—"

"How's he built?"

"He's a thin fellow. Not sickly, mind you. Not broad-shouldered nor wide-hipped, is all. More like a woman in body. He dances well. A handsome face – so some say. Talks up a fine play, I've heard."

"His fighting skills?"

"Like I told you before, he can fence. Good at it. But his weapon is a rapier. That narrow blade's enough for a sporting match. It's not for battle. And they wear wire masks and leather jerkins while in a sport-duel. He's never been in battle, I'm certain. Ah! Yes. He did sit alongside his uncle, the older duke – Barto's his name – perched on their horses to watch the Battle of Cahokia from a safe distance. I presume to learn military strategy. The youth's got no mind for it, I heard. Not sure how much he could learn from that battle anyway. Militia from Louis easily overpowered that band of Illini ruffians. Could've played it out on the sporting fields instead of a battlefield, but that's only my view."

"Seems like an easy opponent. What's his schemes?"

"Schemes? I've not heard of any cheating nor tricks. He plays the fencing straight. A damn rule keeper. He'll cite you rules from the book if you fault."

"There's rules for the duel?"

"None that I know," said Rory.

"Then it's free style, eh? Best blade wins?"

"They'll surely mark you foul if you dare cut the corners. Stay in line. Now, brother, here's the plan."

Rory glanced around as though spies might be lurking. Stank also gave a look.

"You will speak an offence to him. He will challenge you. You accept. He will attempt to cut you quick. Mind you, he's light on his feet. But you only need a good blow from your greatsword and he'll go down, possibly in halves. Ladies will shriek but pay no mind."

"I'm not sure of that. Speak offence? Isn't he in this tournament everyone's been talking about?"

Rory paused, thinking. "That will take longer. You have to fight others before you get to him – if he succeeds as well as you. You may get another opponent in the final clash. No, it's better to push him to challenge you to a duel."

"Would he?" Stank had a smirk for Rory. "If he sees me he won't want to fight me. He won't challenge."

Rory understood. "If he sees you and everyone else sees, too, he can't shy from the challenge. His honor will be at the stake. Like it or not, he must challenge you."

"Then I shall slay him in short order, before the Court, and you will be free to wed that princess you fancy. What's her name?"

"You best be kind to the love of my life, brother. My beloved's name is Majory. And you better not forget."

Along the Royal Road they came upon the ruins of a great mystery. A sign gave no indication of its purpose. Behind a high fence stood giant loops, rings so wide a pair of four-horse teams could pull a wagon through its center. Past the towering rings stood bent pieces of a long iron track that rose up and sailed down on a tender frame, though parts had fallen. Other venues sparked curiosity from the travelers, and they halted to investigate.

"I've heard of this place," said Rory, climbing down from Fergie.

"You haven't gone this way before?" asked Stank as he surveyed the strange arena of mischief.

"On my previous visit I came from the west, on the road through Jeff City."

"That is what they used to call an Amusement Park," Dandruff happily announced. "For the elite, of course."

"Elites?" Stank stood puzzled beside Winnie. "Looks more like a way to torture criminals. Put them up there. Let them hang a while. Won't be no trouble after."

"I'm certain it was considered a fun place," Dandruff countered. "You can't see that now. Look at that track rising beyond: although partially collapsed it once held a wagon, or a string of them, that ran along the top."

"Wagons on top of that track?" Stank was amazed. "That would be frightening. It could easily falter and down you go."

"That was the amusement," said Rory with a laugh. "The thrill of coming close to death yet not meet it."

"Your brother's not wrong," said Dandruff.

"I won't go up there!" cried Mabel.

She stood close, her face showing fear at the sight of the ruins and what they may have beheld back when they were in operation.

Dandruff put his hand on her shoulder as if to calm her.

"After the age of battles, the elites enjoyed pushing themselves into such horrifying escapades as what we see here. As close to them facing death as they could manufacture short of battle."

"Less of amusement park," Rory sang, "more like torture park."

"Then it fell," said Stank solemnly, as though the place was now a graveyard. "Like most of our world. Cities becoming mere towns, towns to villages, villages...gone. What a lonely world we have now. To think how people used to willingly face death for...amusement. It was a vain world we lost."

"At least the flags of the six kingdoms still fly," said Dandruff as he pointed to the tattered banners waving in the breeze.

"Six? Why six?" asked Stank. "Is this where six kingdoms met?"

"Something like that," said Dandruff. "Anyway, it's history long past. Not in my school lessons."

"Nor mine," said Rory.

"I like those flags," Mabel declared, standing proudly. "They got many colors. I shall choose one for myself."

"Which one do you like?" Rory asked her as Stank scoffed.

"I like the one with the big star," she answered, pointing at the one on the end.

"I believe the kingdoms those flags represent," Dandruff began, "are the Missourites, of course. And possibly the Illini. The Arkans, maybe. One could be the Okala territory. I'm not sure."

"That's only four," Stank teased.

"Possibly Tejas is one of them," said Dandruff. "Yet that was still foreign soil in those days."

"Ruled by Slammers," Stank cursed.

"How about when the east stood tall?" Rory suggested. He meant the great cities on the eastern seaboard, before they were destroyed by a vast fire that burned for an entire year. When all the kingdoms were one nation, a joining of fifteen states.

"Could be," said Dandruff, squinting in thought. "It was called.... I think they called it United American States.... I think."

"The Americus," Stank announced, words coming into his head. "We learned of the Americus in my school days. Banding of fifteen kingdoms to form an empire. Well, not a true empire. A collection of what places managed to survive all the great *this* event and *that* awful thing that ruined us, that ruined this whole land all the way from the east coast to the western territory."

"Easy now, brother," said Rory, holding up his hand. "Save your fury for the duke."

"No, I recall that flag," said Dandruff. "It's a gray and red flag. I don't see that one over there."

"One looks like it's got an eagle on it. The red, white, and green one," said Mabel.

"That's Mexi," said Dandruff. "South of Tejas."

"Tejas stretched this far north?" asked Rory, not believing.

"I'm an actor, not a historian!" Dandruff barked.

"I like the one with the red and white stripes, too," Mabel offered to calm Dandruff from the onslaught of questions.

"Yes, it's very nice," he responded.

Stank grew tired, saw the others in their group ready to go. "Let us be on our way. We've no need to guess about the past. Even if you told a newly-wrought tale and changed everything, the true events remain. The ghosts will know it better than me or you."

"Well said, brother." Rory patted Stank's shoulder. "Much passed before we were born, and much will go on after we die."

Satisfied that the past would not haunt them, they gathered the group of travelers and marched onward up the Royal Road, which lay in better condition than the southwest. The creaking cart could roll easily over the stone and Stank let Winnie try it but veered to the grass after a while. Rory kept his mule beside the cart, talking with Dandruff and Mabel as they went along.

History returned to their talk, each trying to draw out what was learned in childhood. Mabel, though a child, had no school lessons to draw from so the men were happy to educate her, telling the stories they knew. A few hours making a timeline in the air of their breaths made them grow drowsy. Yet the mule continued at a gentle pace. The passive pony patiently plied the path, as well, sensing the right way like evening following day.

And in that way they came within sight of the great silver arch of the city of Louis, where King Karl held his Court.

15

THE CITY OF LOUIS

KING KARL THE ELDER, it has been said, came down from the far north riding a mighty snow sledge pulled by two great white bears. One of the Wenn clans from that forested region, following the river down to the Missoura marshes where that river poured forth its last draught. Upon the long bluff overlooking the mud-road he made his camp. He took the name Louis from what local scoundrels called it, saying the heap of ruins around them used to be a city in the distant past, named for a much older king.

"A king, eh?" he was heard to cry. "Then I'll be the new king!"

None dared challenge him. And that was that.

The camp grew, gained followers: folks sensing he was a serious man, a strong leader. In time the camp became a village. The village became a town, drawing its building materials from the ruins of the older city long-fallen – save for the tall silver arch that curved over them, a gift from the gods. King Karl swore it must be a gateway to another world and waited to see who might appear through it. Yet none ever came. None ever went. He set his drinking hall facing the arch so he could keep watch.

The elder Karl knew nothing of the plagues sweeping along the eastern wastes, nor the endless fire that smoked the skies. His was a world of wanton wilderness and wily warriors working their way down from the north, boasting of battles and singing songs of sordid satisfaction. Of rough-hewn families, hairy horses, wolf pelts, bear claws, and eagle feathers. They made an ale that could knock a man out for days, let him visit the gods, and feasted weekly in great halls cut from the earth and hewn timber, with a blazing fire never left to embers.

Then time came upon King Karl and he knew the life he'd lived would come to an end, the long road bringing him to his destination – yet not in fighting his neighbors, but from a warping of his inner flesh. A devil's complaint, pestering his posterior. He gathered his sons and their sons around him, maybe twenty in all, told them how to live their lives in a new way: in peace with their neighbors and in harmony with what the earth provided them. Puzzled, the sons and grandsons led forth their armies in fresh incursions across the land, claiming patches of soil, fields and forests, here and there, enlarging the realm before they had to honor the King's dying wish.

"It may not have been what King Karl wished," Rory explained, "but he understood a way of life couldn't easily be changed in a few days – or even a few weeks. They had a city. Rules were different in a city. Had to turncoat, wear the new rules on their sleeves."

"So they went soft," Stank spoke, gazing ahead along the road.

"Ay, they lost their warrior spirit," Rory conceded.

"Happens to all in time," said Stank, giving Winnie a pat. "You fight for peace. You grow fat in peace. Then a new-born wolf wants what you've gathered but you're too besotted to defend against the attacks." He gave a snort. "Best build high walls while you grow old and fat, safe within your sanctuary. Train the youngers to fight."

"Or do like people did a couple hundred years past," said Rory, "hiding in the woods or going under the ground to wait for peace."

Stank nodded. "They were sad days."

"A few great-grandsons later and we have a new King Karl, who is number five or thereabouts." Rory mugged. "He's a softy now, as you said. Old and fat. Lives in luxurious gowns, hair grown down to his waist, all curly and adorned with ribbons. Always a hair-keeper at his becking and collaring. Not a threat to any of us – lest his hair falls into disarray and the hair-keeper cannot be found."

"I pity the coiffeur," Stank laughed.

"I as well. Yet he's got an army. The generals are true warriors. They know how to fight. And they hold the kingdom together as best they can as they wait for King Karl's prissy son to take over. He's a 'late Karl' like his father. Fidelio is his name. He has three older sisters: Bertilda, Melody, and Gann. The younger—"

"Gann?" Stank almost burst into laughter.

"Ay, she's called Gann. The best-looking of the three, I'm told. Yet I'm only interested in Majory, the younger sister of his. She is my destination. My beloved."

"So you say, brother."

Rory called back to Dandruff and Mabel riding on the creaking cart. "He's one like you: a patron of the stage. Like you. Yet more a dancer than actor."

"I can dance, too," Mabel blithely announced, jumping up as if to show her steps, quickly pulled back down to the bench by Dandruff before she could topple off the cart.

As the group approached the city, fellow travelers took leave, a turn to the left or right where old metal signs stated *Exit*. They'd give a wave or a call of thanks for protecting them on the journey. Stank dipped his head in acknowledgement, though he felt he'd not done much by his own account. His mere presence at the head of the column was enough to deter most vagabonds or dumb savages who considered an attack. There were plenty who might give thought to action were not for him. He saw them standing at the edge of woods, ready to pounce or laying traps to spring, deciding whether to act after seeing him on his warhorse, then deciding not.

He did have to swing Longclaw a few times, feeding the soil with fresh blood.

One overnight camp went sleepless when a band of savages tried stealing their packs only to trip and stumble, making noise as they departed. Stank had risen half-naked and grabbed his greatsword, stalking through the woods after them. He found them and cut them down, reclaimed the stolen goods. Long for breath coming back to the camp, he let the other travelers go haul what was theirs left in the woods. Every attack or attempt wearied him, made him more reluctant to chase after thieves or engage in fighting.

Yet Rory continued to tease him, saying he could make fair wage escorting travelers back and forth along the Royal Road.

Stank scoffed at the idea.

"I'll slay your duke and see you wedded," he replied, "then I am straightaway to Mona. To the home we shall make together: Mona and I, and a brood of new sons to fill the town and country. I ponder how many sons she can make. Seven? Even three would be bold of her, making light of her age. She's got a sturdy body."

"Ay, brother. I wish it for you. Yet we know a woman won't wait. The next handsome buck to bound through the town is fair game for her. You'll be lucky to find her free upon your return."

"It's not that way. I'm sure," said Stank. "She has a calling. And if not for me, she'll keep at it: mending the lame."

"I pray for you, brother," said Rory. "May our two families meet again upon some far-off day and feast greatly together."

"Agreed."

Behind the brothers plodded the pious pony, pulling the creaky cart while Dandruff sat engaged with Mabel on the bench, teaching her the lines she must say in whatever play he planned.

Stank and Rory could hear the chatter but gave them no mind.

"It's like when we left Rolla," Stank spoke, still thinking of a few episodes along the journey, "when that old magistrate told us all to leave and we tried to go but for that damnable constable disliking the verdict."

"Ay, that fellow wasn't worthy of the job," said Rory. "Poor fellow chased after us, brought his guards, made a spectacle of it. What's this world coming to if a magistrate's verdict isn't honored?"

"And poor Mabel. Caught up in such foolery."

"Had to show those guards what a warrior can do. Good on you. They brought it themselves. You had to use your greatsword. It was only fair. Four of them and only one of you. Hardly a fair mêlée for them. Yet you persisted."

"I would've preferred they let us leave as the magistrate ordered, and not try to capture us again."

"So you left them a good story," said Rory with a few chuckles.

"Once mounting Winnie, raising Longclaw, they should've felt a turning in their hearts."

"Yet the damnable constable urged them on. It's on him."

"I tried to give them a free lane, let them depart from us."

"So you left them free of hand or arm. Ay, that's the deal they so struck with a greatsword. A fair outcome."

"It didn't have to happen that way," said Stank.

"You must strike that from out of your mind, brother. Think of the duke. Think of your duel to come. Prepare."

"I'm too weary to fight." Stank grinned at his brother. "It should be you. You should best him with your wily words."

"Ah, he has the words to best me, he does!" Rory shook his head. "No, it must be you, meeting him in fair combat. First, an insult. Then the challenge. Then a deadly duel. That is the only way."

The Royal Road ended in a wide plaza before the tall silver arch, a place beset with market carts and stalls, shoppers gathered about but for a path forward marked by guards in red uniforms, keeping the way clear to the city gate.

The bright sunny day made the plaza a place of play. A wayward leather ball bounced before Winnie and Stank drew rein, let boys pass before him to retrieve the ball. Once clear, they proceeded to the main gate, Rory behind him, and the creaking cart pulled by the compliant pony plodding in the rear.

"Halt," ordered the guard standing with a halberd, ribbons in the city's colors of red and white hanging from it. The guard seemed to shiver in his red tunic at the sight of the warrior on his warhorse.

"Halt? Why?" Stank demanded, ready to stomp forward.

A guard captain in red and black tunic stepped out from a guard hut, bent his arms behind himself in polite pose, and gazed up at the mighty Stank.

"Hail, warrior," cried the captain. "What concern have you today in Louis?"

Rory urged his mule forward. "Good sir!"

The captain turned to the red-haired man on the red mule.

"I am leader of this group." Rory gestured to Stank, then turned in the saddle to point back at the cart bearing Dandruff and Mabel.

"This one's my protector. And they are also with us. They come as my entertainments. We are here to see the duke. We have us a bold business to conduct." He grinned at Stank.

"The duke? Which duke?" asked the captain.

"Duke Leto," said Rory confidently, then had to think. "Ah, Duke Ledo. Hmm? No, Layto.... No, it's Lela.... Leelu? Lolo? Lado...I think. Perhaps. Hmm, what others have you got?"

The captain remained stiff. "Perhaps you refer to Duke Lindo?"

"Yes! That's the one. We have business with that one."

"What business might that be?" asked the captain.

"We've fine business, that's what it is," Rory insisted. "Between me and him."

"Stand aside," Stank commanded his brother. The mule resisted. "I've come for the tournament. And those folks on the cart are here to perform for the Court. It's a play they've put together from the peas of their porridge."

"Ah, sir," said the captain with a wry grin. "the tournament has already begun. Well played this week. Today is the final day. Only the final four fighters remain. It is too late to enter the contest."

Even Winnie seemed to sigh at that revelation.

Stank grumbled at Rory. No doubt they'd taken too much time on the road, had too many disruptions. They'd missed their chance.

"Missed it?" Rory checked with the captain.

"The final four are set for this afternoon. A grand mêlée to seat the final foe who will stand as the new duke-apparent."

"Well, that's a bold thing!" Rory let fly a vile curse. "You've the best mêlée master right here. This is Stanley K. Baumann, warrior! Come all the way from Wichita. We've been delayed by all manner of skullduggery and mischief, had to fight our way up the Royal Road, attacked by Zarkers left and right, only for us to arrive on this, the final day? It's positively preposterous!"

"Easy, brother," said Stank.

He remembered his brother had the plan before the Royal Road and they learned there was to be a tournament in Louis. He thought back to their talk in the Ozark woods, what the plan was when Rory first revealed it. The tournament idea came later. If he had no need to fight in a mêlée then his visit would be mild. Except for a duel.

"Do you recall our talk? Before we found the Royal Road?" Stank prodded his brother.

Rory thought a moment. "Many things we talked on."

Stank looked down at the captain. "Tournament or not, we can enter the city, true?"

The captain stood defiant. "You have concerns within?"

"We wish to witness the final mêlée. See what they've got here. Partake of a fine dinner. We shall be what they call 'tourists': on a tour of a few interesting sites."

"Very well," said the captain, giving a curt nod. "Because of the tournament you may find the city lacking in accommodation. There are a few camp grounds which may have space for you to bed down. Fair luck to you."

"And to you," Rory responded with a snide tone.

They proceeded through the stone entryway into the walled city, found an equally crowded square full of merchants and shoppers to navigate their way through.

Stank was easy to see, riding tall on his warhorse. He attracted stares from people as they passed. If this warrior rode among them he must've been defeated in the early rounds of the tournament, he believed they must be thinking. He tried hard not to let them shame him. He wanted to announce that he was never a participant.

"I know the way," said Rory, pushing Fergie up aside Winnie.

"Then lead," Stank snapped.

Rory's mule plodded forward, jostling the crowd, getting a full stream of rebukes. But mules don't care. Winnie followed, while the cart got stopped by the curious, eager to have a poke inside to see what there might be worth stealing. Slapping back the sticky hands, Dandruff called frantically up to Stank and Rory. Mabel stood on the cart's bench waving her wooden sword, shouting at the people to stand back and let them go free.

"You've no concern with us," Mabel shouted, flexing her sword.

Stank wheeled Winnie around, urging the steed to push through the crowd. He kept a hand on the hilt of Longclaw, ready to draw the blade. Easy to swing a greatsword through a crowd, halve many shoulders and arms, a waist or two if need be, but this was a city, the capital city, and there must be laws pertaining to violence. He wasn't interested in being charged with mayhem.

"Stand back or risk injury," Stank shouted at the throng around the cart. Did they not recognize him as a warrior? Had no fear about them? Or too desperate for an actor's tidy trinkets to dare challenge a warrior-protector? "Stand aside or kiss the blade!"

Pushing through the crowd were three guards in red and black tunics set upon mounts. They waved their riding crops at the crowd.

"Stand down," one guard shouted to the crowd. "Move along."

Stank held fast, leaving Longclaw sheathed, as the three guards came to him and ordered the crowd to withdraw, stand back at least five paces from the cart. He relaxed, gave a nod to the guards.

"Glad you came," said Stank with a grin. "I'll not be set on such as this."

"You must have a warrior's commission," the guard spoke.

"Ay, it's in my bag, on that cart," Stank responded but blinked at his falsehood. Warriors could act as sheriffs in the outlands, yet he'd not been so honored.

"Be well, sir," the guard intoned, turning to go.

Once the cart was free, the group proceeded onward into the city, led with confidence by Rory.

"This way!"

The wide avenue remained filled with people pressing the street, coming and going every direction.

"Must be Sunday," said Stank, counting the days.

"It's always this way," Rory called back. "It's a prosperous city."

"I'll not be pressed upon by so much prosperity."

Rory halted ahead, and Stank drew rein, glanced behind him for the cart. He saw it, also stopped but not for Rory's decision. Ahead they'd come to a crossroad. His brother was determining the correct direction to go – like a fool on an errand, Stank mused.

The cart had stopped because it appeared Dandruff was engaged in talk with a man in a bright yellow costume with small bells sewn along the sleeves and leggings. The man pranced beside the cart like a fool. Mabel stood on the bench laughing.

"What's this?" Stank cursed.

He urged Winnie to turn and pushed back through the crowd to reach the cart. Another attempt at thievery!

"What's this?" Stank asked Dandruff, arriving beside the pony.

"Ah!" Dandruff exclaimed, finding the warrior towering over him as he sat on the cart's bench.

Mabel stood, waving to Stank like he was her wealthy uncle.

"This is my friend," the actor announced, gesturing at the clown-garbed fool. "Yes, a fool."

"Greetings winsome warrior!" cried the jester fellow, displaying an elaborate bow with flourishes, fluffy hat in hand, bells jingling. "It is a feast day, and all are welcome. Come be a fool with us."

"You know each other?" asked Stank, unimpressed.

"Oh my yes," Dandruff responded. "We go back to theater school. Ten years past. I became an actor and my friend, Jamal here, took another path and became a jester."

"There's more coin in jestering," said the jester.

"Jamal is the Royal jester," Dandruff announced.

"I can also perform clown acts," said the brownish man with the curly black hair, fluffed out full with the fetid breeze of the crowded street. "And plenty of magic tricks. Would you care to see a sample?"

"No need of it. I believe you," Stank responded.

"He can join our play," Mabel declared. "He can be the sergeant. The one that dies." She laughed and the jester feigned amusement.

Jamal the jester immediately played a dramatic death, grabbing at his chest and stumbling about.

"The sergeant who dies?" Stank pondered.

"That one's bound for the theater," said Jamal, smiling at Mabel.

"She's learning *The Way of the Son*," said Dandruff to his friend. "Isn't she the most adorable 'Isla' you ever saw?"

"Oh, yes. I can see her as Isla. Truly. Where did you find her?"

"We didn't find her. She found us. On the Royal Road."

Stank didn't want to stay for the talking but he hated to leave the cart while it remained surrounded by so many potential thieves.

"Come, let us keep moving," he told Dandruff. "My brother finds the way."

"Care to ride with us?" Dandruff asked his friend.

"That would be a great pleasure," Jamal the jester replied, and climbed aboard.

Stank gave an approving nod to Dandruff and turned Winnie to find Rory in the street ahead. He didn't see his brother among the throng. May have turned down a new street, Stank considered, and prompted Winnie ahead through the crowd, dividing people coming and going through the passageway with stone walls on either side. A perfect spot for an ambush.

They arrived at the crossroad, let the people pass.

Stank held court in the open space, turning his warhorse to each direction, a check for approaching attacks and looking for Rory. He saw no red-haired man nor any red mule. Nor vagabonds bearing knives coming at him through the crowd.

"Rory!" Stank cried out. People pressed against the walls cringed at his mighty bellow.

The cart and pony came up behind him.

"What's the trouble?" Dandruff stood up from the bench, pausing the persnickety pony.

"Lost my brother," Stank grumbled back. He drew out Longclaw, raised it in the air, ready to receive an attack. "Any of you see a red-haired man atop a red mule pass this way?"

People around him cowered, but one older man lifted his hand, pointing behind Stank.

"I saw such as what you say," said the man. He didn't stand any taller than those who cowered. "Went that way a moment past."

Stank waved the greatsword at the man, a salute, then whirled Winnie around with a snort. They pressed through the crowd, down the passage. He kept Longclaw ready, lain across Winnie's withers, eager for the fight. His sense was that he was being led into a trap. But on a Sunday? In the capital city?

"What manner of ambush is this before me?" he growled as he turned the corner and saw his brother standing stock still amidst a throng of citizens gathered in the small plaza before him. He slid his greatsword into its scabbard, took a deep breath as the creaky cart pulled up behind him.

"Ho! There he is," cried Dandruff.

Mabel stood and cheered like a proper theater-goer, and Jamal the jester jostled his sleeves to make the bells jingle.

"What's he doing?" Dandruff pondered.

Stank and his companions watched from the rear of the crowd as Rory, at the front, stood on the bottom step of a long stone staircase that curled up to a balcony two levels higher. There on the balcony sat a fair woman in a fine silvery garment, a feathered nest of fabric fashioned by five females. He stood frozen at the sight, didn't hear his brother calling to him.

When he did, he dared not look away but jerked his hand at his side to let Stank know not to bother him.

"What's your trouble?" he called to Rory. Even some in the crowd *shush*ed him, so he fell silent and gazed up to the balcony.

A woman, he mused. Then he understood what had so entranced his brother. She wasn't prettier than Mona, he decided, just dressed better. The younger women around her continued to play with her elaborate public gown, placing the proffered pieces into their proper positions as the winsome woman stood still with a plain expression upon her stone face. A living statue. A fleshy model for a clothier's display was all Stank thought of it.

He prodded his mount forward, splitting the crowd, gaining hate for disrupting their admiration of the woman on the balcony. As the only horse-borne figure in the plaza, he stood high among them. He had no intention beyond retrieving his brother, already dismounted from the red mule now nowhere to be seen – Ah! There, across the plaza! – Stank found himself the center of the crowd's attention.

The woman upon the balcony broke from her practiced pose, let the fullness of her face shift into an expression of surprise. Then she arose, leaving her many maids to falter. With the crowd murmuring, the woman stepped forward, put herself against the stone columns of the balcony railing, placed her bare hands upon the smooth stone as though giving a blessing to sinners from far and wide. Her gentle touch sent a rage of chatter through the crowd.

"Hail, warrior!" the woman called, then leaned against the stone in an unlady-like pose.

Stank didn't need to look around to see whom she might've been addressing. He knew he was the only warrior in that plaza, sitting tall upon his warhorse and bearing his greatsword.

So he acknowledged the woman with a salute of his sword.

It was the worst gesture he could've done.

"No, no, no, no," Rory cried out, seeing the woman's gaze set not on him but touching someone behind him, turning to find it was his brother mounted upon his warhorse, getting her attention instead of him.

16

SHE OF THE SCREW-EYE

A BALCONY OF POLISHED WHITE STONE set with the crowning glory that was Princess Majory: she of the raven hair, swept to the heavens like angel wings, bejeweled and bedecked with six silvery strands that rivaled her pale blue eyes when the sun shone a certain way; a regal nose as sharp as a scribe's quill; cheeks as curvaceous as a baby bottom; rosy mouth like crumpled roses, teeth within like thorns on its stems; her throat a molten river of fire pegged with pustules of redder scorn; and her body, at once a feminine delight, stood well-fed like a bovine ready for the slaughter, beefy arms and shoulders like the butt-ends of hogs; legs hidden by the long gown yet strong like the ramparts of a stone fortress with a watch tower full of dizzy guards fearing a fall; set upon feet as large as small boats, slipped into specially stitched slippers, the odd prime toe of each foot protruding askance betwixt the leather strands yet sturdy enough to bear her weight with an unsteady precision.

And her eyes, blue like a robin's egg dipped in acid, whiter than dog-piss snow, must become the observer's focal point: a distraction which one may wish to be distracted from: the bold left eye as keen and aware as any in the land, the right orb directed elsewhere as though a conjoined twin had left it out of spite: the screw-eye, the salacious public had deemed it, refusing to look upon it yet unable to look away. She of the glorious silver gowns and up-done hair, the gaggle of giggly girls tending to her every desire as she might roam, keeping Her Majory within their protective circle. As King Karl had decreed, deeming the dear damsel deficient in daily demeanor and, indeed, of defense.

And in a fine-toothed instant She of Castle Louis had found her own focal point: a rugged mountain of a man, at once handsome yet rough around more than his edges, wielding a greatsword in only a single hand's grasp, seated sturdily upon the muscular back of the mighty warhorse, posed like a stone statue, a war memorial, among the throng of her admirers.

Stank couldn't turn away, transfixed by the woman – a youngish woman. Despite flowery design, haughty accoutrements, and regal pose, she dared appear only at the edge of womanhood. A maid of maybe twenty was all Stank could accept. And yet she held a rare ambiance that landed about him like a sweet perfume, seeping into his thick skin, filling his senses, overwhelming him and leaving him vulnerable to attack.

"Look away," Rory demanded, giving Winnie a shove.

The jostling shook Stank from his gaze. "What?"

"Don't look at her! She's mine. Majory is my bride."

"Bride? Who said anything about a bride?" asked Stank.

"This whole journey is about her being my bride," Rory told him. "You must remove yourself from the square lest she invite you into her wily ways."

"What wily ways?"

"Her wily ways! She's got the eye—"

"What eye?" asked Mabel, picking her way through the crowd to Stank and Rory. People she pushed past gave her rude looks.

Dandruff and Jamal stayed on the cart at the rear of the crowd, against the city's stone walls. They waved when Stank looked back: all was good.

"It is said she has special sight with that eye." Rory tried to keep his voice down. "Can see the future. Can see into your heart – your soul. And tell you all."

"I've heard of that," said Stank, shaking his head.

"She looks like a queen," Mabel pronounced, gazing forward.

"She's only a princess," said Rory.

"Well, princess or not, she's not my type," said Stank, and Rory breathed a sigh at his brother's confession. "Eye or not. Mona is my destination."

"I'm glad to hear you say that, brother. Now look away."

Stank kept his focus forward as he spoke down to his brother set beside Winnie. The princess continued gazing upon him, so he dared not turn away.

"She's got the stink eye on me," Stank muttered to Rory while keeping his eyes forward. "I can't look away."

"You must, you must."

"Will it be an insult to her? Will I be charged with offense?"

"You must dismount," said Rory anxiously. "Just do it. That will break the spell."

Stank set his greatsword in his other hand and loosed his booted feet from the stirrups, slid off the saddle and stood beside Winnie, a moment to break the bond yet still be excused from any offense. You had to look at certain places when dismounting a horse, after all.

"Yes, yes," sang Rory. "That's it."

And yet Princess Majory continued to gaze upon Stank even as he righted himself and stood beside his horse among the crowd, like one of them but a head taller, shoulders broad enough to bear a pair of children, one upon each.

A pair of kinder? the thought screwed into his head.

Stank knew he had at least eleven children across the land, yet this thought was different. A new pair of offspring he seemed to feel were coming his way. He puzzled over it—

"Every morning," Rory was speaking to him, "she comes out on this balcony to take in the sun. People gather to see her. But she never speaks to them, dares not even acknowledge their adoration. Yet you've caught her eye, brother, made her speak, and now you must return the speech."

"What speech?" asked Stank, not looking over at his brother but keeping his eyes fixed on Her Majory. A spot of shadow betwixt her chesty mounds as she leaned forward against the stone rail held his gaze, had him in a trance.

"Address her. You must speak back to her." Rory insisted.

"I'll not be made to give speeches. That's an actor's arena."

"Not a speech," Rory said desperately. "Just greet her. Say a few words. It's protocol."

Then Dandruff was beside them, cutting through the crowd, his jester friend left to guard the cart.

"I can speak for you, sir," said Dandruff to Stank. "If you cannot find the words. It is a service I've provided many times to the shy. A fee is not needed in this case as you've protected me all this way."

"Speak then," Stank demanded.

Dandruff cleared his throat, standing as tall as he could beside Stank. He raised his hand so the princess could notice him.

"Most humble greetings, Your Majesty!" Dandruff called out, his hand raised to Stank's head. "We come today to gaze upon thy eye —err, uh, upon thy countenance, the glory that is your countenance, to praise your beauty—"

"You've done this before?" Stank muttered.

Dandruff proceeded: "Whatever words come to me, they fly away when I'm in your presence. A scatter-brain under your control! Yet I'll offer what I can summon to the cause. A wild cluster of words! Wrapped as a careful bouquet! Indeed, Your Majory—I mean, Your *Majesty*—we suffocate with words. Let us fling them your way, like the mighty dongs of silvery bell-sounds—"

"You're sure you've done this before?" Stank pressed, starting to feel amused. The spell had been broken.

"When we think of Your Majesty's great majesty, we tremble, and great bells shake and ring out your name. Princess Ma! Jo! Ry! Like so. A beautiful bell, a glorious ringing that stirs my heart. Yet even though we gaze upon thee, a fine painting doth hover upon each fine surface we see, the imprint of your graceful countenance everywhere displayed."

"Now he's done it," Stank grumbled, looking at Rory.

"Ah, yes! 'Tis the true love! We are filled with love. Fierce and jealous, and sad, yet never selfish. We would gladly lay down our own happiness for yours. And should we arrive in a far away place, that love shall extend back to you. If only we could hear a word as a fine echo of your soul, an utterance of mirth, a cry of revulsion, even a grunt of foul gas – all is always welcomed from Your Majesty. A small sign of your acceptance of us upon the earth, beneath the sky, ever-present in your heart and mind. Each mere glance from you makes us virtuous and brave in new and unknown ways."

Her Majesty's hand rose from its placement upon the stone and dared hover in the air, uncertain where to reach or where to rest. A hand possessed of fleshy fingers and callused palm from many hours with the crochet arts, not as a labor woman but as an artful aside.

"Do you feel our soul climbing up to you? Through dark of night and fleets of arrows? Ah, it is too sweet to speak! In moments when our hopes rose too high, I could never hope for so much hope! If my words give wing to soaring thoughts I flap them feverishly toward you, like...like an eagle looking for prey.... No, like a falcon slung to your bosom...or, yes, to alight upon your cuff, as befits a lady of the Court. For are we not drawn to such beauty? Could we not dare to approach? For thy glory is complete—"

"End this!" Rory snapped at Dandruff.

"He has a way with words," Stank muttered.

"Our respect and obedience is total, Your Majesty! And we pray we should never offend but offer a sample of our entertainment. The Lyle Danderoff Players are ever at your service."

"What's this?" Stank grunted, glaring at Dandruff.

At that instant, a sliver of silence cut the crowd, the placement of hands together, the creation of applause. Before everyone's eyes Her Majory stood straight on her own two legs, thick as tree trunks beneath her wide gown, and likewise put her hands together.

"You!" she called out, her good eye locked on Dandruff. "I shall see this play. Arrange it." She turned back to her maids, gave them instructions. A few of them hurried off to new tasks.

"What?" cried Rory. "First my brother, now this...this *actor*?"

Dandruff lifted Mabel up, held her before him. "This minor actor shall play the famous Isla, the magic child in *The Way of the Son*. For your amusement. For your entertainment."

"Arrange it. This evening shall do nicely," spoke Her Majesty. "I wish for that warrior to be on stage, too. Find a good role for him. And put him in garments less cumbersome to my view."

Rory was livid. "No, no, no!" He paced the room they put themselves in as tournament visitors began to depart the city. "This is not what I planned. Not close to it. We had everything planned." He glared at his brother. "You! Trying to steal her from me."

"I didn't steal her—"

"And you!" he accosted Dandruff. "Wiling her heart away from me with your...your *words*!"

Dandruff was consumed by applying cosmetics for the play and helping Mabel fix her hair for her role.

"I did my part," the actor responded without remorse.

"It was fine," said Stank. "Got me excused from her grasp."

Mabel pronounced a string of compliments about the princess.

Rory shook his head repeatedly. "No, no, no. This isn't the right way. We need to return to the plan. My plan!" He spun around as if slapped by a new idea. "We need to find the duke. You need to insult him, get him to challenge you. Then you fight. And win!"

"And what'll you do then?" asked Stank, showing a tortured grin. "You go up to her and suggest marriage? You weren't so bold today."

"It will be quite all right," said Rory. "Once you defeat the duke, she will see me and welcome me. I have no doubts."

"You may have no doubts but a blind man also sees no cracks in the street." Stank dared laugh at his brother, making him angrier. "The trip and the fall are his fate."

"My plan will succeed," said Rory, steaming. "There is no blind-man's crack."

But Stank could only laugh. He wasn't even considering how he appeared in his costume for the play.

"I do apologize if I've disrupted your plans," said Dandruff as he put away his cosmetics kit, smiling through his face paint. "Yet my act got us a performance. We are back. You'll see. Free tickets for both of you." The brothers glanced at the jester.

Jamal, sitting to the side, gave a dramatic wave. "I'll be playing the leader of the marauders, so I need no ticket."

"He's played the role before," said Dandruff. "A long time ago."

"One never forgets one's lines," Jamal recited.

"Maybe we'll find the duke there." Rory rubbed his chin.

"No, you don't," Dandruff barked. "No duel at my performance, please. This is our big chance. We can get a Royal commission if Her Majory likes the play."

"Her Majory?" Stank laughed.

"Yes, we call her that behind her front," said Jamal, chuckling.

"Her *Majesty* shall enjoy it," said Dandruff.

"If the duke appears," said Rory, scheme in his eyes, "we shall be civil throughout the night. Yet upon the final curtain close we shift to the insult. Make our way out, veer toward the duke, make a fair bump upon his person, get him to react." Rory glared at Stank. "You listening to me?"

"I hear you," said Stank, unconcerned. He adjusted his costume, finding it uncomfortable.

"As we exit, the perfect moment for an exchange." Rory checked with Stank. "Right? You accost the duke. He reacts. You speak an insult to him. He reacts. You speak another if you must, get him to react. Goad him. The crucial word is *goad*. But – and this is crucial – *he* must challenge *you*."

"No duke would challenge this big fellow," laughed Jamal. "Not me. I wouldn't go against this fit fellow, and I'm no duke."

"Sir Stanley is a big fellow," Mabel announced gaily.

"It's precisely because he is a duke that he must challenge him," said Rory. "Otherwise he loses his honor before his circle – in front of the whole Court, or whoever attends the play."

Stank stood tall in his ungainly costume, stretching his naked arms, flexing his muscles. His belly tight. Legs taut.

"This will do?" He swept the black cloak aside, allowing a view of the sparse garment: leather braces and a red loincloth, feet in his usual boots. "You're sure this is what the princess wants?"

Rory looked over his brother. "She said 'less cumbersome' – what I heard. It's less – but is it less cumbersome?"

"It has some cumber, that's certain," Stank grumbled. "I haven't been so naked in the public arena since...since that—"

"No need to speak of that poor incident," Rory cut in, saving his brother from talking about the 'battle of the three wives', as they'd decided to call it. "This will be on a stage before hundreds."

"He's not completely naked," cried Mabel, to correct them.

"You'll play the chief marauder," Dandruff spoke up. "No lines to speak. Just stand on stage and look mean. When Jamal calls to you, you flex your arm muscles as though you're intimidating the clan members. Make those muscles pop. The princess should be aghast – a thrill for her. Listen for the ladies in the audience to swoon. Then we exit."

"I think I can do that," said Stank. "And I carry Longclaw."

"Yes, carry that sword. It fits your costume," said Jamal. "Back then, of course, they used different weapons. They were called 'rifles' – shot out metal bits into the flesh. A very crude method of harm."

"Enough!" Rory waved everyone to stop talking. He turned to Stank who admired himself in the reflection on a silver serving tray Mabel held up.

"That journey up the Royal Road did me in," Stank grumbled. "I must've lost a fair amount of weight."

"Your muscles are fine," said Rory, on edge.

"I got my sister, LaTonya, to play Hannah," said Jamal, like he should make them aware. "She's played the role before."

Rory shut him up with a look.

"Now," he announced, "let's go over our insults."

"We did that already," said Stank, "all the way here to Louis."

"Let's review, shall we?" Rory was trying hard to stay calm.

Stank gave a hearty laugh. "Go on."

"Always use three words. It's two descriptions and a thing. Like this: 'Artless Beef-witted Barnacle'. You see the pattern?"

Mabel laughed at that, repeating the words in the best 'Stank' voice she could muster. The others laughed at her.

"Not for you, child," Rory cautioned. To Stank: "Another: 'You're nothing but a Cockered Clack-dish Clotpole'. Hear it? Three items. Now you say it."

"Are you sure that will sway his ire?" Stank said, grinning. "You said to talk about his mother."

"No, no, no. She's the duchess. Can't insult her. It's him we want to challenge you. No insults about his mother."

"I can't say 'Your mother is home port to many crews'?"

"No, no, brother. No insults to the mother. Think of *our* mother."

"Not 'Your mother has so much heft that whales shun her'?"

"What's a whale?" asked Mabel.

"A giant fish," said Dandruff. "Although I've not seen any except in a scroll or on a painting. But a fellow named Jonah rode in one sometime back, as I recall—"

"Rode in a whale?" Mabel shrieked in amazement.

"Your mother is so poxy that map-scribes mistake her for Ozark hills," Stank continued. "And they're aflame, at that."

"No, Stank! No mother insults," Rory raged.

Stank shook his head, turning from the polished tray.

"Then what's the worst bit to say to this duke?"

"He fancies himself a clever lad, so an insult directed to his head should land. Try this: 'Loggerheaded Leather-jerkin Lout' or...say: 'That loggerheaded leather-jerkin lout would forget his own name if it wasn't sewn into his clothes!' Like that. Now repeat after me."

"You're a loggerheaded leather-jerkin lout, sir!"

"No! Don't say 'sir'. Don't give him that rank."

Stank shook his head. "I should simply bump him. Make him to tumble. He will jump to his feet and show his rage, demand apology. And he shall not get it. Thus he'll be shamed before his company."

"Yes, yes, yes! That's it," cried Rory. "Then, after he rises, after he demands apology, then you give him the insult. You can say: 'You should be watchful, you spur-galled sheep-biting scut.' That should do it. Then he must challenge you."

"Do we fight upon that spot? Or we arrange another day?"

"If the crowd is thick, offer another day," said Rory, looking at Jamal the jester for a nod of approval; got it. "The dueling plaza is the usual place, is it not? If the crowd is loose, you may get a duel in that moment, there among the crowd. That is best, I think. Defeat him among his circle."

"Get it over with at once," said Stank, nodding.

"I don't like a duel in a crowd," Jamal spoke. "Too much chance of bystanders being run through."

"I've never run through any bystanders," said Stank.

"What are the rules these days?" Dandruff asked Jamal.

"Oh, dueling is allowed," Jamal replied, "but the dueling plaza is the preferred place. Two fighters will often draw a crowd around the plaza, watching from all three levels. If they know in advance, some sell tickets for a good spot. Others wager on the victor."

"I'll not be fighting for sport," Stank grumbled. "Not for another's coin. I fight for honor."

"The dueling plaza – as I suspected," said Rory. "Likely the duke will opt for a later duel. He'll say he'd rather not fight with friends gathered around to see his downfall. That's fine. Let him schedule it for later. Then he has time to flee the city, eh?"

"I've no quarrel with this duke," Stank said, standing half-naked before them in his sparse costume. "An easy blow and down he goes. Done. That's not a fair fight. Actually, it's stupid. Have you thought of that, brother?"

"I've thought of it all the journey here. And you agreed."

"It seemed a fair thing. And honorable. But to slay a man for no more than a posed offense seems not so honorable."

"It's fair if he challenges you. Then whatever happens, happens. And all who see it count it as fair."

"That could be." Stank gave his brother the stare. "Thus he must be removed so you may pursue the princess."

"That is the plan." Rory regarded his brother, who looked sullen. "Have no worries. You do a good thing for me. And much good shall come from a simple act. Being a duke myself, I will do great things across the land. Slay the duke, wed the princess."

"Slay the duke, wed the princess," Stank repeated thoughtfully, as though memorizing the instructions.

"Slay duke, wed princess," said Rory. "Got it?"

"Time is small," Dandruff announced.

"Yay!" cried Mabel, posing proudly in her costume and cosmetics.

"Let us be away to the theater plaza," said Jamal the jester.

17

LADY MAJORY'S GAMBIT

IN THE CENTER of the theater plaza sat the great chair, padded with grand cushions within its high stone arms, facing to the east so the setting sun might light the stage. That became the viewing seat for Her Majory, with her gangly gaggle of giggly girls seated around her tending to every want and need. Their entrance into the plaza a spectacle in itself, the audience stood in lines to form a human chute leading the princess to the great chair.

Those who wished to view the theatrics soon settled into one of many possible poses of legs and bottoms, the majority choosing the cross-legged repose defined by doctors as decidedly decent unless a maiden were aflowing. Older guests brought cushions upon which to seat their bottoms. Some had chairs without legs and could repose against the raised back for the duration of the theatrics.

Dandruff and Jamal took Mabel behind the purple curtain and prepared for the play, greeting fellow players. Stank followed them, feeling abused, keeping his cloak tight around his body.

Rory took his place to the side of the great chair, hoping he could observe the princess while she watched the play. He chose that side which her screw-eye would gaze upon while her true eye would look forward upon the stage. In that way, he hoped to have half of her divided attention.

A septet of musicians sounded the overture. After a few minutes of song, the great curtain parted. A speaker garbed in old-fashioned clothing of *jeans* and a plaid button-shirt with the sleeves rolled up came onto the platform. With a hand raised like bards do, he called to the crowd, announcing the play and giving its historic foundation. As he spoke about the play, he took on the ambiance of one of the characters.

Rory looked closer, saw it was Dandruff in that role, the hood he wore covering his long coiled locks. The actor struck a pose.

"I am Sandy, only son of Polly whose great horn commanded the heavens to open," the actor proclaimed. "In plague times were we – were all people – stricken, made to falter and fall, to our knees, then our chests to the ground as we spewed forth our essence. We held fast to our kin, at once pious yet always protective."

"Beware the sight is not of glory," spoke the woman coming on stage, nearly a twin of Jamal the jester, "nor of beauty. Yet we must endure! We must survive or else the world will die. Would you have a world without us? Let us grasp this island for dearest life."

Other actors joined them on stage, a ragged lot looking forlorn.

"We have the child," declared Dandruff as Sandy. "Our little lady is our hope. She is magic, an elven child. She will guide us."

"Miss Isla Augustine," spoke LaTonya as Hannah. "This magical babe we have birthed, born on this island in the month of August. She will meet the dawn and lead us on. A new hope!"

"Yes, my dear Hannah, wife of my bed, cousin in my head, we go together, you and I – we two, and baby makes three!"

A thunderous noise rose from behind the back curtain as Stank stomped up the wooden steps onto the stage, no longer wearing the cloak but standing nearly naked in calf-high boots, a red loincloth, and leather straps across his chest – much to Rory's amazement. He looked at Majory to catch her reaction: completely enamored by the stirring sight of this mighty warrior coming on display. He saw the princess raise her hands, clap them together repeatedly.

"Go then!" cried a new actor. Jamal played the Island Prince and swept his arm up to point off-stage. "We welcomed you to our island home. We protected you. Yet you dismiss us. You dismiss me! Much riches you could have if only you chose me instead of that simple lad. Let you both be away now, to the outerlands!"

Stank stepped over to the proud couple, took hold of Hannah's arm and escorted her off the stage with Sandy following, bearing a bundle that was meant to be the baby Isla.

"No," cried Majory from the great chair. "I want that one, the big fellow, to remain on the stage!"

Stank startled at the interruption, unsure what to do. Jamal, in character, went to him, brought him back to the center of the stage. He whispered something to Stank, made him blush. A blush to the delight of Her Majory, who clapped her hands loudly.

"Yes, there is his spot," she shouted to the stage. "Let that one be a mountain that moves not."

"And away they go," said Jamal, in character and inventing new lines, "away to the outerlands, there to face horrors untold, and seek a safe space for the years to come. While the Island Prince's guard remains. Barring them from ever returning."

Stank stood stock still in the center of the stage, a look of disdain about him. He remained unsure what to do, kept glancing at Jamal for guidance. When he gazed forward, he couldn't see the audience because of the lamps lighting the stage, but he heard the pompous princess cry out her instructions.

"Let this fine fellow," Jamal spoke, waving his arm at Stank, "be a reminder of the dangers our couple faces in the outerlands. Were he to step from this island sanctuary we would forget what threats a couple might encounter in the outerlands."

"Bravo!" the punctilious princess projected. Her girly gaggle gave weight to her response as they cheered along with her.

Rory noticed how Majory's screw-eye maintained an angled view of the world which included him. He focused on the odd-turned eye, his eyes fixed on it, hoping she might see him even as she gazed with her favored eye forward to the stage. Yet all her responses lay clearly upon the actions of the play, not to the side where he stood dutifully adoring her comely countenance.

Words came into Rory's head: "That Majory's got the screw eye, looks off to the side." He hated people talking that way about her. "If you're atop a woman like that, she could look to the side, flirt with another fellow there even as you make your joy with her."

There was a fight on the stage when he shook the memory out of his head and focused on the play.

A quartet of marauders attacked the couple. Sandy fought them as Hannah led Mabel as the child Isla past Stank's statuesque pose, on to the other end of the stage.

"Fight, Daddy!" cried 'Isla' from the side of the stage. Mabel was in rare form. "Fight them all! You are my hope and my salvation!"

"I shall fight for you, Isla," 'Sandy' called back. "I shall fight for all who would raise a family, cut into the soil, plant seeds and hope for tomorrow, for the sun to rise, for folks to come together, to heal the world and for us all to rise once more!"

Dandruff really put the feelings into his performance, Rory had to admit. Mabel was a natural actor, too. Jamal returned in a new costume as the marauders' leader. Stank remained as stiff as an oak tree. If only Stank could help, could intervene in the fighting.

Yet that is not the way the story goes, Rory knew. Sandy dies in a fight eventually and Hannah and daughter Isla are taken away to become slaves of the marauders. Later they manage to escape – but Sandy remains dead. In this fight, however, Sandy prevails, kills the marauders' leader as the others run away.

The amazed audience cheered as marauders stumbled stupidly through the curtain, out of sight.

Rory, caught up in the play, forgot to observe Majory. When he looked, the princess was transfixed. She seemed to be weeping. He liked seeing that. She was indeed a woman of strong feelings.

If only Majory knew that he, Rory, was a Baumann just like the people in the famous play. A direct line, his mother always told him: from the southeast coast to the ugly capital in the northeast, to the dusty town out west, and half-way back to this Missoura. Then the princess would sweep her arms around him, lead him into her heart-dungeon, locking him there forever.

Rory let out a great sigh, drawing looks from those around him. They watched the play; he watched Majory.

In a later scene, staged as one of Isla's prophetic visions of the future, Hannah has died. Mabel as Isla kneels on stage with flowers in her hands. She places the flowers upon her father's old grave, and beseeches him to look after her mother. She tells him how Hannah died: by hanging herself. It is a gruesome moment in the play and the actors pause to let the audience's weeping pass.

"Take out that scene," cried Majory to the stage.

Rory sniffled back tears, had to honk to clear his nose. Even that noise didn't catch the attention of Majory's screw-eye.

Many in the audience were crying – or cheering – or calling out from the depths of their bellies, as though the play was a true event and they couldn't help themselves but submit to their feelings.

Rory glanced around, saw how much the audience took to heart the pretending of Dandruff, Mabel, Jamal and his sister, and others on the stage. It truly was an art: to make people imagine with a few words and gestures. When he became a duke, thought Rory, he'd require a play each week. To go to such an event, be put in tension, then allow it to be released was medicinal, he decided. Better than a proper poultice.

After an hour of the performance, Sandy and Hannah reach the forest with daughter Isla and are welcomed by the survivor families already settled there. Several scenes later, Isla is being wedded to the son of one survivor family, and the musicians begin playing the song made famous by opera composer Maggie Baumann, Stank and Rory's distant ancestor. All those present on stage dance to the song and join in singing. Some of the audience sing along and the whole plaza turns into a great stage with three-hundred people singing!

Rory gazed about the packed plaza, amazed how the people could believe it was a magical thing. How could they be so dumb? To think what they saw was real? Their belief in reality must be suspended; they couldn't keep hold of it. Yet he had to smile, focusing on Stank posed on stage in leather straps and red loincloth, his magnificent figure everything a Royal lass could wish for. He felt pride in his brother: tough, strong, skilled in battle, yet willing to suffer such humiliation in that silly costume and posing for Her Majory just to help him win her heart!

Rory broke into song. He didn't know the words yet he invented what he could and in the crowded plaza no one knew otherwise. He followed the wedding scene as though he stood in that forest himself as the young couple spoke their words. Mabel looked so regal in her white gown and headdress, he had to admit. Tears came to his eyes. Someday the warrior girl would be wedded in true fashion, and he felt a pang of regret gurgle deep in his belly. As though she were his own true daughter. How the world turns! How life goes on! If only he could join in that vain rush to glory before he got too old to make a brood of kinder. He wished for nothing more than to sit and tell stories to many grandkinder.

A militia arrived to interrupt the wedding and the crowd erupted in jeers. Princess Majory stood and waved her arms frantically. She demanded the nasty militia depart and leave the lovers in peace.

"Ho!" Majory cried out from her great chair. "Leave them!"

Yet the play demanded the militia appear. Soldiers had to fight with Sandy. They had to assault Hannah. They had to knock Isla's betrothed into dream land and take her and her sisters away to lead lives of quiet desperation in the fine homes of northern families who couldn't bear children because of the plague, not to mention the bad medicine they'd received. It was scribed that way on history scrolls, everyone knew, the scrolls set within a library here and there across the land. And the original pages of the play were thankfully placed in safe storage somewhere, the musical transcription as well.

"Repeat the scene!" Majory demanded, shaking her hand at the stage. "Without those militia fellows coming by."

Dandruff, playing Sandy, startled. He stood unsure how to turn the scene over. Jamal, playing the militia captain, gave a glance at Dandruff for a clue. Mabel stood in her white dress, holding hands with the actor playing Little Joe.

Then Stank flexed his muscles, big arms moving into pose after pose, like his morning stretches, drawing *oo*s and *ah*s from ladies in the crowd. He broke from the character of militia soldier – a brown sash had been added to his costume – and stepped up to his captain. The warrior took hold of Jamal, lifted him up, and carried him off the stage to the cheers of the crowd. The other actors portraying militia had to follow them off the stage. The audience applauded.

Stank returned to the center of the stage after the militia had departed and resumed his defiant stance as lord-protector over the forest families.

And he spoke his only line: "I grow tired of this."

Dandruff, playing Sandy, breathed a great sigh, swept his hand over his brow, and invented new lines: "They are welcome to leave. Let us continue our nuptials."

"Thank you, Sir Stanley," Mabel spoke out, her line not in the play. She gave a bow of her head. Her play-husband, a boy named Neal, also bowed. "We go on," she spoke, half her true lines, half of her own invention: "The land is wide yet empty, and we shall need to make many children. I shall have this babe inside me come forth soon. Then I shall have more. By my dying day we shall have legion, and the world shall be saved."

The crowd cheered her speech, the noise almost keeping Rory from making out Mabel's words. The truth was Isla only had four children who lived, Rory recalled from his mother's tales.

The wedding scene in the forest was the final scene of the play – of the original opera, too. Musicians played the final song, building upon what the actors on stage, and the audience, had sung in the wedding scene. It had to be music composed for the opera, thought Rory, feeling proud of his ancestor. He liked the tune, tried to hum along. The music continued as the actors stood in a line across the stage to accept the audience's praise.

People rose, singing along and applauding, cheering for the good outcome the changes provided: a lovely wedding but without Sandy being killed or Hannah and other women and girls being led away. Yes, this actually was a better outcome than the original play – or, indeed, the history itself.

More satisfying, Rory agreed.

Princess Majory stood and her gaggle of giggly girls gladly reset her gargantuan gown, waiting for the crowd to fall silent. Once they noticed she had stood, the chatter ceased.

To the stage, she set her good eye.

"Come forward, playmaster," she commanded.

Dandruff gave a proud glance to Jamal, then stepped to the front of the stage. He gave a deep, humble bow, bending over double then upright again.

"Bravo!" cried Majory. "Well played! I like the ending better this way. This shall be the ending from this eve forward."

A smattering of applause from the audience.

"Now, tell me about that big fellow who had but the one line. He spoke truth. I decree he shall be in all plays henceforth. Now name him, playmaster."

Dandruff shrank away, giving a dip of his head, disappointed the princess had nothing to say about his performance. He waved Stank over, told him what to do.

"I am Sir Stanley of Wichita, warrior, Your Majesty," spoke the big man in the leather braces and red loincloth, chest layered in hot sweat and looking weary of an evening on stage.

"You appear as a warrior, a fighter for someone's hot bed, I dare say," spoke the princess. Her gaggle of girls giggled. Many knew she had a quick tongue and a rapacious wit about her and held nothing back when she opted to speak. "I applaud your performance. Best of the entire troupe, I say. How long you stood still! Truly amazing. A beacon of mighty masculine motive. Such a rigid pose! How stiff! I could not look away – dared not take my good eye off you. You are to be commended."

Stank understood the rules and bowed to her compliment.

The crowd cheered, clapped hands, and a few ladies dared voice their pleasure at his appearance with well-placed whistles.

A pair of castle guards in their red and white finery, who had stood at each end of the stage throughout the performance to hold back a frantic guest who might rush to the stage, now came to life. They swung their silver halberds in ritualistic fashion and stepped forward, up to the front of the crowd as though pushing them back. It was the signal for the audience to disperse for the evening.

"Now let us go into the night," Majory directed the crowd with a wave of her hands. "Merry eve, everyone! Joyous slumber to all! Try heartily to be a joy to someone tonight."

Wishing to be entertained further, the audience balked, instead chose to mill about, chattering about the play, the princess, and the warrior who stole the play although he had but one line to speak.

Rory watched carefully, a little on edge as the audience failed to exit. He would meet his friends after the guests left. Perhaps they'd go have a fine dinner under the stars. That was typical, Dandruff told him. A celebration of a fine performance. And that Jamal fellow, the funny one, with jokes as poor as his own. When he became a duke, he decided, he would keep the jester on to amuse him.

A messenger with a tall, feather-tufted hat cut roughly through the milling crowd, pushing his way to the great chair, holding up a note on paper for the princess. He called to her.

The people still assembled in the plaza suddenly quieted as the messenger's arrival made them curious. The gaggle of girls formed a fine phalanx for the messenger. The closest girl accepted the note, passed the paper up hand by hand through the other girls until it reached the meaty paw of Her Majory. Yet she missed the exchange and the note bounced off her thick palm, sailing downward to be snatched by the messenger before the note could touch the unroyal plaza surface. Again the note was passed up to the princess.

"What is the news, Madame?" asked the chief girl, cautiously.

Majory viewed the note: a simple paper folded over with a wax seal which had broken in its downward flutter and retrieval by the quick-handed messenger.

She rose, at first unsteady upon her marble-column legs, tangled within the silvery gown, and waved her hand bearing the note.

"To all!" she declared. "I have just received notice that upon this fine performance, a Royal Commission is granted to this troupe that calls itself the Lyle Danderoff Players! Congratulations! A grand eve! I look forward to every play you shall perform for us." She gave a pronounced wink to the crowd. "And be sure that manly man is in every play, mind you. That is what I shall require. Put him front and center."

The crowd of guests remaining voiced their pleasure at getting to experience the Royal decree. The note served as a delightful dessert to the evening.

"As decreed by our own delicious Duke Lindo," Majory continued – and Rory's head snapped around as if struck by a mace.

"Duke Lindo!" he snorted.

Rory dared glance about the crowd, looking for a frilly hat that might mark the dastardly duke. That one? No. Him? No. How about the one over there? No, a duke wouldn't be seated at the edge of the audience. Yet he hadn't been placed beside the princess, thankfully, so there was still hope for him.

Duke Lindo! Rory had to curse. Lindsay Doolittle of Kirkwood. The very name stood for Stank to grab. Stank could take him! That smallish Court-dainty man wouldn't have a chance. Yet where was that duke? The fellow must've seen the play, must be present.

He saw the princess rise, her gaggle of girls adjusting her gown with every step: down from the Great Chair, up the walkway formed by gracious guests, on to the corner of the theater plaza.

Rory stretched toward her, his feverish hand hoping to touch her gown if not her own handsome hand. She would remember him, he felt certain. They'd met eyes, after all. Once more their eyes meeting and the deal would be done. She would surely recognize him as that special one she saw before, the lingering gaze they had shared: the furtive feeling, a plan for more. His body sizzled in anticipation.

Then a quick club across his wrist from a guard striding between him and the princess.

"Back, scalawag," the guard chastised him.

Even in discomfort, Rory wouldn't be dissuaded.

"Your Majesty," he cried out, holding his wrist. "I—I adore you! We met before. We locked eyes. I've returned for you. I brought my brother – that man on the stage you so loved. We are Baumanns – like in the play. Please! Look my way, Majory!"

At that vain outburst, the princess motioned for her entourage to halt. The gaggle of girls encircled her as she turned toward the voice which accosted her. Never had Rory been so close to her. He could smell her perfume: a sickly sweet scent softening his soul.

"What is this rubbage you speak?" she erupted.

"Your Majesty," Rory stammered. "I meant no ill-will. Only—"

"Stand back," the guard demanded, giving him a shove.

"You believe we met on a previous day?" the princess spoke, not looking at him but keeping her face forward.

"Yes, Your Majesty. We met eyes. It's true. I felt it – felt you."

"How dare you suggest such things!" she snapped.

"I mean no vile suggestion, Your Majesty."

"Vile is as vile does – or speaks."

"I only wish to worship you—"

"A vain man seeks only his reflection in another," the princess quipped. Then, to her gaggle of girls: "Let us be away now."

"No – wait!" Rory cried out but the guard pushed him back.

He stumbled, then caught himself but hit the plaza anyway, got up clumsily as the princess and her entourage moved away.

"I only wish to talk – to converse with Your Majesty – about the things we must have in common ways – so we might grow closer – closer together...."

The Royal group proceeded out of the plaza, followed by the last of the audience, enjoying the company of the princess.

Finally Rory was left alone in the plaza, quite unsure what had happened. Perhaps he was mistaken. It was a while back, he knew, counting the weeks. Months. She should remember him. He held her gaze longer than what would've been polite. That meant something. Perhaps she had only acted the way she had tonight for the sake of the crowd. She couldn't let them see how she'd fallen for a crafty fighter from Kanza. She actually did remember him but couldn't let on in this public circumstance. He recognized that and grew strong again, confident. She couldn't let on about the duke and his affection for her either. A brilliant gambit!

Now he would have to find his brother. The next step awaited.

18

A Coarse Action

DUKE LINDO and his circle of sycophants and the hangers-on that licked the trailing hem of his cloak, burst into the backstage area as the troupe of actors gathered to congratulate each other for a perfect performance. Cheers, too, for earning a Royal commission on their first night – without needing application to the Academy of Arts.

"Well played," sang the duke, lightly clapping his hands. "I dare say: played as fine as I've ever witnessed. Her Majesty's outbursts not withstanding. You are to be commended. And rewarded with a Royal Commission. We of the Court are pleased."

Dandruff humbly bowed, surprised that the duke himself would bother to come backstage to greet them. Beside him, Jamal and his sister also bowed and arose with delighted smiles. As residents of Louis, they knew the duke, a constant patron of the Arts. Mabel, however, transfixed by the frilly frou-frou courtly countenance of the dazzling duke, stood stock still, gazing up at him as though he were a conquering hero freshly back from a fashion war.

"We, as well, are very pleased, sir," Dandruff spoke on behalf of the troupe. "We are delighted you take some of your precious time to come and join us in these small hours when you surely would prefer dancing the night away with your circle of friends."

"Thanks, Sir Duke," said Mabel, out of the ragged costume of her final scene and in the plain dress worn on the road with her wooden sword once more tucked in her belt.

The duke took notice, grinning, and crouched before her.

"And you, little one, are surely the best Isla I ever did see upon a stage. How you spoke so many lines, girl. It was truly amazing." He gazed up at Dandruff. "She is quite adorable. As fine a child as I've ever seen in this city, although I've never been one of those ruffians who look for children. Wherever did you find such a tiny talent?"

"We traveled here along the Royal Road," said Dandruff, rising and realizing he was taller than the duke. "Miss Mabel found us, I confess. She was a bold one, with sword skills unbecoming of a child. Yet she found favor in our troupe. She has quite a theatrical mind. A natural actor. Perfect for the role of Isla, the magical child."

"Then she was born to play the role," said the duke, standing up straight. He continued to gaze down upon the girl – until the duke's glamorously accoutered lady gave a pat to his arm and regained his attention. *Darling, I'm so bored, let's go*, she seemed to indicate with her fluttering eyes and taut lips. He'd gazed upon this handmaiden often enough to know her back and fore wards, it was clear to see if one were to observe their interacts, though they believed none could notice their playful posturing.

Jamal and LaTonya noticed yet hid their smirks, trying to back away from their greeting and tend to the packing of the play props with others of the company. They ushered Mabel away to help them but she continued to glance back at the duke, waving farewell.

In that instant, just as the duke took a turn to exit the back of the stage area for more fulfilling frivolity elsewhere, he took notice of a foreboding menace watching him.

Stank stood to the side, awaiting an excuse to leave the theater plaza, only to find the duke he sought bounding off the stage steps into this rear area. The moment his brother had foretold was thrust upon him at last.

Stank eyed the smaller man in his comfortable Court clothing: a girly get-up of garments designed for a pretty party or perhaps two, which he and his company seemed next to engage.

"And you," the duke spoke to Stank, halting his exit even as the lavish lady lingered on his left arm, "how delightful was your daring presence on stage, a central position. We cheer your strength, how you stood for the full two hours. Bold of you! Never a small smile nor frosty frown to wax or wane the moment of theatrics." He turned back to Dandruff. "And where did you find this mighty one?"

Dandruff blanched. "Ah! Our warrior. This is—"

"I go by Stank," growled the warrior, not moving a muscle much beyond his mouth. "You can call me Stanley K., if you must. That's Stanley K. Baumann to you and the lesser others." He took a pose as though presenting for conflict, Longclaw still in his grasp.

"Baumann, you say?" asked the duke bearing a suspicious glare.

"I said," Stank responded firmly.

"Baumann, is it?" In a flash he made the connection between the warrior's name and the play he'd just enjoyed.

"He is a warrior," Dandruff interjected, as if needing to explain; clearly Stank was no actor. "We met along the Royal Road, as well. He and his brother were on the way to Louis, so we joined them and gained protection. Many travelers joined. Mind you, sir, we travelers need protection along the way, for the way isn't now a safe passage. I might suggest—"

"I see you bear a mighty sword," said the duke to Stank, with a glowering glimmer of gaiety about him. "A fine prop for the play."

"It's no prop for a play," Stank growled, keeping his anger tight. "It's my greatsword. The mark of my rank. Warrior. To be true, I've notice of sheriff back in my home. Warrior-Sheriff, with the right to exact justice as I see fit."

"Well now, warrior, we do find that welcoming, indeed," said the duke, offering a theatrical shiver for the amusement of the others. "To have such a swordmaster in our presence. I welcome you to our fine city. You shall have whatever you desire for your service, both tonight and for the weeks past. We thank you for your service."

"It isn't service," Stank grunted, much to the duke's disdain, not showing him official deference. "I came on behalf of my brother, not a reason more. Others joined, as you heard. And this is what we've come to: a pretend-thing set on a made-up world of wood and cloth. The great amusement folks such as you seek – rather than facing the real world of blood and steel, of thievery and murder, of disease and death."

Stank continued setting complaints before the duke.

"What's he going on about?" asked the duke's lady.

"I think he must have a play within him, fighting to come out," the duke spoke to his lady.

"If you had any sense of the world," Stank continued in his low voice, "rather than the pillowy pleasures in a castled city such as this, then you would see with your own eyes the misery the fullness of folks endure each day."

"Ah, right you are, warrior," said the duke sheepishly. "I go out and see the world, as you say. Not much joy in places, it is true. Yet most, as I see, are gainfully grounded in good work for both the land and the Court. They are—"

"The Court!" sputtered Stank, amused – or feigning amusement.

"Have you a burr up your backside, warrior?" the duke asked in a sharper voice.

"Not a burr," said Stank, standing firm, "but a bellyful of bovine bunk." He swept his big arm around to indicate the entire theater, plaza included. "This pretend world and all within it who pretend to a pompous purpose are not worthy of welcome."

"What do you mean?" asked the duke, now curious and willing to debate. His lady tugged at his arm but he shook her hand off.

"I mean," Stank started, remembering what he was supposed to do: insult the duke, get the duke to challenge him to a duel, "that you show yourself to be a Puking, Plume-plucked Pustule! Nothing more. Yet you—"

The duke took offense – or appeared confused. "What say?"

Stank pressed ahead: "You Ruttish, Rump-fed Ratsbane!"

"I'm what?"

"You heard me: you and yours, the bane of this building, are less than Wayward, Weather-bitten Wagtails." Stank thought he had the words right, what Rory taught him. He launched further assault: "You're a Clouted, Clay-brained Clack-dish!" That should do it. Yet he wasn't getting the response he expected.

The duke seemed flabbergasted. "What are you saying? It makes no sense."

"It makes sense because it's true. All of it. If you are the duke, it is meant for you, you Impertinent, Ill-nurtured Inchworm."

"Impertinent?" the duke responded, finally showing ire. "I should think it were you who claimed impertinence. You understand I am a duke. I'm first-born and eldest of my House. You do not hold candles well-enough for me to see through the dark. The only work you have skills for is standing upon a stage like a prop tree. Only a fine oaken figure. Oh, the ladies among the throng will have their delight, 'tis true, yet for two hours you stood as a simple barbarian without a single gate to break open!"

That slapped Stank into the heat of the evening. The duke had a fair frazzle of insults himself, and ready to fling them forth.

"As a warrior-sheriff I can dispense justice to all ranks, in any county of the Americus," Stank spoke firmly. "It is decreed. You are no better than me. I shall arrest you. You sully the very name of a Pribbling, Pigeon-livered Popinjay."

"Is that so?" cried the duke, getting rattled. "I'll have you know that I claimed first-prize in both school letters and sporting ground ball games. I have doubts you can spell your own name." He seemed amused. "Stank. What kind of name is that? Are you quite certain you heard them clearly?"

"It's a good name. My mother gave it to me. Others turned it to what it is today: Stank. Stanley K. – Sir Stanley, if you please. I'm known both on battlefields and in tournament quarters. I've likely killed more than two-hundred foes, counting savages in the Ozark hills and Slammers in the field. Not to mention fiends far and wide bent on my purse. Not to mention daring-doers in tournaments such as ended here the previous eve. Yet I come not for the sport, nor for a play of preposterous pomp. I come—"

The duke held up his hand. "Not the 'play of preposterous pomp' as you suppose, but a play of precious perfection, as you must have noticed – if you gave notice at all from your stern stance mid-stage." The duke grew bolder, seeing the troupe pause their prop packing to appreciate the debate. "That was the best they could find for you to do tonight?"

"I joined as a personal request of Her Majesty, Princess Majory, you Nut-hooked, Nose-jeweled Ninnyhammer!"

"So be it then," the duke demanded, forming a fierce fighting fit.

"So be what, Onion-eyed, Over-grown Oaf?"

"Enough of these silly word games—"

"Not word games," said Stank. "I speak insults. Vile insults. You must take notice. I fling them at you, Duke Lindo, like a bucket of waste from a sickly old mule. I mean to insult you."

"You're a defiling lout, knowing nothing of protocol, of courtesy, of speaking to your betters!" The duke was enraged now, but Stank held back his grin.

"Such a Quailing, Quake-buttock Quaffer!"

Stank took a might step to the fore, letting his taut belly brush against the duke's soft mid-bilge, his satin cummerbund smudged by the moisture off Stank's bare belly – a hasty move that struck ripples through the duke's fine figure, causing him to make lost his balance and stumble a step or three to the back, catching his tilt at the last instant and righting himself proper.

The duke returned with an angry scowl. "How dare you touch my person!"

His lady swept further away as his company widened the circle about him, allowing for the next action to unfold in their midst.

"Should any person approach your person it should be a courtesy to you, I would imagine, for as dainty a dandy as you dare display. Who would wish a wanton wipe of your winsome waste-wag?" Stank wondered where the words had come from. Too much time with his brother! And that Dandruff. The words stuck in his head, refused to depart, could only be spoken out.

"You have gone far too far, warrior!" the duke raged. "Warrior-sheriff or not, you have no standing within these walls." He turned to his entourage, safely spaced from him. "Get the guards!"

Stank let go his long-awaited grin. "You need guards to protect you from a war of words?" It was working. He saw the duke melting.

"Not for a war of words," cried the duke, completely flustered.

Stank shifted his greatsword from one hand to the other like a delicate work of artifice, admiring the weapon, letting the lamp light glisten over the blade's surface.

"Ay, do you?"

"Do I what?" the duke demanded, striking akimbo.

"Do you feel lucky?"

"Lucky? How—"

"Ay, do you?"

"Luck is the least of my concerns," spoke the duke, touching his waistband, perhaps expecting a blade to be there but finding none.

"I've come this far," said Stank, balancing Longclaw in one hand with ease like it was Mabel's wooden sword, "to face a fair fight from a fool such as you, if you're bolder than a bin of bitter butter, you Zorful Zebraling Zombite!"

"Zorful Zebraling Zombite? What does that even mean?"

Stank smiled, realizing he might've gone too far. An insult not understood falls free and is not insulting.

"Daddy, Daddy," came a little voice. Then a small hand reached for Stank's mighty paw, the one free of Longclaw, and clasped it.

Mabel took Stank's hand, gazed up at him.

"What are you doing?" asked Stank, daring to take his eyes off the duke and look down.

"Daddy, I wish to go to our room at the inn and there sleep," said Mabel, once again acting. She gave an overwrought yawn.

"I'm not your daddy," said Stank rudely. He shook off her hand.

"You said you were," Mabel rejoined.

The duke dared a laugh. "A warrior with many kin flung far and wide, father to none, eh? There's the bastard for all to see!" He spun around to glance on his entourage, goading them to agree. "You see this one? Often a father."

"No," Stank grumbled. "It isn't supposed to be this way. I insult you. You take the offense. Then you challenge me. I accept. We duel. I win. Obviously. And my brother can make a wedding with Princess Majory. That's how it's supposed to be."

"Princess Majory?" The duke seemed surprised. "What's she got to do with this unpleasant uproar?"

"You, poor duke fellow, must be removed so my brother can wed the princess."

"Wed the princess? Majory? Who is this brother of yours?"

"Ay, he's smitten. They have plans, though I admit it does seem vague at best. And she, with the screw-eye, seems to favor him less after a period of posturing. She would seem to want myself in my brother's stead."

"It's a foul scheme," said the duke. "You are certain of it?"

"So I must remove you from any consideration by Majory," Stank continued.

"Consideration? I have no interest in Majory." The duke glanced around, feigning amusement. He decided in the moment to go ahead with his secret: "I am dissuaded from any alliance with her, truth be told, despite the fortune due upon aligning my House with the kin of King Karl. It would be purely an impure mergerance of unpleasant umbrage."

"You've no interest in Majory?" asked Stank, confused.

The duke reached for his lady companion, gave a sharp wave of his hand and she hesitantly joined his side. She kept her face turned apart lest she be swept by a bitter blade.

"You think I want a princess with the screw-eye? The tree trunk legs and that ham-hock face?" The duke smiled warmly at his lovely lady companion. "Her? When I have this one? This lady? Oh, no."

He gently foisted her forward, knocking off her finer façade for a ghast of worry.

"May I present the Lady Lily, my dear betrothed."

Stank stood stark still, still stuck on the strange strappings of a strict structure. His brother would have questions he must answer.

He smiled at the Lady Lily. She appeared too frail, too faint to endure a naughty night with a warrior.

"Ay, it's true?"

"I assure you, warrior, I have no designs upon Princess Majory. None at all. And I wish not to fight anyone for her hand in wedding. That would be foolish, for I have my lovely Lily. So be at peace. Tell your brother Majory is all his, if he truly wants her. I cannot fathom why he would, her being the sordid sort she is, all mealy and soft, with that eye of good fortune – ironic, indeed – yet instantly insipid and insightful."

"I see," Stank responded, thinking it through. Where was Rory? He had questions needing answers.

"Daddy, please don't fight," Mabel sang, affecting a weepy child.

Stank looked down at the girl. "I won't fight. Not with the truth turning out. It isn't the way."

The duke smiled. "Then we are agreed. I have no interest in Her Majory. Whoever your kin is, he is free to pursue her as he wishes. I will not object nor step in his way. He should court her *tout-suite*."

"I shall tell him of this arrangement." He looked the duke in the eye, grim-faced, then raised his big hand to the duke.

"Ah! The clasp. Country folk like to put hands together," mused the duke and extended his hand.

All gathered present were amazed how small the duke's hand fit inside Stank's mighty paw.

"There it is: an agreement," announced the duke. He took a long look at Stank as they withdrew hands. "Look! I've made agreement with a fellow nearly naked, appearing as a play's slave. What will King Karl think of such an amusing scene?"

"It's a costume," said Stank. "Her Majory requested it."

"She does have a lust for muscled ones. Someone strong enough to bear her form." He laughed and his entourage followed. "She will be inviting you to her chambers before the dawn arises."

"Not likely," said Stank. "I have a lady of my own, away at Fort Branson. Daughter of a doctor. I shall return to her upon concluding this majestic mistake."

The duke gave a nod. "Then a good journey to you, warrior!"

Yet as Stank turned to take his leave, the duke called him back.

"Unless you may wish to meet Majory. You could speak with her. Perhaps apologize, just to make the world a little less insane – the way she sees things."

He gave a laugh and Stank got the reference.

"I'll go for a bit," he agreed. "Let's sort out this mess."

"Then let us go, you and I, off to the party, and there we may die. Ah, 'tis a mere expression. Fear not, for I'm certain you will be quite amazed with how we amuse ourselves."

19

EVERYTHING'S EVENTIDE

"NO, NO, NO!" CRIED RORY as he gazed across the empty plaza, only a few torches lit behind the stage curtain. He could make out figures standing there, silhouettes moving over the cloth. On the unpeopled plaza, he could feel the slings and arrows of outrageous insult. Moreover, he could ascertain that no barb had landed. None had left wounds so dire that a fight must ensue.

He stuck his fists hard to his hips.

"How could he? My own brother!"

He waited a while, looking for the cart to be loaded and the poor pony to plod out of the plaza. Then he would address all of them, the whole bunch: his deceivers, his disruptors. How could his plan have gone so wrong?

"Ah hah!" shouted Rory when the cart appeared from behind the stage, Dandruff and Mabel seated on the bench, Jamal and LaTonya walking alongside. And where was Stank?

"And my brother?" Rory demanded.

"Gone the other way," said Dandruff with a yawn.

Rory started a list of complaints and none dared a counterword. Accusations of deceit, of the casual disdain for his dastardly plan, of deliberately defiling his destiny! The cart drivers insisted 'twas not. They had nothing to do with the cascade of events. Actions had their own movement, like dumb machines, and they hadn't even a widget betwixt them.

The players tried to repress lively guffaws, with Jamal insisting all was actually well. LaTonya praised Mabel for her performance to ignore the criticism of Stank's bold standard. It had ended fairly.

"I'm soooo tired," moaned Mabel. "Can't be two people for long."

"You can return to yourself now," said Dandruff.

"He is a mighty man," LaTonya confessed, warm glow about her cheeks. "Has he a woman to woo? Or is he a weary warrior in search of a happy home?"

"None of that!" Rory barked. "This is about me, mind you."

"We mind you, sir," said Dandruff, a smirk playing at the corner of his mouth.

"Sir Stanley goes to see Her Majory," Mabel announced.

"The duke gave invite," said Dandruff.

"Your brother seemed interested in the party," Jamal offered.

"Oh! Party!" cried LaTonya. "I've heard much about happenings at those private parleys. Pure decadence. Unrestrained acts—"

"Indeed!" cried Rory. "I saw how she lusted for him throughout the play. It couldn't be hidden. How she stopped the play in several instances, made him stand there for her to gawk at. Poor brother! I knew him well. What is he now? A plaything for a princess? A petty pet? Will I go home alone now?"

He hung his head, moped not for sport but in earnest.

"Don't cry, Sir Rory," Mabel insisted, fighting back a yawn. "The world does not end tonight, nor even at dawn."

"Ah, she cites lines from the play," Jamal acknowledged. "Clever girl. The final speech of Isla."

"Yes, she is truly the center of our play," said LaTonya.

"It isn't about the play," Rory growled.

"We're all weary this eve," said Dandruff.

The cart started rolling away. Rory strolled beside it, skipping to keep up as the theater siblings strode easily.

"It's about my brother," Rory continued, unable to calm himself. "He has destroyed me! Defeated my desperate plan. Why would he do such a thing?"

"He didn't defeat any plan," said Mabel, then broke for a yawn.

"He did as you asked him to do," Dandruff explained. "He spoke wonderful wild insults at the duke. Absolute offenses. And the duke returned them, as well. Yet the two of them discovered...."

The yawns had spread around the group.

"The girl is tired. Let us go to the inn and sleep," said Dandruff. "I saw it all. They fought with words. Fought with wit – only to see how they met no end, had no resolution and, truth revealed, the plot you had planned."

"Not a devious thing," Rory insisted, trying to keep up with the cart. "I inspected every angle, fixed every hole. It was perfect. It would work. The fault is in the execution."

"You only wanted to enjoy the princess," said Dandruff with his smirk finally disappearing. "So many others might."

"I did speak with her. She spoke back to me. She halted her exit to speak with me. I knew she had appearances to keep and had to maintain a certain sensation for her followers. I understood that."

"What did she say to you?" asked Jamal, amusement on his face, ever the jester even off stage. "Was it: 'Get away, foul fiend', hmm?"

"Nothing of the sort," said Rory. "She spoke respectful."

"Leave the sour man aside," LaTonya spoke up. "I shall wave at him to make him smile."

"He needs more than a wave," Jamal told her.

"Her Majory told me she remembered me from before," Rory said boldly. "We made a plan to meet later. And yet, what my brother did – what he failed to do – may threaten our betrothment."

"Betrothment?" Jamal laughed loudly.

"Let the man have his dreams," said LaTonya.

"Not mere dreams, friends – if I may yet call you such a vain word." Rory remained at full fury. "Now then: where's my brother? Where's he gone? Hiding from me? Can he not face me after what he's done?"

"He has been invited to the party," said Dandruff, repressing his own yawn on the bench. Mabel already leaned against him to sleep. "It is late, and for us who acted heartily, a party must wait another day. Yet I promise us a party before we part."

"Your brother goes to the party in the Court," said LaTonya.

"In the Court? Is such a place meant for a party?" Rory quizzed.

"It is a celebration," said LaTonya in a bright tone. "Our Mister

Danderoff has won a bold standard."

"Hail, Sir Danderoff, the Royal Lyle, King of the Stage!" Jamal cheered. LaTonya applauded and Mabel stirred.

"Now is not the time for a party!" Rory erupted.

"Be calm, sir," called LaTonya, motioning to Mabel on the cart. "The child sleeps. Let her slumber."

Rory realized not much could be accomplished by his ranting and railing over the ruin of a rough routine. So Stank had gone off to a party, what members of the Royal Court pronounced *par-tay*. So he had joined with them, his rivals. Such loyalty! Off to partake of a *partay*! Maybe he should kill the duke himself – as was meant to be. Then the way would be clear for him. Majory would understand, perhaps praise him for his verve. Yet he had no blade sufficient to the task. He couldn't lift Longclaw with both hands, much less wield the hefty weapon.

"Good evening to you, sir," Jamal called back as the cart rolled out of the plaza, leaving Rory to plop himself down on the stones to mourn his final fate.

The duke swept back his red satin cloak in deliberate imitation of Stank's big arm adjusting the black cloak about himself as if to free his mighty man-form for assorted activities. Actually Stank wished to let a breeze dry sweat from off his naked flesh, yet such motion provided a particularly daring display for the lust-eyed ladies of the Court, not to mention a portion of the pool of page boys, garbed in loincloths themselves.

"Come this way," called Duke Lindo. "The *partay* awaits."

Stank wasn't welcomed at parties in other towns, feared for his fine features as a warrior – "He might slay us!" – and his history in the bed trade – "He's a known breeder!" – yet he wished to set aright the stage, as Jamal and LaTonya had said as he departed.

"I only follow at your invitation," Stank said in a gravelly voice, "to explain to Her Majesty and apologize for my brother's rudeness. My wish is that she'll forgive him."

"Oh, I'm sure she has forgiveness in her heart," said Lindo with a vicious guffaw.

The two strolled through a different kind of crowd, all in gaiety-displaying sloth and mirth. Fashions of streamers and balloons, the cheers of delight and chuckles of vanity between calfskin gloves and lizard-skin collars. Many of the naked belly, others of the marked up chests, drawings upon flesh, the symbols of status. Silver rings hung from noses and ears and chins with care, in hopes that an adoring partner might gleam there. Dancing hand in hand, foot to foot, toes dipped in glee or in a fruity fountain, with a hip shake or rearward shimmy. A *twerk*, they called it. Like a fair steed, thought Stank in his first sight of the party players. He took note of them, their vain costumes, or lack there of. Ho! He fit among them, and many took him for a party prop.

A well-fed woman brushed up to him, offering a sequined glove.

"Sequined gloves are this season's fashion *faux pas*," said a girl in a twittery voice, eyes fluttering in a fittingly foul form. She had feathers about her, a comely cockatoo costume, yet she had the look of a full-grown person set in a small size.

"*Faux pas*?" pondered Stank, gazing down at her. "What's that?"

She smiled up. "Shall we depart for private embarrassment?"

"I've no need," said the warrior to the thimbly girl. He lifted his leather-clad fist off the hilt of his greatsword, resting in its scabbard there upon his mighty hip, ever-ready for action.

"You'll be known as a misanthrope if you shun the trends," cooed the girl. "They watch with care."

"I wear what works for me," he growled as polite as possible. As a guest, he must maintain decorum.

"Leave him be," snapped Lindo at the glittering girl, flicking her away with a swat of his cloth-gloved hand. He turned to Stank. "We must forgive the penny-pinchers. They try so hard to earn their coin. Yet I see that they gather a fair reward at the end of the night. If they do not annoy me so."

"They annoy me so," Stank offered.

"Be not annoyed, big fellow," said Lindo, "for all that's here is for your pleasure. Look about. Take what you want. Anything at all. It is time to *partay*."

Stank glanced about, saw what there was available to take: each party guest a unique fixture of movement or display – perhaps he also was meant for display: an oddity of amusement for party guests – and others fine examples of what a night in Louis could offer. He had no doubt his joys could be joined with a rude gift of flesh, should he desire such. He could make easy coin from ladies bent on a bed.

His gaze followed the duke's hand as he waved it toward the side of the room, to a range of tables overset with fabulous foods from far and wide. Many he'd never seen before, some he wouldn't dare take a sample. A few items he wasn't certain were a kind of food at all.

The duke swept his hand toward another station.

"And try our beverages," said Lindo, indicating the counterboard filled with bottles large and small.

Behind the counterboard stood a trio of young ladies in barely anything, cloth streamers at best, fixed from collar and waist, which fluttered free by breezes wafting from wagging tongues throughout the crowd. They served drinks poured from bottles or delivered from beneath the counterboard as magic tricks or slight-of-hand schemes that made Stank wary. What potent potions might those be? A guest beside him took a simple drink and sweetly swooned.

The counterboard girls giggled gaily, as they let their streamers flutter, let guests grab a bit of handful then drop a coin. A box sat on the counterboard with a sign stating *Thank You*. And as he watched a coin left the gloved hand of a guest, giving a thanks to the girls for a drink and a pinch, a wink and a kiss of the air.

Stank worried he had no pouch of coins on himself, still stuck in the stage costume of red loincloth and leather braces, plus the long cloak he kept alternatingly between a tight clasp around his body and swept free to give air to his slick skin.

"Go on, take a drink," Lindo offered. "No coin needed. You are a guest." Stank stared at the rows of bottles. "Or does a warrior fellow shun the brew? Try one. Perhaps a lager? An ale? We make them all in this city. Send them far and wide. What is your poison?"

"Poison?" Stank exclaimed, then quieted at the alarmed looks of those close to him.

"Well, I suppose you could claim the brews have a bit of poison in them," said Lindo, amusement on his cheery face. "All of those who indulge do fall weak and weary, sink to the surface. The ones who cannot endure a poison, eh? We tolerate them, for we are not unkind in Louis. We—"

"They drink poison?" Stank couldn't believe it. All he'd sampled was juice of the berry, one kind or another, for a celebration only. Many had fallen from that drink, he knew. Yet a warrior must be ever-ready to fight and dare not fall under the spell of brew or wine unless others stood guard.

"Oh, it's not truly poison. Don't be glum. Enjoy. Tonight's fun is for you to enjoy. Take what you will."

"I wish only to speak to Her Majory," said Stank gruffly.

"Her Majory?" Lindo laughed.

"Pardons, I meant Her Majesty."

"Of course you did. We all do. Yet the porky princess is one who also enjoys juvenile jocularity."

"Where is she? I do not spy her in this crowd."

"You cannot miss her, I'm afraid. She rules every party, yet few favor her. In such dismissal does she depart, generally well-before dawn. Off to her chambers to indulge in herself, the wiles a woman wants yet in its absence makes do with dallying digits. Her gaggle of girls report such."

"Ah, like long-serving soldiers take upon themselves at night."

"That, too. The truth of many nights."

"I care not what she does with herself," Stank grumbled. "I need to speak with her. It's not about her wiles."

"Oh, she will speak of many things," said Lindo, "and you best prepare to endure her topics. She favors not counterpoint."

"Will she speak with me?"

"I shall ask about her for you." The duke grabbed a serving lass, told her to pass a message through the crowd, hoping it would arrive at Her Majesty's ear. "Now we wait."

Stank frowned. "Should I do a thing?"

"Do as you like. However, should Her Majesty agree to meet you, you would be well-advised to refrain from the beverages. Keep your wits about you, warrior, for she has many wiles and weaker men fall prey to her plots."

"Plots? She has plots?" Stank thought of his brother, wondering what he must be thinking now. He would have figured by this hour that the scheme had failed. How would Rory react?

"Ah!" Lindo snapped. His face brightened seeing a familiar guest among the throng. "Damien!"

A middling man in strange garb cut through the guests to clasp hands with Lindo and slap backs. They grinned at each other like old friends.

"Sir Stanley," called Lindo, "this is Damien Harper. Or, like we here at Court call him: Damper. He's...well, a sort of traveler. Says he comes from a far distant place. We indulge his fantasy, purely for our amusement. He tells about his time and we laugh and laugh. It's great fun, isn't it?"

"I should hope so," said the man, dressed in a strange outfit not like other party guests. He turned to Stank at Lindo's urging.

"This is Sir Stanley," said Lindo. "A true warrior. Fought many battles, won many tournaments, here to woo the princess, I believe."

"Not so much as that," Stank grumbled, standing tall next to the new fellow.

"Pleased to meet you," said this Damper, gazing up at Stank.

Stank noticed a faint accent, sounding as though the man only learned their tongue after his school years. He remained suspicious. Yet the man's unusual garb of a blue work-cloth jacket, a red scarf fixed around his neck, and white shirt with buttons down the front left him looking oddly restrained among the variety of guests. Could fit right in at prayer stations in Wichita, thought Stank.

"Good to meet you," Stank thought to say, offering his huge paw for the man to clasp, his smaller hand finding a suitable position as Stank's fingers curled over it. A brief pause, then a release of hands – and Damper pretending his hand bore pain from the experience.

"What a fine fellow you've found," said Damper to Lindo.

"Yes, yes. He comes to us from...where is it, Springer's Field?"

"No, from Wichita – further west. A good ways west. At the edge of known civilization. Beyond there is the wilds of woe where none should go."

"The Wilds of Woe?" Damper gave Lindo a curious look. "I should write that story. It would sell bigly back home."

"You see, Stanley, his home...." Lindo gave a silly smirk. "This fellow's home, he claims, is this very spot upon which we stand but many years in the past. That is, *our* past. He claims to be a traveler from that distant time. He steps into a silvery machine and whisks away to our time here."

Stank stood stolid, pondering the pronouncement.

"It's all true," said Damper. "You've never heard of time travel?"

"Sure I have," Stank grumbled. "You go to sleep and you awaken in a new time."

Damper and Lindo chuckled together at Stank's joke.

"No, my large friend," said Lindo. "He means traveling from one year to another year, as simply as one gets on a coach and travels from Louis to...to Chicageaux, for example. A five-day journey. Yet for him in his machine, it is—"

"It is instantaneous. A mere blink of an eye." Damper grinned at Stank like he believed the warrior was impressed. "It's like stepping through a doorway into a new world."

"What is the use of it?" asked Stank, sternly.

"Well, uh...you can go to other times and see how life is there. And come home again. You can compare life in your own time with how people live in the time you visit."

"What is the point of comparing?" Stank pressed.

"A very good question," said Damper, and glanced at the duke.

"He means to say," said Lindo, "what can be made from that gain of knowledge? With the comparison between different times?"

"History," Damper responded. "The only way to make changes. A project to prevent future life from becoming that way. You see, I can report on how this life, what you have as the level of civilization in this time – What's the year now? Twenty-three-fifty-three? – how it has degraded to such a degree to what we see about us now."

The man dared grin as he happily surveyed the party.

"What's askew about our life?" Stank quizzed him.

"You don't see it? The decadence? Going back home, back to my own time, I can report this, all that I witness here. From my report, people can make changes so we don't fall to your level by this year."

Stank stared at the man, noting his beady eyes, his lively, raving countenance while speaking.

"I understand," he said gruffly. "You think us dull and foolish."

"Not like that," Lindo cut in.

"No, it's true," said Stank, remaining serious. "He finds us a poor administration as he compares here with his own time. He wishes to report how awful this time is so that his time won't fall to what we have today. Fall, he says. He thinks us poor and uncivilized."

"Ah!" cried the duke. "It's but a game. Pay no mind."

"It's a valuable effort, sir," said Damper. "We in my time simply don't wish to become what you are in your time. That's fair, isn't it?"

"It's a fair insult," said the duke, giving Stank a glance.

"Yet we are already here, in our time, doing what we do," Stank spoke louder. "You obviously failed. You've fallen. Look about you. You in your time couldn't overcome fate. Here is what was wrought, to your dismay. We here are doing what we do, so nothing you did mattered, didn't change one thing."

"Ho! The insults beckon," cried the duke, taking a step back as if a blade had been drawn.

"I—I'm not finished with my exploration yet. There is a lot more information to gather. I haven't reported anything yet. I have yet to return and deliver my report. Nothing's been done to change your time. Not yet."

"We are onboard with his curious claims," said Lindo, grinning like a sickly dog. "'Tis our amusement. He's been given free-rein to examine our city and read our old scrolls of knowledge. He can make of them what he will. See what the years have wrought. Report back as he will. We wish him well in his project. Soon we shan't see him."

"I will return to my time and make my report," said Damper in a decidedly dapper tone.

"And what is your time?" Stank demanded.

"I come from the year two-thousand," Damper replied smugly, as though it was a year filled with great events, a peak of civilization. "Returning there is a virtual celebration of advanced technology. We managed to survive the dreaded Y-2-K virus, then leaped ahead. My team created the device I use."

"It's kept secure in a room of the east tower," said Lindo. "Would you like to see it?"

Damper began chuckling. "Maybe he would like to return with me, back to my time. I can show him to everyone there—"

"I don't want to be a display thing," Stank growled.

"No, not at all. But we would like to study you anyway."

"I think you like studying yourself more," said Stank, glancing from Damper to Lindo and back. "What you do, even to travel from past to present, it's all a journey of your mind, not a real thing."

Duke Lindo tried to shush Stank, put his hand on the big man's shoulder to clue him to be quiet.

"We wish for a good report," said Lindo. "The King wants it."

"Isn't it true?" Stank glared at the time traveler. "Your travel is only in your head. Your report also in your head."

"No, it's true," Damper insisted. He looked to Lindo for help.

"He believes what he says," Lindo responded, "and I believe what he says. There's no harm done, either way. Let the man explore."

Stank wasn't swayed. "Better if he goes ahead and tells us what happens here next year. Crops coming in fine? Wars on the horizon? Or next week. How what's happened this evening changes anything for tomorrow. That's the only good use of your machine."

"He's quite right," said Damper, pursing his lips. "You see, what the device takes in terms of energy precludes so many random hops between close time points. Like one day to the next day. It's a waste of valuable energy. So we go the longer distance. And back again."

"Then I wish you well on your backtracking," said Stank, staying unimpressed. "I have important tasks to get on."

"Oh, yes," said the duke. "He wishes to meet *Her Majory*."

Damper appeared amused by the moniker. "We all wish to meet the princess. She has that odd eye. The all-seeing eye. Can see the future. Just as you said: tomorrow, the next day, whatever you need her to tell you."

"I'm not here for that purpose," said Stank.

"Well then, Damper," said the duke. He placed his hand upon his friend's back to guide him away. "Let us leave our fine friend here to a messenger. He has important business with our princess."

Duke Lindo led his time traveler friend away through the crowd as Stank gazed about the room, seeking a flag-waving messenger to approach him with news of his arrangement with Majory. If she accepted his address, he'd go and straighten out the whole mess his brother caused. Then they could turn homeward, a journey to Fort Branson and reunion with Mona.

A dutifully dainty woman in flowing flowers swept up to Stank, her perfumes clouding his judgment.

"Might you be a bedman? You appear as one," said the matron, older than Stank, She flicked her feathered wand at him. "I could have need of such as you tonight."

"I'm not that, ma'am," he responded, trying to be polite.

She continued to toy with him, running her wand down his bare chest. "Are you sure? I have many coins to offer."

"I have what I need," he replied, tone less polite.

A quartet of nearly naked nymphs pranced prettily through the crowd, singing a bawdy song, flailing fingers at the gracious guests, a performance of prodigious pomp that pushed many to applaud the bold offering. The gorgeous girls passed by Stank, smiling upon him. One sprite reached for him, wrapping her dainty hands around his muscled arm, cooing at him, drawing the attention of the others. His cloak fell open at his consternation, leaving the nymphs to admire his fine figure, to the chagrin of the matron, They enthusiastically invited him to their chambers.

"We solicit customers, sir," said the girl hanging on his arm.

Stank shook her hands off his arm, set his hand upon the hilt of Longclaw. "I've no coins for you!"

The glamorous girls showed shock, then swept themselves away and immediately engaged others.

"As I told you: all is for you. Take as you please," said the duke, returning to his side with Damper no longer in sight. "Many comely country girls come to Court in hopes of earning coin."

"I please not," said Stank.

Lindo laughed. "In true warrior fashion."

"I shall have food, as you offer," said Stank. "I've an empty belly after this length of pretending."

"Yes, indeed. What a performance! You were superb. You played it fine. Please: indulge. Eat as you wish."

Ignoring the compliments, Stank sidled up to the counterboard where all manner of foods had been set out for guests' consumption. He started pinching a piece of meat, slivers of a well-grilled cow. He took a hank of hog. Gathered strings of noodles, bits of beans, slices of tomato, squares of cheese, and the end of a loaf of brown bread. The girls behind the counterboard stood in amazement how much he put away. They offered him a plate, which he refused. They offered napkins, which he took at the end, wiping his mouth and then his hands. They showed him a large pie. He took the cut quarter in one hand, quaffed it down like a beverage.

"Ah! There you are," called Duke Lindo, returning to Stank, like the warrior represented an innocent isle in an ocean of biting beasts. "Her Majesty has agreed to see you. I'm surprised, yet not. This is a great honor, so pull on your best behavior."

"My behavior is my behavior," Stank replied, wiping his mouth of berry juice with the back of his hand.

"Yes, yes, certainly." Lindo looked over Stank. "Are you fit?"

"I ate food," he responded with a stern face.

"Yes, well, *Her Majory* has eaten food, as well. You're safe."

"I wish to explain my brother's rudeness. That is all. I have no designs on Her Majesty for myself. Then I'll go."

"Yes, I see that," said the duke. "Yet she may see you in quite a different way."

Stank glared at the duke. "Let us agree thus: there is no further quarrel between us."

"Bygones be bygones," said Duke Lindo. "In those insane insults we do not indulge. No harm is done. A playful jousting, a mere rude romance of wily words, what say you?"

"I say it's finished."

"Then off you go to see Her Majory. Best of luck!"

20

A FINE BEDDING

THE PRINCESS sat on her tuffet, surrounded by a gaggle of giggly girls, constantly arranging her gilded gown as she leaned this way and back, ever shifting her balance upon the furniture.

"Your Majesty," said Stank in a serious but polite voice. He knew what to do and lowered himself to a knee, bowed his head, then rose before her.

"Well done," said the princess, her rosy cheeks aglow. "Not many know the protocol. Not many *follow* the protocol. Pointless to have a protocol if none obey. True?"

"I say it's a fair thing." He stared at the princess, seeing her in such close angle for the first time. His brother must've been smitten or how else would he accept this large lady, so vividly vulgar in her ways. He couldn't keep from gazing at the screw-eye, looking off to the side, its white hemisphere towards him.

She noticed his expression: curiosity and frustration dueling for supremacy.

"You have a gaze not unlike most city ruffians," she said.

"Pardon me, Your Majesty," said Stank, forgetting the speech he had put together.

"I'm well aware and much acquainted with the look," she said, "a notable attribute of our Royal House, they say. People come from far and wide to catch a glimpse of this oddity. Like a fine jewel set in a museum display. I've become quite used to it and take no offense."

"Again, I beg your pardon," said Stank, trying not to look harder at the odd eye. His gaze focused on her forehead instead: the high block of flesh that rose from her eyebrow ridge.

"I shall tell you a secret," she spoke on. "If you must know, I can't actually see with the eye in question. Many rumors and cruel tales have risen concerning this feature. Yet the orb sees not."

"But my brother—" He stopped himself, anxious at breaking the protocol. The gaggle of girls gasped.

"Your brother?" She smiled, chubby cheeks jiggling. "I was told you had something to say about your brother."

"I mean only.... I came to apologize for my brother."

"Apologize? For your brother? For what offense?"

"He...he believes there is a connection between himself and Your Majesty. He has the idea that you two met eyes, and in that glance made a pact. I know it may sound something in jest, but—"

"Much that is ever said sounds in jest. Speak on."

"He believes, as I said, that he made an amorous connection with Your Majesty. In fact, he expects.... It's outlandish, I know. Yet he... he wishes.... He thinks because Your Majesty and he met eyes once before – must be nearly a year ago by now – he believes...."

"An admirer! I have many. Your brother saw me and fell into his britches, is that it? How sweet!"

"It's more than that, Your Majesty."

"What then? He wishes for a token of our esteem? A trinket from the Court to show his friends? We can offer that. I shall have a maid bring one."

"No, Your Majesty. I mean, thanks. Yet I think it's much worse. He has the idea.... He believes Your Majesty shall be happy to wed with him. He is quite serious about it. Yet I now know the truth. He was mistaken. It has been conjured entirely in his head. So I have come to offer apology for him, so Your Majesty will hold no ill-will against him – or me, or our family. That is all I wish."

"That's bold of you," said the princess. With a thought, she gazed at her gaggle of girls a moment before waving them away, sending the group twiddling out the doorway, giggles trailing. "Now, tell me: your true reason for wishing to see me?"

"As I have said." Stank stood still, unsure what the princess may be assuming. He remained in his sparse costume from the evening's play – and the duke's party. Not a courtly combination.

"I, too, have a belief. That a mighty fellow such as yourself might have no eyes for a figure in full such as myself. Although I do bring with me much that men crave. Did you know? Being my father's last daughter, I'm the only family member left to woo and wed, to bring a scoundrel into the family fold. So there are those who feign delight yet look askance when wooing me."

"I would not look askance, Your Majesty," said Stank.

"I do see that. You have honor. You look me straight into my eye. My good eye." She broke into a gay frolic. "I understand it now. Your brother, desperate man that he surely must be, saw my other eye and believed I gazed back at him."

Stank nodded. "That could be the thing."

"Well, sir, that is what gets men into a trouble. Your brother saw my odd eye and believed I could see him in return. Yet, truth to be told: the eye cannot see. Your brother looked at and thus became enamored by a dead thing." More laughter, letting her cheeks jiggle and her great belly shake. "What a joy! A foolish delight! To think the poor man locked eyes with my dead eye and believed we made a pact in that moment. My evening's entertainment is complete!"

"That's very gracious of you, Your Majesty."

"Yes! True! As we are alone now – although my girl gang awaits my cry should anything become untoward, summoning the guards – we can speak frankly."

Now Stank felt his nerves fire. "Frankly?"

"I saw you upon the stage, a mountain of a man, and I knew I chose the right play for this eve. Not that silly thing *The Waylayers Comportment* over in the west plaza. Not *A Fool's Errand* in the east court. Seen it. No, I chose rightly. Yes, a dramatic review of history turned to myth. And there you stood, so mighty, so rigid, so...perfect. Indeed, a perfect man. I'm embarrassed to say so, yet we are alone so I say so."

"My thanks, Your Majesty."

"I do not compliment to win your esteem. I share my thoughts at that event so you know how I felt. I truly wished you to come down off that stage and come to my seat. I wished for you to climb over me and sweep aside my gown and before everyone take me as you would your wedded bride. I'm talking hard and fast, a forceful thrusting, a steady beat into my feverish loins, all humping and pumping, and the nasty wetness of it our enragement as we come together as one wild beast, a single fleshy fury, one glorious union, noisy and sloppy, for all to see, for all to know I am yours and you are mine and we so engaged we care not for the opinions of the Court!"

She had to take a breath, fanning herself. Noises from an array of small cages to the side of the room arose. Stank noted the cages held small lizards in greenery, like pets. Green slithering things. A red one dashing up a branch within the cage. Another with purple collar flaring at him, hisses of challenge.

She let go a moan. "But it wasn't so. You didn't see me."

Stank snapped his attention back on the princess. "I—I couldn't see anything with the lanterns about the stage, Your Majesty."

"Oh, let's stop all the Your Majesty protocol. It's tiresome. Call me Majory. You will earn that right tonight if you proceed properly."

He gave tilt to his head. "What do I proceed?"

"Why, have you no head upon your shoulders? I invite you to join me in decidedly unroyal patronage. Word in the corridors has it you maintain a service for the barren among us. True?"

"Yes, it's true. *Was* true. Yet I'm now—"

"Then you know well what to do. You have skills." She regarded him, her good eye caressing his body from his bearded face down over hairy chest and forested groin, his legs down to his boots, and upward again. She drew in a long breath, eased out the wind with a lusty hiss. "It is a bonus to bear your scent from the stage, as well: a virile, manly musk that excites my loins."

"Your Majesty—"

"It's Majory, remember."

"Yes, Majory.... I should not be so available, as I've another I will return to."

"Oh, that makes no difference. Is she a princess? Will she make you a duke?"

"I do not actually want to be a duke. It's my brother who does. In fact, he has great plans for the kingdom. He will—"

"Is your brother like you? Big and tall? A warrior?"

Stank looked down, hiding a grin. "No, not like me. He's a fine fellow, I'll say, though shorter than me. He's a wiry, clever man. He can fight but he's no warrior like me. And he has red hair. But he loves you."

"Love is not the sole requirement," the princess proclaimed. "We have many accounts to settle. If bearing a son or daughter will join our ranks, we shall make it happen, no matter the persons involved would like it or not. The bedding must ensue. It is the Royal way."

Stank smiled to be polite. "You will get no royal union from me. I have no lands, no title other than warrior to offer."

"I crave no Royal union from you. Only the mad, wild bedding I deserve. Only that. If you wish more, then perhaps you should find another among the Court who will settle your affairs in the bed."

He shook his head slowly. "I mean to apologize for my brother, nothing more."

"There is more. You've come to the right room in the right hour, and what's more is you have all you could ever want now at my beck and call. Ask and you shall receive – once you've given me what my heart and loins desire."

Stank stood frozen, unable to think clearly. Everything had gone wrong. He was supposed to kill the duke, not join in friendship. He was to help his brother win the favor of the princess, not let himself be seduced by her. Perhaps it would be best if he simply withdrew. If he did, then they could join the road and soon be home, laughing about this sorry sojourn.

A sweet voice called to him: "Sir Stanley, would you bed me were I to ask nicely?"

The warm voice sounded like Mona's yet he knew it belonged to the princess. She of the double chins, the rosy cheeks, the fullness of figure, tree-trunk legs, chesty hillocks set on a wide berth, and the screw-eye gazing into the future—

"They say...." Stank looked straight at her. "It is rumor that your eye can see into the future. Is it true?"

That halted her seduction, made her sit back and scoff.

"That's what you wish to know most? I can do far more than see into the future. I wish to show you all I can do. I have talents that none may guess."

He tried to smile. "But can you see into the future?"

She glared at him. "Sometimes. Yes, once in a while. When I try to look with that misfortunate eye I can see things inside my head that are not present before my good eye. It's rather like seeing into a looking-glass but seeing a new world there instead of my reflection."

That impressed him. "And what have you seen?"

She thought a moment. "I see things of no interest to me. Like horses. Men on horses. Riding over a weary plain. Going to a high tower in the distance. A baby cries there. An army gathers around the tower, shouting for war. A man appears at the window high on the tower. He holds up a baby wrapped in his battle flag. He calls down that the baby will unite their two kingdoms."

Stank pressed: "And that will happen?"

Majory's cheeks brightened. "I only see them. I don't make them happen."

He took a step forward. "What kingdoms will unite?"

"How should I know? I am only a poor princess stuck at Court."

"How did the battle flag look?"

"It was black and orange. Had the face of a bear on it."

Stank repeated the description to himself. "Is it Chicageaux?"

"I have no idea."

Now Stank was interested. "What else have you seen?"

Majory shook her head sadly. "You don't want to know. Terrible things. They keep me awake in the night. Only a fine fury of lustful lunges gives me peace, lets me go into sleep. Yet a determined maid wielding a benevolent wand is not the satisfaction a princess craves. Will you, warrior, aid me thus?"

Stank grew concerned. "What terrible things?"

She shook her head, let out a breeze, giving up. "I sometimes see dark skies filled full from one horizon to the other cast with lizards. Flying lizards. They wing to the east as if on attack."

Amazed, Stank reached the foot of her great seat and sat himself there. "Tell me more."

Majory observed him a moment, gave a flip of her hand as final permission to sit with ease within her presence. "First, warrior, we must come to an understanding. How will you think of me after the bedding? Will I be merely a plaything of yours? Only a memory that makes you grin when you are with another? Will I be your mistress? A secret love? You wish to be a duke, so I shall make you a duke."

"It's my brother who wishes to be a duke, not me."

Majory grinned. "Then I shall make your brother a duke. After you give me what I want. You don't want to be rude, do you? I am a princess, the last of my father's daughters. I'm the final chance for suitors far and wide. Yet I welcome only you into my love chamber." Her hand swept over the great seat, inviting him.

"I am a guest in your castle, true," Stank spoke slowly, choosing his words carefully. "Thus I do not wish to be rude. I'm a warrior, so rudeness comes easy to me. Yet I know the rules of the Court for the most part. As your guest, I won't be rude to you."

A melodious laughter burst from her. "There are different kinds of rudeness. Some better than others."

"Which kind would you have me employ?"

"A rudeness where we both hide beneath the covering of a grand bed, trying to make the other one fall into a spell."

"A spell? What kind would that be?"

He remembered the displays along a table against the wall, saw movement within the cages. His eyes followed her hand gesture.

"These have a spell about them. What do you think of them?"

He studied the cages a moment, saw the small beasts attentive to her voice. The purple collared lizard watched him as though it hoped for a bite. The green ones paused to listen to their mistress speak, the greenery around them quivering in anticipation. A red one appeared between leaves, its yellow eyes mocking him.

"You have lizards in your chamber." He felt like laughing, held it back. "Unusual in a Royal Court. I didn't know they were suitable as pets. It could be the cause of your dreams."

"Not in my dreams. That was what I saw with my odd eye." She smiled at him. "Anything – any *person*, as well – may be a pet. An old magician comes daily to tend to the creatures. I think they will grow larger. How large, I cannot know. The old magician feeds them special potions."

"You raise lizards...." Stank contemplated.

"Doesn't everyone?" She chuckled at her joke. "So then, we shall try the test of tribulation. Satisfy me and your brother shall become a duke. No need for him to wed me. Oh, there's a protocol, you must understand, yet it amounts to little. On a document we shall be wed, yet no further. A frivolous failure I want not. For such a fair play, I shall welcome you into my bed for my weekly wellness whims. Come as I call and your brother shall be a duke. He may go about spouting his duke-ish deliriums as he deems desirable. That should annoy my father to no end." She laughed, then smiled lustfully at Stank. "Do you agree?"

Rory's face was as red as his shock of hair when Stank returned to the inn still wearing the absurd costume from the play.

"Where have you been? I was told you went to a party? With the duke! Is it truth?"

Stank halted in the street, confronted by his brother's fire.

"All I have done has been to better you, brother."

"What's this *all I've done*?" Rory burned with anger. "What did you do? Make friends with Duke Lindo? He beguiled you with his intense insults. Was that it? Got you tracked aside into some sort of swaggering swoon. Got you liquored up then dressed down. Found you a comely companion for the eve. And look at you: still in that silly costume in broad-daylight!"

"All comes to an end," said Stank as calmly as he could, "once an error is smoothed. I spoke for you. Thus it is settled now."

"What's settled?" Rory breathed hard, ready to roar again.

Stank had to take a breath. "This whole adventure."

"What adventure? My scheme to wed the princess?"

"Ay, that one."

"What did you do?" Rory demanded.

"I settled it. Everything. Done. Now we can turn homeward."

"What?" Rory exploded. "We?"

Stank took his brother by the arm and pulled him into the inn so the passers-by wouldn't be entertained. In the front room they went on with unwelcomed words.

"Listen to reasons," said Stank, holding his brother by the arms.

"What reasons are there in all of this? My plan is ruined."

"No, it's not."

"Not?" He dropped his anger. "How so then?"

"You've a calling on the morrow, upon the thirteenth hour," said Stank, a wry grin breaking. "You must go. And dress your best."

"A calling...? Dress my best...? What does this mean?"

"It means you go to the Court at that hour. Perhaps buy a new outfit, something regal. You go and you will be happy. As happy as you're ever likely to be since we met back in the woods when you was strung up by the savages. Then you'll thank me. Then I'll be returning to Fort Branson and to Mona."

Rory shook his head. "You've a new plan, don't you? Leaving me here. Done with me."

"Isn't that what you want? A life in Louis?"

Rory seemed confused. "Yes – if my plan is complete. Then I will stay in Louis. I will be a duke, in that case. I presume with lands. So how will I be a duke now? With no plan?"

"Go to the Court on the morrow upon the thirteenth hour," said Stank. Holding a faint smile, he let go of his brother's arms. The confusion had weakened his brother.

"Very well," said Rory. "I shall go to the Court. I'll go and see of what amazing amusements you've arranged. What foolishness!"

"'Tis not foolishness. 'Tis hard-won victory. I fought for you."

"You fought for me?"

"Ay, for you. Did my part. More than called upon, I'll say."

"Called upon? What is that?"

"You had your plan, true? I tried my best to follow it."

Rory fumed. "And did you succeed? I think not."

"Succeed, in a manner of speaking. What was the goal?"

"To wed the princess and become a duke."

"So you say, brother. Yet, which would be your prime result?"

"Prime result? What mean you in that?"

"To wed the princess, or to become a duke?"

"Ay, it's both, brother." Rory clasped his hands. "They go hand in hand, like a bride and a groom go together."

"Then you must have both?"

"Ay, both."

Stank's look sharpened. "If only one may be earned, which would you have?"

Rory had to think a moment. "I never have thought to gain only the one without the other. You make me a jest?"

"Not a jest," said Stank, glaring at him. "Not a game, neither. I did what I had to do to bring you what you asked for."

"What I asked for?"

"Ay, what you asked for."

Rory glared at him. "What did I ask for?"

"You know what you asked for."

"What was what I asked for?"

"You know you asked for what you asked for."

"Ay, but what was it that I asked for?"

"You asked for me to confront the duke, that Lindo fellow."

"Ay, that one. I asked for him?"

"You asked me to remove him. That's what you asked for."

"That's what I asked for?" Rory threw up his hands. "That duke you were supposed to offend and get him to challenge you to a duel, then defeat him?"

"That's what you asked for, and it's what I attempted."

"What I asked for didn't get answered then. The duke lives."

"Didn't seem to need him defeated, no matter you asked for it."

"Not defeated? Who are you to make a judgment like that?"

"You asked me to defeat him, yet I saw no need of it."

"I asked you to do it, brother. And you failed."

"I failed not. I attempted not. There was no need of it."

"Yet I asked you to defeat the duke."

"Ay, you asked for it. Yet I found no fair reason for it. I gave him insult after insult and he fairly fought back, words upon words."

"As I asked for!"

"Yet in the word-duel, truth sprang forth."

"I asked for no truth to spring forth. What is this jest?"

"What you asked for was for me to remove the duke from this game you've devised."

"Ay, it's what I asked for."

"Yet the duke need not be removed. He was not in your way. He professed no interest in the princess. The way was clear for you."

"That's not what I asked for!"

"Ay, perhaps not. Yet what is better than finding a way forward which removes not a living being?"

"Again, that isn't what I asked for. I never asked you to choose to let the duke live or not."

"You asked me to remove him. I found no need to remove him. It may not be what you asked for, but it seemed a far fairer finish than what you asked me to do."

"Then it's done? What I asked for?"

"If what you asked for was to see the duke removed from your path to the princess, then yes: what you asked for was done."

Rory stopped, took a breath, let it out slowly. "Ay, brother."

Stank laid a paw on his brother's shoulder. "Now you only need go to the Court upon the thirteenth hour on the morrow to receive your official scroll of rank. Then you will be a duke."

Rory's eyes narrowed. "Me? Be a duke? Just like that? With a damn scroll? Like that?"

"Isn't that what you asked for? To become a duke yourself?"

"Ay, yet it's not all. There is Majory – my majestic Majory!"

Stank shook his head. "And what did you ask for?"

"I asked you to remove the duke so my path to her was clear."

"So I made the path clear—"

"Did you? I feel it not. Why, Dandruff and those others saw it all and reported to me. You went to a party with the duke. What major mischief made you make my day?"

Stank dropped his hand from Rory's shoulder. "I did what you asked for: I fought the duke with words. That was what you asked. Beyond that, I can think for myself, see with my own eyes."

"And what did you see with your own two eyes, brother?"

"I saw the truth of everything."

"That wasn't what I asked for."

"Ay, perhaps not. Yet it stands up to be seen. You have to see it, have to give your eyes over to it, for it shines so brightly."

Rory scoffed. "Not what I asked for."

"What you asked for was me to fight the duke. Elsewhere in your plan you could manage on your own. I followed your plan up to that point and saw beyond your plan that I need not go further."

"That's fair. I think. You acted on your own motive, eh?"

Stank glared at his stubborn brother. "I did what I had to do. In the end you will be a duke, just as what you asked for. Now go to the damn Court and get your damn scroll. Be fine about it. Follow the protocol. Nod and bow. Say good words. And do not grow any anger from this. It was not an easy task to perform."

Roy started to smile, then lost it. "What task to perform?"

"It's what you asked for."

"Again! What did you do?"

"I did what the princess bid me to do. To win you a dukedom or whatever it may be called. Your dukeness."

"The princess?" Rory reddened, his head again catching fire. "Bid you? What's this?"

"Ay, she bid me do a thing for her. And to promise more. For you, brother. I agreed for you. To make you happy. So you will be a duke. And you will be happy."

"No, no, no, no," cried Rory. "I want to be wed with my Majory."

"That was only to become a duke, was it not?"

"That was not what I asked for."

"Here we go around once more." Stank grunted. "What you asked for was me removing the duke so you can wed the princess. Yet the duke has no interest in the princess, so there was no need to remove him. Turned out to be a fine fellow, odd at times, fruity like those others preying upon party-goers, yet in the end a decent duke."

Rory shook his head, disdainfully. "You let him live. That will be upon you."

"No duke in your path, so I proceeded to the princess, promising her what she desired. And more to come, as unpleasant as it may be.

It is what I do for you, brother. You shall be a duke for it."

"What I asked for, *brother*, was for me to wed my Majory, which would be association to confer upon me a dukedom."

Stank grinned. "Done and done."

"Done and done what and what?"

"You will be a duke."

"And...?"

"And you will wed the princess."

Rory fell back, delight bursting upon his face. "Truth?"

"Ay, truth." Stank froze, then unfroze when words came to him. "As long as you follow two protocols."

"She does like her protocols," Rory mused. "I'll be glad of her and her protocols. What says she?"

Stank took a breath. "You ask for so much, brother, it's hard to deliver all things."

Rory remained excited. "Then deliver what you can."

"I did."

"Her Majory shall wed with you, yet you shall live apart and be as strangers except for a few official duties throughout the official year. 'Go do his own activities' was how she put it."

"Go do my own activities?" Rory turned sullen. "That's not what I asked for, brother."

"You shall wed with the princess. She agreed."

"She agreed? Such ample words you must've employed. How did you speak them?"

"Not words. Ay, not much so. More *her* words. She saying what she wanted. What *she* asked for. A short list of demands."

Rory refused to believe. "What did she ask for?"

"It's not so much what she asked for, it's what she asked for that met up alongside what you asked for."

"You riddle with me, brother. What did she ask for?"

Stank looked away. "She asked for me."

"You?" Then all the words hit Rory like a burst sack of manure. "She wanted you. *You?* Ay, I see it now. Everything I've worked for, all I've done this past year to make this moment appear, all *what I asked for....* It's now ruined by your lust! Ay, I should've known you could never do what I asked for. I should've known."

Stank met Rory's angry eyes. "I didn't want to. You know I love Mona the physician. I'm for her. Yet I had to—"

"Ay, you had to make coin in Rolla. That was no black mark on your plans with the doctor. It was a must."

Stank nodded. "Same for here in Louis."

Rory stood back and glared at his brother. "What did you do?"

"What I had to do. When a princess demands it, you do it. All the more so to give your brother what he asked for. I weighed the costs with the rewards, found I could effectively force myself to fulfill my brother's worldly wishes."

"I didn't ask for you to do *that*."

"She demanded it."

"Demanded how? Like you winked on her and she fell fast apart? Or she stood bold before you, guards ready to skewer you should you refuse?"

"Somewhere in the between. She made an offer. No other offer. I considered you, brother, and chose wisely."

"That's wisely? I wed Majory and I'm a duke, yet we live apart and we have no bed together? That's what's wise?"

"It seemed the best, or the only, choice among what she offered. I knew it would be a harsh sentence for me, given her attributes, yet I've made maternity with a few worse than her."

Rory shook in rage. "Worse off? She's beautiful!"

"Ay, if you believe so, there is a dukedom I offer to you."

"Ay, the dukedom...."

"Be of good cheer, brother. She may grow fond of you. She may welcome you into her bed in time's passage. If you play nicely with your words, keep clean, and play gentle with her pets. Praising her lizards can elevate you in her good eye."

Rory was struck dumb. "What lizards do you speak of?"

"Oh – and another thing: that screw-eye of hers. She can't see a thing through it, actually. She's blind in that eye. So when you had locked your eyes with her, she never saw you – couldn't see you."

21

A Woefully Winsome Wedding

DRESSED IN A FINE NEW COSTUME of cream and crimson, Rory proceeded up the grand staircase of white stone to the great doors of the Royal Court, muttering over and over "This isn't what I asked for," shaking his head repeatedly.

At the top a line of impressively uniformed guards awaited him in their cardinal red. So, too, stood his fast friends: an actor with a Royal commission and his own company. Lyle Danderoff posed in a fine cloth suit straight off the clothier's rack, of black and white with cardinal red neck scarf. And Mabel Maddox, warrior-girl, in her fine red jerkin. Jamal, jester of the Court, dressed in his yellow costume with bells jingling, beside his sister, LaTonya, dressed in a lavish burnish gown with golden wings and orange trappings, her huge hat also displaying feathered wings that tripled the size of her head – plus other members of the troupe in costume as if they might prance on stage at any moment. And tallest of all, his brother, Stank – Sir Stanley, for whom all things were possible.

Rory smiled proudly if not with a shade of sheepishness. Nothing he'd done had brought this day into being. Only Lord Fritz smiling down upon him, bringing the sun out and bestowing upon this red-haired lad, half of his wishes coming to truth. "This lad has suffered enough in his poor life; we shall make his life easy from this day on," Lord Fritz would say. It was what all the others had done that made it happen. He felt foolish – like he had to go ahead and play it out. Then he'd go about his activities like the plain ruffian he was.

"All hail!" a crier in red cried out, producing a scroll, unscrolling it before the crowd in dramatic fashion.

Rory stood at the proper position upon the upper plaza, having mounted the grand stone staircase, where everyone below could see him. He held his breath – had a weird sense of something bad about to happen, like a team of swordsmen rushing him, cutting him into pieces for the Court dogs' dinner. Or, worse, the crier announcing it all was a joke proffered upon him and the throng of citizens below would laugh at him. *What a great play!* they'd cheer. This outsider rube gets his comeuppance!

Four trumpeters stepped upon the plaza and blew notes through the long brass tubing, making a song in Court style resound over the stone of the stairs and the plaza filled with curious citizens. *What's the event today?* they surely wondered. How amusing these folks up there standing so solemn, like Lord Fritz would come down to greet the assembled, kisses all around, and a welter of wisdom bestowed like a newborn babe in gift-wrapping. Like that! Rory had to grin.

More notes from the trumpeters and all eyes swept to the side of the upper plaza as a regal entourage arrived, a gaggle of giggly girls encircling the mistress of the moment, the largely lavish lady known as Her Majesty Majory of Louis, youngest daughter of King Karl. A wave of cheering filled the plaza. The lady raised her thick hand, flicking her fingers at the crowd, as she strode across to her central position, barely a hand's width apart from this country rube. Rory dared not glance to her, keeping his fair face to the crowd, following the damn protocol.

"You must be Aurora," a womanly voice spoke, soft in noise yet firm in demeanor. "Your brother said you had red hair."

Rory resisted, then fell short. He turned to the lady posed beside him and in that instant beheld the magnificence that was Majory.

"Yes, Your Majesty, I am he – *er*, him." His breath failed to send his words far. "The one who worships you."

"Ah...." She gave him a quick look, her chins nodding for her. "As your brother told me. Exactly such."

"I pray he spoke truth," Rory replied, keeping his fake face to the excited crowd.

"He did," responded Her Majory.

The crier called for attention, raised the open scroll once more, and read off the accomplishments of Her Majory: this organization founded, that club advised, another activity anointed by her, a few civic improvements honored, and the final praise: "Instigator of the reptile exhibit at the Louis zoological garden, fixator of lizards, and investigator of lizard attributes!"

The crowd cheered for their Majory, darling of the Royal Court.

Not like her elder sisters who wedded top-grade politicians of the neighboring kingdoms and lived among them in order to set a seal to important treaties. Only Majory remained in Louis – and should she dare wed a lower-grade fellow she would remain in Louis and, who knew? become Queen after her father the King passed into the long, dark, bitter void. What kind of Queen would she be, citizens might wonder, given her proclivities to enjoy the arts and not to diplomatic endeavors? Few wondered of the succession at this point in her life: a dozen years remained in her maternity window. It would take a fierce fellow to plump her up and press out princes and princesses to follow after. Could it be this short, red-haired man standing there?

Rory noted how she stood a head taller than him and considered the height her elevated shoes hidden under the silvery gown might give her. He'd never seen her standing, only seated. Yet she had the height, clearly, even without the surety of shoes. And width! Twice his breadth, more than his muscled shoulders. He would surely be lost in her fleshy folds, he knew, and yet that – more than anything, perhaps – enlivened his sour soul. How maternal Majory must be! A glorious ocean to envelop him! Ah, much as his mother once held him, and she was his entire world, surrounding him....

He took in a deep breath and drew in Majory's sweet scent, all of flowers and sniffling, like a garden grew beside him, its air pressing against him. And thanks to Stank for a cake of soap for his bath so he wouldn't offend his bride!

The crier raised the mighty scroll once more to trumpet blasts.

"To the grateful groom, Sir Aurora Bret Baumann—"

The crier had to pause. What accomplishments had he to read off the scroll? With a clearing of throat gup, the crier proceeded slowly, inventing a list of great events that the groom, one Rory Baumann, had successfully accomplished in his storied life. Words of the man's origin first. Much made of the long line of the Baumann clan going back four-hundred years. Then there was the Battle of This and the Skirmish of That, the Raising of Something, and Defense of Here and There. Designer of the Famous Thing. Inventor of Tools for the Modern Warrior and Weapons for Blacksmithing. Now come for his greatest triumph to Louis!

Joyful applause from the crowd assured Rory that he'd actually accomplished quite a lot in his half-life, a mere thirty-five years to measure against Majory's twenty-five fair turns of the world.

He stood proudly beside her, his bride. His bride!

"By Royal decree," pronounced the crier from a fresh scroll, "His Majesty, King Karl, at the behest of his daughter, Princess Majory, hereby bestows upon Aurora Bret Baumann the title of Duke, junior rank, with all manner of rights and privileges allowed to accompany such title."

More applause from the crowd.

"Heretoforthwith, this mister standing before us today, known to public account as Aurora Bret Baumann shall adopt the Royal name of *Robau*. Henceforth known as Duke Robau!"

"It's actually like 'cow' not like 'toe'," Rory spoke to the crier. "A common mistake in my youth, all the kinder calling me Ro-Bo. Like I was a prince, eh?" He chuckled, then caught Majory's serious eye — or was it the one that didn't see?

"All Hail Duke Robau!" the crier declared, using the suggested pronunciation. "His Majesty, King Karl, awards this Duke all lands around and including Lindenwood to the west, from the cross-ridge south to the river shores in the north, including the dismal swamp, given as his ducal domain, although residence there is solely by the Duke's choice. A place in Louis shall be maintained for the duke."

"Hail Duke Robau!" the crowd cheered.

"I always wanted a duke for a brother," Stank was heard to call.

"Yay, Rory!" Mabel cried out.

He beamed with pride, chest puffed out, the sunshine hitting his face, coloring his cheeks as red as the hair on his head.

"Now that you are a duke," the voice from the woman beside him strangely struck his ear, "you are fit for wedding."

Rory broke into a grin, wishing to turn and gaze upon her, the object of his desires, his magnificent Majory.

"Yes, indeed, Your Majesty," he spoke solemnly without turning his head. "Thank you."

"Oh, don't thank me," she responded. "It's the protocol. You must be a duke or better to win this hand. It's how we play the game of Royal Flush."

Rory knew the rules. After first seeing Majory, he'd consulted a law-speaker back home, got the protocol stuck in his head. That was the reason he needed his warrior brother to remove the dastardly Duke Lindo from the game. And Stank had somehow. The game was a blur as he stood moments away from everything he'd ever wanted.

"We shall be so happy," he blurted and heard her laugh.

"I shall count upon that daily," Majory replied, her voice full of amusement. "Now be true to the plan, Sir Robau."

"If you please, Your Majesty, I prefer Rory. Please call me Rory. Yet I'll welcome 'Duke Robau' in official places. If you please...."

"If I please?" A chuckle, then she turned to gaze at him, a sweet smile unfolding between her chin and cheeks, like nothing he'd seen from her in public venues, indeed something meant only for him. "I fully intend to be pleased. I can assure you of that."

The crier gave way to a priest, a tall man in black robe with red lines crossing this way and that, with a peaked red cap marked by a white cross. He came bearing a thick book in black cover. He opened the book, flipped to the proper page and read from it:

"Two persons come before us, the community, being humble and good of manners, here to share with us their full praise to the Lord of All for abundance and safety, protection from eastern disease and cleansing fire! We gather today to witness these two members of our family join together in official union, joining their hearts in a blaze of passion, and to bestow upon this couple the right of reproduction and promotion of population proliferation. Let our community grow! Here we today acknowledge the official pairing of this couple. May they bear many babes, as the law requires."

Cheers rose from the crowd.

Rory turned and regarded Majory, his smile unable to be slapped from his face even by Stank's mighty paw.

"Give you fair value to this partner?" the priest asked of Rory.

"She is the most marvelous maiden I've ever s—"

"It is a yes or no question, sir," the priest interrupted.

"Yes," Rory sang out. "Fully yes, and also yes!"

"And do you likewise give this person permission to join with you for purposes of proliferating population?"

"I suppose so," said Majory. "I'm willing for it."

The words rang in Rory's ears and his smile stretched wider.

"Very well," spoke the priest, balefully batting his eyes as though unimpressed by her lukewarm dedication to improving the populace count which had been falling for the past century.

"Is it done?" muttered Rory to Majory.

"There's more to say," Majory replied with a giggle, like they had shared a joke. That was promising.

The priest launched into passages from the Book of Wise Words, a sermon on the plaza, compelling the crowd to begin slipping away.

Rory couldn't wait, had to touch her. He reached out, took hold of her pudgy hand, clasped it like a pouch of coins. Only then did he look at her, his eyes turning to her face: seeing the splendid smile set there among the facial hills, a reflection of his own.

"My Majory," he muttered, throat tight with emotion, "this is the happiest day of my life."

Her great smile continued, cheeks and chin aglow.

"I look forward to the wedding night," she spoke to him.

"Ay, me as well. It shall be glorious. I promise you."

"Glory is what I expect. As your brother has promised."

"My brother promised? What did he promise?"

"He promised to make the wedding night glorious."

"He *what?*" His voice boomed louder than Court protocol allowed, and the priest frowned at him.

"Sir Stanley promised to please me if I would wed his brother – you, Sir Robau. And I agreed."

Rory raged about the grand hall newly assigned to him, still bearing his Court costume. He had no opinion of its furnishings, its décor, or servants put to him. The closets of fine fashion didn't impress him. Nor the boundless bed he found full of fluffy frou-frou cushions and ample blankets. Not even the fine dinner brought in for him and his friends to enjoy. Only Stank was absent.

"I'm sure he will arrive presently," said Dandruff, with Mabel by his side looking worried.

"Sir Stanley has much to do," said the girl.

Jamal and his sister sat on gilded chairs, their eyes gazing about the room, admiring every little decorative touch, remarking on what they saw. Those of the Court lived such ornate lives. The citizenry had no idea how lavish their living lounges were.

"This is not what I asked for," Rory grumbled, pacing the room.

The floor shook and all of them turned to see Stank in his finery pounding down the corridor toward the room. He burst through the double doors swung open by a pair of solemn guards. He didn't seem in a fair mood – then to be accosted by his brother's red face.

"What did you do?" Rory demanded, grabbing his brother by the sleeves of his tunic.

"Do?" Stank seemed angry as much as Rory. "I saved you."

"Saved me? From what? I'm a duke now."

"Ay, everything you wished for. True? I came all this way to help you get what you asked for. And you got it. It's done. So I'm ready to return home – to my new home in Fort Branson with Mona that we shall make together. It's my turn to be happy."

Rory reddened at that rebuke, let go of Stank's sleeves.

"When do I see my bride?" asked Rory, trying to calm himself.

"You may go see her now," Stank replied. "You know the way?"

"No, of course I don't. I'm new here, brother. They haven't given me the house plan. Only led me to this room, which they said is my quarters whenever I'm resident in Louis. I expected to share a room with my bride."

"The Court has protocols," Stank said.

Dandruff and Jamal nodded. LaTonya agreed with a smirk.

Rory stared hard at his brother. "You know the way?"

Stank gave a nod. "I do. A staff fellow showed me." His voice and the grin suggested a joke.

"Then show me," said Rory sternly. "I wish to be with my bride."

"I can show you, but now is not the best time."

"Why not now? I want to see my bride."

"Now is not a good time. Let us say, Her Majory is feeling ill at the present. It would be best not to disturb her."

"Disturb her? She's my bride!"

"She is yet your superior," Stank reminded him. "A princess does outrank a duke. It's how the game is set."

"And there are, with you, fifty-six dukes in the kingdom," Jamal offered, then shut up at Stank's glare.

"And you've had so little to achieve to earn it," LaTonya added, then got Rory's angry stare. She apologized. "Perhaps we should be leaving you two sirs to tend to your protocols."

"Right," said Jamal, and they seemed happy to depart.

Rory resumed his pacing. "Wait, wait, wait...."

Stank moved to an elegantly designed chair, gave consideration to its sturdiness, then sat. He found it not so comfortable. Too small for his hips. After a few minutes he got up, stood beside the chair as Dandruff and Mabel watched Rory pace.

"You will wear a hole in the carpet that way," said Stank.

"He will," Mabel laughed.

"Then send me to my bride," Rory exclaimed.

"Give us an hour more," said Stank. "The physician is tending to her. Nothing serious. Caught by surprise."

Rory grew wary, suspicious. "What did you do?"

It was time to come clean, Stank decided.

"I did what I promised. Her Majory agreed to make you a duke and to wed you in exchange for my services."

"Your services?" Rory exploded. "How could you do that, brother? You know my feelings for her. *Her?* She's my bride! *My* bride."

"Ay, it was the only way she would agree to give you what you asked for."

"Damn what I asked for!"

"I didn't want to provide such services, yet she insisted." He took a big breath. "Yet today nothing has occurred. She fell ill, as I said. Not a thing to do with my services."

"Nothing at all?"

"I went as required. She commanded me. Guards led me there, lances ready should I refuse. She is a cruel lady. Yet when I arrived at her room, the gaggle of girls always around her informed me that she had taken ill. I worried, naturally, and inspected her. She had a wound on her hand. Seemed to be an animal bite."

Rory felt a shock. "An animal bit her?"

"I told you about her love of lizards. I suspect one of them took a nip of her hand as she held it. Likely taking some time with her pets while waiting for me."

"As she waited for you? My own brother! Snatching my wedding union from out between my legs. How dastardly!"

"I delayed as much as I could. I invented a fantastic tale for the guards who came to escort me. It went on a while. So she likely grew bored and proceeded to play with her pets."

"A likely story!"

"It's true. Ask her staff. The physician arrived and so I left."

"How delicate of you." Rory was shaking his head.

"It's true. I didn't want to do anything of the sort. Not with her. Not with Mona on my mind. Yet I agreed to the terms she set forth, and what warrior goes against a fair compact?"

"Would you have gone further? If she hadn't taken ill?"

"I prayed I wouldn't. I delayed as much as I could. Perhaps Her Majory would forget, become engaged in other activities. Perhaps a calling to other tasks. I don't know. Ay, there must be a way to get away from the promise."

Rory shook his head, began pacing again. Then he stopped.

"You can head home, as you say. Go back to Mona. I'll make an excuse for you. I'll apologize for you. She may hate you for leaving, you understand. Will that make her turn to me? I doubt that would happen. She already stated we shall live apart and meet only for official functions. What kind of life is that?"

Stank forced a grin. "You have a union. It's a start, brother. You can build upon that. You can draw closer. Woo her with your wily words. She's weak for words. In time, she will come around to your bedside. I'm sure of it."

Rory threw up his arms. "You're sure? Hah!"

"Perhaps that is the best way," said Stank, thinking it through. "I shall leave tomorrow. After I bid Her Majory farewell properly. It is the polite thing to do. I'll be quick yet polite. She will understand – I hope. She's a reasonable woman."

22

HOMEWARD REBOUND

STANK ARRIVED at the Court stables to find Winnie enjoying the finest grooming a warhorse ever had, the groomsmen lavishing their most attentive efforts to the beast's care.

"Ay, Sir Winthrop, how you love being at Court," cried Stank at the sight. "You'll be too spoiled for battle now. Have to put you out to stud, eh? A different mare each day." He thought a moment. "Like me. I'm ready for a good pasture, too."

The warrior stood before the stable boys in his finest jerkin over the leather braces he wore for protection, and new trousers of rough brown tweed. His boots were now highly polished. He held Longclaw in its scabbard at his side, then strapped the greatsword to himself as the boys watched admiringly.

"And you, too, can be a warrior," he told the boys. "Eat the meat. Play-fight every day. Learn your weapon."

He gave a glance back out the stable doors, as if expecting to be called for another task. Already the morning had been busy enough. Rory got hold of a map of the Court and finally found his way to Her Majory's room.

That was a scene!

"I bring your husband, Your Majesty," Stank had announced, as the gaggle of girls gave way for them. "He's fraught with fear upon your wounding."

"He is?" Majory called from her bed, looking a mess from her bad turn. Her giggly girls hadn't made her ready for public display. The sight astonished Stank, who'd seen her after the party in fine form. Rory seemed confused, struggling to gaze upon her with a glad face.

"You do recall wedding my brother, Duke Robau, don't you, Your Majesty?" Stank spoke carefully, adding a bow of his head.

"There was a little red-haired man," she muttered.

Stank grinned. "Yes, that one."

"My dear Majory," Rory spoke and got a dismissive wave.

"So be it," spoke Majory wearily, holding up her bandaged hand. "I had no sleep whatsoever over the night. Pain constant. The bite of a red-necked rufus. Couldn't believe it. It's always been kind to me."

"Even our best friends can bite us," Stank offered.

"And bite the hardest," she responded.

Movement in the corner got Stank's attention, and his hand slid to the hilt of Longclaw.

A tall figure in purple robe draped down to purple slippers, long white beard to his waist, entered the space surrounding the great bed from a shadowy corner, bearing a beaker of pink potion in one hand and a gnarly wand in the other.

"You must be the physician," said Rory to the man, acting like he knew it all along. "I need to be allowed to tend to my bride."

The tall man looked down at Rory with a stern face, then turned his eyes to Majory.

"I called my physician," said Majory, wiping feverish moisture off her broad brow before an attending girl could dab a cloth. "I always call on him when a thing happens." She waved her good hand at the tall man. "This is Nightshade. He's a magician of sorts. Up from the Or-Lean. He knows voodoo. Father doesn't like him, yet he tends me well. He mixes many potions."

"Glad to meet you," said Rory dutifully but with a sneer.

As an afterthought, Majory pointed at Rory. "This one it seems is my husband. You saw the ceremony yesterday?"

"Yes, Your Majesty. Very impressive," said Nightshade, ignoring Rory's greeting.

"Pleased to meet you," said Rory again, but got no response.

Stank stood back, moving Rory forward with a look.

"You know now what silliness I've done," Majory spoke, a sigh to the magician. "Foolish pleasures bought me cheap. Perhaps the poor party put my protocols in play. Now I've become a wounded woman while awaiting welcome wonders. Oh, woe is me."

"My dear Majory," Rory spoke tenderly, going to the bedside and kneeling. He gazed upon her. "I would've come sooner, but I was told to wait. I was told you had been bitten by a lizard. What foil is that! Lizards about the Court?"

"Be not a silly fool. They are my pets."

She proceeded to tell how she took her pet out from its cage and spoke to it, bemoaning her foolish venture, wondering if she'd made a mistake. She'd asked the lizard for advice – playfully, of course, as lizards don't actually speak. However, she thought she got a reply: He will come. *Who?* she asked the red-necked rufus. That wonderful warrior she would woo were she not a properly prim princess.

"I expected this time – *this* time – my wish would be fulfilled and I would be filled fully by a mighty man."

Stank did arrive – late but never absent – and found her bitten, crying in pain, with this Nightshade fellow tending to her.

"Your Majesty is in no condition to meet our agreed conditions," Stank had said. "I shall leave you with your physician."

Majory begged him to return later, after she'd mended. Then he would complete his obligation to her, for the promises made earlier that got his brother the ducal scroll and a thick hand to hold in the wedding. It was done.

Stank had given a nod and exited.

"Is that how it was, my dear?" Rory begged the question by her broad bedside.

Stank stood back, humbly, letting them have time together.

"Oh, it is misery now," she moaned.

Then her face brightened at the sweet sincerity of Rory's abject adoration. Even laying whale-ish upon the well-braced bed, a gleam of glistening glow enlightening her feverish face, ravenesque hair in a tussled mess, night-breath unminted, slippery sheets of seduction tangled about her forest-thick legs, Rory still gazed with passionate doe-eyes upon her – this random red-head rogue!

She pushed her lips into words: "Give me time to heal."

"Take as much time as you need, my dear," said Rory, offering a serious smile. "I will remain ever-ready to return at your immediate call. For I am your most-devoted husband now. I shall be ever-ready for you."

"Thank you...mmm, what was your name again?"

"Rory. Call me Rory. Otherwise, I'm now Duke Robau."

"Yes! Robau. Now I recall it."

"But call me Rory."

"Rory?"

"Yes, Rory."

"What's it mean?"

"My mother thought my red hair was bright much like lights in the northern sky so she named me for those lights. Aurora. But the boys teased me for it, so I go by Rory."

"That's a fine tale," said Majory in a weary voice. "I am named for my size at birth. A *major* offspring, they said. Sad it is, I was too wide for my mother to push me out. They had to cut open her belly to retrieve me. Alas, she passed from life because of my birth."

Rory expressed shock at the tale, understanding why she was so shunned by the Court.

"The others – my sisters Bertilda, Melody, and Gann – they had easy births, grew up slender and romantic, well-wedded to unite us with foreign lands. Even our brother Fidelio is a slender fellow. He has fine features although manly he is not."

Rory detected tears forming in her eyes, saw one roll down her round cheek.

"Yet not me," she whimpered, then sniffled. "I'm as big as all of them together on one carriage. Father says I need my own carriage. He says I bring embarrassment upon him. He prefers me gone yet none will wed me to unite our lands. So I dare wed a scarlet ruffian just to spite Father."

Rory took her unbandaged hand, held it gently and patted it as he gazed into her dull eyes, pained at the poison pumping through her plumpness.

She let out a yawn. "Many thanks, Ra...."

"Rory," he gave her.

"Rory...." She seemed to slip into sleep.

"It will take time," Nightshade spoke after a moment of silence. He stood at the foot of the great bed. "Let the potion do its work. She will sleep for a while. Then we shall assess whether it is effective. If needed, I have a stronger potion to give her."

Satisfied, Stank had left Rory to watch over his bride, and went to see to Winnie's care, readying the warhorse for the ride home.

Jamal did his best to keep the jingling of the bells on his costume to a minimum as he performed his acrobatic tricks before Duke Lindo and various guests at the private show. He tried listening to their chatter. As he performed, LaTonya sat among the guests, showing them string pictures and gaining praise at each iteration of a full menagerie of animal shapes. Most of them she made still existed within the bounds of the city's famous zoological park.

"It has to be a ruse," Lindo spoke to an older man sitting beside him, Duke Olden – previously Oliver Denton, sympathetic barkeep, before his ducal elevation. "That red-topped fop hasn't done a thing to earn the title. And such a smallish man! Yet he bears that full fellow about him – that warrior who tried insulting me, yet failed to draw me out. A pair of fools! He admitted as much: the game they purported to play. All for winning the wedding of a weighty woman. What a pair to want her!"

"You saw it coming," Duke Olden confirmed.

"Yet not the whole scheme," said Lindo.

"Now they are wed – if only on a Royal decree. You have not lost. Not as yet." He studied Lindo. "You were never drawn to her at all, were you?"

"Not drawn so much as painted," said Lindo with churlish chuck. He put his hands up to clap at Jamal's latest spin movement. "A fine portrait of my Royal commission delicately stroked. That, more than anything, comes with the joining to a member of the Royal family, no matter her appearance, no matter her attributes. It is her name that matters. Then I may go as I please."

"Majory?" asked Olden cautiously.

"No, her family name: Kurtz." Lindo forced a smile at Jamal. "It was I who should receive the Royal right to restitution. Shouldn't be some red-haired country bumpkin tripping backwardly over his big brother into her battened bed."

"Yet you never had want of her," Olden said, a wry grin playing upon his face. "Too large, you said. And the screw-eye."

"Those are deal-breakers, I admit. Yet she could still be an asset. Wed her, gain power, then put her away somewhere. Let her attend her stage-plays or such. Ah...too late to act now."

"She's the youngest daughter," said Olden. "I think nothing to be missed were she to go missing."

"With the older daughters wedded to distant princes, treaties be damned, they are far away now. That leaves Majory with a toe-hold upon the throne here. If that fumbling Fidelio fails to find it."

Olden grinned at the mention of the King's son. "He's pleased to play with others of the Court."

"He'll never be a good ruler for Louis. No, despite her expanse, she does have wit and wisdom within her – if she doesn't set it aside for amusements. She can be cruel – excellent attribute for a ruler."

"I've also noted such." Olden perked up. "I heard she was bitten by a petty beast in her bed chamber."

"Yes, it's rumored. But what can we do? Rumors upon rumors."

"They say she hasn't yet taken the new duke into her fleshy folds so there is still time to act."

"I haven't any urge to slip into his place," said Lindo, rolling his eyes at the image. "I would surely drown in that ocean."

Olden chuckled. "If she were to succumb to her wounding – the lizard that took a bite of her flesh, poor lizard – then the King would have no one for the last chair. It's an opportunity for you, being the senior duke of the kingdom. You and your lovely lady would be next in the line, certainly. You should go on and wed your lady. When the good king, whence his loss, realizes the truth, you will surely be appointed to her seat."

"That is a brilliant scheme." Lindo rubbed his chin, got a look of annoyance from his lovely betrothed, Lady Lily. He gave her a frisky frown and she feigned a return to the performance while keeping ears on their talk. "I can see how it unfolds like a new shirt from a clothier's wrapping. If Majory is made ill and doesn't recover, then it falls to me to take her place at Court. It is stiff duty, yet I'll abide."

Duke Olden pinched his lips at Lily's lingering look.

"She's already been bitten by the boisterous beast. If a portion of poison were applied, as well, all would think it was a matter of the lizard's activity. It's what lizards do. Who could blame a small lizard for having a bitter bite?"

"You could blame the lizard. Then kill it. No one would care." He paused, thinking, as the jester did his flips.

"Then you approve the scheme?" asked Olden.

Lindo turned roughly to him. "What? Are you serious?"

Jamal landed with a serious split that would've sent a less spry fellow to a physician to string his sinews afresh. Yet as limber as he had trained himself to be, the maneuver cost him no pain nor an overwrought tangle. The group gave applause and Jamal took hands with LaTonya, joining him, and they bowed in appreciation.

Olden gave a nod. "We are."

"We?"

"All of us will do well with you advancing."

Lindo gazed about the gathering, seeing who close at hand might have caught their conversation. None seemed to have taken notice. He glimpsed his lovely Lady Lily who gave her glamorous gaze.

"You have a poison suitable?" asked Lindo – and Jamal took note and stood rigidly as the applause fell away.

"The physician," said Olden, turning tightly to Lindo to hide his lips. "He has many potions. Mix the wrong elixirs together and harm is achieved."

"And do you know which to mix?"

"I do not. I'm not a physician."

"You used to make up fabulous drinks at that tavern in Webster Grove, *The Lucky Losers*, as I recall."

"A long time ago," said Olden. "Well into my youth. Now I'll need to press that fellow she has tending her, the one in the purple robe, to mix up something proper. Let him take the blame, too."

Lindo smiled like he hadn't during the entire acrobatic show.

"You've a crafty mixology about you, Olden. Good to have such a friend as you. Or that fool from the past, Damper. He's an odd one, yet amusing at parties – the tales he tells!"

In the high tower, behind locked doors, stood the silvery machine, a shiny armoire yet without a stitch of clothing hung within. Enough space for an adult of standard size to pose upright, with everything necessary placed in half-an-arm's reach. No seat to sit one's bottom upon. One inner wall beset with buttons, lights and levers, switches and screens: glass windows showing numbers during its flight.

They asked what flight would that be? Not into the air, the man named Damper explained to Rory and Stank.

"You move through time," said 'Damian Harper, Time Traveler'. His new Court uniform stated as much on a brightly sewn label. "It is virtually instantaneous. The blink of an eye."

"Looks like a prison cell," said Rory, festooned in his Court finery of gold and cardinal red, short cape hanging on one shoulder, boots of red calfskin with golden toes. He seemed to stand a bit taller.

"A cell for maybe a half-minute at the longest," said Damper. "It depends how far one wishes to travel."

"How far can you go in it?" asked Rory.

"This is the farthest I've ever traveled," said Damper, his silvery garb gleaming like it was an official uniform of the time travel guild. "Actually, it's the only trip I've taken."

"Can you return?" asked Stank suspiciously.

"That remains to be seen," said Damper, a catch in his voice.

"One trip and you are done?" asked Rory, amused.

"Sadly, this is the only trip we've sent the device on. We spun the dial and chose a year. Twenty-three-fifty-three. I volunteered for this maiden voyage. We sent it into the future because we expected to see a lot of advancements in technology, maybe learn from them and bring it back to our own time. That was the plan, anyway."

"Ay, we've not so much as what you wanted," said Stank with a warrior's guffaw.

"How far in the past can you go?" asked Rory, acting serious.

"We have no information about that. My friends think we could never go back beyond the time we left from. Only into the future and return to our own time. Never further back than our own time."

"You can't see where you've come from, eh?" Stank teased. "Only ahead to where you're going, eh?"

"Yes – in theory." Damper couldn't shake off his frown. "First, I must return. Then we can figure out what went wrong."

"Seems you're here, so it must have worked fine," said Rory.

"Only thing not working is the King's guards found you," Stank roared. "A poor outcome."

"Yes. But he promises to let me go soon. I hope."

"I'll request it," said Rory, presuming much.

"How's it get power to go places?" asked Stank.

"A very good question. I'm glad you asked." The man hesitated.

Stank grew impatient. "You have an answer?"

"Ay, he's got one," said Rory with confidence.

Damper mugged, stretching out the time.

"It's complicated, as you may well imagine." He rubbed his head. "The numbers are staggering. Yet all the equations are quite sound. My friends did the math. I'm only a test subject, but I do understand some of the figures. And I'm here, aren't I? So it obviously works."

Stank continued gazing inside the chamber.

"How's it work?"

Damper stood back, grinning proudly. "The principle is to create a kind of folded space around the device. A bubble, to put it in terms you'll understand. Worry not, for you remain quite safe within the capsule. Directions set inside at the control panel send you to the period or time of your choosing. You don't move left or right, up or down, but you remain essentially in the same spot. If I were to go home, I would need to take the device from this room back to where I first landed."

"Landed...?" Rory quizzed.

"Yes, landed!" Damper laughed at a joke only he seemed to think was funny.

241

"It's humor?" Stank demanded.

Damper grinned as if he thought of happier times. "I didn't fly. Hence no 'landing' as such. Entirely land travel, time point to time point. Our starting point inside a building was apparently the same point in your time that is now Royal hunting grounds. It was outside the castle walls, in a grove. The King's patrol found me, thought me a curiosity and took me to the Court for inspection. King Karl, bless his heart, granted me residency. But he ordered the device locked up in this room so I couldn't escape."

"Looks too heavy to move," Stank noted.

"Yes, that's a problem. Takes at least four strong men to carry it – or, as they did, lift it onto a wagon for transport to the Court. They didn't damage it, thankfully. Only way to know for sure is to send it back to my time. And I'm quite ready to go."

"And what places do you find when it stops moving?" asked Rory, acting princely, chin tilted up, brow somewhat higher.

"I expect to find my home. Inside a garage. My cousin's garage. My friends and I from the university, we built it there. That's where I'd return. To the garage again. One hopes they haven't rolled one of their old sports cars into the garage during my absence. Been nearly two years by now."

"Seems not a fair way to travel," Rory decided, frowning.

"What is 'sports cars'?" asked Stank, lifting his head from inside the device.

"I've learned since arriving that you call them 'motor carriages'. That is, when you look back at pictures of old times. I mean the time I come from. We have particularly fast 'carriages' which we called 'sports cars'. Ford Mustang. Dodge Charger. Like those."

"I see," said Stank, not liking the way Damper spoke to them.

"He means the horse-free carriages. They had a noisy motor that pulled them along," said Rory, as if Stank didn't know. They'd both looked at plenty of torn-up books in their west Wichita camp when they were mere lads. And they saw plenty of rusty hulks.

"Ay, I'm ready to go," Stank announced, "on horse-free carriage or on my warhorse." He stood up straight yet seemed still interested in the device, rising taller than him. He couldn't possibly fit inside the device. Rory could fit inside easily. Maybe he'd send his brother back to meet the ancestors. What was the year? Two-thousand? See what trouble they'd gotten into.

Damper cringed as Stank reached inside.

"Like this?" He thumbed the scroll of numbers until it read *2000*. That was the year Damper said he'd come from. No, thought Stank, better give some lead time to recover from the journey. He adjusted the numbers to *1999*. He set the next tabulation to *12*, which he took to be Twelfthmonth. There would be the holiday feast, so he chose *30* for the day. That would give him time for a good welcome.

"Careful," Damper warned. "Can't go past our starting point."

"Many times I've wished to go past a starting point," said Stank light-heartedly, "then do things different, eh?"

"Mind you," said Rory when Stank glanced back from the travel chamber, "I've gathered a traveling group for you to escort along the Royal Road. All paying customers. You'll be rich when you arrive at Fort Branson."

"Not if savages come for me or I've fallen and cannot arise," said Stank, standing straight with a grin.

Damper ducked his head inside the chamber to see what Stank had played with. He switched some levers.

"I can see you wouldn't fit inside this device, sir," he said with a sigh of relief.

Stank stayed focused on what Rory said. "And my horse, Winnie. He must ride free. No, we'll go the usual way. I'll take your mule to bear my supplies. I'll bring many gifts for Mona."

"I give my mule to you, brother. Good wedding for you."

"Thanks, brother." Stank turned to Damper. "And thanks for the timely lesson."

"Ay, thanks for showing us your machine," Rory echoed.

"My pleasure, gentlemen," said Damper.

"It's Duke Robau," Rory snapped playfully.

"Sorry, sir. Duke Robau...."

A smirk played on Stank's face. "It's just what we need: another duke to bow to. Even a junior duke."

They bid farewell to Damper and proceeded down the plethora of steps, one case after another, spiraling toward the bottom.

Coming down from the high tower, Stank and Rory found Jamal in a jingling way, the jester acting frantic.

"I found you," Jamal spit out breathlessly. "So many stairs."

"You search for us?" asked Stank.

"Calm yourself," urged Duke Robau, posing regally.

Jamal breathed hard. "I—I need to tell you...."

"Tell us what?" asked the duke, transforming back to Rory.

"I was performing...for the duke...Lindo and guests...."

"Take your time," said Stank, then gave a chuckle as he glanced back up the stairs to where Damper lingered.

"I heard him...and another duke...."

"Yes?" Rory pressed.

"Duke Olden."

"Not heard of him but go on."

"He's Lindo's friend in the Court. They conspire...against you."

"Conspire? What's this?" Stank spoke, his words echoing in the stone stairwell.

"Her Majory is not safe...."

"What?" Rory roared. He regarded Stank. "We must go to Majory at once."

Stank and Rory rushed down the stairs, hurried through a long corridor, up more passages, out along the ramparts, and boldly into the Royal family quarters.

When they arrived at Majory's chamber, the doors were left wide open. Inside, no gaggle of girls, no sign of Majory. No Nightshade either. And no guards.

At the center of the battened bed, the white coverings rumpled into disarray, lay a red-necked rufus bleeding out, a dagger through its white belly.

23

A RED RUSE

"WHAT DOES THIS MEAN?" cried Rory, staring at the empty bed and the dead lizard upon the sheet.

"That lizard must be the foul cause," Stank said, pointing at the red thing: its mouth open, red tongue falling out. "The magician said as much. Thought it had poisoned her."

"Where could she be?" Rory spun around inspecting the room. He went to the corridor and shouted for guards to come.

A male attendant in red finery appeared, white lace at cuffs and collar. The man didn't seem distraught in the least.

"What needs have you, Duke Robau?"

"Where is Her Majesty?" Rory demanded.

"Her Majesty has been taken to the magician's quarters," he said like he read it from a news-paper. "She took a poor turn. They said she needed a new potion."

"Because of that lizard?" Stank demanded.

"Yes, sir." The attendant stood rigidly.

"A small lizard like that one?" Stank shook his head.

"And they stabbed it through with a dagger? Seems a bit much," said Rory.

"Can't bring a new potion up here?" asked Stank.

"I heard it said she needed to be under the magician's care," said the attendant, now acting as though it was all a great secret.

"Why not care for her here?" Stank pressed. "That pesky purple fellow came up here before. I saw him."

"I do not know the answer, sir," the attendant replied.

"Where is that Nightshade's quarters?" Stank pressed.

"In the far tower. In the underground chamber. I can lead you to his quarters," said the attendant and turned sharply.

"Another delay to my journey home," Stank grumbled.

When they arrived in the dark, damp corridor, stone walls moist and stinking, they paused as if expecting an ambush. The attendant seemed suspicious, like he'd fulfilled his role in a scheme and would soon be paid. He tried to hide a smile but they noticed.

"What've you to be glad about?" Stank asked the attendant.

"I serve you and all members of the Court, sir." A tic on his face popped in a steady rhythm. "We reached the destination you wished to find. Therefore, I am glad."

"That's a fair answer," said Rory, raising his eyebrows. "It's good to be glad."

"It's a suspicious answer!" Stank roared.

Rory caught on to his brother's idea. "Seems you've information to hide."

"This is the chamber of Her Majesty's magician, Nightshade," the attendant said. He waved at the big oaken door, moss growing in the cracks between its braced boards.

"Here?" asked Rory. "Seems no place for Her Majory. Not if she's in a dire way. A clean place is what she'd want."

"This is all a ruse," Stank growled. He went up to the attendant, grabbed him by the collar. "Tell us the plan!"

"Sir, there is not any," the attendant stammered, eyes showing fear. "None I have heard."

"There is!" Stank roared.

At the noise, the wooden door gave a pop and loosened from its stone seating.

"You see? It's open now," exclaimed the attendant.

"Like a magic trick," Stank grumbled.

"Ay, vile magic," muttered Rory.

The door pushed open and darkness spilled out into the corridor, followed by a man in purple robe bending low to keep his peaked cap from brushing the stone arch of the doorframe. He straightened up once free of the doorway.

"Nightshade," Stank announced.

"Where is Her Majesty?" Rory shouted at the magician. "I must see my bride."

The purple-robed man remained calm, hands folded together at his waist, long sleeves hanging below his long white beard.

"Where is she?" Stank asked, ready to act upon the answer.

"Duke Robau," spoke Nightshade in a stiff manner, "your Lady is in a better place than any that could be fashioned for her."

"What?" cried Rory, sounding annoyed.

The magician remained grim, unmoving. "I hesitate to speak the words, sir. Yet I know I must. And so I tell you: Princess Majory has unfortunately succumbed from the deadly poison of that red-necked rufus bite. The poison took hold of her quickly—"

"She what?" Rory burst into rage.

"Just like that?" Stank spoke. "One bite? Why would she keep a poisonous lizard as a pet?"

"Perhaps she did not know the lizard bore a poison," Nightshade offered, his plain voice heavy with the dankness.

"I surely would want to know were I to consider such a pet," said Stank. "Are you sure it was the lizard?"

"It is our only clue, sir. The poison caused a reddening of her face and body, as though the sun had born harshly upon her flesh, a rude rash which ran afoul of her natural color."

"She turned red?" Stank tilted his head.

"Quite red, sir." Nightshade turned to Rory, "More red than this one's hair."

"Listen to whom you speak, for I'm a duke now," Rory raged. "It can't be true my Majory is gone. Now where is she? Red or not, I will see her."

Nightshade inhaled deeply. "Alas, sir, she is gone."

"Gone? Gone where?" Stank joined in. "Where is her body?"

"I want to see her body," Rory insisted. "I mean, I wish to gaze upon my bride's fine features."

"Taken from her chamber when her heart beat no more."

"That staff fellow brought us down here...to this swamp chamber to see her. She's not here?"

Nightshade bowed his head as though on a stage and the play, a tragedy, had come to its dramatic conclusion.

"Her Majesty's body was carried upon a trolley, rolled away to what we call the chill chamber, where she often chose to go to escape the summer heat. It is a room set with blocks of ice."

"I've heard of that," said Stank, curious more than angry.

"They should've waited for us," Rory demanded.

"How many should bear her body up from this place?" pondered Stank, staring at the magician.

Nightshade kept his grim demeanor. "Her Majesty is no more." He attempted a glitch of despair, yet Stank remained unconvinced. The magician bore strange waves which Stank could sense shaking in unnatural patterns – as certain as if the man were about to strike with a blade.

Stank heard Rory sniffle back tears and clear his throat.

"Where is she?" Rory asked, voice rough, begging. "Where's her body now?"

Nightshade spoke: "They have taken away her body—"

"To the chill chamber," Stank cut in, concerned for his brother. He gazed harshly at the magician. "That quick? And why bring her down here to this messy place?"

Nightshade continued the play. "This chamber has potions she needed. It was best she be here so I could administer a remedy—"

"Which didn't help!" Rory cried out.

"In the end, they did not."

"She trusted you."

"Yes, Her Majesty had trust in me. I did my best to aid her."

"Not enough," Stank growled. "Should've had a boy gather your potions and elixirs and bring them up to her chamber. Let her lay in peace there. Let her husband be at her side. At least that."

Nightshade stood still, letting the men's anger bounce off him.

"We were just there," moaned Rory. "No Majory. No nobody—"

"Just the lizard stabbed on the bed," Stank cut in.

"What do you know of that?" asked Rory.

"The lizard?" Nightshade appeared to blink, too quick for Rory to be certain. "Of course it must be killed. A poisonous bestie. I would think a dagger would be adequate for such a purpose."

Stank noted the odd detail. He hadn't mentioned the dagger. The magician must've been there to know about the dagger in the lizard. Perhaps he'd put the dagger in the lizard himself, or it was done at his direction.

"Seems too dramatic."

Nightshade didn't bat an eye. "No drama. No stage-play. It's a true scheme."

"Ay, a scheme," said Stank.

"What have they done with my Majory?" Rory howled.

"Easy, brother."

Nightshade seemed to fight to keep a grin hidden. "I cannot say. She is no more. That is truth. Her body, given her great girth, could not fit most anywhere. A special container must be built to bear her body. Now the King is in mourning – as well as all who knew her."

The magician choked up, then acted like he'd shed tears, wiped them from his eyes. Stank watched carefully.

"And her husband," Rory sobbed. "Her new-wed husband."

"My sympathy, sir," said Nightshade.

The heavy wooden door swung shut. The brace slid across to prevent anyone from opening it. Steps across the stone floor, over the woven rug, to a quaint bed of straw and old pillows with a rough blanket tossed to the side. Light from a pair of candles glowed.

"It is done." The magician stepped across the chamber to a basin and washed his hands. "Those two country ruffians...they sensed a scheme. Yet we have passed the first part adequately."

A half-chuckle, half-cough from the woman on the bed.

"It is a firm cot, I must say. Well-strung. Served the purpose."

The tall man in the purple robe turned to her. "The bed was not the main thing, Your Majesty."

"I know, I know."

"They have gone away and likely you are free now."

She let out a sigh. "I was stupid. Like a cow in a field. A poor gal looking for love in all the wrong places."

"You, like most, deserve to find love in one place or another."

"Easy to say. Not so easy to do."

"You have another chance, Your Majesty."

"Perhaps I should keep that red-haired ruffian. He adored me. I do like adoration."

"The fool is half your size. Had no manners about him."

"He was rather pretty in his duke garb. And he spoke kind words to me. He was sweet."

"Is that all you require?" asked Nightshade, raising an eyebrow.

"I require a lot," she said willfully. "I do not get a lot, however."

The magician studied her, saw how his cot sagged under her.

"Now we must find a place for you. A place where none can find you. There you will be apart from those who curse you, and the fools who find you foul and furtive."

"You told me that red-haired fellow, Duke Robau, is not for me. I should have listened to your advice. You know so much. You can see the future better than me and my bad eye."

Nightshade smiled like a doting father.

"What do you see, Your Majesty?"

"Right now? Nothing." She *tsk*ed. "While you chatted with those two outside this chamber, my bad eye saw a long line of soldiers in red and black marching across the land, heading to war."

"You did?"

"Yes." She grew frustrated. "It's always been like that. They are always marching. Always going to a war. It shakes me awake."

"I counseled you on the proper potion to put in you. Did you heed my counsel? Or did you play with your precious pet and let it bite you so you had an easy escape from your dutiful life at Court?"

"I did as you advised me."

"You did. And now we must go to the second phase. To hide you. Send you somewhere safe."

"Where can a large woman like me ever hide?"

"There are places unknown to most. Places where a woman such as Your Majesty can live a care-free life unhindered by any protocols of the Court."

"You mean I can prance about without a gown on? Run barefoot over the soft grass? Eat as I please without gaining a bit of bulge? Enjoy a festival of plays and concerts of music and delight in all I survey? Like that? Is that where I should go?"

"There is a place for you, Your Majesty."

"Then I won't be any *majesty* after that, will I?"

"No, you will not. You will be only plain Majory Kurtz. And you will not be the daughter of a king. It shall be a simple life. Yet you will find it a fine respite from what you have now."

She struggled to rise from the small bed. "I'm ready for my move. Let us be away. Will you come with me? I'll need your counsel."

"Alas, I cannot go with you. My place is here. Remember: I serve others at Court beyond you."

"I know. So you'll tend to my pets? Only you understand lizards. They need special care."

"I shall care for your pets, Majory." He gave a slight grin, a rare expression. "How does it feel to be called by your name? Majory...."

"Not many call me by my name, true."

"You will become familiar with it. People will take you as one of them. You will be like the citizens of Louis: a woman named Majory. No more 'Your Majesty' – that era is done."

"I do love a done era," she said, full smile expanding her round cheeks. "I think I'm ready. So let the play begin."

The stone walls were slick with moisture, an echoing drip here and there, a startled rat scurrying away as Stank and Rory ascended the steps from the lair of the magician. The passage turned and turned as it rose. Voices from above seeped downward and Stank and Rory halted, listening.

"She's not one for schemes, clever girl," said one voice. "Not ours, least of all. Not anyone's. Yet there must be a scheme of some kind. Let us consult with her physician to gain answers."

"Fair play," said a second, deeper voice.

Stank looked back curiously at Rory. They understood what they heard. The foul fiend! Duke Lindo was coming down the steps in the passage. Stank put his finger to his lips to signal silence.

But Rory retrieved his blade, which made a noise that echoed up and down the stone walls.

"What?" the voice of Lindo expressed to the other with him.

Stank loosed the leather strap on the hilt of his greatsword, and suddenly became aware of the tight space of the passage.

Within the few breaths taken and spent, the two men from above and the two below met in fury.

"You!" cried Duke Lindo, pressing against his companion, a man Rory recalled from the roster of dukes bore the name of Olden.

"Lindo," Stank grunted.

"How can it be you are in this step-well?"

"We've rights to go anywhere in the Court." Stank kept his hand on Longclaw's hilt. "What's your excuse?"

"We come to speak with the magician," said Lindo.

"The physician," his companion, Olden, added.

"He's no physician," Stank growled. "I know a physician and he isn't the same. More of a magician, that's certain."

"Stand aside, big fellow," Lindo ordered, Stank blocking the way, his shoulders reigning wall to wall. "We have urgent business."

"As we," Stank growled back at him.

"Easier for you to stand aside than my brother," Rory called from behind Stank.

"It is our right to pass. Now stand back. Let us pass. Or shall we command guards to dispatch you?"

"Dispatch us?" Stank laughed bullishly. "You think they could?"

"What business must you attend?" Rory called up the steps.

"Our business is none of your business," Olden called down over Lindo's shoulder.

"Business is business," said Stank. "Tell us yours."

"If you must know," Lindo began, affecting an air of superiority, like his business was more important than any business the lower pair might have, "we seek the magician. We mean to get answers as to where Her Majory has gone. We must speak with her at once. It's a delicate matter—"

"You wish to know where Majory has gone?" Rory called up, idea forming in his head. The two dukes obviously didn't know that she had died from poisoning by a lizard.

"Yes," said Lindo, then turned wary.

Stank noticed. "What scheme have you?"

"No scheme," cried Olden, his words echoing against the walls.

"It is a scheme," Stank growled.

"We come this way to speak to the magician," Lindo repeated.

"About your business?" asked Rory.

"Yes, our business. Now let us pass."

"There's no passing in this passageway," said Stank. "You'll have to back up, return to the top."

"No, you will have to back down to the bottom."

"We've an impasse," said Stank.

"Impasse or not, we must make our way," Lindo demanded. He stood taller to look at Rory behind his brother. "You are just made a duke. You have small standing in the Court. It's you who must yield. You and your ruffian brother."

"I'm no ruffian," Stank growled. "I'm a warrior. What have you? Not even a guard squad to protect your posterior from abuse."

"So, we return to the insult dance? Is that your plan?"

"Not with words this time," said Stank, "but with blades!"

Lindo stepped up, reaching for his side blade, a short sword ideal for a close passageway.

Stank slid Longclaw out of its sheath a bit, found the problem. A greatsword would not fit in a tight passage.

"Ah hah!" cried Lindo, holding out his short sword. "You've never thought long and hard for a short sword, have you?"

Stank couldn't pull his long blade free of its scabbard in the close quarters. A panic swept through him.

"What shall you do now, my brave lad?" Lindo ejaculated.

24

THE LONGCLAW OF VENGEANCE

STANK HELD THE HILT OF LONGCLAW, deciding what to do. Before Lindo could also think what to do, Stank let his mighty fist shoot out toward his opponent, still grasping the hilt. It was a swift punch that sent the sword's heavy pommel straight into the duke's unshielded nose.

"Ow!" cried Lindo, dropping his short sword and reaching for his nose, finding blood there. "You broke my nose!"

"Stop shrieking," shouted Rory. "You brought this on yourself."

"It is you two who caused this," Duke Olden spoke up, examining his friend. "You shall pay for this."

"Pay what?" Rory countered. "A coin or two? A physician's fee?"

"Done," said Stank.

He slid his greatsword down into its scabbard and punched at the duke, landing a mighty fist to the duke's narrow jaw that sent him crumpling hard upon the stone steps.

Lindo reached for his back, claiming pain there, cursing at his opponent and citing the rules of combat. As a warrior, Stank knew them backward and forward.

"So, we go," Stank instructed Rory.

"I shall have you put in the jail for this!" Lindo exclaimed.

"It was a fair fight," said Stank, searching for the best route to take in stepping over the fallen foe.

Duke Olden backed up the steps, pressing himself flat against the dank wall.

Stank took a step over the fallen Lindo, but the duke grabbed his short sword off the step and desperately swung it up. The tip struck at Stank's hip, cut into his tunic and hit the leather brace he wore, then slid off the leather and into flesh. A weak push from Lindo's hand and the blade entered.

Stank noted the offense yet did not cry out.

"There!" cried Lindo. "I've got you, you big oaf!"

"Oaf? I should think you are a stinking sack of offal."

"Not true, mountain-man-wedged-in-a-corridor."

Stank tightened his jaw. "You're a Lily-liver Paisley Pooch who can't even lift a greatsword! A measly man-child bending to sneak attacks! A limp-handed loser lost in limited luxury—"

He pulled the blade free, saw blood on it.

"—who can't wield any sword worthy of a name. Wish I had let Longclaw take a bite of you. Perhaps another day. Not like this toy of yours. Mabel's wooden sword could beat you."

He tossed the duke's sword backward over Rory's head, down the passage, hearing the steel clatter upon the stone steps.

"You're wounded," Rory declared.

"Ay, by the sneak of a snerdly snuffle snoot, whatever that might be! It's this fine figure of a man. So bold, this one. A champion."

Lindo grinned. "So you recognize—"

Stank gave him a hard punch to the face, cracking the nose and leaving His Dukeship's face bloody. Stank raised a boot, stepped on the duke's belly, pressing him to release his inner materials in dual directions. The soiling from the downspout filled the passage in vile wretch. The mouth gave up its last meal.

"This isn't done, big fellow," Duke Olden called out on behalf of his friend. "We shall have you taken to the jail for this!"

"Bring a squad," Stank grumbled, stepping on up the passage. "I require no less than a dozen, if you're serious about taking me."

Rory, alarmed yet feeling pleased in the moment, leaped over the fallen Lindo. Once clear of the man, he turned to look back at the bloody face, smiling warmly.

"You want to know where Majory has gone?" asked Rory.

"Yes, that is the question," Olden responded while tending to his poor friend. He'd retrieved a handkerchief, dabbing at the nose.

"We wish to know the same," said Rory. "For there appear many schemes in this Court. Yet schemes will not save you."

"There's no scheme," grunted Lindo.

Stank, up the passage, gave a great guffaw that echoed down the stone walls. "You were born to schemes like other babes are born to suckle. This is not done."

"Agreed. Not done," Lindo howled up the passage. "Prepare to be arrested."

"I shall sharpen my sword!"

A warm breeze carried the city's sorrow across the plaza, tugging at the sleeves of Rory's Royal tunic. He wiped his eyes, trying to stand tall and be strong for his friends.

"He never loved her," Rory had to explain to Dandruff, standing with him in the plaza. Feeling lonely, he'd come out to see the Royal troupe prepare the stage for another performance. He let out a long sigh, his world now devoid of pleasures. "His was only a scheme to gain standing, to rise in the Court. He thought he could become the king once King Karl passed on. That poor prince, Fidelio, is never to follow after him. Not bold enough."

"Yes, he's a fine dancer, loves the theater," Dandruff responded. "We should invite him to take a role."

"You do that." Rory winked. "Keep him out of troubles. Not like my brother has."

"Yes, we heard the report from the town crier." Dandruff had a fair show of sympathy for the man.

"It took two dozen guards to capture him." Rory took a breath. "I thought he could defeat them. One dozen, I'd bet on him. So they did send a dozen, then a dozen more. A king's dozen! Unfair at best! And they took him away in heavy chains."

"Unfair, indeed."

"Said he had to stand before a judge and say his words. Make up a good tale. Yet it's truth that will stand tall for us. The scheme will be exposed! He will be freed and the duke will be put in chains."

"Or worse—"

"Let Longclaw take a bite of the crime! Off with his head, I say. Senior duke or lesser, it matters not. A scheme is a scheme!"

"How might we help?" Dandruff kept glancing back at the stage. The company were busy setting up the large painted screen.

"Now we cannot find Her Majory," Rory went on.

Dandruff turned back to Rory. "Didn't you say she died? Got bit by a lizard. That's all we heard."

"That's the story they tell through the streets. Schemes within schemes. The whole business would provide a fine play for you."

Now that Rory was a duke, Dandruff tried to speak carefully. Not that he believed the man would call guards upon him for a slip of tongue. With Duke Lindo in question, he recognized Duke Robau as a new patron to woo.

"A bold idea, sir. A play about this scheme."

"Yes, a scheme! It will be exposed. Then Lindo will be brought out, words will fail to save him, and life will go on." He blinked. "I saw my brother in a fight with an opposing warrior: lopped off the fiend's head with one swing of his greatsword and in the next swing batted the head over the camp. Must've been hundred yards! That's the dream I have for Lindo: losing his head like that, while all those about him keep theirs."

"It would seem a fair final form." Dandruff started to be anxious about getting back to his stage-craft. He had to shout at his troupe a few instructions about the screen. "Sorry, sir."

"No mind. I know you've tasks to get on." Rory watched them working on the stage. "Like a play.... That's the thing. We must play a part, it seems, willingly or not. Do our best to fool everyone. That's a life.... A series of scenes, constituting nothing...." His tone turned sour, his thoughts darkening. "No, I do not take it as truth. Majory must be hiding."

That drew Dandruff's attention. "Hiding? From her husband?"

"Ay, it's not such an uncommon thing among the wedded folks." He rubbed his eyes. "We hadn't even gotten together in her vast bed, I dare say. Pardon the private revelation."

"What a sad story," said Dandruff.

"I'm still learning to say 'pardon' over 'sorry' – more duke-ish."

"What're you talking about?" asked Mabel cheerfully coming to them garbed in her costume, ready to play Tiny Tilly in *The Lives of Trolls*. The long pointy ears amused Rory.

"Her Majesty is missing," he said. "Feared dead."

"They prepare a funeral for her," Dandruff spoke up. "Sadly, that is what Jamal tells me."

"Funeral?" cried Mabel, disbelieving.

"Do they?" Rory regarded the girl. "It is all make-believe. A stage play for the citizenry. And I must play my part. Act with sorrow. Yet how can I cry on cue?"

"We have an ointment for that. Dab some in your eyes. I'll give you a tin of it."

"I can cry on cue," said Mabel, then promptly demonstrated her teary persona. Dandruff grinned at her act.

"That's very clever," said Rory, then to Dandruff: "I must get my brother out of the jail. Too many guards. I have little power in the Court being a new duke. I have a petition prepared for his release. Lindo didn't die, so there's that. He wants a chance to fight him again. Thinks he can win in a fair venue."

"Can he?" asked Dandruff.

"Sir Stanley can best anyone," Mabel declared.

"It's good he went peacefully when they came for him," Dandruff offered. "Didn't fight them. Should be easier to get a quick release."

"I'll bring the troupe," said Dandruff. "We'll cheer for Sir Stanley and he will know we stand with him."

"I thank you for that," said Rory, raising his hand and giving a pat to the actor's shoulder.

The magistrate sat on the high seat gazing down over the gathering: prosecution on the right, defense on the left. Stank looked weary in his dirty gown, not sleeping well on the cold, stone floor of the cell. A sextet of armed guards stood around him, more ceremonial than any ability to keep the warrior under their control. Stank had enough of the Court protocols and stood glumly.

"Hear my judgment," spoke the magistrate, brushing his long, gray beard aside. "All facts stated, each side heard, a verdict is now produced. Being a duke yet aggrieved, Lindo is awarded justice. The opponent, Sir Stanley K. Baumann, warrior-sheriff, must accept the awarded justice or be sent to the greater prison in Florissant for a period of one year." The magistrate regarded Duke Lindo, with his associate, Duke Olden, by his side. "What say you?"

"We accept the awarded justice," spoke Lindo in official tone.

"And you? Do you accept?" the magistrate asked of Stank.

The warrior, looking gruff and surly, gave only a nod.

"So be it. The awarded justice is accepted." The magistrate held up a scroll, unrolled it and read: "The offended party, Duke Lindo, requests the choice of fair duel to be set between him and the other party, Sir Stanley."

"And what's a fair duel?" Rory quipped in a low voice to Dandruff and Jamal beside him in the gallery.

"Fair duel to be set thus: Lindo shall have a single weapon of his choosing, and free movement about the field. Opponent shall bear a weapon of his choosing yet be restricted in movement in the field, as given the advantage his size provides him. One foot to be fixed to a stake. One arm to be lashed to his back. No armor or helmet worn."

"That's unfair!" cried Rory, jumping up.

"Silence!" roared the magistrate, waving a pair of guards to rush to where Rory stood.

"Do not make this worse," cautioned Dandruff, nearly bumping Mabel's head in trying to restrain Rory.

"Do you accept the terms?" asked the magistrate of Stank.

Again a solemn nod from the warrior. Rory could see the hatred boiling in his brother's eyes.

"Your Honor," Mabel called out, startling Dandruff and Jamal, "I am grateful to these fine fellows for saving me from harm as I was left alone on the Royal Road, savages all about, ruffians pursuing me, and too many lustful men cajoling me for poor means and evil purpose. Then Sir Stanley saved me, took me under his protection. I can state he is not a bad man and deserves not this unfair play." She let streams of tears run from her eyes.

"That may be true, little one," said the magistrate, taking note of her tears, "yet in this instance, he is at fault. He should have stood back for a duke, let him pass. He should not have engaged in a fight with a duke. He should not have struck the duke and wounding his person. While I appreciate your gratitude for the warrior's timely assistance, the awarded justice has been decided."

"But...he's my daddy," she cried, shedding more tears. "What of me were he to fall? Who will watch over me? I cannot lose him."

"If this warrior should fall, we shall assign a person of the Court to watch over you." The magistrate glared at Rory. "Or the warrior's brother, a duke, can become your guardian – if he is so moved."

"I accept her, Your Honor," Rory called out.

"Then it is settled. If the warrior falls, this little one is hereby joined to your House, Duke Robau." He turned to the scribe sitting at a lower desk. "Record it so."

Mabel resumed crying and Dandruff fought back a smile.

"Let us go forth to the dueling ground," declared the magistrate.

Still in his dirty jail gown, barefoot and disheveled, seething with a raw rage, Stank stood solemnly as his ankle was tied to an iron spike hammered into the ground. His opposite arm was bent back and lashed to his body. His sword hand remained free, and he held Longclaw in his firm hand.

"I like his chances," said Rory to Dandruff and Jamal. "Only man I ever knew who could wield a greatsword with a single arm."

Mabel kept jumping up trying to see over the wooden wall that separated the spectators from the dirt of the dueling ground. Finally Jamal lifted her, set her on his shoulders to see.

"I think he must win early," Rory went on. "The longer it goes, the more fatigue he will suffer. The greatsword will become heavier. His arm will slow, his swings become weaker. And Lindo is using a rapier. Could slip the narrow blade through a gap easily."

"Broadsword versus rapier," Jamal muttered.

"Fixed target versus prancing fop," Rory corrected.

"He looks like a bear," said Dandruff. "Used to tie up a captured bear back in Sedalia, let the dogs taunt it. This looks the same: bear versus a crazed wolf."

"It's an atrocity," said Jamal.

"What's 'atrocity' mean?" Mabel asked.

"This duel," answered Jamal.

The gathered crowd let a cheer arise, starting below the viewing stand where the magistrate and staff sat and spreading through the three levels of spectators.

Duke Lindo marched out in his ducal finery, all in cardinal red with black fringe, short cape flittering in a light breeze. The dashing duke! His rapier remained in its scabbard as he strode to the center of the ground. Spectators cheered. They had their favorite, clear to see. What had they to cheer for gazing upon a dirty fellow from some other land? Lindo retrieved his rapier, held it out as though pointing to his enemy, and the crowd cheered.

"Look at him, acting so brave," said Rory. "Not like Stank. Look at him: he seethes with rage. It's building in him."

"Can he win?" Dandruff posed.

"Sir Stanley must win!" cried Mabel from Jamal's shoulders.

Another figure in Court uniform strode out from the gate.

"Let the awarded justice commence," the young crier called out. He held a red flag flapping from a pole in one hand, the pole jabbed into the dirt, and a scroll in the other hand. He let it fall open and read loudly to the crowd. "A fatal wound wins. Blood itself shall not halt the duel. Three middling wounds shall equal a fatal wound and the duel shall end. Two middling wounds for each and the duel ends. If both combatants have survived to the end, each shall never more engage the other within an interval of seven yards."

With a curt nod, the crier took the flag and scroll and quickly ran to the side, remaining against the wall.

At a long blare from a trumpet, Duke Lindo circled before Stank, swinging his rapier like it was a broadsword, acting the fool, gaining cheers from the crowd.

"Watch this," he called out. "You will be entertained."

Stank stood ready, Longclaw in his free hand, held up across his body in defense. The nasty rapier could slip through a narrow gap if he had loose form. He had to stay guarded, using the wide blade to block a lunge. At the same time, if he could knock the rapier aside he might get a moment for a swing of the heavy weapon toward his opponent. The weight of the blade or its sharp edge could be enough to lay out his opponent – yet only if he could get an instant for such a strike, fixed as he was to the spot at the center of the ground.

"What say you now, warrior?" goaded Lindo, prancing freely. The rapier sang through the air. He slipped closer to Stank. "Not so bold now, are you? The scales are made even."

Stank didn't waste his breath, instead waited for the first lunge.

When it finally came after much taunting, he easily blocked the attempt with minimal movement of his broadsword, the wide blade an effective shield against the narrow tip of the rapier. Likely Lindo expect a wider parry, one which would open a space for a *riposte* and the decisive wound.

"Good catch," Lindo chided, circling. Then to the crowd: "I shall toy with the beast for your amusement."

Flicking the rapier, Lindo danced around Stank, moving behind him and back in front. That forced Stank to twist awkwardly as his ankle remained lashed to the spike. If he tripped and fell—

Lindo lunged again, the rapier going for Stank's back quarter, a foul move. The crowd knew it and jeered at the dastardly act. Stank threw his hand at the jab, Longclaw meeting the rapier's tip, which slid away and landed a nick on Stank's wrist. The crowd erupted.

"Blood!" shouted the crier. "Middling wound one."

Another try by the duke could give Stank a chance to snip off the tip – and leave flat metal to pierce his body if he failed to block the strike. That square-end blade would go in painfully.

"Come on," cried Lindo sporting a wild grimace. He let his short cape flap behind him. "Give us a firm swing, warrior. Show us your strength."

Stank knew the vain man wanted him to try a strike, then he'd slip the rapier under his arm and into his ribs, so he bided his time.

If he were free of the spike, he would raise the greatsword over his head with both hands and bring it down decisively upon the measly man, slicing him like a loaf of bread.

Lindo circled, plotting, making Stank have to turn around the spike which caused the lash to tighten on his ankle.

"Have you fear yet?" teased the duke.

Another lunge, another parry, the greatsword's block being hard enough to cause the duke to stumble back, nearly lose his balance. The cape blew around him, briefly blocking his face. Shouldn't have worn the cape, thought Stank, but the man was a frilly filly of fair favor. Appearance mattered more than life itself.

"Come at me, you bastard!" Lindo shouted, forgetting that Stank was fixed and unable to go at him.

Bastard? That did it! His mother was a dear soul, a kind woman who worked hard to provide for him and his brothers and sisters. No matter how she made her coin, hers was as noble a life as anyone's in the Court. She knew how to run a family, could run a Court.

Stank gave up protection and swung Longclaw hard at the duke who easily danced out of its range.

"There you go," laughed the duke. He'd managed a flick of the rapier to Stank's forearm, drawing blood.

"Blood!" shouted the crier. "Middling wound two."

Lindo swept about the ground, regarding the crowd. "I promised you entertainment!"

The crowd cheered again, sensing an end to the spectacle.

"Let us try again," the duke called to Stank.

Stank held Longclaw ready for the attack.

As the duke came forward, his cape also blew forward, blocking his view. In that instant, Stank slapped his blade down at his ankle, cutting the leather strap fixing his ankle to the spike. He left a cut to his bare ankle but it was minor. His foot shook free of the spike as Lindo swept the cape aside and beheld an unfixed warrior, now free to move.

The crowd erupted at the new situation.

Lindo struck a ducal pose, affecting the defiant hero. "That isn't allowed." Then he lunged straight at Stank, perhaps hoping to catch the warrior not ready to defend.

Instead, the greatsword caught the rapier's narrow blade on its edge, bending the last third.

"This is not the awarded justice!"

The duke backed away, nearly stumbling. He held on to his bent blade, righting himself. The rapier was still useable. He only needed to get one more middling wound to win.

Stank stood mighty before the little man who challenged him to this ridiculous rout. He dared not look to the viewing stand where the magistrate and other officials of the Court observed the awarded justice. It appeared that the magistrate might be consulting with his fellows about the rules.

"Is that allowed? To free himself?" asked Jamal of Dandruff.

"The only rule I heard was that he should be fixed at the start."

Mabel cheered loudly for Stank.

"I suppose he's allowed to cut the ties, if he can," said Jamal.

Free of the ankle strap, Stank stepped forward, holding up his greatsword, daring the duke to come at him. At the same time, the warrior pulled his lashed arm outward until he broke free of the restraining straps. He shook his arm to regain strength, then took hold of the hilt of Longclaw with both hands.

Holding the greatsword up before his face, he glared at Lindo, who suddenly cowered with a poor bent rapier his only shield.

The crowd jeered at the duke. He had to do something, enough to regain the crowd's support. Maybe the crowd actually cursed Stank's new freedom instead, deeming it a violation of the rules. Others had eyes fixed on a final furious *finalé*.

Stank stepped forward, greatsword posed for a strike, looking at the duke straightening up, sorry rapier in the *en garde* position like he was in a mere sporting match.

"You've broken the rules," Lindo cursed.

"There are no rules in combat," Stank declared, "once you've a marked target."

He gave a mighty swing of Longclaw with both hands on the hilt, down to the soft unshielded shoulder of the duke, in the very instant the man started to cringe. The furious blade met meat there in the clean cleft and the follow-through motion severed head from neck, releasing a fountain of blood.

His strong backswing of Longclaw lofted the separated head up and into the crowd, the shrieking spectators scrambling to avoid the bloody thing.

"Does he win?" Rory asked excitedly.

"I should think so," said Dandruff.

"Yay, Sir Stanley!" Mabel shouted, her hands cupped around her mouth, matching the roar of the crowd.

Stank returned wearily to the center of the dueling ground and tapped the iron spike with his toe. He set Longclaw to rest, tip to the dirt, its hilt held in his two hands like he offered up a prayer. As he knelt against his greatsword, the spectators shifted from an anxious murmuring to mild applause. Yet, as Stank raised his right arm to the sky, clearly thanking the Great Spirit for his victory, the crowd got up and shouted their praises.

"Yes, yes, yes," Rory cheered. "It is done! Stank has won! And no more dastardly duke to duel with."

25

WORMWOOD

"THE WARRIORS BAUMANN!" sang Rory. He smiled around at his circle of friends, each with a stein of ale to enjoy. He bought them the city's finest brew at the *Iron Codpiece*. Even Mabel was allowed in the tavern at the order of this duke, although she drank a lemon fizz, burping like a drunken riverboat man.

Stank sat glum at the end of the table, cleaned up and dressed in a dark blue tunic, his middling wounds tended with ointment and bandages on arm and ankle that were more display than need. Rory had insisted: only the finest care for his brother.

"I put my money on you, I want you to know," one patron told Stank on the way out of the tavern. "Won a handsome fare."

Another said the same. Then another.

"Lost coin because of you," snarled one patron, then left.

"Good that dastardly duke's dearly departed," said another.

"I should've put coin on you, brother," said Rory. "Sorry for that. I knew you would win, certainly, yet I stood too struck for thinking of the betting."

Stank didn't answer, just offered a half-smile.

"What's got you?" asked Rory. "You won, brother. A great end! No more Lindo to make a deal. It's done. You should be pleased. You should be happy."

All eyes at the table turned to Stank. He sat his stein down.

"Ay, pleased the duke is no more given to harass us," said Stank in a low voice, sounding tired and sad. "Yet...to speak truth...I hate cutting down a mere fool who thought himself a warrior. Seems a bit unfair. It didn't need to happen."

"But they had you tethered to a spike. Strapped back your arm. How was *that* fair?" Rory countered. The others agreed.

"Ay, rules. He who makes rules, dies by the rules." Stank gave a little chuckle. "No, brother. The whole thing was a farce." He turned to Dandruff. "Like a stage-play, true? Like we acted for the cheering of the crowd. Everything planned."

"And executed," Rory added.

"That may well be true," Dandruff responded solemnly.

"I would rather not kill men who mean me no harm," said Stank. "I intended to take only an arm, and not even his fencing arm, yet he moved – cowered like a coward – and Longclaw came to meet his neck, found purchase, and off comes his head."

His friends quieted, seeing again the fatal moment.

Rory grinned. "He did have a surprised look on his face—"

"All for words. Only foolish words. The insulting. A mere game. That's all he had. And whatever schemes he thought he'd put into play. What's still in motion? Who among us knows?"

"Ah, don't worry yourself," said Rory.

"It was all within the rules," said Jamal.

"It looked fair to me," LaTonya added.

"Not a word spoken against cutting yourself free after the duel begins," said Rory. "Nothing declared afterwards either. He had his chance. Fair on the square. You are free now."

"It isn't about that. I know I'm free," said Stank. "I've always been free. None can hold me back. It's that duke."

"You're soft for that dastardly duke?" Rory pressed.

"I have no like of him, true." Stank took a deep breath. "Listen, brother. I came on this journey to help you win the hand of Majory. And to do that you set me to removing the duke from the Court. To open the way for you. And yet all has gone wrong."

"Not wrong," Rory said. "You removed the duke. And I did marry my Majory. Just can't find her anywhere now. Like she's run away, hiding somewhere, ashamed to be wed to such as I."

Stank shook his head. "She's pleased to wed with you, brother."

"Then why does she hide from me? I mean her only the best. I've a kind heart."

"I know you do," said Stank. "Yet it seems you had a scheme of your own. Get your brother to fight for you, getting rid of a man who, in truth, had no ill will towards you nor intentions upon Her Majory." He let go a sigh. "All a twisted thing. So it's done now. Your scheme done. Most of it. I leave you to find your bride. I shall set my way for home on the morrow. My new home with Mona. I can only pray she's waiting for me. Yet another month of Sundays to return...."

Those around the table sat in silence. Dandruff soon dared lift his stein and drink. Jamal followed. Mabel, smiling, lifted her glass of bubbling yellow water.

"To Stank!" Mabel spoke out, glass held high.

"Ay, to Stank!" Rory joined her.

"To Stank!" they cheered.

"Mightiest of the mighty!" Rory added. "My brother the warrior!"

Stank waved them quiet. "It's not all mine. 'Twas Lord Fritz who watched over me. I felt it. An extra set of arms swinging Longclaw that final stroke. Don't think I could've won without His aid."

"May be true," said Rory. "Lord Fritz works in mysterious ways."

"Who is this Lord Fritz?" asked Jamal.

Rory grinned. "He is our great ancestor, He of the Old Country, bearer of the Great Horn that calls us into battle. He rides the sky bridge now, watching over us, His kin."

Jamal held a quizzical expression, so Dandruff stood, holding his stein. "We have a warrior among us. We have no lack of protection. We are safe beside him. All hail the warrior, Sir Stanley of Wichita!"

"West side," Stank made sure they understood.

Everyone cheered, including other guests in the tavern. Several applauded. Others shouted their praises for him and what he'd done on the dueling ground. The boisterous barrage broke into two bands: the squad of Stank supporters shouting at a diminished den of duke defenders. It became loud, with bare-knuckle blows threatening.

The barkeep called for calm.

"You quarrel over crumbs," growled a voice from the shadows.

The crowd quieted, sought out who had spoken.

"You would pity the dust in corners of a tavern over the ways of men." Letting his words settle, the rough voice again spoke: "The ways of the world are wont for wiles you wouldn't wish upon your worst foe."

The guests fell silent, turning to see an old man sitting in the shadowy corner. No brew on his table. His was a magical apparition: bald head, white beard not long yet not neatly kept. He wore soiled travel clothes like he'd just arrived in Louis an hour earlier and this was his first stop.

"Ho! What say you, stranger?" called someone at another table.

"This is Sir Stanley," another guest spoke up.

"Winner of the duel."

"He should've been in the tournament—"

"But he got here too late."

"Settled his affairs in the dueling ground, fair enough."

"Sent that foolish Lindo to hell in high water!"

"You daren't speak ill of our warrior friend!"

Again they fell silent and waited for the old man to speak, either to join them in praising Stank or to speak words against his victory. The room boiled tension. If he spoke against their champion, a fury of response might be unleashed.

"Victory.... Defeat...," the old man spoke from his table. "It's all the same. Little men's tasks."

The barkeep brought over a glass of soda water to him, set it on the table, but the man didn't reach for it, kept his eyes on Stank.

"Ay, he's just one of those playing at wiseman," Rory teased.

Rory's table guests laughed uneasily.

"There are no wisemen," said the man. "You must have confused me with some person from another time and place. When wisemen were a *dime* a dozen." He saw puzzled looks upon their faces. "You know what a dime is? An ancient coin. Ten cents. Ten of them make a *dollar*. Then dollars were changed. And changed again. And once more. No more of them today. It's only coins. Everyone wants coins to measure their worth. A circle of metal pressed with the likeness of one of your betters, watching you. Yet what's a coin worth today?

I see three counts: one, ten, hundred. Is that all they make now?"

"We have five and fifty coins, too," said Dandruff meekly.

"Are any of them worth much?" the old man spoke. "Buy a stein of ale? Is any coin worth your soul? How much for your soul?"

"Ay, he's a fool," Rory muttered to his friends.

"Sir Stanley, what's a 'soul'?" asked Mabel but the warrior waved her quiet.

The man spoke on: "A fool is what you call someone who doesn't know what's going to happen next. Only a guess. Or something read on a scroll. Or in a book. Remember books? Sheets of paper, pages sewn together? Or news-paper? The old days before the flash, before the Glow, what they called it back then before it burned itself out. Remember any of that?"

"None of us can remember back that far, stranger," said Stank.

The old man sat still, eyes hard on them. "I do."

"You do? That far? How old are you?" asked Rory, then he had a new idea. "Do you come from that distant past? I know a fellow like that. Name of Damper. Comes from the year two-thousand."

"Not that," the old man responded from across the room. "I lived all of it. I was there. Many, many years ago. Do not cross me. I felt the plague. Saw the ravages. So I had to flee. I had to make a home far away from other people. I had to start anew, making this world from scratches in the dirt. I used my own two hands. Built a town, filled it with healthy people, hoped for more to ease my life, settling down with a family, watching grandchildren play in a fragrant yard, flowers and bushes, trees and soft grass, with plenty to eat. Had no worries. That was our goal. I think we may have gotten there for a few days over a few years."

"Wait," Dandruff cut in. "You lived through all of that history?"

The old man's face reflected nothing. "I did."

"Then how old must you be?" asked Rory with concern.

After a moment the old man spoke: "I am as old as time."

The guests in the tavern chuckled. This fellow certainly was of a crazy clan, spinning his tales to get odd reactions, an amusement of travelers, they understood. Many such persons came through.

"But how old is time?" asked Mabel so innocently.

The question from a child made the old man sit up straight, look sharper at her. He seemed to be a fit man, after all, old only by the appearance of his head and face. Beneath his burgundy jerkin, he could be well-muscled, able to fight. How old was he actually? Rory studied the man more closely.

"Time, child, is without end. Begins before time itself. Goes on long after time ends."

Mabel laughed. "Time is older than time?"

"Your words make no sense," said Dandruff. "Like something put in a play, words for the audience to enjoy yet without meaning."

"Words are but tools," said the man. "Tools to convey messages. Nothing more. Numbers can do the same yet in a different way. Not all can hear or see them and understand. That is a special talent. I see you have that talent."

Dandruff blushed at the compliment.

"We understand you just fine," said Stank, growing impatient. He finished his stein, set it down hard on the table.

"I assure you, warrior – if that is how you call yourself – I am not about simple stuff. I have a message for you."

"Ay, what's that?" Stank responded gruffly.

The old man put his hands together, interlocking his long-nailed fingers, and stared seriously at Stank.

"The message is this: Don't."

"Don't?" asked Stank, pinching his eyes.

"Don't what?" Rory asked.

"Everything," said the man.

Stank and Rory grinned, knowing a fool with words to play.

"Don't take on excuses. Don't let a day slip out of sight without a simple task done. Don't let feelings sway you to action against your gut. Don't let—"

"He's just a preacher with some common axioms. Good things to do, like our mother would say." Rory caught Stank's scowl. "Yet he's strange. Like a thief spying on us. Knows things none other would know. He's—"

"I know much, Duke Robo," said the man.

Rory frowned. "It's Ro*bau*. Like 'cow'; not like 'toe'."

"And how are you called?" asked Stank.

The old man kept a stern face. "The original pronunciation was like 'toe'. *Boh*-man. I heard it said in the early days. Two clans. One stayed. One left. It is a mystery to you, I am certain."

"He's speaking of Lord Fritz," Rory told Stank.

"More than that. It is a whole tale. A history. A thick book of the tales we tell to teach and preach, in order to pass messages from one generation to the next, to the next, and the next, and now to you – both of you. And you should spread it to your kin, all of them. Tell all of them to beware."

"Why, he sounds like one of those Illini rubes," Jamal blurted out to the amusement of several in the tavern.

"The Illini are not to be trifled with," said the man, by his calm demeanor clearly not Illini, known for barbarism. "Yet you think so, Jamal, the jokester. A man of amusement."

"I have a Royal appointment," Jamal came back proudly.

The man nearly smiled. "Royal appointment? A license to amuse the Court. A worthy calling. Yet you are little more than one James Malden, formerly a repairer of wagon wheels. One nameless duke found you to be amusing and brought you to Louis to ply your trade. You have done well."

"How do you know all that?" Jamal demanded, jumping up.

LaTonya grabbed his arm, urging him to sit down. "Easy now."

"And her," the man spoke, pointing at LaTonya with his chin, "your *sister*. Also known as Ladonna Tonya Jones, who is not your sister but in truth your niece. And, if I may say so, also your lover."

"How dare you!" Jamal shouted.

The man appeared to smile. "Is it not true?"

"Who *are you?*" Jamal challenged.

"He's one not to be trifled with," Rory cut in. "You heard him."

"Sounds like an Illini," Stank offered, unamused.

LaTonya got Jamal to sit again as Mabel checked that everyone returned to calm, nodding at each one in their group. Rory grinned at the girl, then turned to the man.

"You said beware. Beware of what?" asked Rory cautiously.

The man, already sitting straight, shuffled the chair closer to the table's edge, pressing against it.

"Wormwood," he spoke and the tavern drew quiet once more.

"What's that?" asked Stank.

"A star."

"A star named Wormwood?" asked Rory with a chuckle.

"It's a plant known for its bitter taste," said Dandruff to Rory. "A book from ancient days tells of its use in punishments."

"Do not mock it," said the man. "A star which brings death, that will bring bitterness to the waters and death to the earth. I tell you now the star shall fall, shall come this way, shall blaze upon this world and leave nothing in its wake. I tell you now there is but one way to survive. You must—"

"Build a castle with thick walls?" Rory offered.

The man grinned, like he'd gotten the response he expected.

"He means we should offer prayers," said Jamal.

"Who are you?" Stank demanded, raising his voice.

The man's grin expanded. "I am you." He set his eyes upon Rory, then on each of them. "I am you. And you. And you. I am also the child. I am all of you."

"He's a specter, a ghost come to haunt us," Rory sputtered.

"None of the above. Yet I warn you, all of you," he looked around the tavern at the dumbfounded guests. "Wormwood comes. In the next year that star which guides you, around which your ships can steer, your armies march, your calendars fixed, shall become dark. Not dark like a hearth put out. No, dark by the discharge of fire, reigning out upon the sky, like the Glow that destroyed everything along the eastern coast, every city there. This will be much more destruction. Most of you will not survive. Those who do might wish they had been burnt to ash in the first moments rather than suffer the years that follow. It is time for you to prepare."

"Prepare? How?" asked Mabel, getting scared.

"Do not build castles," said the man, narrowing his eyes. "Build dungeons. Go beneath the ground. Make a city there. Put all your families into it. Gather all animals and plants that you can find. Put food and fuel and fresh water, and all your documents there with you. Keep them safe. Wait for the fire to end, for seas to disperse, for the air to clear. Then you may rise again. Then you may build again. All will be ash and sorrow, yet you must build again. You must go on. I will watch for you to come out of your underground city. I will cheer for you on that day. Now go and prepare."

"Who are you?" Stank quizzed.

The man closed his eyes. "Some call me Fritz."

Stank blinked a moment, then started to rise from his chair but saw the old man had faded into the darkness of the corner, unseen, his glass of soda water untouched.

Duke Robau's chambers were quite cozy yet comfortable, the suite lavishly decorated in cream and cardinal red, a bit frou-frou but he determined the style would befit a princess like Majory, and he was happy to call the chamber his own despite the feminine touches.

"A weirding worrywart," Stank grumbled, setting down a heavy bag of supplies he'd bought along the merchant streets before they'd met at the tavern. He was eager to set forth on the road again and stopped at the livery to be sure Winnie would be ready to ride.

"Yet he claimed the star exploded years ago," said Dandruff. "I'm not aware of any such event written on scrolls."

"He said the light takes some time to arrive," Rory responded. "I expect it's instant. I light a fire and it flames."

Dandruff pinched his lips. "If the light is far away...."

"What he said was the star burst forth," Stank spoke, "way back in the year of twenty-twenty-five, long before any of us were born. It's before our time. Maybe the scroll saying it was lost. About the time of the plague, I recall our mother saying. She had those paper-books from her kin. Passed down to her. Papers they wrote on long ago. They're surely crumbling by now yet she can read them, having the same marks we have. Nothing about a star flaming out. Nothing about its fire coming to us."

"It's a ruse, I told you." Rory settled down into his great chair, expecting it to be used by Majory. He looked small in it, like a child. "A man telling tales. I suspect he had a good laugh after we left." He directed Mabel to a chair fit for her.

"And then he disappears right before our eyes," said Stank.

Dandruff stood ready to depart for his new quarters, next to the rooms for troupe members. Mabel had her own room there.

"I wish you could stay to see our new play," said Dandruff. "I'm certain you will enjoy it. You need not be upon the stage this time. You can sit yourself back and watch. And sing along, if you know the songs."

"I can teach him," Mabel announced.

"So the fire burns through the sky," Stank wondered aloud, "and the distance makes it take sweet time. This must be the year it will finally arrive. That is what he's saying."

"Nothing special about this year," said Rory from his chair.

"Perhaps the arrival is what is meant to be what is special about this year," said Dandruff, leaving Stank to ponder it.

"Is that what's special?" asked Rory, sitting comfortably.

Stank turned to him. "It's what is meant to be special."

"What's special is what comes this year," Dandruff clarified.

"Then it comes, if that's what's coming," said Rory.

"That's what's special," Dandruff added.

"Special or not, it's what comes," said Stank.

"Ay, what comes this way," Rory said with a sigh.

"What comes this way in this year is what's special about this year," Stank grumbled at Rory.

"I can't wait to see it," cried Mabel happily.

"You're not afraid?" asked Dandruff her.

"I like the lights in the sky," she replied.

"It may be more than lights," said Rory, voice turning solemn.

"Death comes for us all," Stank spoke up with his back turned to them, starting to organize the contents of his bag, large items on the floor and smaller items set upon the cosmetics table against a wall. It was where Rory intended his bride to sit and apply her face paint.

"In our own time," said Rory with a sigh.

"Ay, in our time," Stank echoed.

Rory clapped his hands. "Well, brother! We needn't worry about a stranger's tattle tale. You're off to your home on the morrow. And I have my tasks as duke to tend. So many I might have to think again about accepting the title."

"And we have a new play to write," Dandruff announced.

"Tell him," Mabel commanded.

"Ay, there's too many plays," Stank moaned. "Life is a play."

"Yes," said Dandruff. Then he turned dramatic: "And a new play is written every day. With new players playing their roles. Straight from the news-crier's call. A story in truth becomes a story on stage. I am blessed to witness it upon my first hand. I speak of—"

"You two," Mabel exclaimed.

"Us?" said Rory, then broke into disbelieving laughter.

"You have given me the idea, both of you, from your actual acts, your many tasks, your determined goals, and all of the tribulations and the trials you have endured. I am proud to be a witness to your dramatic events. True drama! I applaud you both."

"Ay, we thought it all up for you," Stank grumbled. "Didn't we?"

"Seems that we did," Rory confirmed, nodding.

"I speak in serious means, sir. I shall pen a play from all of this, the event you have only now completed. I mean the famous duel. It's being written now, sending the story to other cities. Yet I shall write of the whole journey and our days in Louis. All of it."

"How will you recall our words? Things we've said?" asked Rory.

"He invents them from the whole cloth," Stank growled.

"In a manner, truth. I shall tell of you two, all of us, from when we first met in the woods, fighting savages, to finding Mabel, to us arriving in Louis, full of your longings and expectations. Then the schemes, the play within a play...within a play! The dastardly duke. And Her Majory. My friend Jamal. Everyone we've encountered. It shall be glorious and grand. A true spectacle! And the end shall be Duke Robau's wedding to Her Majesty, Princess Majory."

"Ay, there's a way to see it through," said Rory sadly.

"It is after the duel." To their quizzical looks, Dandruff said: "We can move events here and forth to make a good story. That is always allowed by the theater gods. They look another way."

Stank mugged. "If Lord Fritz agrees, who am I to make trouble?"

"And I, Lyle Danderoff, playwright, shall hope to become nearly as famous as your dear ancestor, Maggie Baumann, who composed the opera that made foundation for our play. You and your kin shall live onward in a stage interval."

"It seems a good thing, to live on," said Stank. "Yet I've little for living on. Only Mona, if she waits still."

"Won't you still be my daddy?" asked Mabel, displaying sad eyes. "You promised. Back at the inn in Rolla. Don't you remember?"

Stank regarded the girl. "Ay."

He went to her, stood towering over the girl, and placed his huge hand over the top of her head, his fingers stretching ear to ear. He tussled her short straw hair, which fell straight again when he lifted his hand.

"I did say I would be your papa. Yet what's it now? Seems you've taken to the theater folks. There's your family."

"I have," spoke Mabel, turning shy. "Yet I'll always be able to say my daddy is a warrior. Folks mayn't believe it. I'll say to them if you give me harm, he will come and slay you. I want to say that."

"Ay, I give permission for you to say it...when you need."

"Would you come then?"

"If I got word that Miss Mabel Maddox needed help, I'd hurry to her and turn things aright."

"Would you tell folks about your daughter, the actor?"

"Well, child, I have daughters already. Four of them. I think. Yet I'll welcome you into my clan. I'll call you Mabel Baumann. How's it like that?"

"I like it." She beamed. "From this moment I'm Mabel Baumann, daughter of Sir Stanley the warrior."

"There it is: a deal that's done," Rory declared.

Stank took Mabel's tiny hand in his, shook it. "Done."

Dandruff clapped his hands. Rory let go a cheer. Mabel grinned like it was the end of a play, and took a bow.

"Everything is settled," said Stank with a warm smile.

"Now let us be off for the night," said Dandruff, feigning a yawn.

"One thing," Stank called to the actor as he turned to go. "What shall the name of this play-thing of yours be?"

Dandruff faced him, letting his long, twisted locks shake against his back. He glanced at Rory, to Stank. "I would call it only by a true name. I shall make its title *The Warriors Baumann*. It's a title that fits the story."

"Agreed," said Stank, clapping the actor upon his shoulder. "Let me know when you perform. We shall come and give criticism."

"If you can find a figure to play Stank," Rory quipped.

"Yes, indeed. A search!" said Dandruff. "That comes later. First I must compose the words."

"And I shall play Mabel Maddox, swordswoman."

"Swordsgirl," Stank corrected her. "No, *warrior girl!*"

Dandruff gave a nod to each man. "Now we should be away. The night grows darker."

"As it will before it's light," said Rory and laughed.

"And we have a new play to write," said Dandruff.

"May take most of the night," said Stank.

"Perhaps you're right," said Dandruff.

"It surely might," Mabel agreed.

Dandruff spoke his goodnight wishes then waved Mabel to follow him, taking her by the hand and finding the exit.

"Those two," said Rory with a contented sigh, "they'll be famous in the theater, I think. I'll support their work. I'll get other dukes to fund them. A play every week. We could have a traveling show, too. Go to other towns, let them see a play – not one of those reviews like what we saw. Wouldn't that be lovely?"

"Ay, come to Fort Branson and I'll bring Mona to see it."

"That's fair." He began unlacing his tunic for the night, taking the wide bed while his smaller brother accepted the cot for this one night. "Lord Fritz watches over us. All is well. All is settled in the end – ay, brother?"

"If not for Lord Fritz coming to my aid, I shouldn't be returning to Mona." He pulled off his shirt, set it beside his tunic, and took a moment to stretch in the light of a dozen lamps.

"Ay, Lord Fritz is always there for us," said Rory, kicking off his soft Court shoes. He preferred boots but he wanted to fit in.

"So now you're a duke," said Stank with a laugh. "My brother the duke! I could never believe such. Yet without his bride. The scheme was to become a duke, was it not? Wedding with Majory was only a means to that end, true?"

"You're mistaken, brother. Wedding with Majory was always my first concern. Only later did I learn I must be a duke or better to wed with her. Yet she awarded me the title. With only a few words of my adoration presented to her. She saw me, saw I adored her so. She must've been enamored. That's a truth. No other reason. Screweye or no screw-eye, I had feelings in me for her."

"Ay, she would hold you like our mother did: all fleshy warmth and unending love. That's what you want."

"Maybe so, brother, but what's the harm?"

Stank made a face. "Her Majory reminds you of our mother?"

"No, no, no, no."

"She's a rather large woman, your Majory. To a babe, a mother is large, a whole world."

Rory chuckled. "I don't mind at all getting lost among her folds, all hot and moist, swimming within her, finding her soul and joining mine to hers. Meshing, I think it's called. Becoming one. Like that, brother. Like that."

"Have her flesh to yourself," Stank teased. "You had our mother nearly four years, all to yourself. Then my father came and put me in her. You were jealous when I was born."

"But my how you've grown, brother!"

"What a mystery...how she disappeared. And none can find her." Stank shook his head. "Do they still intend to play a funeral?"

"Not until they know for certain she has died somewhere." Rory shook his head to match Stank. "I expect it, I'm sorry to say. I can still have affection's thoughts of her. She's still a part of me. In my heart and mind forever. I did wed Majory. It's written on a scroll. That makes it truth. I shall bear it with me the rest of my days."

Stank watched his brother thinking. "It does."

"I will make a memorial to her and it will be as grand at that silver arch they built outside the Court. It will be higher, and wider, and more silver. I swear."

"Then I shall return someday to see it. Send a message."

"I will, brother. I owe you so much."

Rory grimaced, then reached for a hug.

Releasing each other with back slaps, he spoke: "You shouldn't have to worry about that travel group I put together for you. We can make another if you will wait a while. I wish you gain some fair coin on your journey back."

"No bother. So I was arrested and sent to duel. They would turn against me for that? Better they left. They can go on their own way. Good luck to them and the savages they'll meet there. I ride fast and alone."

Rory clapped his hands. "True, brother. Sometimes it's better to go alone. Hear your own thoughts. It's the only way to live."

26

Y2K

THE SHAKING FINALLY CEASED but her head still swirled like a whole sky full of stars set to a left-footed gavotte. Squeezed into the tight space gave her nowhere to release a bellyful of bile. She tried, couldn't hold it back, yet only a thin liquid slipped from her mouth.

With a panel of buttons before her, pressed against her face, she noticed how she stained them. She couldn't move her arm, jammed in as it was, pressed along her sides, to wipe them off. She noticed how wet her armpits ran. She could hardly breathe, cramped as she was in this *thing* – this device, what that odd fellow Damper called it: a 'time machine'. She'd called it the Tick-Tock Closet and laughed boldly at the man's explanations.

"What crockery!" she gasped.

If only someone would come to open the door, release her so she could breathe again.

"Where's a chamber pot when one has need?"

She squirmed, trying to bring her thick arm up, aiming her hand for the red button to her upper right. He said that was the release button. Good that she took attention when he explained everything. At the time it had all seemed a jest, a tale full of amusement for the Court, much like a droll play.

"Not. Going. To. Fear. This," she told herself with each breath.

Her hand couldn't raise high enough to reach the button, so she squeezed to her right, stretched up, pushing from her toes, leaned forward and touched the red button with her nose.

Pop went the door. A long hiss, then movement. The door panel slid away, opening to a strange new world.

"Looks not like my lovely lounging loft," she muttered.

She still needed to squeeze out of the thing – and try not to hit any other buttons on the panel. No idea what might happen if she did hit one. All Damper said was to avoid the buttons on the left and the big green button overhead.

She tilted her head up to see it, looking like one of her froggy pets perched on a lily pad in a pool. Ah, if she could just return to her chambers, to her proper place, safe with her pets, then she could pretend it had been a bad dream.

"Whoa!" cried someone outside the thing. "What's this?"

She saw out the opening a middling man approaching. He wore a single garment of faint orange, covering him from collar to shoes. He bore a wide broom upon his shoulder and pushed a cart containing other tools. Clearly a tradesman.

"Can you give aid?" she called, not so high and mighty now.

"You needing some help?" asked the man, coming up to the open door. He looked over the thing from top to bottom, shaking his head. "What is this? Never saw nothing like this up here before, huh-uh."

"I don't know," she spoke, voice wavering.

"I guess y'all got stuck, huh?"

"I'm stuck, yes."

"Lemme help you get yourself outta there."

He set down his broom and grabbed her closest arm, tugged it. Tugged hard. Harder. No movement.

"I think you gotta push some, too. Maybe hold in your breath."

She sucked in air, pulled her belly tight, as the man yanked on her arm. She moved, pushing herself toward the doorway, inch by inch. The man was breathing hard but she urged him not to give up. He promised he wouldn't.

Out she popped then, like pus from a prodigious pustule, falling on her thick knees and gasping for air.

"I thank you, fine fellow," she struggled to speak, trying to catch her breath. "I shall reward you. Give us your name and we shall call you to Court."

"Y'all talking funny," he said. "Now what's your name, hon?"

She righted herself on the floor, wondering why this fellow didn't recognize her. When she tried to get herself up on her feet, he lent a hand, taking her arm and easing her up.

"I dare say you must know me," she spoke.

"Ain't never seen you before."

"Why, I'm—I'm Princess Majory," she said, acting offended.

He looked her over, noting the gown she wore, and she could see him pondering her: Could be something a princess might wear. Does look fancy. A bit ruffled being stuffed in that silver capsule.

"Of course," he said softly. "Of course you are."

"Fine," she said, back in form. "Now that we are known. I must return to my chambers. I very much need to rest."

He waved his hand to indicate the large room they were in, dark in the corners, boxes stacked up all around them. "Here?"

"Certainly not here," she said with a dismissive grunt.

"I don't know where your...chambers? Where those are."

"Why, they are in the Court. In the west wing. Everyone knows."

"Sorry, ma'am. Guess I forgot." He gave her a warm smile. He'd seen people back in the neighborhood who had some extra space in their heads, filled it with made up stories just to get through their days. It was sad.

"Tell us your name, fellow," she demanded, her famous double chins a bit higher now.

"Me? I'm Earl."

"You shall be rewarded for your aid to me, Earl."

"Uh...thanks, I guess. But weren't nothing. I just come up here to do my work. Like usual. Sweep the floor and clean up any mess I find. That's all. They pay enough for that. I get by."

"You shall pass more proudly, I assure you."

"Well, if you say so."

"As princess, youngest daughter of King Karl, I can give rewards to those who aid me. It is my pleasure to award such."

"Thanks again, ma'am."

"Now, good fellow, lead me to my chambers. Or, a better thought, onward to the *toilette*, for I have need."

"I bet you do," he said, repressing a snicker. "Well, let's get to the elevator and I'll see that you find your way outta here."

"That is indeed what I ask."

"Glad to help."

"You are a fine fellow. Perhaps I shall add you to my staff."

Earl grinned. "It'd be my pleasure, ma'am."

Majory looked around at the large room stacked with boxes.

"I have never seen this place," she spoke up, gazing at the grid of rafters above. "Certainly not the same room I was in before. When I got into that thing. The silver capsule."

"Now about that silver capsule thing...." He regarded her, after a moment got her attention. "What is it? How'd you get in it?"

"A place to hide," she confessed, her cheeks glowing in shame. "I went to hide. They were after me. Tried to poison me. They wanted to kill me. All so he, that dastardly Duke Lindo, could rise in Court. With the King's last heir removed, he could be elevated...."

She saw how Earl stared at her, a pleasant face yet disbelieving. How could anyone of note believe such a story? Yet she swore it was true. They had come for her in her amorous hour, seeking to poison her and blame her lizard pet.

"You know...?" she pondered, ignoring Earl. Perhaps it had been Nightshade who conspired with them. He had all manner of potions. She couldn't trust the magician any longer.

"Y'all right, ma'am?" asked Earl cautiously.

"Where is this place? Here, where we are at present?"

"Here? This is Macy's. It's a Macy's warehouse, don'tcha know?"

"Warehouse?"

"Yes, ma'am. They keep everything here. When something gets low in one of the stores, they stock it up again from here." He looked around. "Not much up here, being the top floor. But it gets dusty."

"The top floor?" She gazed in wonder. "How many floors?"

"This building? We got ten floors."

"Ten floors...." She appeared to grow faint.

"Something wrong?" asked Earl.

"The same rise as the tower. The tower where that Damper rube keeps his precious capsule." She glanced down the aisle of boxes to

286

the silver capsule. "It is the same height."

"Same as what?"

She suddenly glared at him. "The same height as the chamber where Damper put that silvery thing. In the far tower."

Earl frowned. "Damper?"

"Yes, Damper. Damian Harper. He who created that thing. The time travel device."

Earl tilted his head. "Time travel?"

"Yes! He insisted he came from a year of the past. Two-thousand, he claimed it was."

"Well, ma'am, it's gonna be two-thousand in a couple days. What people been calling Y-two-K. But it's only December thirtieth today. Nineteen-ninety-nine. Kinda cold outside but no snow, at least." He gave her a once-over. "You better not be going outside in just that frilly gown."

Her chubby face reddened. "I was properly clothed within my bed chamber. What else should I wear?"

"But this ain't your bedroom," said Earl.

"An obvious observation. Yet I was made to flee...."

Earl grinned sympathetically. "Flee, huh?"

She stared hard at him like he was a magician just performing a grand trick, amazed at the revelations falling over her.

"This is Louis still?" she asked desperately.

"You mean Saint Louis? Yep, sure is."

Rory wore his finest cardinal red outfit, daring to bear a cape of the same color since he would not be engaged in any duel. His staff had to also wear red. He had selected uniforms for them: red with black trim, flourish of white on cuffs and collar. Quite a beautiful display, the Red Duke declared, seeing them all lined up before his carriage driven by a team of four horses, decorated also in cardinal red.

"Welcome to Lindenwood, Duke Robau!" cried the head steward of the estate, an older man with cropped white hair. He approached at a lively pace out the double doors of the grand house. Staff stood respectfully along the veranda: seven maids and cooks in white and red, four stewards in red and black, as he ordered.

Rory accepted the bow of the head steward, acting superior even though it wasn't his nature to stand taller than others around him. A short man with red hair wasn't seen as any kind of Royal person, but here he was: a duke. A widowman. Lord of an estate.

The head steward introduced himself as Dalton, born in Fenton to the south. He escorted the duke into the great house, telling him of its features: thirty-one rooms, with eight for beds, six *toilettes*, two game rooms, pool for swimming in one room, and a grand stable for ten horses. The grounds extended for sixty acres, including forest and field, and swampland down the slope along the river flowing by. No neighbors for two miles in any direction.

Rory eventually arrived on the upper floor, stepped out through the double doors there onto the long balcony. He took in the view, then leaned against the railing, happy to survey his estate as noon sunshine provided a comfortable warmth. Yet he saw less of the rich manicured lawn before him, the woods beyond, than the Royal Road laid out in his mind. He saw his brother riding there, sitting upon his great steed, making his long way home. To his new home, Stank had declared, to take up with that physician woman, Mona. He had wished his brother a fine life. Better he had stayed, thought Rory, giving him someone to talk to.

"Is it to your liking, sir?" asked Dalton, posed stiffly.

"Ay, I like it. Like it fine."

"Will there be anything more you desire today, sir?"

He turned from the railing, eyes landing on the head steward.

"I'll start with a nap. Then I'll stroll about the grounds. Then get supper. Let's have a roast of something, with whatever vegetables can be found, and hot bread. And lots of butter."

"The kitchen has a full stock of foodstuffs, whatever you wish."

"Then that's what I wish for," said Rory with a wink.

"Very good, Your Dukeship."

"One thing," said Rory, and the head steward stopped mid-step. "You can call me Rory when we are in the house. Just you and me. I feel better that way. My brother calls me Rory. I'm only Duke Robau outside, for official events. You understand, don't you?"

"Yes, Your...Rory...?"

"That's it. Just Rory. That's all. Like my mother called me." He smiled to himself. "I'm not like one of those high and mighty dukes in Louis. I'm from the country, a place called Joplin, although born in Wichita in the Kanza territory. Humble beginnings."

"You have achieved much, M'Lord."

"Rory, I said."

"Yes.... Rory."

At that moment a boy arrived in the doorway to the solarium. He waved a small envelope. Dalton retrieved the envelope, a few inches square, and sent the boy away.

"A message has come for you, sir."

"A message? Already? But I've only just now arrived." He smiled nevertheless. "Couldn't be from my brother, Sir Stanley," he said for Dalton's benefit. "Not been long enough for him to return home and write out a page."

He took the envelope, studied it a moment. It had a musty smell. Looked old, like it had been kept in a desk drawer for many years. The seal was dry, cracked, yet appeared unmoved.

Annoyed more than curious, Rory tore open the flap and jerked the paper out, snapped it open. The page had lines across it, writing done by hand along each line. Wishing Stank were here to read it to him, Rory regarded the artful writing, the curly lines much like his mother used to draw, but he couldn't make any sense of them.

"Here," he called to Dalton. "My eyes are tired. Can you read this to me?"

"Certainly, sir." He took the paper, straightening it, read aloud: *"My dearest Rory, my husband! How I have missed you these many years! I can hardly bear it. If you are reading this, then know that all is well for me and the process has worked as intended. This message has reached you on this day, as I planned."*

Rory grew faint. "It's from Majory."

Dalton read on: *"Two great errors occurred to split us. The first is a crime. Duke Lindo tried to poison me. He slipped a potion into a drink, let me fall ill. Yet my great girth, it seems, prevented me from being taken from life. He miscalculated the dose. Tried to blame the illness on my pet lizard, the red-necked rufus. Killed that lizard, too. Then I find he has lost his head in a duel? Strange events unfolding as I lay weary in my physician's underground chamber."*

"As I suspected," Rory said with a disappointed grunt. "Go on."

"Second, my husband, is the silver device brought to the Court by a fellow named Damper. It is with much regret that I hid within its tight interval. I did so to escape from Lindo's men who sought to take me and end my life. I nearly died of losing breath as I climbed up the stairs to Damper's room. I knew nothing of the device but what he told us when he first arrived. Yes, he spoke true words: moving from his time to our time in an instant."

"Ah hah!" Rory cried, starting to pace the room. "I warned Stank it was evil. Should've gotten rid of it."

"In my error I set the device churning," read Dalton, *"hidden as I thought I was, safe from my assassins. Yet I must have pressed on a button or two, or several, and suddenly it began to whir, making a frightful noise. I found myself in one moment in a different place, one which I soon discovered was the same place yet into a year of the past. In my great consternation, I discovered I had arrived in the old month they called December, in the year Nineteen-ninety-nine. I now believe that Damper fellow: the device does indeed transport a person through time. Yet I know not how I may return to Twenty-three-fifty-three."*

"Can it be so?" Rory began to weep. "My Majory lost in time? Set back so far?"

Dalton paused, letting Rory cry. "There is more, sir."

"There is always more," said Rory, gathering himself.

"She writes: *Finding myself in a new place, without Royal rank, I made myself a fair life, setting myself as a cleaning woman. It is not as I would wish yet I have time to think, time to ponder time. I came to realize how I miss you, my once and future husband. All is error, yet all is not forgotten. And so I write this message for you. I have instructions for my advisor, a wise professor of the language arts, to see that it finds you, there in your time, so you may read it and know the truth of things and my heart's desire. Many years have I thought of you, my husband, and considered what could have been were we to never be so attacked. You alone saw me for my heart, dismissing my poor screw-eye and my unyielding folds of flesh. BTW, I'm very much thinner now, with all the work I have to do. I think you would be pleased."*

"What does that 'B-T-W' mean?" asked Rory.

"I do not know, sir."

"Go on then."

"FYI, If you are reading this, know that I am long dead, centuries before your time. It was likely a handsome ceremony and a few of my co-workers might have attended. Nothing fancy like at the Court. My advisor will take actions to deliver this message to you, in your time, should your time still exist what with some kind of disaster coming for you. I can only hope you survive. As always, I wish you the best and I pray you will not hate me and will make a good life for yourself and whomever you may take as wife after me. I bid you farewell and give you all my love, my dearest husband, Robau."

In the silence of the room the final words seemed to echo against the walls. Rory stood frozen at the center of the room.

Dalton lowered his hand, holding the aged paper tenderly, then a moment later stepped over to the desk and laid it gently there.

"Will that be all, sir?"

Rory broke from his trance, looked at the head steward.

"Yes – that seems to be all there is."

Epilogue

THE WOMAN LOOKED IN BAD SHAPE, her gown torn and dirty, hair a mess, a scar on her bare arm from a cut that hadn't healed properly. She sat on the bench under the awning of the bus stop outside the Walmart, the dark evening hiding the cold falling rain. Not a night to be out and barefoot.

I didn't want to sit beside her but I recognized she needed help, so I pulled out my cell phone and called 9-1-1. A squad car arrived after a while. I asked if I could ride with her, see that she was taken care of. Officers said it wasn't allowed but they gave me the name of the hospital they would take her to.

Long story short, I found her. She recovered, looked a lot better. I felt happy I'd helped. She was thankful. We talked in the hospital room, a nice chat.

She said her name was Majory, a little odd but anyway.... She told a fantastic story of how she came to be so destitute at that bus stop with no money for fare, rejected by three busses. When she told them who she was, they shut the door on her. I had to smile at her tale, something that would make for a good anecdote in a magazine. I urged her to tell me more.

Awaking in a warehouse and stumbling outside, she could make no sense of where she was, tried to ask for help. Tried to go home but nobody would help her. Wandering the streets of the naked city, she met with undeserved violence and cruel taunting. I felt sorry for her the more she told. So I promised to help. Got her into a shelter, cleaned up. Not on any drugs, thankfully. Passed a psych eval. They got her set up for a job interview. Cleaning staff at a department store. Easy work. Night shift, of course. She could do it, she agreed.

I checked on her, daily at first, then weekly. She moved into a small flat for low-income. I took her shopping for supplies, what she needed for cooking and a few items of clothing. Large size. I didn't care. I took her out for dinner but she didn't eat much. Maybe she was dieting. She told me more of her story. About the castle and the king, being a princess, and the plays performed on a plaza. It was a fantastic narrative and I told her she should write it down. It would make a good novel. Fantasy's popular these days.

"You can write it, if you wish," Majory told me. She had an odd way of speaking, sounding educated but not from around here.

I suggested we could write it together. She would tell me about an episode and I would put it into novel language.

"Don't be silly, Stephen," she said, and laughed like Christmas ornaments. "I don't know everything. I only know what happened to me. Everything else you will need to invent."

"I suppose I could do it." Then I dove into complaints about not having enough time, needing to prepare lessons, and grade student papers. Finals were coming.

"You needn't be quick. There is no line of death," she said, and I had to grin.

We arranged regular sessions after her work. That was morning. Early morning – before I went to teach my classes at the university. I brought her with me a few times, let her sit in my classes, see what they were about. My colleagues asked if we were dating. No, I said, we were writing partners, working on a novel of a princess and a rogue who meet and marry. But not until after a lot of dramatic events, of course. That's how fiction is.

"What should we call it?" I asked her one day, eating breakfast at the local Waffle House. "*The Baumann Brothers*. How's that?"

She gave a smirk. "I thought this was to be about me."

"But all you've told me is about them. Those two warriors."

"It started with the arrival of those two," she said, chewing a bite of link sausage. She swallowed and set her fork down. "The brothers were called Baumann. One was a big fellow. Said he was a warrior. Said his name was Stank – short for Stanley, as I recall."

"As you recall?" I smiled, amused by the way she told her story, like it had really happened that way and she was part of it.

"Yes, Stephen. I recall it. And the shorter brother was Rory. The one who became a duke. Then we called him Duke Robau." She had to pause, stabbed a fresh bite of sausage, stuffed it into her mouth. "He was my husband."

"Your husband?" That surprised me. But I played along.

"We wedded, as I said before."

"But you never said he was your *actual* husband. Your lawfully wedded husband."

"Didn't I? You weren't listening, Stephen. We were wedded only a single day before I was taken ill. From the poison. That was Duke Lindo. But, thank the gods, he lost his head and that was that. So I had to hide then – as I also told you. Remember? I thought you were taking notes."

"I was – *am*." Pen in hand, I scribbled a few words on a napkin.

"You know, Stephen, if you want to write a book then you have to actually write," she said, proffering a grin.

I had to agree, and gave a nod.

"No," she said, waving the waitress over to refill her coffee, "it was that warrior. Stank – Sir Stanley." She thanked the waitress. "He promised me a night I'd never forget. One look at him and I knew it would be so. Good God what a figure! That was the reward for wedding his poor brother. A mere trifle. A document. Then glory among the sheets." She let out a great sigh, causing the waitress to turn and look. "Yet he never did come to me. Only a potion of poison. Then he was gone."

"And then so were you," I said, and called for the check.

In the dank quarters where potions are mixed, Nightshade holds up his latest test. The glass jar bubbles with pink fire, furious sizzling loud in the lair. Cages full of lizards along the walls hiss, perhaps sensing something evil comes. Nightshade endures their complaints; they know better than most people. He hates them. He loves them.

"Come here, my pretty," he speaks in forced gaiety to one green and yellow lizard, one of Majory's favorites.

He lifts the wary beastie from its wire cage, holds it between his fingers, regards it like a gift. The lizard grins, tongue lashing out.

The magician lifts a beaker of potion, letting the lizard gaze at it a moment.

"This should do. If you don't spit it up like the last one."

He gently pours a thin stream of the pink liquid directly into the lizard's wide gullet, measuring it carefully so the lizard won't choke. Instead of swallowing innocently, however, the pet lizard shakes its head furiously, flinging the potion about. Pink globules land on the floor and upon the magician's purple robe where they sizzle.

"Again you disappoint me, Newton," cries Nightshade, no longer willing to act like he enjoys the lizards he has adopted. "So much to disappoint. Like the pitiful princess. Nowhere to be found. My entire plan destroyed. No reward after all. Despite the drama, she's away. Let it be far. Our derelict duke is also away, wandering the high sky headless." He lets go a ragged sigh half-soiled with amusement. "So the gods curse us once more. Idle time will do that to any of us."

He puts the green and yellow lizard back in its cage.

As he closes the lid, he spies movement in the corner of his eye. Another lizard, the black and blue one, has slipped from its cage by squeezing through the wires. It pounces upon the stone floor with a pronounced plop and scrambles to the droplets of pink potion.

"No! Don't drink that," cries the magician. "That's not for you."

Yet the black and blue lizard laps up the pink globules on the floor, seems to like them and looks around for more.

"Ah, now what did she call you?" he addresses the lizard. "Was it Bruce? Is that your name?"

The lizard gives a glassy-eyed glance up at the magician, then waddles over to other pink drops, licking them up.

"That's not for you," insists the magician. "You eat that and it'll give you wings. Make you fly. You're not meant to fly."

He leans down and closely studies Bruce, noting what effect its slurping of the pink potion might have.

First come hiccoughs, and the magician thinks Bruce is about to spit up the potion. But no! The dark lizard appears to slip into a trance, turning bright-eyed – then moves. Moves upward.

"What's this?" asks Nightshade.

As he watches, Bruce begins to rise, levitating off the floor. From its small shoulders new lumps appear, like extra shoulders forming. The potion works, in a manner of speaking, yet differently than it is supposed to. Or he tested it on the wrong lizards.

"Now you've done it," mutters Nightshade, watching the black and blue beastie being buoyant, a balloon of flesh and scales, tongue flicking out as if steering a path through the air—

A bright flash cuts through the narrow windows of the chamber. Filtered down from above, the windows do not allow enough natural light to keep the room from needing to employ candles. This flash fills the room completely – an entire inferno, a world-burning blaze – and Nightshade cowers.

Forgetting Bruce, the magician rushes out the oaken door, as he fears the worst. War? Royal celebration? The arrival of the gods? He hurries up the winding stone staircase, finds himself on the rampart with a few others of the Court, everyone gazing up to the golden sky. Some of them shield their eyes from the brightness. He tries to look but can't let his eyes open. It is too bright.

"What is happening?" many cry out.

Some of the Court are moaning. Others praying.

"Is it the end?" asks a steward, falling to his knees.

One figure among the group, wearing the golden robe of a Court officiant, raises his arms to the Glory, announcing: "In the Year of the Red Duke comes the star called Wormwood, as it was foretold, come to burn away our sins and make us whole. As it is written."

"Ah, shit," one named Damper was heard to utter.

And Nightshade, the magician, spying several pets from his lair rising into the air like milkweed, knows it to be so.

ACKNOWLEDGMENTS

Poet T.S. Eliot expressed the idea that poetry – and by extension, all imaginative writing – requires various influences to come together in random fashion to initiate a story.

The *Flu Season* series began as a deliberate thought-experiment as the world entered the coronavirus pandemic. Based on the film *A Boy and His Dog* (1975), from Harlan Ellison's short story, a sardonic adventure set in an odd post-apocalyptic landscape, the first book (and at that time the only intended one) was given the working title "A Boy and his Mom and her tuba". However, the situation turned serious as the SARS-CoV-2 ("covid-19") pandemic worsened. Only as the crisis was coming to an end did I find a way to start *The Book of Mom*.

I wanted to focus not on those initial days we all experienced, when everything was immediate and real, but further into the future, when the worst we had experienced had gotten even worse, say, six years into the future. Book 2, *The Way of the Son*, continues the story through another year of post-pandemic misadventure. Everything is irrevocably broken and the only way forward is to rebuild from scratch.

In Book 3, *Dawn of the Daughters*, the rebuilding begins but our family isn't aware of it for a while. When they enter the new society, they find it being rebuilt in horrible fashion. Book 4, *The Book of Dad*, shows us the beginning of a society heading straight into tyranny. But in Book 5, *The Granddaughter*, family members escape the tyranny of the capital for a kinder, gentler chapter in the west.

Book 6, *The Grandsons*, is intended to wrap up the saga by exploring what the continent has become, as seen through the experiences of a headstrong young man and a trio of sisters he meets out west. An epic tale should conclude the series, I believed, yet I had more to write. So I jumped ahead two hundred years and set future family members in a ribald comedy in a medieval Missouri: *The Warriors Baumann*.

As always, I select music that helps me create the appropriate emotive soundscape for writing sessions. The aural support unlocks my muse. I found the ideal soundtrack in the following music: various music from the game series Elder Scrolls/Skyrim composed by Jeremy Soule and Brad Derrick, though I took no story elements from it; some of *Adiemus* composer Karl Jenkins' album *Diamond Music*, featuring "Palladio" and others; Scott Buckley's music continued to serve me well.

ABOUT THE AUTHOR

Stephen Swartz is the author of twenty novels, including this present volume, as well as several short stories for anthologies and literary journals. He has also published scholarly articles and a Ph.D. dissertation. He taught English at several colleges and universities over a thirty-year career. While teaching English courses at a university in Oklahoma, Swartz realized his ambition to publish his previously written novels. Thanks to the notoriety of the Amazon Breakthrough Novel Award competition, the first of those novels, *After Ilium*, was published – followed quickly by the sci-fi tome *The Dream Land*, which became a trilogy, and the anti-romance *A Beautiful Chill*. New novels soon followed.

Prior to graduate school and earning an M.A. (English) and M.F.A. (Creative Writing), Swartz lived in Japan where he taught English at middle school and high school levels. His experiences there helped to inspire his novel *Aiko*. Swartz later taught summer courses at a university in Beijing, China. His wide travels and interest in cultures and languages has propelled his fiction into explorations of situations where a main character is a stranger in a strange land and must find ways to adapt – much as he has done during a lifetime and career of various excursions.

He borrows from those experiences for the *Flu Season* series. From his reading of medieval comedies, he offers this current entry in the series. He is presently at work on a much more serious epic set further into the future.